Ruth Hamilton was born in Bolton and has spent most of her life in Lancashire. Her previous novels, *A Whisper to the Living, With Love from Ma Maguire, Nest of Sorrows, Billy London's Girls, Spinning Jenny, The September Starlings, A Crooked Mile, Paradise Lane* and *The Bells of Scotland Road,* are also published by Corgi Books and she is a national bestseller. She has written a six-part television series and over forty children's programmes for independent television.

Ruth Hamilton now lives in Liverpool with her family.

THE DREAM SELLERS

Ruth Hamilton

CORGI BOOKS

THE DREAM SELLERS
A CORGI BOOK : 0 552 14566 1

Originally published in Great Britain by Bantam Press,
a division of Transworld Publishers Ltd

PRINTING HISTORY
Bantam Press edition published 1997
Corgi edition published 1998

Copyright © Ruth Hamilton 1997

Set in 11/12pt Baskerville by
Phoenix Typesetting, Ilkley, West Yorkshire.

Corgi Books are published by Transworld Publishers Ltd,
61–63 Uxbridge Road, London W5 5SA,
in Australia by Transworld Publishers (Australia) Pty Ltd,
15–25 Helles Avenue, Moorebank, NSW 2170,
and in New Zealand by Transworld Publishers (NZ) Ltd,
3 William Pickering Drive, Albany, Auckland.

Reproduced, printed and bound in Great Britain by
Cox and Wyman Ltd, Reading, Berks.

In memory of Eric 'Rushie' Rushton
and all the laughter.

AMBER

My sweet and gentle Labrador, thank you for twelve
wonderful years of loyalty and perfect innocence.
If there were dreams to sell, merry and sad to tell,
and the crier rang the bell, I would buy you back
tommorow. Goodbye, my lovely friend.

Acknowledgements

My thanks to:

Diane Pearson, my long-suffering editor.
David and Michael, my sons.
Sergei, Olga and Julia from Chernobyl, who brightened my summer.
Helen Barford and Susan Acton for making me laugh.
Spike, who lived in my house for five months and who remains in my heart.
My animal family – Benny, Scooby, Soapy, Bodie, Ladybird, Jack and Vera.

A very special thank-you to Sandra and Josephine of Sweetens Bookshops for all the help with research.

Dream-Pedlary
Thomas Lovell Beddoes, 1803–1849

If there were dreams to sell,
What would you buy?
Some cost a passing bell;
Some a light sigh,
That shakes from Life's fresh crown
Only a roseleaf down.
If there were dreams to sell,
Merry and sad to tell
And the crier rung the bell,
What would you buy?

ONE

Alderman Edward Shawcross was a striking figure of a man. He was tall, erect of stature, and he owned a full set of well-trimmed facial hair whose original darkness had become streaked with small amounts of silver. A solid gold albert was stretched across his waistcoat, while all cufflinks and tie-pins were of the same precious metal.

Sadie Martindale, a doffer of sufficiently long standing to warrant bunions and corns, waited for the wrath of Teddy Shawcross to fall on her head. He looked regal enough to warrant a place on British coinage, she thought. Anybody catching sight of him now might think he had always been grand, but Sadie knew better. She remembered Teddy Shawcross's beginnings, recalled seeing him on his way to school with holes in his trousers, iron-bottomed clogs on his feet and enough wild life about his person to start a miniature zoo.

The alderman took the hunter from his pocket, looked at it, listened to it, polished it on his hanky. 'Sadie,' he began. 'I am saddened. What are you thinking of?' He hated pretending to be cross with the woman who had done so much for him, but he could not afford to allow bad examples and dangerous behaviour in his mill. 'Well, Sadie? What's on your mind?'

Sadie Martindale was thinking about her bunions, but she said nothing. Years of running about to don the new and doff the filled tubes had made the joints of her feet resemble gnarled bits of tree. She lifted a shoulder, remained silent.

'Smoking in the toilets,' he continued, the tone still mournful. 'There should be none of that.'

Everybody smoked in the bloody toilets. Where else could they smoke? Over a pile of cotton or a can of oil?

'How long have you worked for me?' he asked.

Sadie narrowed her eyes and stared at the window. She counted backwards, got lost, started again. There was Bernard and Mary, then Tommy. She'd had about six years off, then she'd done evenings, back to days, back to evenings when her mam had got ill . . .

'Sadie?'

'I'm counting. More than twenty-odd year, Mr Shawcross, on and off, like.' Out of work, everybody called him Alderman, but within his empire, he was plain Mr Shawcross. There wasn't much side to Teddy Shawcross, which was just as well, because he'd had no fancy start in life, not by a long chalk. And anyway, this was his wife's firm, really. It was common knowledge that he'd only married Alice Fishwick for her money, Sadie reminded herself inwardly. And who in his right mind would have married Alice for her looks or her personality? Alice Fishwick had a physog like a month of wet Sundays, miserable, all down in the mouth and scraped-back hair. Temperament to match, too—

'You shouldn't be sneaking away from your work, Sadie.'

The doffer pulled herself up, reined in her wandering thoughts. 'No, Mr Shawcross.'

'Time is money.'

'Aye. Right you are, Mr Shawcross.'

He didn't always feel comfortable in the company of Sadie's generation. Like him, Sadie had come from the streets of School Hill, had been raised in poverty. But Sadie was older than he was. She had a long memory, too, could probably recall looking after him and his brother after their mam's untimely death. The colour had risen in his face, and he was glad of the whiskers. 'Don't do it again, please, Sadie.'

'No, Mr Shawcross.' She hobbled to the door.

'Sadie? What's the matter with your legs?'

She stopped, turned slowly and grimaced. 'Bunions,' she said. 'I'm a martyr to them. Corns and all. Feet swells in the heat, Mr Shawcross, then they rub and your skin gets all sore. There's more dangers in a mill than just smoking in the lav, you know.'

He rose slowly and walked round the large desk. She was wearing heavy clogs that seemed far too big for her. 'Are they yours?' he asked. He wondered how she managed to drag herself around the spinning mules in order to do her job – the footwear looked as if it weighed a couple of pounds. There were irons on the soles, not rubbers – he had heard the clattering when Sadie had mounted the stairs to his office.

'They're our Tommy's. He grew out of them years back and I don't like waste.' She fixed a gimlet stare on Teddy Shawcross's watch chain. It would have kept a family of six for a month with enough left for the Saturday rush, pie and peas, plus a pint or two of brown ale.

'No slippers?'

Sadie clicked her porcelain dentures. Her slippers had given up the ghost weeks earlier, had curled up with the heat like everything else in this place. She was curling up herself, was having trouble with her back, her knees, her feet. 'They got crusted with rings,' she said. The tiny circles of metal became embedded in soft-soled shoes, sometimes cutting their way right through to the skin. Though most folk wouldn't feel any pain, she pondered, because the skin on their feet was tough enough to take soling, heeling and, if necessary, a full set of clog irons.

'Buy some more.' He pushed some money into her hands.

Sadie eyed him warily. He was a boss. She had wiped his snotty nose, had changed his mucky clothes, had wrapped him up against the weather. His mam had died of gin, his dad had died eventually of whisky, but Teddy Shawcross was a boss. 'I can't,' she said sadly.

'Why not?'

She raised her shoulders, felt her bones creaking and clicking as if they, too, had shrivelled and become desiccated in the scorching heat of cotton-spinning rooms. 'It'd be favouritism, Mr Shawcross, if I took this money off you.'

'Don't tell anyone, then.'

His logic was undeniable. If she kept her gob shut, nobody would know. Sadie was fifty-three going on ninety. Her thin hair was prematurely white, her husband was dead and her eldest lad was a drinker. Even young Tommy, who had been a promising boy, had come home several times in a medicated state.

'Why do they drink?' she surprised herself by asking.

He closed her fingers round the money. 'Sadie, I don't know. Why did my parents drink? Because it's grim and grey out there.' He pointed to the window, remembered dragging his father home, recalled his mother's decline into delirium. 'A dark world,' he muttered softly.

'Sun's shining,' she replied.

'You know what I mean,' he said.

She knew. She knew that her house was grey, that no amount of summer weather would make it bright. The meatsafe was empty, and their Bernard was drinking half his wages before tipping up on a Friday. They'd had bread and scrape for supper three nights in a row, and the boss had just given her the price of a nice cow heel tea and a bit of gammon to boil for Wednesday and Thursday. She'd likely get a drop of pea and ham soup out of the gammon, too, because there was pearl barley in the cupboard and a few lentils. Her mouth moistened at the thought of marrowfat peas soaking overnight, getting plump with water, then a couple of bacon ribs and a crust of new bread to complete the banquet.

Edward Shawcross walked to a cupboard and reached inside. 'Remember Dolly Minton?' he asked.

Sadie smiled broadly, though a dampness in her eyes spoiled the grin. Everybody remembered Dolly. She'd been about twenty stones, as wide as she was tall and with a laugh that might have frightened a bull terrier out of its coat. Dolly had worked at Fishwick's from leaving school until dying in the mill yard and in the middle of telling a very rude joke. 'A grand old lass,' said Sadie. 'We'll not see her like again, Mr Shawcross.'

He lowered his head, shook it slightly. 'I remember the riot she started over tea-breaks,' he mused. 'A big lady in more ways than one. Big, but her feet were small.' He lifted out a pair of shoes with bunion holes cut into their sides. 'We collected Dolly's bits and pieces for her family, but her daughter left these in case anyone might need them. You need them, Sadie. Try them on later,' he suggested.

Sadie accepted the shoes, decided to make a stab at politeness. 'How's Mrs Shawcross?' she asked.

'Very well,' he answered.

'The children?'

'In good health, thank you.' He paused, made sure that she had finished with the social niceties. 'No more smoking in my time, Sadie,' he said.

She looked him up and down, remembered him crying into her shoulder the day his mother died, recalled how frightened he had been, how young and vulnerable. 'I won't smoke in your time,' she promised solemnly. He'd be off to one of his council meetings soon. While the cat was away, she'd sneak the odd puff.

He returned to his desk and watched through the upper half of his door while Sadie hobbled back to work. Smoking in the toilets was the least of his problems. There were bigger fish to fry, bigger problems to solve. With his soul in his boots, Alderman Shawcross prepared himself for another evening at home.

Alice Fishwick had expected to be loved universally. An only infant of doting parents, she had been cosseted and cajoled through childhood, had attended a nice little school for gentlefolk, was now an expert needlewoman and arranger of flowers. The trouble was that embroidery and snipping rose stems took up too little of her time. Alice brooded a lot. She brooded because she had turned out all wrong, had inherited her mother's originally podgy frame and her father's heavy facial features, plus that supposedly good man's large hands and feet. She was ugly. Nobody loved ugly women, so the promises of her childhood had never been fulfilled.

Nature was a player of cruel tricks, Alice told herself. Constance, daughter of the Shawcross marriage, was a comely young woman. She had dark blonde hair, blue eyes, a dainty nose, dark eyebrows and lashes and a flawless skin. Constance's figure was well proportioned, while her singing and piano-playing were becoming legendary in genteel circles.

'Sit up straight,' snapped Alice, hating herself for envying her own daughter. 'You are playing beautifully,' she added apologetically. The girl had to do something with her life. Often, Alice wanted to scream at Constance, wanted to tell her to get out and make a life, make a place for herself in the world. But Alice had been raised as a lady, so she said little or nothing.

Constance straightened her spine and devoted all her energy to the practising of a Chopin étude. Mother seemed to be in a bit of a flap again. Gilbert, lucky Gilbert, was out of the way. He had gone riding with some people from Top o' th' Moor, the rather grand house which sat like a crown above Aston Leigh. Aston Leigh, a slightly less salubrious mansion, had been lent to Mother by her parents. Constance had never known her maternal grandparents.

'Was that the right note, Constance?'

'Yes, Mother.' Constance would never hit the right note, she told herself. As far as Mother was concerned, many of the things Constance did turned out wrong. She was accused of practising too often, of practising too seldom. She played over-loudly, too softly, too quickly, too slowly. What Constance failed to understand was why Mother insisted on sitting here, in the library and right next to the piano, whenever Constance played.

'That was another wrong note,' snapped Alice Shawcross. Edward would be home in an hour or so, and Alice's temper shortened as the hour of his return approached. After a meal, he would probably go out again to sit on some committee or other. In Alice's opinion, Edward did not love his wife. He was pleasant to his children, his colleagues on the council, his workers, his customers. Alice ground her teeth. It wasn't his mill. It wasn't hers, either, because it really belonged to her parents, a pair of nomads who had chosen to wander the face of the earth. Edward was the owner of nothing at all, yet he managed to love everyone. Nearly everyone, that was. Where loving his wife was concerned, Edward Shawcross was an utter failure.

'May I go upstairs to change now, Mother?' asked Constance.

'Yes.' Alice fanned her face with a limp handkerchief. The day had been far too hot for a person of large build. 'Will Gilbert be back in time for dinner?' Dinner at Aston Leigh was a splendid, quiet meal. Everyone chewed as noiselessly as possible in order not to break the silence by allowing a crass bodily function to be audible. If a person gnashed accidentally, Alice glared. A noisy swallow could be enough to send her reeling from the table before finishing her meal. Alice ate secretly and voraciously in her room. The secret was an open one, though none dared to mention it.

'He said he would be back,' replied Constance. Gil could have stayed out, could have eaten among normal people who actually talked at table. She rose, pulled down the piano lid, walked to the door.

'The deportment lessons did very little for you,' was Alice's parting remark. Alice leaned back and closed her eyes. She was becoming snappier by the day, was picking at her daughter, was sharp with the house staff, was deeply, horribly unhappy. 'It's myself I hate,' she whispered into an uncaring, empty room.

Constance lingered in the hallway. It was a square-ish area with a fireplace, two sofas and a low table for coffee and teacups. Grandmother and Grandfather Fishwick had probably withdrawn to the hall after each evening meal, would have taken coffee and petits fours here. The floor was of marble mosaic with a huge star in its centre. Lamps and occasional tables stood around the walls, while a dead tiger lay in front of the hearth. Constance could never bring herself to look this poor creature in its glass eyes.

She began to ascend the curving staircase, her gaze fastened to a portrait of her grandparents. They were alive, in good health for their time of life and in Africa. The older Fishwicks had taken up residence in a decent climate where they could find a decent bridge partnership and some decent conversation. Their daughter had disappointed them by marrying a man of poor blood, so the Fishwicks had upped and offed in a flurry of tempers and eccentricities.

Constance sat on the top step. This was a very

strange family. Not once had her grandparents visited her or Gilbert. A letter arrived occasionally for Mother, but she never discussed the contents or passed on any messages. 'I am the disappointment of a disappointment,' she told a painting. 'And it's almost certainly your fault.'

The portrait stopped a hair's breadth from life-size. A whiskery man who bore a marked resemblance to Father and to King George V stood next to a seated woman of great beauty. The artist had sculpted Grandmother Fishwick with care, had shaved off a few dozen pounds of flesh in order to be paid a goodly sum for the work. Constance had overheard people talking, knew full well that Grandmother and Mother were similarly cursed. 'I wish you two would come home,' sighed Constance. 'At least there would be something new to talk about.'

The Fishwick grandparents were a pair of enigmas. No-one seemed to know them thoroughly. Mother, upset by what she chose to interpret as their abandonment, would scarcely discuss them. Constance was forced to admit that they appeared peculiar to the point of insanity. Who on earth started a new life in a faraway country at the age of fifty or so? Who on earth were these strange ancestors? Mother answered few questions, invited no dialogue on the subject of her family. Yet Constance knew that this house belonged to her mother's parents. What would happen if and when they returned from Africa? Well, they would provide a topic for discussion, at least, Constance reminded herself.

Nobody talked. Mother snapped, because Mother was a lonely and embittered woman. Father nodded and looked at his watch a great deal. Gilbert had a life outside, while Constance filled the role of Mother's companion. She should get a job. This was 1950 and history's various dark ages were long over. What might she do? Mother wanted her to go to university, had forced her to apply several times, but Connie had deliberately flunked entrance examinations and interviews. Although she had not chosen her future path, she realized that she did not belong in the heady atmosphere of true academia.

'Constance?'

'Yes, Mother?'

'Stop loitering. Go and dress for dinner.'

One interesting thing about Mother was that she knew everything. If the maid sneaked outside to meet the gardener's lad, Alice Shawcross knew. When the cook brewed an extra pot of tea for the small staff, Mother always chose that day to examine the caddies. She was from a different age, was carrying on in the footsteps of the mother who had deserted her.

Constance entered her bedroom. It was a plain area with cream walls, cream carpet, beige curtains and bedspread. A door of varnished oak led to a bathroom with white tiles and white fittings. She sat on the edge of a stool and stared at her reflection in the central mirror of her dressing table. There were three mirrors, two that hinged against the larger one. As a child, Constance had angled the glass, had stared at Constance after Constance in seemingly eternal repetition.

Mother was unhappy. Mother didn't understand the world and was unfit for it. She picked on other people all the time, was particularly hard on her daughter, because Alice Shawcross, née Fishwick, had been rejected by her own parents. 'Come home,' said Constance softly. 'You loved her once, yet you abandoned her when she married my father.' Why had the Fishwicks allowed Father to move into their house? Grandfather Fishwick had scuttled off with his wife to the other side of the world, had left Edward Shawcross to take charge of the mill. Why?

Gilbert tapped on the door. 'Another moody day, I take it?' he asked his sister.

Constance smiled wryly. 'We live in a very odd household,' she said.

'At last! She has noticed!' Gilbert threw himself onto his sister's bed. 'Mother wants you downstairs.'

'I'm changing.'

'Into what? A pumpkin?'

Constance jumped up from her stool, slapped her brother's hand. 'What am I going to do with my life?' she asked.

Gilbert sighed dramatically and placed the slapped hand on his heart. 'Get thee to a nunnery,' he suggested. 'Or take lessons in train driving.' He felt sorry for Connie. She was a grand-looking girl and a good sort, but Mother was trying – albeit quietly and subtly – to direct Connie's life. Mother was a miserable old soul whose attitude to Connie vacillated between envy and frustration. Alice was jealous of Connie's beauty, yet she wanted her daughter to go forth, enjoy a good education before making a sensible marriage. Mother was a mess. She stuffed herself silly with sweets and chocolate, moaned and groaned at the servants until they left, had all the charm of an ill-tempered viper. Loving Mother was difficult; disliking her was dreadful. Disliking a parent made a son guilty, so he stopped thinking about Mother for a few moments. 'James

Templeton's been looking at you again through the binoculars,' he said. 'All wistful and sad, like a dog who never had a bone.'

Connie lifted her eyes to heaven. 'I shall report him to the police,' she declared laughingly. 'Poor James. No-one will have him, I suppose, because of the limp. If his mother knew that he was looking down the hill at me, she would die of shame.' The Templetons were not trade. The Templetons enjoyed a private income from land and properties all over Lancashire and Cheshire.

'You could do worse,' said Gilbert.

'I know.'

'And you'd get away from Mother.'

Constance Shawcross had no intention of using marriage as an escape. If and when she did tie herself to a man, she would not be running away. No. Marriage should be the beginning of a future, not the end of an unsavoury past. 'I'm going nowhere,' she replied tartly. 'Except, perhaps, to the technical college.'

Gilbert closed his mouth with an audible snap. 'What? She'll never buy that one, old girl. She wants you to do history or music, something decorative.'

The 'old girl' gave him another thump. 'I'm twenty,' she told him. 'And you're twenty-two. I'm going to learn shorthand, typing and other office skills.'

Gilbert sat up. 'Have you asked her?'

'No. I'm going to ask Father.'

Gilbert jumped up and saluted his sister. Constance was capable of causing uproar in the household, he told himself. After National Service with the Air Force, Gilbert had returned to find his sister at the complete beck and call of Mother. But

Connie had a fuse of a certain length, Gilbert reflected. Once she chose to light it, she could go off in a dozen directions all at once. 'How's the *magnum opus* coming along?' he asked.

Constance dragged a frock from her wardrobe, spat on a finger and rubbed at a stain. 'Gravy,' she grumbled. 'I should have had this laundered.' She pulled out another garment, cast it across a chair. 'I haven't done much,' she admitted. For a while, she had been bent on becoming a writer. But writing was boring. Writing meant sitting down with a lot of pretend people and trying to make them interesting. 'My life has been too dull,' she advised him. 'So I have very little to write about.'

Gilbert ruffled her hair, received another mock blow for his pains. 'Get married, Con,' he said. 'Find a chap and clear off out of this place. It's all right for me. Another few terms at the university and I'll just follow Dad.'

Connie nodded. 'It isn't his business, Gil.'

'I know.'

'It isn't even our house.' They had discussed the subject for hours in the past, had invented all kinds of scenarios for grandparents whose absence made them glamorous and mysterious. 'They could come back tomorrow and throw us out,' Constance reminded her brother.

'They could, indeed.'

'What happened, Gil?' she asked. 'If Father wasn't good enough, then what on earth persuaded them to rush off and leave him in charge?'

Gilbert shrugged. 'I know what you know, and you know what I know.'

'Exactly.' Without a trace of self-consciousness, Constance heaved off her day dress, powdered her upper body and pulled on a smarter gown. 'She'll know I haven't bathed,' she said. 'She listens to the pipes. I should have run the water.'

Gilbert Shawcross smiled at the girl he sometimes called Minnie the Minx. 'Don't worry,' he said. 'Save that for when she hears about technical college. Compared to that, unwashed flesh is nothing.'

Sadie Martindale stirred the stew, licked the spoon, then added another dash of salt. She lowered her tired body into the fireside rocker and gazed around at her worldly goods. Thanks to Teddy Shawcross, she had managed to get hold of some scrag end and spuds, so there was the smell of cooking to cheer things up a bit. And, in the meatsafe, a small joint of ham promised a tasty tomorrow.

The window boasted three sections of glass, the fourth having been replaced by strips from a demolished orange box. Outside in the yard stood an air raid shelter. Sadie had never managed to work out why money had been spent on brick shelters. If somebody had to die, he'd be better dying in his own bed rather than in a freezing shack in the back yard. No-one had ever been inside the single storey building. Cats and rats probably used it, she thought, because it stank like an open sewer.

Sadie's kitchen was not clean, as she was too weary for housework, but things were more or less in order, pots on a shelf above the range, pans on a rack next to the hearth. The room was dominated by a large, square table with bulbous legs and a dark green cloth. This had been Sadie's mother's table. All that remained of Sadie's mother was this table and a pot dog from Blackpool. The dog sat next to a pile of plates above the mantel, paint missing from a lolling tongue, his tail a bit skew-whiff after being glued back on by Tommy.

Tommy was a good lad, she told herself determinedly. Bernard was a bugger, Mary was an energetic and lovable pest, and Tommy would turn out all right if he just stayed out of the pub. He had a good job at Walker's Tannery, had served his apprenticeship and was waiting, alongside others, for dead men's shoes to carry him towards promotion. The poor lad ponged a bit, because the stink from Walker's was enough to bring tears to the eyes of a corpse, but he tried. He got an all-over wash every night, and a total immersion each Friday at the slipper baths. Bernard, a miner, took a shower at work when he came off shift. The trouble with Bernard was that he couldn't seem to hang on to his money. Sadie's eldest went from shower to pub, arriving home in time for a meal only on the nights when his beer money had run out.

Sadie closed her eyes. A corner of her mind could still hear the clatter of machinery, a sound that had been an integral part of her life since school. She was worn out, wearied to the marrow. For how much longer would she manage to earn her keep? The days blended together, were becoming one endless succession of chores with the odd break for sleep and food.

'Hiya, Mam.'

The woman in the chair jumped. 'God Almighty,' she said breathlessly. 'You frightened me near to death, Mary.'

Mary, bright as a button, bent down and kissed her mother's hair. Mary helped to run a sweet stall in the Market Hall. Bubbling with goodwill and enthusiasm, she had become a firm favourite with Bolton's shoppers, because she invariably had a good word and a smile for everyone.

'You're a pest,' declared Sadie.

'I'm a manager,' replied Mary. She stalked up and down the kitchen with a hand extended, tried to pose like a model. 'They're putting me wages up, Mam. And there's a rumour going round that toffees could be off ration soon.'

Had Sadie owned sufficient strength, she would have leapt for joy. 'You're going up in the world,' she said. 'And good luck to you, girl. You're a worker, I'll give you that.' Sadie had forbidden her daughter to go in the mill. She didn't want Mary ending up with aching bones, horrible feet and ringing in her ears. 'When do you take over?'

'Two weeks. I'll have a white overall with a pink collar, Mam. And a brooch thing with me name and "manager" on. Mr Smith's had enough, because he's seventy. He says I'm the only one in the world he'd trust with his money. They've bought a little bungalow somewhere near Blackpool, but they're keeping their house up Chorley New Road. Their son's going to live in it and run their other shop.'

Sadie blinked away some drops of happiness. She wanted their Mary settled. The lads – well – lads went their own road and shamed the devil. There wasn't a lot a widow could do for sons. But Sadie intended to see this girl of hers set up for life and well away from the cotton industry. 'I've made stew,' she said.

Mary pulled a parcel from her basket. 'Here you are, Mam. A little present for you.'

Sadie stared down at the package. She hadn't received a gift for ages . . . oh, yes, she had. Teddy Shawcross had given her a few bob today. But this was different. This was wrapped up in dark blue paper.

Mary had taken the care to make the offering special.

'Open it, Mam.'

It was half a dozen little lavender bags with pink ribbons.

'For your underwear drawer, Mam.'

Sadie's underwear drawer was usually empty. She had three pairs of knickers – one for on, one in the wash and the third drying on the pulley line above the kitchen fireplace. 'Lavender,' she whispered. 'You remembered how I've always liked lavender.' She would wrap these little bags inside her one and only underskirt, a poor thing with the hem wanting stitching and a shoulder strap broken. Perhaps Mary's present would goad Sadie into getting out her sewing basket.

Mary saw her mother's weakness, heard exhaustion in the voice. If Mary Martindale had to work her socks off, she would do it. Mam deserved a better life, a life away from this dark house. 'I do love you, Mam.' Those words had not been said for a long time.

'I know you do, Mary.'

'You need a rest.'

Sadie tried to smile. 'There is no rest, lass, not for the wicked.'

Mam had never been wicked. Mary looked down on her mother's prematurely white hair, tried to remember a time when Sadie's brown locks had not been streaked with strands of silver. Mary's hair was brown and curly. It shone with health and regular shampooing, and it had a life of its own. There was so much of it that Mary often gave up and tied the whole lot of it into a bundle. At work, she wore a white mob cap into which the disobedient mass was tucked, but she struggled with it at home.

'I'll just taste the stew again,' said Sadie.

Mary took herself off into the front room, a tiny square with oilcloth, a rug pegged out of old clothes onto sacking, two uncomfortable armchairs and a table next to the window. Mam's blue-and-white bowl sat on the table with a large, evil-looking plant growing out of it. Mary could not remember a time when the plant had not been there. As a child, she had often wondered whether it might come to life and take over the house. It sat smugly in its container, shiny leaves thrusting their confident way up towards the ceiling. It produced no flowers, wasn't a cheerful piece by any stretch of imagination.

She sat down, wriggled until a loose spring settled. How did a person go about making a decent life for a worn-out mother? There must be something, Mary told herself, a bit of evening work that would bring in an extra pound or two. Sometimes, Mary's heart felt broken when she looked at Mam. Mam expected little and got less. Bernard was a stupid lout and a drinker, while Tommy's wages were still not quite up to scratch.

'It's always down to the bloody women,' Mary whispered into the unwelcoming room. 'Men think they've done it all when they've managed a week's work.' Men should be ashamed of themselves. Their wives, sisters and mothers had jobs. After their paid work was finished, they were expected to come home, cook and wash for a family, do the shopping, clean the house, tend the sick, look after the young, stone the steps and sweep the back yard. For women, there was no freedom.

When the front door opened, Mary leapt from the front room and into the narrow lobby. Bernard had arrived. Bernard was a useless great lump with no discernible conscience and very little sense. All the same, Mary beckoned him into the so-called parlour and tackled him. She noticed that the coal was eating into fine lines around his eyes, that there was a bluish tinge to his skin. 'Bernard, Mam's had enough,' she began.

Bernard took a step back. Their Mary was all right until she got riled. She took some riling, but she wasn't the sort of person a man would choose for an enemy. 'We've all had enough,' he replied.

He didn't understand, and Mary told him so. 'She's up at six messing about with porridge and butties for you and Tommy, then she puts in a full day at Fishwick's. Now, she's got the tea to make, and God knows where she found the money for it.'

Bernard sniffed the air. Thank God it promised a bit more than yesterday's bread and dripping. 'What do you want me to say?' he asked.

'You've got to stop drinking.'

He looked at his sister as if she had suddenly gone mad. It was obvious that Mary had no idea, no idea at all. 'What the bloody hell are you going on about? A couple of pints? Do you want me to sign the pledge while I'm at it? Have I to join the Sally-Anns and run about with a trumpet or a sodding tambourine?'

'Salvation Army wouldn't have you,' came the quick reply.

He scratched his head. After a full eight hours beneath the earth's surface, Bernard was not in the market for a fight. 'I need a drink now and again,' he said.

'You spend half your wages in pubs,' snapped Mary. 'While our Mam struggles to put a bit of tater hash on the table.' She drew herself up to full height, which was a not inconsiderable five feet and seven inches. 'I think you should leave home,' she advised him quietly. 'If she didn't have you to feed, she'd manage better.'

Bernard's mouth hung open for a few seconds, then snapped shut. 'Are you off your head?' he asked. 'I tip up every Friday, don't I?'

'Not enough to keep yourself, no.'

The oldest of the three Martindales leaned against the wall.

Mary continued her attack. 'There's rooms for ten bob. You can feed yourself, but remember pennies for the meters. Oh, and you'll have to do your own washing. No fetching bundles home for Mam to tackle.'

'I can't afford ten bob,' he said.

'You'll have to. There's nowt for less. Ten bob'll get you a bed and a gas ring if you're lucky.' She strode up to him and grabbed the front of his jacket in her fist. 'You're not putting my mam in her grave, Bernard Martindale. I hand over every penny of my wage, because she's looked after us all our lives. And, if you're not careful, you'll be dragging Tommy into the gutter and all. She's fair, is Mam. She'll give you your spends if you cough up all the wage. But just remember, Mam listens to me. I can get her to show you the door if I work on her.' She released him, stepped back. 'Well? What do you have to say for yourself, then?'

He was fed up to the back teeth, including the four wisdoms, all of which had led him a dance while breaking through. He sighed, ran a hand through his hair. His hair was receding already because of the flaming pit hat.

It had been one hell of a shift. The foreman had

been on at him all day, and their gang leader had gone and got cramp in the middle of a propping job. Bernard had finished up using his back to stop the seam from collapsing on himself and six others. 'It's not a bobby's job, you know,' he said. 'I nearly got killed this morning. There wasn't one of us without dust in our eyes, and Loony Lundy got the rosary beads out again. What good is he up to his neck in Hail Marys while the rest of us are up to ours in muck and coal? Eh?' He was warming to his subject.

Mary was ready for him. 'Listen, Pie-can. You've had it easy and no mistake—'

'Easy? Try blinking National Service for a kick-off, girl. Two years of running round like a mad hike, some stupid fart of a sergeant telling you to polish your buttons, swill the lavs out, stand on your head for half an hour in the rain.' He stopped, pondered. The army had been a sight better than the pit. Any damned thing at all would be better than mining. 'You women don't know you're born.' His voice rose in conjunction with his temper.

'You weren't the only one called up,' snapped Mary. 'Our Tommy went and he never complained.'

The door opened. Sadie looked with great sadness upon her children. 'What's all this?' she asked.

'It's him and his beer,' snapped Mary. 'He should swallow less and cough up more.'

Bernard had the good grace to blush. He stood up properly and looked at his mother. She did look a bit peaky, a bit on the worn-out side. She had removed her shoes, and the bunions were bright red and angry. Mary was right. If he didn't start pulling his weight, Mam might become really ill. 'I'll try to cut down on the beer,' he mumbled.

Sadie glanced from one to the other, knew that

they had been arguing fit to burn. 'Your tea's ready,' she said. 'And keep your voices down in my house, will you?' She returned to the kitchen, her head shaking in despair.

Mary spoke to her brother in a whisper. 'I don't care what I have to do, Bernie, but I'm getting our mam out of that mill.'

Bernard listened to Mary, heard his grumbling stomach. After a nice plate of stew, things would look brighter, he told himself.

'Did you hear me?' she asked.

'I heard you, all right.'

Tommy was already at the table. He had come in the back way, was halfway through his bowl of stew. 'Good day, Bernie?' he asked.

'Brilliant,' came the sarcastic reply. Bernard took the edge off his hunger before fixing his eyes on Mam. Mary was a pain in the backside, but she was right, as usual. 'You can go back on evenings,' mumbled Bernard. 'Or mornings, if they're offered. Me and Mary and Tommy'll look after you.'

Sadie froze, her spoon halfway between plate and mouth. She couldn't eat, couldn't have swallowed to save her life. Bernard was the man of the house, she supposed, and he had spoken.

'You're doing too much,' said Mary. 'My wages are going up, then our Tommy should get more soon.' She smiled over-sweetly at Bernard. 'And Bernard's going to hand the full packet over from now on. Aren't you?'

Bernard nodded.

Sadie put down her spoon and wept silently. Teddy Shawcross had given her three bob and Dolly Minton's famous Bunion Beaters. Mary had bought lavender bags, and now all her children were going to leave themselves short just for her sake.

'Don't cry,' said Tommy. 'Having a bit more time at home should make you happy.'

Sadie dried her eyes on her pinny. 'You're good to me,' she said. 'Pass the beetroot, Mary.' Her appetite was improving fast.

He would be with her, of course. He would be paying court to that reed-thin woman in her corporation house on Tintern Avenue. Vera Hardman was the name. Vera Hardman was the love of Alderman Shawcross's life, and it was time somebody spoke up about his carryings-on.

Alice Shawcross stuffed another chocolate into her mouth and continued to stare blindly at the mirror. She didn't see herself, didn't see anything, because she was concentrating on mint creams and being angry. Edward Shawcross was a mean-spirited man with no thought for his family. Oh, he pretended to love his children, but shouldn't he also love their mother? She had given up so much for him, had lost her once-adoring parents, her child-hood friends, her figure. It had taken ages to get decent people to call at the house – after all, who wanted to associate with a common weaver? It had taken just a few years for Alice to lose her youthful frame. Two children, she had borne him. And what did she have to show for it? A wardrobe filled with outsize frocks, and a starved soul that craved sweets because love was no longer on offer.

She screwed up the empty bag and rummaged in a drawer. The coupons were running out again. If sweets didn't come off ration soon, she would be bereft of all comfort. Cook did her best with biscuits and cakes, but chocolate was Alice's balm. Oh well, she would telephone a few people tomorrow, would beg for help on some pretext or other. Alderman Shawcross would perhaps need sweet coupons in order to buy presents for needy children.

Alice glanced at her watch, wiped her mouth on a handkerchief, made sure that her hair was decent. It was time for dinner. He had not telephoned, had not bothered to inform his family that he would be late. Why had she married him? Why? Her face crumpled for a second as she remembered how she had loved him and needed him. There had been few suitors, as Alice Fishwick had been less than comely. Then, all of a sudden, this charming fellow had turned up, had spoken to her, had nervously invited her to walk with him down the lane outside Aston Leigh. And she had been hooked almost from the start.

She looked at a photograph of her parents. Eleanor and Samuel Fishwick had allowed the marriage. They had, in a sense, created the situation by introducing their daughter to Edward. Then, soon after the wedding, they had disappeared to another continent. Why? Had they hated Edward so strongly? No, no, she reminded herself. Samuel, in particular, had grown very fond of Edward Shawcross, had owed his very life to the young man.

Before her engagement, Alice had sensed her parents' anxiety, had been aware that Mummy and Daddy had worried about her remaining single. It was all a muddle even now, the sudden appearance of a suitor, the quick marriage, the disappearance of Mother and Father. She prayed that they would return to claim back their house and the mill. She hoped fervently that Edward would be cast out, sent back to the slum from which he had crawled.

Her shoulders slumped forward. None of that

could happen, she told herself. Even if her parents did return, Edward would have to stay with her. The disgrace of separation would be too much for her to bear. Unless, of course, he chose to go off into the sunset with the skeletal redhead.

Tomorrow was whist day. Alice's partner, wife of a wealthy and rather common butcher, would accompany her to Top o' th' Moor. There, in the splendour of a true mansion, Alice would struggle to remember trumps and court cards while keeping a careful eye on the lady of the manor. If Alice could manage to play all her cards right, Constance might be married to that crippled boy of theirs. If the silly girl continued to refuse a university education, she would have to make a good marriage. Constance was of a trade family, but James Templeton's limp was a great leveller. Perhaps she should drag Constance along to the game. No. That might be too obvious, too clumsy. It would soon be Constance's birthday. Alice might summon the energy to put on a party for the young people, could perhaps steer her daughter in the direction of the money that dwelt up the moor.

The dinner gong sounded. Alice picked up a pile of sweet wrappings and placed them in a drawer. No-one knew about her private little habit, she told herself. She stood up and walked to the door. Just before leaving the room, she caught sight of a very bulbous woman in the full-length mirror. A few seconds passed before she realized that she was looking at herself. Life was so cruel, so unfair.

On the landing, she almost bumped into her husband. 'Oh,' she squeaked, a hand to her throat. 'I thought you were with . . . I thought you were elsewhere.'

'Not this evening, Alice.' His voice had modulated

itself over the years, yet traces of flat, Bolton vowels continued to colour his words. 'We must talk,' he said.

'But the gong—'

'Never mind the damned gong,' he replied. 'Your parents are coming home.'

She staggered away from him, steadied herself against the door to her room. They had not shared a room for . . . for how many years? And what had he just said? 'I beg your pardon, Edward?'

'Your parents are returning soon.'

'But—'

'Go back.' He reached past her and turned the handle.

When they were inside Alice's bedroom, he waited until she was seated. 'I had a letter this morning,' he said.

She stared hard at him. 'You had a letter? My parents write to me, not to you.'

Edward pushed his hands into his pockets. He didn't know what to tell her, whether to tell her anything at all. For many years, Edward had guarded a secret, had kept a certain group of big bad wolves from the door, had protected Alice, her parents and the children. The truth was unpalatable, yet it might prove useful at this point in his life. Gilbert and Constance were grown. There was nothing to keep him here, nothing at all. And Bolton Council could take a running jump, because he would rather be a free man than an imprisoned alderman. Yet he had enjoyed his civic work, had liked planning and sitting on committees. And, as he looked at his unlovely wife, he knew that he could not hurt her at this moment, could not say those words. Could he leave her? he wondered. Yes, he probably would leave, but he had no intention of destroying Alice by revealing a secret that really belonged to her father.

'Edward?'

'Yes?'

'Why are they coming home?'

'Your father is in uncertain health,' he told her. 'He needs treatment and a good doctor.'

Alice was suddenly frightened. Her marriage had been a sham, and she had always felt that the whole situation had been delicate, even manufactured. She fixed her eyes on her husband's face. 'Why did you marry me?' she asked.

He offered no reply.

'And what is wrong with my father?'

'I'm not sure.'

She would get no answers, she decided. 'We must join the children,' she said. No matter what, the rhythm of Alice's household must remain steady. It was all she had. The domestic certainties provided steadiness and comfort for her insecure soul.

As his wife left the room, Edward Shawcross looked up at the ceiling and exhaled. He was such a coward. The speech had been rehearsed perfectly. And she had given him the ideal opening by asking why he had married her. But he hated hurting people. 'I have to,' he mouthed silently. 'I have to get out of this house before I go mad. But Samuel can do his own bloody dirty work when he gets home.' All in all, Edward had done far too much for Alice's parents. From now on, they could take care of themselves.

Edward Shawcross straightened his tie and followed the mother of his children down the stairs.

TWO

The Fishwick family bible was a weighty, leather-bound tome with its fragile, pristine leaves edged in gold. Constance lifted it down from the shelf, pressed open the clasp and gazed upon a page she had studied many times.

The book had been a wedding gift for Matthew and Sarah Fishwick, who had married in 1836. Their children had been Hannah and Abraham. No attempt had been made to announce the births of Hannah's children, as they would not have been Fishwicks. Abraham Fishwick, born in 1840, had married an Elizabeth Beswick. Two sons were announced in careful copperplate – a Simeon and another Abraham.

Constance sighed, stared through the window as if trying to work her way out of some difficult problem. Simeon, the elder son, had not married, but Abraham, in conjunction with Rachel Hanson, had produced a Samuel in London in 1884. Samuel Fishwick was Constance's grandfather. He was in his early seventies, as was his wife, Eleanor. Neither Constance nor Gilbert had ever heard from their nomadic grandparents.

She ran a finger over her great-greats, through the

greats and into the grands. Her mother's birth had not been announced on this first page of the volume. In her hands, Constance held the evidence of the dying Fishwick family. Aston Leigh, the Fishwick homestead, was now occupied by the Shawcross clan.

Gil entered the library, a finger to his lips. He closed the door silently. 'Dinner at last,' he whispered. 'I think there are on-goings.' The Shawcross children had attached the label 'on-goings' to the rare periods when their parents actually communicated. 'They were both in Mother's bedroom,' Gil added. To add an air of high drama to his statement, Gilbert shook his head and sighed heavily. 'Parents,' he tutted. 'What will they do next?'

'Together? In an upper room? Good God!' exclaimed Constance. 'Surely you don't mean real and actual on-goings?'

Gil smiled ruefully. 'Calm down, Minnie Minx,' he said. 'Parents fully clothed, as far as I know. And the whole on-going lasted about two minutes.'

Constance shook her head. 'No,' she said. 'It couldn't happen in two minutes. Not while they were dressed. I bet Mother's a virgin all over again.' They joked and laughed as usual, because the tension in the house needed easing. 'We'd better go in, then.'

Gil pointed to the bible. 'You weren't reading that thing, were you? Are you looking for inspiration for your great novel?'

'No. I was just wondering. How different things might have been if Great Uncle Simeon hadn't died without issue. Great-Grandfather Abraham might have stayed in London, and Grandfather Samuel would have been a southerner and—'

'And you wouldn't be sitting there eulogizing,

because you would not have existed, Minnie, old thing.'

Constance laughed at her brother. 'Where is your soul, Gil?'

'On the bottom of my shoe, Con.'

Arm in arm, they went into the dining room.

Alice sat at one end of the table, a disapproving frown creasing her forehead. She glanced meaningfully at the clock, then waited for her errant offspring to be seated. Alice's appetite, dulled by chocolate, was almost non-existent. Her parents were coming home. She should be happy, excited, but she wasn't. Something in Edward's face was troubling her. He looked like a man who was about to climb a mountain in order to reach safer territory. Edward was nervous, yet happier than usual.

Edward picked up his spoon and began on the soup, a watery concoction of vegetables and meat stocks. The woman he had married was stirring the liquid, was pretending to take delicate sips. Alice had already eaten. She would be stuffed to the brim with sugary confections.

Gil winked at his sister, was sorry when she choked.

Alice eyed her daughter. 'It is a good thing that we do not have company, Constance,' she barked. 'Sit up straight and give your digestive system a chance to work.'

Gil, a shining, dark-eyed angel, winked again.

Constance promised herself the pleasure of battering her brother later. He could get away with just about anything, because he was so terribly good-looking. Like Father, he was dark-skinned and dark-haired. Unlike Father, Gil was clean-shaven. Father's beard made him so old, Constance thought.

Ada Dobson, Jill of all trades with the exception of

41

cooking, cleared away the soup bowls, then carried sliced lamb and vegetables from warming dishes to the table. Edward no longer carved the meats.

While Ada doled out food, Constance sat like the perfect lady, studying her parents covertly as carrots, potatoes and roast lamb were distributed by the maid. Mother was fatter than ever. Her hair was scraped back too severely, offering neither shade nor shelter to a grey dumpling face whose weighty deposits had settled around deep lines of displeasure.

Father continued regal and handsome. He was tall, broad and powerful. Constance had inherited his uncommonly long and slender fingers, a feature that was very much at odds with Father's humble beginnings. In fact, Mother looked out of place in this setting, while Father seemed perfectly at home. But he was not at home. An 'at home' father would have carved the roast, would have chatted with his nearest and dearest during the ceremony. He was not content, yet his eyes seemed brighter this evening. What was going on here? Constance wondered.

The pudding was apple sponge with custard, a speciality of Cook's. Alice prodded the fluffy offering, yet no expectant juices coated her tongue. Something momentous was about to happen. She had always been uneasy about her parents' abandonment of her, had often had the feeling that Edward knew something vital, something she had failed to notice all those years ago. And, from what he had said earlier, it was plain that Father had kept in touch with Edward over the years, probably sending letters to the mill. There was mystery here, she decided, a form of dark concealment that was about to erupt into everyone's life.

The coffee arrived with cheeseboard and crackers. Edward sipped from his demi-tasse, then took the watch from his waistcoat pocket. 'Tell Cook that the meal was splendid,' he advised Ada. Ada, recognizing dismissal in his tone, left the room.

Edward Shawcross inhaled deeply. 'Gilbert, Constance, your grandparents are coming home.'

Constance managed not to choke a second time. 'When?' she managed finally.

'Soon.' Edward rose from the table, placed his napkin on the side plate, then stepped towards the door. 'I have a meeting shortly,' he said. 'Planning. Something to do with new shops in the centre of town.'

Alice eyed him warily. He was up to something. The pores on her arms had opened, and she forced herself to suppress a shiver of fear.

Meanwhile, Constance worked hard to contain her excitement. She had grandparents at last. They promised to be interesting, not just because of old age, but also because they had travelled.

Edward opened the door.

'See you later, Pater,' quipped Gilbert as his father left the room. 'Grandparents!' he said to his sister. They had no aunts, no uncles, no cousins. Apart from Mother and Father, Gilbert and Constance were bereft of relatives. Father had a brother, but that particular uncle had disappeared to Australia years earlier.

Alice rose from the table, almost stumbled over the chair when it caught the backs of her knees.

'Mother?' Constance saw the unsteadiness, the uncertainty in Alice Shawcross's face. 'Are you all right?'

Alice looked at her children, sniffed, then left the room. She was suddenly close to tears.

Vera Hardman lived in a newish council house in Tintern Avenue, a street that stretched from Tonge Moor through to the ring road. A slender woman in her early thirties, Vera had never married. Her mother, who had suffered from severe asthma, had been Vera's sole responsibility once all the other siblings had left home. As the youngest female of a large family, Vera had fitted the usual Cinderella role until her mother's death.

She sat on a green moquette couch with William, an alsatian of uncertain temperament. William's start in life had been rough, but his new mistress was gentling him towards more acceptable behaviour. 'The postman was just bringing a letter,' she informed the panting animal.

William pricked up the splendid ears and tipped his large head to one side. She hadn't hit him yet, hadn't taken a strap or a chain to him. He was allowed to stay indoors and had been given things to chew, plenty to eat and a level of affection he was struggling to comprehend. 'Woof,' he said.

Vera grinned at him. 'I know the binmen take stuff away, lad, but it's their job.'

He cocked his head to the opposite side. She talked a lot, this one. Still, the new life was better than guarding a rag yard day and night for very little food and too many beatings.

She stroked his head, looked in wonderment at teeth powerful enough to rip her in half. The miracle lay in the fact that this maltreated animal chose not to attack her. 'So stop chasing people, William,' she said. 'And be nice to Edward, because he rescued you.' Edward would be arriving shortly. He always left his car on the main road, though Vera knew that several of her neighbours were becoming suspicious. She sensed it when curtains twitched and when conversations stopped the minute she entered a shop.

William raised a large paw and placed it on her knee.

'Are you promising to be good?' she asked.

'Woof,' he replied.

'Oh well.' She stood up, batted a few dog hairs off her skirt. 'If that's as intelligent as your conversation gets, I think I'll have a cup of tea instead.'

In the tiny kitchen, Vera lit the gas and filled the kettle. She could hear William breathing in the doorway. Whenever she moved, he followed her. The only times he spent alone were when she was in bed or at work. Vera worked five evenings a week at the local off-licence. This was one of her evenings off, so she and Edward would have a few hours together. Usually, he picked her up from the shop after his council meetings and brought her home. Today, he was supposed to be telling his wife about Vera.

She brewed the tea, found a couple of digestive biscuits, threw one into the alsatian's ever-gaping maw. 'You'll eat me out of house and home,' she said absently. Had he told her? What was going to happen? And why, after all this time, had Edward suddenly decided to come clean?

The front door opened. William, hackles rising, bounded through the little living room and prepared to attack.

'Truce!' shouted Edward. The dog lunged at him, tried to lick his saviour to death. 'You'll get no sense out of this chap,' Edward managed between soggy licks. 'He's as daft as they come.' He separated himself from the canine lunatic, kissed Vera on the nose, then settled on the couch.

William sat next to him, leaving a small space for Vera right at the end. He panted first at Edward, then at Vera.

'He's coming between us,' announced Edward gravely.

William grinned.

Vera waited for Edward to speak up. She had learnt not to question him about his life at home, because he looked so miserable whenever he was encouraged to discuss his marriage. 'Cup of tea?' she asked.

'No, thanks.' He cleared his throat. 'I haven't said much yet, Vera. She knows about her parents coming home, but that's about all. I can't talk to her.'

Vera nodded, sipped at her tea, spilled half of it when the dog decided to jump down to the floor.

'I'd got myself all wound up for it, too,' said Edward. 'There I was in my office with poor Sadie Martindale.' He paused for a moment. 'When my mother died, Sadie looked after me. I was six, so Sadie would have been about fifteen. I remember her drying my tears. Dad just went out and got drunk as usual. Her feet are giving her some terrible pain, but it's hard to know what to do.'

While he carried on reminiscing, Vera took care not to prompt him. She loved this man more than life itself, but she didn't want to force his hand. If he decided to leave his wife, then Vera would have him gladly. Pushing or cajoling would be wrong, she told herself. Edward had a lot to lose.

'Where was I?' he asked.

'In your office with Sadie Martindale's feet.'

He smiled. Vera had a way of summing up things in a very droll fashion. He should have married someone like Vera, should have stayed where he belonged, among real people who talked to one another and laughed together. 'It was a mistake,' he said.

Vera turned her head and looked at him.

'I married her out of fear.'

He had never said much before. Vera poured the dregs from her saucer back into the cup.

'My mother and father both drank. Mam was bright yellow when she died. I remember wondering how she had managed to get sunburnt in the middle of winter. It was her liver cracking up, of course. Dad was a boozer, too. All I wanted was to be safe and well away from poverty. So I married Alice a year or so after Dad failed to wake from his final stupor.'

Vera placed her cup on a side table and reached out for him. He was like a child sometimes, a confused infant who could not understand the cruelties of life. 'I love you, Edward Shawcross,' she said. 'Don't explain things, not to me, not unless you really want to.' She stood up, whistled at William, then led the dog into the back garden. As she closed the door, she smiled at a picture that had formed in her mind, imagined how William might have reacted if she and Edward had made love in front of him.

She stood on the hearthrug and peeled off her clothes. With any other human, Vera would have been embarrassed to the point of terror. She was small-breasted and skinny-limbed, and her belly was almost concave. All her life, she had been taunted about her lack of flesh. During adolescence, boys had rejected her and taunted her as a Skinny Lizzy.

But none of that mattered now, because Edward loved her anyway.

He sat very still and watched her, marvelled at her innocence. It was strange how such an unpadded woman could be comforting. In a moment, he would melt into her and all his troubles could go away for a while. For now, he enjoyed simply looking at Vera. At home, his plump wife would be eating something sweet in the cosy isolation of her bedroom. In spite of all her blubber, Alice had always been cold. It had been like making love to a very large iceberg, he told himself. And, like the *Titanic*, he had not emerged intact after encountering such disaster.

Vera lifted up her arms. 'Come on, Edward,' she said huskily. 'Or that damned dog'll start barking again.'

Accepting the invitation gladly, Edward Shawcross knelt on the hearthrug and paid court to a very real woman. She was slender, tough and wonderfully responsive. For Vera, he was prepared to give up just about everything.

Alice Shawcross glared at her daughter. 'Look, I know exactly the same as you know, Constance, no more and no less.' She sniffed, allowing the impression that a bad smell had accompanied Constance into the drawing room. 'Your father said very little to me.'

Constance could not understand why her mother was so quiet, so unenthusiastic. Her parents were returning from abroad after an absence of twenty-odd years, yet Alice Shawcross maintained the same grim, creased countenance as ever. 'Aren't you pleased to hear such news?'

Alice was afraid, but she strove to hide it. Mother

and Father were coming home, and something else was about to end. She hated change. The house was going to be fuller and busier. There would be more people at table, further witnesses to the sham that was the Shawcross marriage. 'I shall be glad to see them,' she answered carefully, untruthfully.

Constance decided that Mother was undecided. If Alice's mind was in an un-made-up state, then this might be a good time for Constance to speak up. 'I didn't do terribly well at school,' she began.

'I know.' Alice folded her arms across the bulge of her stomach, as if cradling and comforting herself against inner pain. 'Even so, I think you would make a good teacher of music.'

Connie was not interested in music. 'There is a course at the technical college,' she said quietly. 'Shorthand, typing, general office skills.'

Alice arched an eyebrow.

'It's 1950, Mother. Girls are doing all kinds of jobs. I don't want to carry on with music and English – I'd rather do something real.'

'You have abilities,' snapped Alice. 'You should use your gifts. Why waste yourself?'

Constance stood her ground. She was lumbered with a ridiculously unfashionable name, an unsupportive mother and a father who was usually absent. She wanted something of her own, a proper, down-to-earth career, a future. 'I shall be starting next September,' she said.

Alice smiled, though her eyes remained icy. 'As you wish, dear,' she said. 'And close the door on your way out, will you?' The mother's heart bled. Why couldn't she speak her mind? What stopped her from telling Constance how much she loved her, how much she wanted for her? I can't show love, she said inwardly. Because I've forgotten about love.

Rejected and pink-faced, Constance went through the French doors into the garden. It was a fine, warm day filled with buzzing bees and chirruping birds. The gardener and his lad were paying their weekly visit, and Ada Dobson, Aston Leigh's maid of all work, was paying her weekly visit to the gardener's lad. Constance winked at the courting couple before walking out into the lane.

Across the lane, at the other side of a low stone wall, James Templeton sat painting. Seated, James was a handsome if rather pale man, with a great deal of blond hair and an attractive, open face. An only child, he had suffered damage at birth, had been dragged into the world by means of some nasty-looking metal contraption. He had managed to acquire a set of forceps, had done a self-portrait with the ghastly apparatus wrapped around his face. 'That's me to a T,' he would say to his friends. 'Special delivery, registered post.' The forceps hung above his bed next to an advertisement for Carter's Little Liver Pills. James was eccentric, but deliberately so.

'Hello, James.'

'Hi.' He added a touch of yellow to an extremely surreal cow.

'Have you been drinking?' asked Constance.

'What time is it?' he enquired.

'About four o'clock.'

He chewed on the end of his brush. 'Doubt it,' he said finally. 'Usually, I start at about five. But one never knows, does one?'

'No, one doesn't.' She sat on the grass next to his stool. 'What sort of an animal is that?' The cow had three legs and the trunk of an elephant.

'It's not an animal,' he said with exaggerated patience. 'It's a statement.'

Constance flopped backwards and shaded her eyes from the sun. 'I'm asking no more questions,' she announced. James's answers were too obtuse for Constance's current frame of mind. 'I'm going to technical college,' she murmured.

'Right away? Is the bus due?'

'In September. I want to do something. If I don't do something, I shall go stark, staring mad.'

'Didn't you do something last year?'

Last year, Constance had worked voluntarily in a little cottage hospital. She had indulged in pleasant activities like reading to the bedridden and arranging flowers. The year before had been spent in a workshop for the blind. 'Mother has me filling in time until I get a university place or a man,' she replied. 'And I've had enough. So I'm going to learn office skills, get a proper job and leave home once and for all.'

James laid down his brush and stared at her. She was excessively beautiful, which was why he treated her so flippantly. If he thought about it, he treated most people flippantly so that they would like him. If he belittled himself, then he might be accepted in spite of being a cripple. 'She won't let you leave,' he said. 'She would send for the army and the fire brigade if you went off. In fact, an Act of Parliament is probably being prepared for statute as we speak.'

'Stop it, James,' she said. 'I'm serious.'

He shifted on the stool to ease his bad leg. 'I have the solution. You and I should marry, then our families would leave us alone.'

Sometimes, Constance thought that her heart would break in two. James was the loveliest person.

He wasn't always silly, wasn't always trying too hard to be amusing. When they talked, really talked, he spilled his soul to her. 'I'm not ready for marriage,' she told him.

'And even if you were, you would not consider me.'

'I didn't say that.'

'But you thought it.'

'James, you are my friend.' She sat up, pushed back her hair and sought a change of subject. 'As a friend, please tell me honestly, what do you think of my name?'

He inhaled deeply and stared at the canvas for a moment or two. 'This painting is your mother and mine rolled into one. Yours is a cow and mine's an elephant – she forgets nothing. Your name stinks, Constance. I am deeply sorry to be the one to break such dreadful news, but it's a bugger of a handle.'

She nodded. 'I shall change it.' She did a mental roll call of names, came up with nothing suitable.

'Angela?' he suggested.

She pulled a wry face. 'Too holy. No, Connie will do.'

'Connie is common-sounding. Your mother won't like Connie.'

'Good,' she replied. 'Connie it is, then. Because, James, I really dislike my mother.'

He spat on his hand and reached out. 'Shake,' he said solemnly. Her hand was so soft, the fingers long, slender and sure. God, how he loved her. Had he been whole in body, he would have fought dragons for her. 'And welcome to the bloody club. We are a select few. Meetings are every alternate Tuesday in the Pig and Whistle. Just wear a silly hat and ask for the Whoms.'

'Whoms?'

'W-H-O-M-s. The We Hate Our Mothers group. Of course, Peter Charleson is a whop, because he nurtures a dislike for parents in general.'

'This is very sad,' she said quietly. 'We're supposed to love our families.'

A frown chased its way across James's face. He dismissed it quickly, replaced it with the usual smile. 'They are meant to love us, Connie,' he reminded her. 'Love breeds love. Remember that.'

Maude Templeton watched the scene, her lip curling when James reached out and touched that girl. That girl was an upstart, a damned nuisance, too free with her opinions and far too plebeian for James. She lowered the binoculars and sat on the edge of her son's bed. He had painted the forceps purple. Maude would not look at them, because they were the evidence of her own failure. Had she pushed harder, had she put in some effort, her son might have been born without all that fuss.

There had been no more children. She had failed to carry another baby to full-term, had been left with just one precious son whose gait was a daily reminder of her own limitations. Eric never mentioned the subject, yet he probably blamed his wife for neglecting to produce a sound heir.

James treated the whole issue as a huge joke. His limp was a joke, the forceps were a joke, his family's sorrow was probably the biggest joke of all. Maude's son was failing to come to terms with the realities of his existence. He had wealthy parents. As the son of landed people, he had a duty to marry well. Apart from the limp, James was an attractive boy with a good brain and much to offer. He had the opportunity to expand the Templeton empire by marrying into a similar situation, preferably one without sons.

Maude picked up a book of English verse, tut-tutted impatiently when it fell open at 'Dream-Pedlary' by Thomas Lovell Beddoes. Poetry, music and painting – James lived in a totally unreal world. She skimmed the first verse, read,

> If there were dreams to sell,
> What would you buy?
> Some cost a passing bell;
> Some a light sigh,
> That shakes from Life's fresh crown
> Only a roseleaf down.
> If there were dreams to sell,
> Merry and sad to tell,
> And the crier rung the bell,
> What would you buy?

A loose page was squeezed as marker between the leaves. Maude took it, discovered among many crossings-out her son's answer to the poem's question.

> If there were dreams to sell,
> I'd buy a leg,
> Of proper flesh and bone,
> Not just a peg
> That scratches on the ground
> A deathly, bloodless sound.
> If there were dreams to sell,
> I'd happy run to hell,
> Straight and rudely well
> In Satan's eye.

Maude's hand trembled so badly that the page fluttered to the ground. He never talked about this, never made a fuss about being less than whole. Yet here, in silent words, he had made his statement. The mother of James Templeton picked up his work and replaced it carefully on his bed. He hurt. The happy chap who spent his days painting the unrecognizable and mooning after Constance Shawcross was in pain.

Maude Templeton did not believe in quick decisions. She voted Conservative, attended evensong every Sunday and played whist eight times a month. As a token of charity and neighbourliness, she allowed the dreadful woman from Aston Leigh, together with the wife of a very loud-mouthed butcher, to join one whist session each week. On a broader scale, Maude worked tirelessly for the young victims of infantile paralysis and made a donation each Christmas to the RSPCA, because unfairness to animals was abhorrent, while cruelty to them was unthinkable.

She rose and walked to the window, tried to imagine how she might feel if one leg were shorter than the other, if one of her shoes had a great, built-up sole to compensate for the lack of almost two inches. James's hip often ached; she had caught him rubbing his side sometimes. The girl had gone. James sat with his head down and the palette thrown aside.

Maude picked up the binoculars, saw Constance Shawcross skipping up the lane on strong, sun-kissed legs. She was a pretty girl. The summer weather had lightened her hair, had made her skin vibrant. She was healthy. Constance Shawcross was a good specimen. She knew James, probably liked him well enough. The Shawcross people were not gentry, yet neither were they paupers. Trade people often 'looked after their own', were usually appreciative and protective when someone with a better pedigree came along to give them a boost.

The telephone rang. It was no matter; the housekeeper would answer it, no doubt. Maude's train of thought journeyed onward, needed little fuel to speed its course. James would stay nearby if he married Constance. Were he to marry some horsy girl from Cheshire or East Lancashire, Maude might not get to see him very often. The Shawcross girl was sturdy, and her name could be changed in a matter of minutes to Templeton. She had good bearing, a pleasant enough if rather forward nature, a lovely face. Given time, Maude Templeton would, no doubt, knock the girl into shape.

The one drawback was Alice Shawcross. Alice was a mean-faced and petulant woman with all the charm of an open grave. But she was not a strong character, promised to be considerably grateful should James take on the daughter. 'Quick decisions,' Maude said aloud. 'I must speak to Eric first.'

Hilda Ainsworth, housekeeper at Top o' th' Moor, entered the room. 'Telephone ma'am,' she said.

'Who is it?'

'Mr Templeton, ma'am.'

Maude followed the woman out to the landing and down the curving staircase. She didn't want her son writing sad odes about walking upright into hell. She didn't want James to be unhappy to the point of suicide. It would be a sacrifice of enormous proportions, yet it promised to make James happy. 'Hello, Eric,' she said into the receiver. She would start working on her husband right away. 'I do hope you won't be late, my dear. There is something we must discuss, something of great importance . . .'

Alice had never been very good at cards. Her partner, Jessica Barton of Barton's Butcher's notoriety, was equally inept, though she always covered her mistakes with a fluttery, 'Oh, silly Jessie, what must you all think of me?' whenever she made what she referred to as a 'pig's ear' of the game.

Maude, who had been seriously considering upgrading to bridge, decided to stick to whist for the Shawcrosses and the Bartons of her acquaintance. Bridge could quite easily send Jessica Barton into a flurry of apologies, while Alice Shawcross was depressed enough by a simple game of whist. 'Tea, everyone?' she asked sweetly.

All four women sighed with relief. Maude's partner, the widow of the Templetons' land agent, was glad of the break. An accomplished contract bridge player, she had little patience with women who could not remember trumps for two seconds together. She cast a critical eye over the Barton–Shawcross partnership. Jessica was resplendent in a dress of many colours, none of which suited her. Alice had stuck to her usual plain suit, this time in an unattractive shade of mud.

Alice fanned herself with a score sheet. 'It's getting no cooler, is it?' she asked of no-one in particular.

Maude pulled the cord to summon tea and sandwiches.

'Very warm,' agreed Jessica. 'Poor Joseph's got his work cut out to keep the meat fresh. They're no sooner slaughtered than they start to go off.'

Irene Cawley shuddered and raised an eyebrow at

her hostess. The subject of tainted meat was hardly a suitable topic for discussion in the face of cucumber sandwiches and fairy cakes. Irene, whose husband had died the previous year, was Maude Templeton's sole confidante. Maude had discussed with Irene her thoughts about James and Constance and, though Irene remained unconvinced, she felt beholden to the Templetons. After Sidney's untimely death, his employers had found Irene a little house and had paid her a sum sufficiently handsome to provide interest enough to exist on. 'How is your daughter, Alice?' Irene asked now.

Alice, unused to personal questions, coloured slightly. 'She is well enough, thank you.'

'A pretty girl,' said Maude. 'Strong, too.'

Alice Shawcross offered up a hesitant smile in exchange for a small sandwich.

'What is she doing with herself these days?' asked Irene.

'She wants to go to college,' replied Alice. 'Not to university, unfortunately. They aren't like we were, are they? We would have given up a great deal for the chance of a university education. But she wants to follow the herd into the world of commerce. Of course, Constance is twenty-one shortly, so she doesn't listen to her mother any more.'

Maude bit into a sliver of angel cake. 'Almost time she got herself married, then.'

Alice made no reply.

'She'll make somebody a good wife,' offered Jessica. 'I've always liked Constance. She seems such a pleasant girl, usually has a smile on her face. I can't be doing with miserable folk.' She glanced at Alice and blushed. Alice was misery incarnate, especially in that dreadful colour. Also, Jessica should watch her language in company such as this. She should not say things like 'can't be doing with', because such phrases made her sound like . . . like a butcher's wife. Middle-classdom sat uncomfortably on Jessica Barton's shoulders. She reached for another sandwich and made an inner vow of silence.

'I thought we might have a young persons' occasion quite soon,' said Maude. 'Just a casual affair – fruit punch, sausage rolls – you know how they love that sort of food.'

Jessica sat up, her vow of silence forgotten. 'Joseph will be pleased to supply the meat,' she said. 'At discount, of course.' She blushed again, partly because she had spat a few crumbs, mostly because she had mentioned discount. People like Maude Templeton didn't know about such things, since they had housekeepers to do the shopping.

Alice swallowed the food and took a sip of tea. She craved chocolate and solitude, longed to feel that sweet, melting mass on her tongue, wanted to savour the sensuous luxury that had replaced her longing for human company. She was, she supposed, rather like an alcoholic. Only when alone could she completely indulge herself. Wrappings were hidden in paper bags and stuffed deep into drawers so that no-one would discover her Achilles' heel. Like a drinker with his empty bottles, Alice concealed all evidence of her criminally stupid behaviour.

'Alice?'

Maude was speaking to her. The desire for chocolate had been reborn because Maude Templeton frightened her and chocolate was a soothing drug. 'Yes?' she managed.

'Come upstairs,' said Maude. 'There's something I would rather like you to see.'

Alice closed her gaping mouth, placed cup, saucer and plate on the tea trolley, then struggled inelegantly to her feet. The chair was low, too low for a person of Alice's bulk. Feeling like a country bumpkin at a hunt ball, Alice Shawcross pursued her hostess into the hallway.

Top o' th' Moor was twice the size of Aston Leigh, was a place where things thrown together artlessly looked artistic and stunning. There was a mish-mash of black Wedgwood, Spode, cubism, impressionism, art nouveau, art deco, Capodimonte, leather, mosaic, sculpture. Every last inch of the walls was covered in some kind of painting, while tables and cupboards groaned beneath the weight of ornaments. Anywhere else, Alice thought, would have looked tacky like this, but Maude had a way of . . . of arranging things. What was she arranging now?

The bedroom was strangely bare, painted white and with a huge four-poster dominating the scene. Alice watched while Maude opened a drawer and fiddled among layers of tissue paper. The room was scented, as if a rose garden sat just outside the door.

Maude let out a triumphant 'Yes,' then brought a package to her neighbour. 'This is not my colour,' she said. 'But it's yours. I do hope you won't be offended, Alice, but it's just the most wonderful silk. Four and a half yards of it, too.'

Alice didn't know how to act, what to say. She remembered long-ago Christmases when, as a specially favoured child, she had risen to find her room filled with gifts. More recently, Christmas had been just another day except for gloves or handkerchieves. 'Thank you,' she stammered.

Maude eyed her neighbour. They had never been friends, but Maude suddenly felt a degree of pity for the unlovely woman. It was that damned poem, she told herself inwardly. James had discovered a crack in her armour, had allowed in the thin end of a wedge. 'Alice, you must start to look after yourself. No-one else will, you see. The men blunder about blindly from one day to the next, no thought except for their own comfort. You know, if I were to die in my chair downstairs, Eric would scarcely notice.' She placed a hand on Alice's fat arm. 'Vegetables are my secret. Vegetables, fruit and a brisk walk each morning.'

'Oh.' Alice's tone was high and squeaky.

'Cod liver oil, plenty of oranges. Cut down on the confectionery, my dear.' The face was pale grey and unhealthy. 'And a good haircut. Look.' She unwrapped the silk. 'Did you ever see a shade like that before? It defies description, does it not?' It wasn't peach, wasn't pink, wasn't any particular colour, yet it shone like a pale sunset.

'It's wonderful,' agreed Alice. 'I don't know what to say.'

Maude clicked her tongue. 'Well, the damned stuff has been sitting in that drawer since 1946. I looked at you earlier and decided that you should have it.'

Tears pricked Alice's thick eyelids. Someone had thought about her, just as Mummy and Daddy had once done. 'My parents are coming home,' she blurted before thinking properly.

'Really?'

Alice nodded, sniffed away the self-pity. 'Father's health has been playing up.'

Maude nodded sympathetically. 'It would. I mean, all those mosquitoes and sleeping sickness and malaria.' No-one had ever worked out what had prompted the Fishwicks' sudden emigration. 'Will they stay with you?'

'I expect so.' It was their house. It was their mill, their money, their land. Alice picked up the package of material and thanked Maude again.

'Don't mention it,' replied the hostess. If Alice could lose a bit of weight and do something about her skin, the silk would look very well on the mother of the bride.

Bernard Martindale, at twenty-six years of age, had just suffered the biggest showing-up of his life. Mary was on the bounce. She was on the bounce because Bernard had not tipped up his full whack. 'What about your bloody market stall?' he asked. 'Shouldn't you be at your own work?'

Mary stood with arms akimbo and head thrown back. She wasn't frightened of her brother, couldn't have cared less about the small gathering of miners studying the scene. 'I am as good as my own boss,' she replied. 'Soon, I'll be manager, so I asked for an hour off and I got it.' She paused for breath, then began again. 'Some use you are, eh? Mam gets the evening shift so she can take things easy, then you go boozing with this motley crew.'

The motley crew took a step back, as if their move had been choreographed.

'Where is it?' she demanded. 'There was near one pound ten less than there should have been.'

Bernard shrugged. 'I must have lost it.'

A young man in the crowd giggled.

'What's up with you?' Mary asked. 'Somebody touch your funny bone? There's nothing to laugh at, I can tell you that for nowt. My mam's wore herself out looking after this daft swine. And he goes and pours good money down his gob.' She grabbed her brother's arm. 'I've found you a place,' she told him. 'Nine bob a week, plus gas. It's down Vernon Street where they put the stray dogs to sleep.' She nodded twice. 'Happen that's what'll become of you, Bernard. Your things are in a bag in the back yard next to the air raid shelter.'

Bernard stood with his mouth agape while his sister flounced off towards the bus stop. She meant it. The one thing he could be sure of about Mary was that she meant what she said. Mam needed their Mary. If Mam had to choose between him and his sister, there'd be no contest.

'What are you going to do, then?' asked another face worker.

'I'm going home, that's what,' replied Bernard. 'She's a cut above herself, is our Mary.'

'Will your mam let you in?'

'Course she will.' Mam would let him in, all right, but Mary would see him off. He dashed off up the street and jumped on the bus just before it pulled away.

Mary was in a front seat. She would always be in a front seat, thought Bernard as he placed himself next to her. 'It won't happen again,' he said out of the corner of his mouth.

'You what?' asked Mary.

'You heard me, right enough.'

She swivelled round and caught the eyes of other passengers. 'Are you telling me in front of all these people that you'll never open another wage packet, Bernard Martindale?'

He shrank down in his seat, wished with all his heart that the bus would crash or do something that would take the attention away from him.

'A sick mother's a big responsibility,' yelled Mary. 'You'll have to start looking after her, won't you?'

'Yes,' he whispered. 'Now, shut your bloody mouth, Mary.' The trouble with women was that you couldn't give them a good thumping and get everything over and done with in a quick, clean fashion. Had she been a workmate, or even his younger brother, he would have sorted the whole thing out in two shakes.

Mary patted his knee and smiled. 'There now. That didn't hurt, did it?' She knew she had him right where she wanted him. Any more messing, and she'd be back at the pit with another mouthful for him. 'Have you got your busfare?' she asked sweetly.

'Course I have.'

'Good,' she said. 'You can pay mine and all. Let's face it, it's your fault I'm here.'

Bernard paid the fares and kept his mouth shut. He'd read somewhere that it was a man's world, but he was not too sure about that. While their Mary was in the world, it was hers. For the foreseeable future, ale would be off the menu.

THREE

Sometimes, chocolate was not enough. When the sun started to dip in the sky, Alice's heart often went down with it. The nights were so long, so silent except for the occasional eerie hoot of an owl or the report of a gunshot in the Top o' th' Moor woods. People hunted rabbits and hares among the trees, often at night, sometimes quite noisily. Inside Aston Leigh, walls closed in, rooms seemed to grow smaller, the ticking of the clock had no rival save for the beating of Alice's saddened heart.

Alice Shawcross, née Fishwick, was simply sitting in a house and eating chocolate, waiting to die, perhaps hoping for that final release. There was birth, there was death, and the space between the two was called life. Life. Living, moving, breathing, laughing, crying, singing, enjoying. Loving. The clock chimed ten times. Was she really going to sit here and wait for that never-time when the damned thing would strike thirteen?

Constance would leave home soon. She would probably escape long before Gilbert made a move. Gilbert was studying maths, physics and chemistry at Imperial College, London, so Aston Leigh remained his base just during holidays. But Constance was restless. She was no more an academic than Gilbert was, but Constance probably had a good business head on her. Gilbert was struggling. For all his immersion in the sciences, Gilbert remained an easy-going chap with a marked lack of drive when it came to books.

Constance. How Alice wished that she could talk to the girl, communicate properly about the future with its dreams and the past with its memories. 'I don't know how to talk to my own daughter or my own son,' she said softly. 'Perhaps that's because no-one talks much to me.'

The chocolates lay on the bed beside her. Alice picked up an orange delight, looked at it, breathed it in, allowed the sickly-sweet aroma to enter her nose. It was a small but deadly thing, no more than half an inch across, smug and secure in its brown, silky-smooth jacket.

She had taken that other silk, Maude Templeton's silk, had placed it in a bottom drawer among layers of tissue. It was too nice for her, too beautiful for such an ugly, misshapen woman. A contest had begun in the core of her mind, a tug-of-war between the orange delight and those yards of wondrous silk. She could not have both. If she took the sweet, she would take another and another until she felt sick. And all those calories would sit about her person in horrible, lumpy rolls of lard.

If she chose the paler silk, that four and a half yards of not-quite-peach elegance, there could be no more chocolate. No more chocolate. How could she possibly enjoy a play on the wireless without a few nice, soft centres? And reading always brought the craving on. Reading made her hungry, avid for the lives in the books, ravenous for involvement, communication, love. Was chocolate love, then? If it

66

was, then the love was a one-way feeling, because she was being sorely ill-treated by the object of her desires. It was melting, was sticking to her fingers, was sticking all over her flesh in great mounds of unsightly fat.

Alice studied her nails. They were polished and shaped, but they had no length to them. It would be lovely to have a bit of pale lacquer on the ends of her fingers. Maude wore discreet colours on her nails. Alice's digits were plump, but a longer nail would extend them. Where was that hand cream? The orange delight was speaking to her, crying out to be eaten. Hand cream, not sweet cream, she reminded herself determinedly. Centre drawer of the dressing table, she thought. There was face cream, too, in an opaque glass jar with a gilded lid.

Sewing. She remembered bits of tapestry that she had begun and grown tired of, recalled a little tray cloth with unfinished daisies round its edge. A person could not sew and eat chocolate simultaneously. Cocoa products and white linen made poor bedfellows. Sewing while listening to the wireless might work, but reading was another matter. The reading must happen downstairs where there was no chocolate. In fact, reading in the garden might be a good idea.

Alice got out of bed and walked to the full-length mirror. She wiped the melted orange delight onto a page of a magazine, then ripped off all her clothes. It was a long time since she had examined her body. Fat women tended to concentrate on their faces, she reminded the fragile inner soul. Hair and make-up, never mind the rest. She looked and she minded.

Her breasts had moved south, as had the stomach and the abdomen. Turned sideways, she looked about seven months pregnant, probably with twins. The tops of her arms were huge, while hips and thighs were dimpled and threaded with new, purple stretch marks. She was forty-three years old, and she had the body of a very ancient woman. Tears sprang to her eyes, but she ordered them to retreat. This was serious business and there was no time for the spillage of emotion.

Walking, vegetables, fruit and cod liver oil had combined to make Maude Templeton younger than her years. 'She's older than I am,' said Alice to her reflection. 'You aren't old, Alice. You just don't love yourself, that's all. If you don't love you, who will?' Nobody would.

She moved in closer and studied her face. Yes, the nose was large, but she had a generous mouth and the eyes were not too bad. With a decent hairstyle, she might look a sight better. Her stomach rumbled, complained about being unemployed, empty and bored. It was now or never, Alice told the fat person in her mirror. And it would be no use telling herself that she could have a little bit of chocolate every day, or at the weekend, or on her birthday. Like an opium addict, she had to quit for ever, no giving in, no weakening of resolve.

The clock seemed quieter and the room was not as small as it had appeared earlier. When an owl hooted, Alice smiled, interpreted the sound as a sign of continuing life. It was only chocolate, she reminded herself. She would still be able to eat, would not become undernourished.

Yet it took a tremendous courage, a strength of whose existence she had been unaware, to finally grab the confectionery and squash it into an inedible mess. When the task was completed, Alice took herself into her bathroom, found lotions and creams, ran a hot tub. From tonight, her real self could begin to form.

The system worked quite well. Mary Martindale had appointed herself Keeper of the Purse. Although this position had been acquired by a method bearing no relationship to democracy, everyone else in the household was relieved. Mary took the wage packets, including her own, and tipped the contents onto the green tablecloth. She then divided the spoils into piles for rent, food, gas, electricity and insurance.

A family meeting was held each Friday after tea, and the remaining money was allocated to the members of the quorum. If someone was missing, no decisions were made until he or she returned.

Bernard got his beer money, as did Tommy, while Sadie took a few bob for baccy and papers. Mary saved. Had there been just a halfpenny spare at the end of the calculations, she would have walked to the post office with it. She made her own clothes, stitched everything by hand, and made do with cobbled shoes until the uppers fell apart.

Sadie was filled with admiration for her daughter. They sat together one Friday night while the boys were at the pub, Mary at one side of the grate and Sadie at the other. Mary had brought a jug of stout from the off-licence, and each partook of this frothy concoction from a white pint mug. 'I don't know how you do it, love,' said Sadie. 'Our Bernard, I mean.'

Mary had her methods, but she kept them under her hat.

'It's never easy, separating a man from his brass,' mused Sadie. 'Your dad would put his last two bob on a greyhound even if we were starving.'

'They have to learn,' replied Mary. 'And to learn, they have to be taught. Women do the teaching.' She stretched out her long legs. 'It's like when you get a dog, Mam. If you leave that dog to go its own road, it'll chew your rug up in five minutes and leave piles of dog-dirt all over your floor. So you train it. You make life better for it, because it can't think for itself. Well, I suppose it can work out how to get food, but that's about the limit.' She took a swig of black beer. 'Men are the same.'

'They've got brains, though,' offered Sadie. 'Well, some of them have.' She chuckled mischievously and added, 'A few of them, any road.'

'I know they've got brains, Mam. A dog has a brain of sorts, enough to look for a bitch and for food and for somewhere warm to sleep. Men are after the same things, because their brains divide their time between their trousers and their bellies. They want sex and they want food and booze.'

'Mary! I've not brought you up to talk like that.'

Mary grinned. 'Things have changed, Mam. We're halfway through the twentieth century now.' She was warming to her subject. 'When you were born, women stopped at home having hundreds of babies. Men went out to work. On their way home from work, they drank all their wages, so most of the babies died, and a lot of the women did, too.'

Sadie nodded. 'They did and all. I've seen a fair few little coffins in my time, Mary. There were one woman down Noble Street buried five. She died after her . . . ooh, it must have been her tenth. So she got carted off to a pauper's grave and all, just the same as her poor little children. And what did he do?' Sadie nodded excitedly, angrily. 'He got wed a second time to some other young woman, and it all happened again. She lasted about six years, the second wife, then she keeled over with consumption – coughing blood, she were. Makes you think.'

Mary smiled knowingly. 'They've not changed, you know. The men, I mean. If we were daft enough, they'd still throw their money away before coughing up for their keep. It's us that have changed. We don't put up with it no more.'

'About time, too,' said Sadie. Mary was going somewhere. In ten years from now, Mary Martindale would not be sitting in a shabby little house drinking stout from a cracked mug. Sadie saw Mary in a comfortable red-brick semi, half pebble-dashed all round, with a bit of a garden, two kiddies and a nice-looking husband with a good job. Happen they'd have a car and two weeks in Blackpool every year. 'What do you dream about?' Sadie asked her daughter. 'What do you hope for, Mary?'

The answer was immediate, needed no thought. 'Me own business,' replied Mary. 'Not a stall in the Market Hall, a proper shop with me name up over the door. I don't know what I'd sell, like. What you sell doesn't matter, it's selling and making a go of it that counts.'

Sadie lit a cigarette. 'Where will you get all that money, though?'

Mary lifted her shoulders. 'Somewhere. Anywhere. Them universities have started realizing that women can learn and do good jobs. All we have to do now is persuade the blokes in banks that we can add up and fill forms in and talk English.'

'So you've to train them and all?'

'Yes.'

'Are you planning to take the world on, Mary?'

'Course I am.' She picked up the jug. 'Fancy a bit more of this, Mam?'

Vera leaned against the stone wall and watched her daft dog cavorting about like a lunatic with bugs. 'I hope he hasn't got them,' she muttered.

'Got what?' asked Edward.

'Fleas.'

'He's bound to have them,' replied Edward. 'Since most of the rags he guarded were full of life.' He turned his head and looked at the moors. They were particularly lovely tonight, because a mist had fallen towards the east, was rolling down from the Pennines to kiss these smaller brethren. 'I couldn't live anywhere else,' he told her. 'Except, perhaps in Yorkshire.'

'That's enemy territory,' Vera declared. 'And aren't they born with their mouths turned down and their pockets sewn up?'

Edward looked at her with mock severity. 'Do not believe all you read, Vera. And remember the rugged brilliance of *Wuthering Heights*. There could be a Heathcliff loitering behind a big black rock just outside Huddersfield waiting for his lady friend—'

'Or for the number twenty-seven bus to work.'

He sighed. 'Do you have no soul?'

Vera dug him in the ribs. 'It's my down-to-earthness that you love, Edward Shawcross.' He was troubled. A few weeks earlier, he had professed to have the answers to all his problems, but his brow had darkened of late. She bit down hard on her curiosity, told herself to remain calm. Leaving a wife, a son, a daughter and a grand house could not be easy.

'I thought it would be over,' he said quietly. 'But now, I'm not too sure. I suppose I'll just have to wait until I've seen Samuel Fishwick.' He fiddled with the chain of his watch. 'They should be here any day. He's not well, you know. Reading between the lines, I think he hasn't long left. So I hope you don't mind if we leave things as they are for a while.'

Vera tried not to mind. She couldn't understand why the return of Edward's in-laws was expected to solve his quandary. According to local folklore, the Fishwicks had buggered off to India or Africa – some hot place anyway – because their daughter had married beneath her. Was Edward afraid of Eleanor and Samuel Fishwick? Vera studied his profile, watched him grinning at the dog. She couldn't imagine him being frightened of an old couple.

'He's chasing his tail,' said Edward. He watched the dog turning, turning in the same monotonous circle, round, round and round again. Edward knew how that felt. Get up, wash, get a shave, eat, go to work. Come home, eat, bathe, go to bed. The same circle, the same damned thing over and over again, with only weekends to look forward to. Weekends? Silence, a deathly quiet broken only by the occasional clatter from the kitchen.

'He's going to jump in the reservoir,' said Vera.

Constance was good company, but she couldn't possibly want to spend her time with her father. Gilbert was away a lot, wasn't very chatty during holidays. Holidays? That lad was having a three-year holiday, didn't seem to do a stroke of study when he was at home. Constance was promising, though Alice did her best to hold the girl back by trying to force her along a 'suitable' path.

'Edward?'

Alice. She lived in her bedroom, stuffed her silly face with sweets, sat at the dining table looking as if she could smell something nasty. These last few days, her pattern had changed slightly. She had started walking about outside, had even dragged Constance's old bicycle from the garden store. The idea of Alice on a bicycle was laughable, though he wasn't particularly amusable just now. Alice was up to something, though, was probably trying to limber up in preparation for her parents' return.

'Edward? Look, he's swimming.'

'Yes.'

The delighted dog crawled out of the water and shook himself. He sniffed the air, caught a whiff of rabbit, dashed off towards his next adventure.

'It doesn't matter, Edward,' Vera said quietly. 'It really doesn't matter.'

'What doesn't matter?'

'If you have to stay with . . . at home. With your family. You know what I'm talking about.'

He stared at her as if she had spoken in a foreign tongue. 'I'm staying nowhere,' he informed her. 'It's just a case of working out what's best.' His brow creased. 'Would poverty bother you?'

Vera laughed. 'No, I'm good at it, passed all the exams with flying colours and got a certificate in it.'

'Things are . . .' He stopped, thought for a moment. 'It's difficult. I entered a contract, you see.'

'A marriage?'

'That as well.'

He was messing about with his watch chain again. Although they had been lovers for just a few months, Vera could read this man like a book, a first-year primer. He was lovely. He was kind, funny, generous, loving and . . . and hurt. Sometimes, Vera thought he might be rather malleable, but she loved him all the same.

Vera closed her eyes and was transported to the off-licence on Tonge Moor Road, a shop that sold beer, spirits, sweets and most other comestibles. She recalled her first sight of Edward, remembered being struck by his bearing. 'When you chose me, I couldn't believe it,' she said. 'When you kept coming in the shop at night to buy daft things like tapes of Aspro and boxes of cooling powders. At first, I thought you were coming down with something.'

'I was,' he said wryly.

'We were getting towards shoelaces when I saw you fiddling with that damned chain. I thought to meself, "This one's nervous." So I let you take me home.' He had taken her home four times without kissing her. Four and a half, if she was going to be honest, because she had done the kissing and he had done the receiving. Even after that, he had been reluctant to go into the house. 'I thought I'd go to my grave a virgin,' Vera said now.

'You're too warm for that,' he told her.

Vera laughed. 'It's no use being warm on your own, is it? Did I tell you about my headstone?'

He shook his head.

Vera riddled about in the ashes of memory. 'I was going to have a poem on it. "Here lies Vera Hardman, she's dead and that's a fact, went to her grave disgruntled, disappointed and intact." Anyway, I won't bother now.'

He pulled her into his arms. 'Too well-read by a mile,' he announced. 'Clever women are so difficult. You are supposed to be compliant and totally devoted to the man in your life.'

'I know,' she sighed. 'It's a bugger, isn't it?'

William chose his moment well, as usual. His owner was kissing the man who had rescued him when the dog leapt over the wall and knocked the pair of them down to earth. A tangle of human and canine limbs writhed on the ground for a few seconds. William, who judged the game to be a good one, separated himself from the rest and circled them repeatedly.

'We're surrounded,' said Vera mournfully. 'Do we wait for the cavalry or wave a white flag?'

Edward waved his handkerchief until the dog grabbed it. 'These natives are most unfriendly,' complained Edward. 'That one's tearing the symbol of peace to pieces.'

They lay back on the grass, watched the dog running out of steam. William flopped and spread his panting body across the remains of Edward's handkerchief. The sun slipped away and left a canvas of bright oranges and pinks in its wake. 'What will your neighbours say?' Edward asked.

'What about?'

'About me moving into Tintern Avenue.'

She hadn't thought that far, had refrained from indulging in rose-tinted reveries. 'Curtains will twitch and tongues will wag. And they'll carry on going to work and worrying about the coal money. Nothing changes.'

'Will you mind?'

'No.' Vera had not expected this. What had she expected, then? A new place, a country cottage, a caravan, a couple of rooms over a chip shop?

'You'll wait for me?'

'No,' she answered, a sharp elbow prodding his midriff. 'I'll run off with Arthur Brazendale from number twenty-seven. He's got new teeth, a pension and a leather bag for his bowls. Stop asking daft questions, love. It's nearly time to go home.'

He sat up. 'You never question me,' he said.

'No.'

'Why not?'

Vera stared hard at the man she loved. 'Because you're the one with the full dance card, not me. I'm a free agent, Edward. You've a family and a mill and folk depending on you. Then there's the council. What about the council?'

'Sod them.'

Vera grinned. 'You love being an alderman. What about when they ask you to be Mayor of Bolton, eh?'

'If you can be Mayoress, I'll consider it.'

She stood up, held his arm. If and when Edward left his wife, he would be drawing a line under his civic work. No-one wanted an adulterer to shimmy about in silly hats and chains and cloaks. 'You've a lot to lose,' she whispered.

Edward Shawcross gazed at this slip of a girl who was really a woman of thirty-two. There was very little of her. She had vibrant red hair, a laughing mouth, eyes of the deepest green. She worked in an off-licence, read the classics for pleasure, loved theatre and concerts, enjoyed a joke and a fish-and-chip supper drowned in vinegar. Vera was his little pixie, his amulet, his luck, his future. 'My love,' he said gravely. 'From where I stand, I think I have every-thing to gain.'

'I hope so,' she answered. 'Now, get me home, I'm fair clemmed, me stomach thinks me throat's cut.'

Maude Templeton was unused to opposition. Her husband, a man of great wealth and intelligence, was not one for putting his foot down. He believed in God, the sanctity of marriage and the indisputable benefits of golf. On the whole, he allowed his wife

77

her head, because she was a sensible woman and a good sort when it came to running the house. But to maintain the integrity of the wedded state, it was necessary to escape from time to time. He did this by reading lessons in church on Sunday morning and by playing the full eighteen holes each fine Sunday afternoon; on less clement days, he and his friends managed just nine holes. So, in Eric Templeton's book, marriage, church and golf were interdependent.

'Eric, you aren't being fair,' said Maude. 'It's only one Sunday, for goodness' sake. We can still go to morning service. I love evensong, but I'm quite willing to forgo it for the sake of my son.'

'Maude, my dear, it is a match at Royal Birkdale. We've a fair bit of money involved.'

'Betting? Betting on golf?'

Eric shook his head mournfully. Maude had never been a scold, and he hoped she wasn't practising to become one. 'It's just a little added incentive. Like a side dish at a meal.'

'A great deal of money, you said.'

Eric was unaccustomed to argument. He was not built for it, was not a man who sought trouble. His financial affairs, with which he had very little direct contact, ticked along nicely, he enjoyed an excellent standard of living and his marriage was perfect. Well, nearly so. 'Maude, I have given my word.'

She sat down and flicked through a magazine. The Templetons had never quarrelled. Arguments were for people of a lower order, people who had to fight to stay alive. 'I should have thought that you might be interested in getting to know Constance.'

Eric swivelled on his heel and walked to the side-board. 'Sherry, dear?' he asked.

'No, thank you.'

He poured himself a double scotch and wondered whether his wife might be sulking. 'We have lived practically next door to Constance Shawcross for twenty years. I see no reason to make a fuss simply because you are putting on a little party.'

'But if she and James are to marry—'

'Have you spoken to him, Maude? Or has James spoken to her?'

'I know how James feels about Constance.'

'Really?' He drained the glass. 'How?'

'A mother knows.'

Eric tapped his empty glass with a fingernail. Maude was behaving quite oddly. Was she reaching that age, that time of life when women started to have vapours, dizzy spells and strange ideas? She had become veritably besotted with the idea of marrying James off to that rather fine girl next door. Hadn't she always disliked Constance? He tried to remember, wished that he had listened more carefully in the past. But women did go on so. 'Are you well?' he asked.

'Yes, perfectly well, Eric. I am eternally grateful for your concern.'

Eric was acquainted with men who were at loggerheads with their wives. They spent their time in gentlemen's clubs playing poker and all kinds of games involving long poles and coloured balls. They never went home except for a change of clothing. He did not want to join that unhappy throng.

Maude waited. Everyone was coming. All her son's friends, some of their friends, people from Smithills and Horwich and Bromley Cross. She, too, had given her word. Maude would have been delighted if James had shown a little more interest in his mother's

79

plans, but she would have to be satisfied with her son's rather amused compliance.

'I must make some calls,' Eric announced eventually. 'Perhaps Dr Soper will play the round in my place. Unless he's on call, that is.'

Maude patted her hair.

'It's a bloody nuisance, old girl,' he told her. 'But I do see your point. My fault entirely, of course. I should have remembered this function of yours.'

She smiled to herself as he went out to the telephone. Eric was a good man, a great man. He had never berated her about James, or about the fact that she had not produced a second court card for him to play. James was frail and special, yet Eric had soothed his wife's brow for years. 'It wasn't your fault,' he used to say to her. 'The boy will survive, and we need no more, we're not royalty, so we don't want heir and spare.' She hadn't pushed hard enough, hadn't tried hard enough, and her baby had been damaged by emerging backwards. Everyone had told Maude that a breech presentation was no-one's sin, yet she had still blamed herself.

Eric re-entered the room. She looked tired, he thought, just a whisker short of her normal self. 'I've had a word with the boy, too,' he grunted. 'Damned ornamentation hanging over his bed. It's not on, my dear.'

'That is his way of managing, Eric.'

'Does he not see what he is doing to you?'

Maude raised her slender shoulders. 'No, he doesn't. Because I have never told him. If he wants purple forceps over his bed, let him have them.'

This was not Eric's territory. The decor of the house, its running and its upkeep were not his responsibility. He provided the money, paid the servants, paid the bills, kept an eye on those who guarded his interests. But the house was Maude's. 'As you wish, my dear,' he said as usual.

It was the poem, Maude kept telling herself. James would 'happy run to hell' on a real leg, the verse said. James would have been willing to sell his soul to the devil in exchange for his own dream. She shuddered. If James wanted Constance Shawcross, then he would have her.

'Maude?'

'Yes, dear?'

'Are you really well?' He loved her, could not imagine life without her.

'Thank you for changing your plans, Eric,' she replied. 'And yes, as I told you earlier, I am very well.'

Constance kept a wary eye on her mother. It occurred to her that the raising of parents was very difficult in this ever-changing day and age. Father was becoming more and more withdrawn, while Mother had started walking briskly up and down The Rise in flat shoes and a large-brimmed hat. They both needed watching.

The Rise was steep. There was a cluster of houses at its base, then a gap until Aston Leigh. The Shawcross house was a large Victorian pile with massive chimneys and patterned brickwork. It was a square, no-nonsense type of building, sash windows, solid doors and four steps up to the front entrance. Top o' th' Moor was The Rise's crown, a massive, rambling residence of Georgian origin. Mother had taken to walking down to the bottom, where the lower middle classes lived, then back again, past her own middle-middle-class house and all the way up to landed gentry.

Constance stood on the driveway of Aston Leigh. When the straw hat hove into view, she bobbed down behind the holly. This really was a worry. Not only was Mother walking about, she was also talking to herself in her bedroom. Mother had never been one for hiking and, as far as Constance knew, there were no recorded instances of insanity within the Fishwick clan. Perhaps Grandmother and Grandfather would turn out to be raving mad, all African beads, nonsense and incense. Anyone who killed a tiger and turned it into a glassy-eyed rug had to be pots for rags, Constance told herself. Was Aston Leigh about to become an asylum, then?

Mother, breathing heavily, was just about three feet away from Constance and on her way to James Templeton's house. Once there, she would stop and wait for her puff to return, then she would amble home. 'I do not know you, Mrs Shawcross,' mouthed Constance at the holly bush. Mother had been snappier than ever of late. Under the vigilance of Alice Shawcross's ever-alert ear, Constance had nervously murdered a bit of Beethoven's 'Moonlight' just after lunch. 'What is the matter with her?' Constance asked herself and the hedge. 'And am I just as daft?' Talking to the greenery was stupid. Though Constance's chances of getting sense out of timber and leaves were as good as any. When had Mother last had a proper conversation with her?

On a sudden whim, Constance turned and dashed into the house. Father was at work, Mother was tramping about outside, while Gilbert had disappeared hours earlier with a tennis racket and a string bag full of balls. Cook and Ada were in the kitchen, and the daily had gone home.

She opened the door of her mother's room and

stepped inside. There was something different on the dressing table, a silver tray covered in pots and bottles. There was vanishing cream, hand cream, nightcream and Foster's Cream Shampoo with Eggs and Beer. Four lipsticks lay side by side, each one pristine and new. 'Fuchsia, Palest Peach, Rose Blush and Soft Apricot,' read Constance aloud. Mother never wore lipstick. Mother's opinion on the subject of cosmetics was that they were probably responsible for the Empire's decline.

Alice's daughter pulled out a drawer, found a large magazine which seemed to concentrate on hairstyles. One page was marked with a cross. The woman in the photograph looked a little like Alice. She had a large nose and thicker than usual lips, but her hair, puffed up at the sides and pulled forward in wisps, made the face gentler, more feminine. A dart of sadness pierced Constance's heart. Poor Mother was trying to improve her looks.

The door opened. 'What are you doing?'

Constance was surprised to find herself shaking. It was as if she had been caught peeping at someone naked or reading a very secret diary. 'I'm sorry,' she mumbled.

Alice remained motionless in the doorway.

'I was worried,' managed Constance.

'About what?'

'About you, Mother.'

Alice Shawcross pulled off the straw hat and sent it skimming onto her bed. Why would someone suddenly start worrying about her? She was used to being alone in the world, had made an unemotional decision on that score when her parents had upped and offed to foreign parts. 'I am well, Constance.'

'Are you?'

Alice raised an eyebrow. 'Certainly.' She came into the room and closed the door. 'You should not pry into anyone's private affairs. This is my bedroom. You are a young woman now, so you must realize the value of personal space.'

Constance decided to hang for the full sheep. Mother's mood was already grim, so what did it matter? 'I could help you,' she mumbled.

Alice sat on her bed and wished that this daughter of hers would go away. It was time for a bath, because the day was hot and clammy, especially for someone who had just walked the better part of a mile. 'Go and do something, Constance. Read, or practise that piece you played earlier, or—'

'Are you thinner, Mother?'

In that moment, Alice could have died a happy woman. It had been noticed at last. 'Perhaps,' she replied casually. 'Just a little.'

Constance stared. 'That skirt doesn't fit you any more. You could carry a picnic inside the waistband.'

Alice's eyes pricked, but it was only perspiration, surely?

'And your face is . . . different. A bit pinker.'

'I've . . . started to walk. It's good for the circulation.'

Constance lowered herself onto the dressing stool. She remembered the magazine, spoke carefully. 'You know, a softer sort of hairstyle would be nice. There are some good salons in Bolton. I could go with you, get mine done, too.'

'You have beautiful hair.'

Constance, unused to compliments from this source, rattled on. 'There's a new shop on Deansgate. They do wonderful clothes for the slightly larger woman. Cleverly cut and lined, really good stuff, quite expensive and exclusive.'

Alice closed her eyes. 'Constance, let me deal with one thing at a time, please. You young ones are always in a hurry, aren't you?' Her eyelids lifted. 'You never crawled. I can see you now as clearly as daylight. You walked at ten months and fell over every two minutes. Slow down.'

Constance nodded. 'I will. But when you . . . I mean, if you want me to go anywhere with you, just ask.'

'I'm buying no clothes,' said Alice firmly. 'In case I change size again.'

The younger woman rose to her feet. She came from a family in which tactile love was non-existent. Father ruffled her hair sometimes, punched Gilbert playfully in the chest, asked how he was, how his daughter was. But there was no real touching. She wished she could dive across the floor and hug Mother, tell her that she was doing the right thing. She couldn't.

'Constance?'

'Yes?'

'Don't discuss this with anyone at all. I am doing it for myself, for my own good. If people choose to comment, be noncommittal. I will not have my regime bandied about.'

'Right. And good luck with it.' Constance escaped to the landing. That had been a near thing, she said inwardly. Mother and daughter had almost had a conversation, had come dangerously close to discovering common ground.

In her bedroom, Alice Shawcross removed her sweat-damped clothing. She hadn't been imagining it, then. The mirror continued to reflect a large woman, but the fat seemed tighter, firmer. Her daughter had noticed, too, so the walking and the abstinence from chocolate were beginning to pay off. When had she last thought about chocolate? 'Don't think about it, Alice,' she said severely. 'Don't let it into your head.'

She ran her bath, soaked for a long time in fragrant water. Clothes were becoming a nuisance, she told herself when she was dry. But Alice gritted her teeth and tightened the belt of a sensible maroon frock. In a week or two, she might take Constance up on that offer. It would be lovely to sit in a salon and allow the staff to pamper her.

Constance sat on a milestone. It said BOLTON 2 MILES, but her skirt covered it. If any lost people turned up, they would have to find their own way from Belmont to the town centre. It was five o'clock. The unconfined joy of a typical Shawcross dinner would be let loose in an hour or so.

Constance sat bolt upright with a jolt. So that was it, that was why Mother was doubly awful at the moment. The poor old duck was missing her chocolate. She probably had withdrawal symptoms, too. The gardener had stopped smoking a few months ago, and he had been very crabby.

Mother. What was she up to? What had motivated her to start improving herself? Grandmother and Grandfather Fishwick were supposedly on their way home, but Mother did not seem to be very interested in the prospect of seeing her parents again. So she wasn't likely to be going to a lot of trouble for their sake. Funny family, Constance thought for the umpteenth time. They were all crackers, and she, daughter of the tribe, was probably as daft as the rest of them.

'Connie.' James Templeton arrived and threw himself onto the grass. He preferred to sit, as his stance was somewhat crooked, and his hip was a source of pain. 'Penny for them,' he said.

Constance studied him. 'What's this party all about? Do we get a balloon and a bit of cake to take home? Is it going to be hide and seek, hunt the thimble?'

James shrugged. 'Search me. She's gone all strange.'

Constance breathed a sigh of relief. It wasn't just Alice. Perhaps there was something in the water that affected women of a certain age. 'I'm to have a new dress,' she told him. 'It's in Modes by Elaine being hemmed as we speak. So you'd better not spill any jelly on me, James.'

'Well, I've drawn the line,' he said. 'I'm not having a new frock. But she wants me to go and get fitted for a new set of hooves.' His shoes were made by a firm in Flash Street. He got one ordinary shoe, and another with a build-up of just under two inches. 'I'd rather have my teeth pulled,' he added. 'At least you get gas with dentistry.'

'Does it hurt, having the shoe fitted?'

'Yes.'

'I'm sorry. It must be terrible.'

James looked over his shoulder, saw rain clouds moving towards them, used them as a change of subject. 'The Pennines will puncture that lot and we'll get the benefit,' he said. 'The rain it raineth every day, upon the Lancs and Yorkshire fellow—'

'But mostly on the Lancs, because the Yorkie pinched the Lancs' umbrella,' she finished for him. 'It's not their fault. We should have lived on the other side of the hills. Then Lancashire could have been Yorkshire and vice versa.'

'The Irish were Scots and the Scots were Irish,' James mused. 'Then somebody built a boat and took all the Scots to—'

'Shut up, James.'

He shut up.

Constance plucked a blade of grass and chewed on it. 'Why has your mother suddenly decided that you should have a nice little tea for your nice little friends?'

'I don't know. I didn't know the first time you asked me, and I still don't know. Stay at home if you like.' If she did stay at home, he would go and seek her out. She was the only one who made him laugh, the only person whose company he really enjoyed.

'They're up to something,' declared Constance. 'Both of them. Yours with her tea party and mine with her Soft Apricot.'

'Do tell,' begged James.

She made him cross his heart and hope to die, then she related her tale. 'No chocolate, James. My mother lives for the stuff. She gets coupons from all sorts of people, tells them they're for charity work. It's become a drug. And she's given it up.'

James nodded sagely. 'There should be special schools for mothers. Somewhere they could go to give their children a rest. Mine is very tiresome. She keeps staring at me.'

'Really?'

He nodded. 'I can feel her eyes on me when I'm in the garden. I can feel her eyes on me now. I think she's at my bedroom window with the bird-watching binoculars – no – don't look, please. I'm beginning to wonder whether I might have some dreadful disease that's going to kill me off within weeks.'

Constance spat out some grass in a very unladylike

fashion. It was nice to be with somebody, especially another person with a difficult mother. 'The grandparents are expected daily,' she said. 'Father's never in. Gilbert will be clearing off back to London when the fancy takes him. I suppose I'll be expected to cope with the old folk when they arrive.' She deliberately fell off the milestone and laid herself out next to him.

'Passing motorists will make comments,' he said.

'Just passing comments, James?'

'We could be lovers lying here.'

She laughed hysterically. 'If I were to take a lover, I don't think the affair would be carried out by the roadside. Anyway, this will steam up your mother's binoculars, teach her a lesson.'

He wanted to reach out and touch her, but he couldn't. Time after time, James Templeton had lectured himself. A couple of missing inches off the length of a leg did not reduce his real stature, his standing as a human being. Yet always, in a corner of his mind, he knew himself to be unworthy of someone as whole and as wholesome as Connie Shawcross.

'James?'

'Yes?'

'Are you ever going to do anything – a job, a career?'

'I don't know. I suppose I'll step into Father's shoes – as long as one of them gets built up, that is. But I'd rather like to be with people. You know, all kinds of people from all kinds of places. Working at a railway station could be interesting, all those crowds, half coming and half going, all on the move and with stories to tell.'

Constance sat up and stared down at him. 'You're

going to be a writer,' she told him. 'I've always envied your way with words. One day, you'll sit on that railway station and give those people imaginary lives.'

'Isn't that what you've always wanted to do?'

She nodded, punched him playfully, jumped to her feet. 'We should team up,' she joked. 'You do the words and I'll put the full stops in.'

'And the commas.'

'If you insist.' She glanced at her watch. 'Time to change for dinner,' she said resignedly. 'Shall I help you up?' She regretted the offer immediately. 'Sorry.'

'Why? Accepting the fact that I need help has been part of my development.' He wanted her help, but not on this occasion. She had the sort of spirit that might lift him right through life, not just off this grass verge. He struggled into an upright position. 'Race you to your gate,' he said.

Constance grinned broadly. 'Home, James,' she said. 'And don't spare the horses.'

FOUR

Mary was offered the job on the spot. It would mean a quick dash across town three nights a week, but she would get a uniform, a torch, and the privilege of seeing a film without paying. By the third night, the celluloid action might well become boring, though the chance to buy ice-creams or lollies cut-price would compensate for that. With a couple of old *Bolton Evening News*es, she could wrap up a block of Wall's and take it home for Mam.

She skipped along Bradshawgate with the good news quickening her step. Another few bob a week, a chance to save up a deposit on a shop of her own. Deliberately, Mary slowed herself down and looked at the businesses along the way. Shoe shops, tobacconists and furniture stores lined her route. At the junction with Deansgate, Churchgate and Bank Street, Preston's Jewellers sat beneath a clock and a gilded orb. She took in Woolworth's, a chemist, a couple of dress shops with uninteresting items plonked into the windows. Butchers, grocers and pie shops were all scrutinized by Mary Martindale. Everything was grey, grim and deeply miserable; everything looked like a scene from a pre-World War One sepia photograph. And wherever she looked, there were pubs with their doors wide open and the stench of work-stained folk and stale beer wafting out into the warm night. It was depressing, sad and weary-looking.

The Second World War had been finished for five years. People should be moving on, should have something to look forward to, a bit of colour, progress, promise. But it didn't appear to be working out quite like that. The country fit for heroes seemed to be stuck in a timewarp of green paint, brown paint and mucky, cheerless windows. It was all depressing and unimaginative. Rationing was not completely over, and people seemed ridiculously content to remain in a world populated by queues and ration points. Mind, what else could they do? Start a revolution? Storm the gates of Westminster and demand a decent standard of living? Mary was beginning to realize what Mam had meant about the winning of a war being costlier than losing.

What did folk look forward to? Mary wondered. At the end of a day spent in a mill or a mine, what joys were available? A pint, a ciggy and a natter with cronies in a smelly pub. Or, for the women, a huddle of gossips on a street corner and a jug of warm beer from the outdoor licence. Was that it, then? There had to be something else. Pubs were horrible places filled by big, soft grown men whose goal seemed to be to drink as much as possible as quickly as possible without vomiting. They'd be better pouring the ale straight down the drain. That way, they could cut out the middle-man and the bellyache and still get rid of their wages.

People needed to meet. Yet not everybody was content to sit in a saloon bar in clouds of cigarette smoke and amid the stench of fetid, spilled beer.

Where else could they go at night? There were dance halls – the Empress, the Aspen, the Palais de Danse. But dancing wasn't everybody's glass of pale ale. The Swan and the Pack Horse did meals sometimes, but these town-centre pubs still attracted hardened drinkers.

A cheerful cafe, she thought. No, more of a restaurant, but with a licence. If clients sat down for a meal at a little table with flowers and a white cloth, there'd be no need for spittoons and dartboards. There might be a gramophone in a place like that, with some peaceful sort of records to play on it. Chopin was nice – she'd heard him on the wireless. There were cookery books in the library, posh ones with foreign recipes. All a cook needed was to be able to read, Mary informed herself. Customers could drink wine with their dinners and have cheese and biscuits after the pudding. According to *Good Housekeeping*, those with money always finished off with cheese and coffee. Mind, it would have to be something a bit better than that bottle of Camp in Mam's back scullery.

Good Housekeeping might be the very place to start, she thought. Mrs Smith often passed copies on to Mary when she had finished with them. There were casseroles, risottos and all kinds of funny salads with grapefruit mixed in with lettuce and stuff. Mam's apple turnovers were great, and there was nothing wrong with decent Lancashire cooking. Wine would be good, because it wasn't as common as beer, didn't have the same stigma. Though Yates's Wine Lodge wasn't exactly Buckingham Palace, was it? Still, you couldn't buy thin pancakes called crêpes at Yates's.

Mary turned to continue onward and homeward,

collided with a young man in white trousers and a V-necked cream-coloured pullover. 'Sorry,' she said, her face heating up. The poor fellow was scrabbling about all over the place, because he had dropped several tennis balls. Mary bent to help him, chased a couple of escapees into the road, shoved them into her pockets.

He arrived at her side. 'My fault,' he said. 'Are you hurt?'

'No,' she answered. 'But I should look where I'm going, shouldn't I?'

'Shouldn't we all?' He glanced at his watch. Twenty minutes remained before he was due to meet Father at the Town Hall.

Mary pushed the tennis balls into the man's green string bag. He was good-looking, so she didn't study him too closely in case her eyes betrayed a hint of admiration.

'Thanks,' he said. An idea entered his head and dashed out of his mouth before he could process it properly. 'Would you like a drink to set you right? A shandy, perhaps?' He liked the look of her. She was very pretty, yet wholesome, and he was acting like a stupid dolt. 'No strings,' he added weakly.

She laughed. 'Yes, you do have a few missing.' She pointed to a large hole in his bag. 'Some strings, but not enough,' she concluded.

Mary Martindale had developed her own philosophy with regard to men. Many were not to be trusted. The not-to-be-trusted category displayed a varied assortment of characteristics. There were those who made remarks, usually when in the company of similar heroes. They were to be found most often after lunchtime and towards evening, as such creatures did not function well unless they had

94

been fed and, as pack animals, they seldom hunted and taunted alone. These silly devils had more muscle than brain and were, on the whole, objects of pity, all mouth and trousers, no discernible symptoms of intelligence.

Another type was the loner, who was similarly pitiable. He wore a full-length coat, sometimes of the old army variety, and he seldom journeyed along proper roads. The Lone Skulker liked back streets and ginnels. Occasionally, he would rip open his outer clothing and display himself as ready and able to take on the world. Mary, a feisty lass, was inclined to laugh loudly whenever confronted by a would-be game bird, as laughter tended to deflate the display, but she avoided back streets on the whole. 'Are you trustworthy?' she asked the young tennis player.

'Not at all,' he replied cheerfully. 'But I'm extremely thirsty.'

Mary was thirsty. She took a step back and looked him up and down. He had dark blue eyes and thick brown hair that was not quite straight, but not curly. There was education in his vowels. He fitted none of the usual 'dangerous' groups, though Mary remained on her guard. 'Are you one of them university students?' she enquired.

Gilbert Shawcross burst out laughing. 'Yes,' he managed finally. This was a live wire, he told himself. Lovely to look at, a very feminine shape, perfect eyebrows above dark brown eyes. Her hair, too, was brown, with lovely waves that owed nothing to a salon, and chestnut streaks bequeathed by the sun. 'We are human beings, you know,' he informed her.

'Don't you run round hanging things on statues and wearing daft clothes?'

'Sometimes. It's just fun.'

Mary sniffed meaningfully. 'It's just fun when you do it, because you're all young gentlemen. If my brothers went round decorating Queen Victoria with underclothes and chamber pots, they'd finish up in prison.'

He found no answer to that.

'Come on, then,' she said impatiently. 'Are we having a drink or not?' Mam would kill her if she found out. According to Sadie Martindale, nobody should talk to anybody without being introduced by somebody else. Mam had read that in a book, Mary thought. If everybody hung about waiting for everybody else to introduce them to everybody else, there'd be nobody talking to anybody. With this confusing thought in mind, she turned towards the pub.

Gilbert guided her into the Hen and Chickens. After appointing her to guard his racquet and balls, he sauntered off to the bar for shandies. Mary watched him. He was easy on the eye, about average height, not muscle-bound, not weedy, and she didn't even know his name. Still, he was no Jack the Ripper.

He set her drink on a cardboard mat that advertised Magee's Ales.

'What's your name?' she asked.

'Gilbert.'

'Oh.' He didn't look like a Gilbert. Gilberts were old with beards all yellow from smoking. 'I'm Mary,' she advised him. 'Mary Martindale.'

'Pleased to meet you, Miss Martindale.'

She'd almost forgotten about her job at the Queens Cinema. She'd been on her way home, all excited about the extra income, but now, she was all excited by a pair of keen, dark blue eyes. 'The shandy's good, thanks,' she told him. It wasn't; it was warm and nearly all lemonade, but Mary was trying to be polite. As she wasn't normally one for being on her best behaviour, Mary knew that she was slightly smitten. And it was no good, because he played tennis, talked posh and went to university.

'What are you doing on Sunday?' he asked.

Sundays, Mary did her washing for the week. 'Nothing,' she replied. And her ironing, too.

'A friend of mine is having a little occasion,' Gilbert said. 'It will be little, because his mother's had a hand in it. Just fruit punch and sandwiches – you know the score.'

Mary didn't know the score. The nearest she had come to fruit punch was being hit in the face with a toffee apple at Bolton Fair. 'Where is it?' she asked, her tone higher than normal.

'Belmont, The Rise.'

'Oh.' There were rich people up The Rise. Mary's mind went through her green frock, her blue suit and that little white blouse with a tear on a button-hole. She progressed from clothes, through footwear and on to talking properly, eating properly and acting the part. 'I don't know whether I can go,' she said. 'It depends on . . . well, I don't know,' she finished stupidly.

Gilbert smiled at her. 'Of course you can go. You can do anything you wish.'

He had the face of a rather mischievous angel, Mary thought. He was the sort of chap who could twist a girl right round his little finger and whip her knickers off with his other hand before she'd got her breath back. Mam had warned Mary about such charming fellows. But, Mam's warnings on one side, Mary liked him, and therein lay this particular man's brand of 'dangerous'.

'Say you'll come.' It would be a hoot, Gilbert thought. All the toffee-nosed upper middles, middles and lower middles would be floored by this girl's brightness and beauty. She was quite capable of giving them a run for their money. 'I'll borrow Mother's Morris,' he said. 'Where shall I pick you up?'

God. The Martindales had moved sideways in the world, definitely not upwards. They had swapped Delta Street for Emblem Street, and they still had an outdoor lav and a tin bath in the back yard. Electricity was a novelty. Mam had sat for three straight nights, almost blinding herself by staring endlessly at her first ever light bulb. She thought she was posh because Mr Smith had half-promised his old fridge. Sadie would have half the street in to examine her cold sausages once the 1929 Frigidaire was installed. Mary could picture her mam running round the neighbourhood with ice-cubes from the Exclusive Frigidaire Cold Control. 'Pick me up here,' she told him.

'On Deansgate? Is this where you live?'

Mary was ashamed of being ashamed. 'My mother would want your name, rank and number before she'd let you take me out. Especially in a car. She doesn't trust cars, says they lead to all sorts of trouble.'

Gilbert drained his glass. 'Come on,' he said. 'I'm getting a lift home from my father. He's been out on business tonight, so I'll have to run round to Newport Street. Will you be all right now?'

'Of course I'll be all right.' Mary stood up, handed over the balls and the racquet. 'What time Sunday?' she asked.

'Five-ish. It's a soirée. Don't ask me for any details,

because I haven't been to a soirée before.'

'It's like a matinee,' she told him. 'Only matin means morning, which is why it's daft having a Saturday matinee in an afternoon. Soir means evening.'

'Do you speak French?' he asked.

'No,' she replied seriously. 'But I always read *Good Housekeeping.*' She nodded at him before turning away. With every step she took, Mary reminded herself that she did know how to behave, how to carry on in company.

Gilbert stood outside the Hen and Chickens and watched Mary Martindale as she sauntered off towards the end of the road. She was going in the direction of Deane and Daubhill, was probably of a poorish family with its roots in the rawer end of cotton. Mother would throw a fit, he thought. But Mother wasn't going to be there on Sunday, was she? And anyway, Mother was too busy dashing about in a straw hat and sensible shoes.

He waited until the girl had disappeared round the bend, noted that she did not turn round to look for him. She was a cool customer, a girl with something extra about her.

Mary rounded the corner, stopped, counted to ten. She had felt his eyes on her, knew full well that he had stood and watched as she walked away. Her heart was acting a bit strangely, like a clock whose mechanism needed a bit of an overhaul. She was a level-headed type. She didn't believe in love at first sight – daft stuff like that only happened in books. Even then, they were the sort of books that had drawings with the talking done in bubbles.

She edged along the wall of yet another pub, peeped round the bend. He was just breaking into a run, was barely twenty yards from where she had left him. And a big, daft smile had broken out on her face. Mary pulled herself together and set off home. She was going to a soirée. And she was going to be an usherette at the Queens Cinema.

Ethel Hyatt knew everything. She lived next door to Sadie Martindale with her husband, Denis. Her children had flown the coop at the earliest opportunity, thereby allowing Ethel to concentrate on the important things in life, such as who was having a baby, whose baby they were having, and wasn't the step at number twenty-seven a disgrace.

Sadie looked the woman up and down. She wasn't going to invite Ethel in, because Ethel was a great one for discussing levels of dust, unswept floors and holes in oilcloth. Also, none of Sadie's chairs seemed fit enough to support sixteen stones of solid animosity. 'Yes?' Sadie asked.

Ethel had clasped fat fingers beneath the enormous weight of bosom that sat above her non-existent equator. This pose of Ethel's was legendary, as it denoted sympathy and near-pity for the receiver of sad news. 'I'm not one for gossip,' she began, her mouth stretching and twisting its way around the vowels.

Sadie sighed, wished that she had donkeyed her step that morning. She felt sorry for poor Denis Hyatt. Every time she saw him, he was scuttling to or from work, or to and from a shop with Ethel's basket on his puny arm. Mary must approve of Ethel Hyatt, then, because Ethel had her 'stray dog' trained to a point where he might have turned professional and joined Chipperfield's. 'I've a pan on, Ethel,' she said. 'And I want to get the sheets in an overnight soak.'

'I won't keep you.' The large woman licked her lips. 'I'm dying for a cuppa,' she added. 'This hot weather doesn't half make me thirsty.'

Sadie ignored the strong hint. She had better things to do than brew up for Ethel Hyatt. 'What is it, then?'

Ethel leaned backwards, looked up the street, looked down, as if she expected the world and his wife to be hanging on her every word. 'It's about your Mary,' she mouthed.

Sadie relaxed. Their Mary was a dependable girl. If Ethel had come to talk about Bernard, then that might have been different. Bernard had a tendency towards rowdiness when in his cups. In fact, he'd kicked an empty marrowfat pea can all the way home just two nights ago. But Mary was different.

'She's been seen, like.'

'Has she? Well, she does go out, you know. I don't keep her chained up.' Denis was all but shackled, though Ethel would doubtless fail to hear the sarcasm.

'With a man,' said Ethel triumphantly.

Sadie folded her arms. 'Half the folk round here are men. I'm not surprised if she has been seen talking to one.'

'With tennis balls.' The pale blue piggy eyes flashed triumphantly. 'In town, too. On Deansgate, broad daylight, late afternoon, like. Going on for evening, really.'

'Oh.' Sadie kept her face in order.

'And a tennis bat and all.'

'Well, I'll go to the foot of our stairs,' exclaimed Sadie. 'What is the world coming to? Tennis bats and tennis balls? Out in the street? Eeh, well.'

Ethel Hyatt had no ear for the various shades of

irony. 'That's just what I thought. I come in and I said to my Denis, "What's the world coming to?", and he agreed with me.'

He would, thought Sadie. Given the weight of Ethel Hyatt's argument and Ethel Hyatt's fist, anyone but a fool would comply with the opinions of this female Samson. 'It's all right,' lied Sadie. 'I know all about it. I think he's summat to do with the Smiths. They're moving to Blackpool in a few days, and our Mary's taking over their business. She'll be the manager.'

Ethel seemed to deflate physically. Her shoulders sagged, and a curler slipped forward to dangle limply beneath the red-and-white headscarf.

'They've got a son,' continued Sadie. 'He's stopping on at their house in Bolton, and with him having his own business – I think he's in newspapers and tobacco down Chorley Old Road – he won't be able to run his mam and dad's stall, you see. Our Mary's been talking to him, like, working out about all the banking and stocking-up and ration points.'

Ethel rallied visibly. 'Well, what did they want tennis balls for?'

Sadie raised her shoulders. 'Happen he was on his way somewhere.'

'They went in the Hen and Chickens. Annie Cartwright from Noble Street saw them. She said they were smiling at one another and all.'

Sadie's head shook sadly. 'Eeh, Ethel,' she said, 'thanks a lot. I mean, I don't mind her doing business with young Mr Smith, but she shouldn't be smiling at him. I'll tell her when she comes in that she has to be more respectful. After all, she owes so much to the Smiths, does my daughter. Fancy, our Mary in charge of a business when she's only twenty-one. I'm that proud of her, I could burst, Ethel. But you're spot on. She mustn't go round smiling at people. No, she's no right smiling out of turn like that. I shall have to give her a talking-to.'

Ethel's jaw hung loose and she blinked slowly. 'Right,' she said, visibly nonplussed. At last, Sadie's sarcasm had made a small dent in Ethel's puffed-up righteousness.

'I'll just get on with me cooking,' Sadie told her. 'You've to be so careful with the better cuts of beef. Not much fat, so I don't want it drying out.' She paused, thought of another bit of fodder for Ethel's tongue. 'It'll be that much easier next week once me fridge comes. Ta-ra, Ethel.'

Ethel Hyatt stared at Sadie's closed door. A fridge? How the hell was Sadie Martindale getting a fridge? If Ethel Hyatt hadn't known better, she would have sworn there was a man at the back of this. The only folk who got fridges were the well-to-do, same as millowners, doctors and suchlike. And women who went with men for money – they would likely have a few luxuries.

She pushed the steel curler back into place under the front of her scarf. Nobody would want Sadie enough to pay money, she decided. Sadie Martindale wasn't up to much in the looks department. So the family must be going up in the world, then. Ethel sniffed. If Sadie was going up, how come she hadn't bothered getting down on her hands and knees first? That step hadn't been donkey-stoned in three days.

'Coo-ee!' called the woman from number twenty-seven. Ethel bucked up. Twenty-seven's step was worse than the Martindales', but the newly-arrived young tenant liked a bit of a natter. 'I'm just coming, love,' called Ethel. 'Give us a minute. Put the kettle on.'

She stepped inside her own house to make sure that Denis wasn't peeling the potatoes too thickly. She scrutinized his efforts, patted him on the head, then sallied forth towards number twenty-seven. There was plenty to talk about, what with fridges and managers of stalls in the Market Hall. The Martindales were stepping well above their station, so they wanted talking about. A bloody fridge? Was Mary doing the extra earning? Was Mary taking money for favours so that her mam could have a fridge?

Halfway across the cobbles, she paused and pondered. She didn't care what anybody said. The Hen and Chickens, tennis bats and balls had nothing to do with running a toffee stall. With a gleam in her eye, she strode on towards a cup of tea and a ravenous ear.

'Who is he, then?' Sadie stood with her feet planted well apart. She wasn't best pleased, because that female gorilla next door had been the bearer of tidings. 'And why did you not tell me, Mary? Why did you go behind my back?'

Mary didn't know why. 'It just happened, Mam. I'd been to the Queens about the job, and I bumped into him. He had all these tennis balls, and they went everywhere. So I helped him, then he asked me did I fancy a shandy, because it was warm, and we'd been chasing about and—'

'Mary, what have I told you about talking to strangers? You might be twenty-one, but you're never too old to learn.'

Mary puffed out her cheeks and wondered what to

do next. She'd bought a nice fent off the market, an end-of-roll with just a couple of little flaws. It would make a lovely frock, scooped-out neckline, not too low, a white belt, some of those popper-beads that had just come out. The cotton was in a pleasant shade of strawberry, rich, but not too red. 'Mam, I'm tired.' And she had to have the dress made by Sunday.

'You will be tired when you start that usheretting job. And there's funny folk in picture houses, funny blokes. They like the dark, these mad buggers, and they watch all them young couples getting steamed up in the back row, then they just go and grab the nearest girl.'

'It's a big torch, Mam. I'll lash out with that.'

'Aye, that's all well and good,' answered Sadie smartly. 'But what about when the picture's over? You've to stop on sometimes and help to tally the takings. There could be one of them waiting outside.'

Mary sat down. She placed an elbow on the table and cupped her chin with the hand. 'Mam, what if our house had got bombed in the war?'

'It didn't,' snapped Sadie.

'It could have. Things happen. They can happen to anybody, not just to some. I've got this job so I can save a few quid a week. I'm not going to let some imaginary queer fellow spoil all my plans, Mam. I'm old enough now to decide things for myself.' She sat up, placed her hands in her lap and straightened her spine. 'I'm finishing that frock tonight.' She paused, inhaled a bit of courage. 'Because that lad with the tennis balls wants to see me again. I'm meeting him on Sunday.'

Sadie was flabbergasted. 'You're meeting a lad you don't know?'

'Course I know him. We had a drink in the Hen and Chickens. He made me laugh. Anyway, he's called Gilbert and he's taking me to tea. Well, it's more like a bit of a party.'

'Where?'

'Up Belmont.'

It was Sadie's turn to sit down. She placed herself directly opposite her daughter. Mary had never been the slightest trouble, had always been easy. But Mary had a strength in her, the sort of power that might just give birth to stubbornness. 'Did he have dark blue eyes and brown hair? Nice-looking, goes to university?'

Mary nodded.

'He's only Gilbert Shawcross. It's funny he wasn't recognized by Annie Cartwright from Noble Street. Mind, I think she works at Kippax's, so she won't have seen young Mr Shawcross. Him with the tennis balls is only my boss's son, Mary.'

Mary was not in the slightest way surprised. She had realized that Gilbert was out of the ordinary. But Mam was staring at her so hard, was making her feel like squirming in her seat. Mary had not squirmed since junior mixed. 'I like him,' she said quietly, angry at having to explain herself. Many girls her age were married with two or three children.

'But he's not for you, love.'

'I'm meeting him, not running away with him. Anyway, I know what's what. I don't confuse cutlery with jewellery, and I've got manners.'

'It's still wrong,' insisted Sadie. 'You're chalk and cheese, oil and water, there's no mixing. You might as well go and knock at Buckingham Palace, ask the king has he any cousins going spare. There's no future in it, love.'

Mary drummed her fingers on the table for a second or two. 'Mam, my future is mine. And I'm not wanting anybody in it yet, with or without a tennis racquet. He's just a friend, just a nice lad.'

'Is he?'

'Yes.'

Sadie got up and carried the steaming kettle through to the back scullery. She filled a white enamel bowl that stood in the slopstone, added some cold from the single tap, then began to tackle the pots. Their Tommy was out in the back yard knocking a hole in the air raid shelter. He was going to put a window in it and use it as a workshop for mending bikes. Tommy had a way with wheeled things. Bernard had sloped off straight after tea, had given himself an extra lick and a promise before venturing out. There was probably some girl involved, because Bernard and soap were usually passing acquaintances.

She hoped that their Mary wasn't going to get her heart broken. They had a knack with women, these educated men. They saw things differently, didn't set as much store by decency as they should, were not as morally correct as people from Sadie's environment. She thought back, remembered Teddy Shawcross with his tears, his worn-out clogs and a nose that dripped like a tap needing a washer. He'd gone up, hadn't he? Oh yes, Teddy had a mill now, and a posh wife, two kids and a car.

When the dishes were clean, she rinsed them in cold water, then started the drying process. Why shouldn't their Mary mix with Teddy's son? Teddy had been no catch in his time. It had all happened so suddenly – the wedding, then the disappearance of Mr and Mrs Fishwick. In fact, most folk had looked for an early baby, but the Shawcrosses had been married a good year when Gilbert put in his appearance.

Sadie punished the dishes, drying them to within a fraction of their glazing. It was stupid, all this class business, who had a car and who didn't, who paid rent, who borrowed a fortune for a mortgage, who played tennis, who was an usherette. This was 1950, for goodness' sake. If Mary wanted to go and look how the mortgaged half lived, fair enough. Though Sadie would have bet her upper denture that the Shawcrosses had no loan on their house.

Mary was sewing when her mother returned from the scullery.

'I'm off out,' said Sadie.

Mary dropped her needle. Mam never went out after tea, even in nice weather like this. 'Where to?'

'Just for a walk,' answered Sadie. 'You do what you want on Sunday, love. You're as good as any of them. Just keep yourself to yourself, if you get my meaning.'

'Thanks, Mam.' And yes, she did get Sadie's meaning.

Sadie got off the bus, looked around at the beauty of Belmont. All the way up from town, she had watched the area getting better and better until the smoke of industry was just a faint and wispy memory. Her lungs opened greedily to gobble up fresh, untainted air. This was where Teddy Shawcross had finished up, then. She knew his house was on The Rise, because she'd seen the address in the paper when young Gilbert had celebrated his twenty-first birthday. She remembered thinking what a difference there was between Delta Street and Aston Leigh. There'd been quite a spread and a big tent in the garden for the lad's coming of age. Well, Sadie wanted to see for herself exactly where her daughter was going to be on Sunday. There was no harm in having a look, was there?

She began the climb past a clutch of small, semi-detached houses, just like the one she had imagined for their Mary. Then they thinned out a bit, became detached with slightly bigger gardens. When the houses ran out, the hill steepened, but Sadie had made up her mind, bunions or no bunions. She had looked after Teddy Shawcross as a nipper, so she could go and peep at his house. Any road, a cat could look at a king without buying a ticket.

Partway up, Sadie noticed a woman in front of her. She was big, with a straw hat and ugly shoes, and she seemed to be talking to herself. Still, it took all sorts to build a world, didn't it?

The woman stopped, turned, looked at Sadie. 'It's very warm, isn't it?' Alice Shawcross would not normally have spoken to a stranger on the lane, but she felt a bit silly, was sure that this person had heard her muttering to herself. That was how Alice kept going, by urging aching muscles to carry her up and up this confounded hill. Three times a day, she did the hike now. 'I hum to keep myself company. The walking was . . . recommended by a medical person, you see. Anyway, I'm not terribly musical,' she concluded nervously.

The voice was posh. Sadie narrowed her eyes, identified Alice Fishwick-as-was. She didn't seem quite as ugly or as grim-faced as she used to be. 'Yes, it is warm,' she agreed. 'Better than the winter, though,' she said.

'I hope my singing didn't annoy you.'

'No. Not at all.' Sadie stood and watched while Teddy Shawcross's wife struggled on. What the heck was she up to? Folk didn't go piking about all over the show just for fun. Though these people were different, she said inwardly. They didn't spend their days piecing ends and dragging skips loaded with cotton cops all over the place. Happen they needed exercise, what with all that sitting down, reading and drinking cups of tea.

When the woman had disappeared, Sadie carried on up the hill until she came to Aston Leigh. It was an ugly house, she supposed. Squared-off, it was, a bit like an institution. There were roses in the garden, and someone was playing the piano. The tune floated out through an open window. Sadie knew it wasn't the wireless, because the player kept starting again. So this was Teddy's house. This was where their Mary would be coming on Sunday.

She crossed the lane to get a better view of Aston Leigh, stopped in her tracks when she saw a young man at the other side of a stone wall. He was painting. The paints looked like oils, and the surface on which they were being placed was canvas, but the picture itself – well – it resembled nothing on earth.

James Templeton turned his head. 'Hello,' he said. 'Isn't this a perfect evening?'

Sadie put her head on one side, tried to make sense of the work. 'What is that?' she couldn't help asking.

James laid down his brush. 'Don't you start. I've had Gilbert going on at me for the past hour.'

She pricked up her ears. 'Gilbert Shawcross?'

'That's the man. Philistine.'

Sadie wasn't sure about Philistines, but she

ploughed on. 'Mr Shawcross's lad? Him that owns the mill?'

'That's the one.' James looked at his painting. 'I think I shall call it Blind Rage,' he announced, a hand waving towards his masterpiece.

'Is it a landscape?'

'No. Not really,' he replied.

'Then why don't you paint in the house? I thought people who painted outside painted what they saw.'

'I do,' he answered.

Blind Rage was about right, Sadie thought, because it looked as if it had been produced by someone with severely impaired vision. 'It doesn't seem like anything,' she told him. The fields leading up to the moors were beautiful, lush and green, yet this man had thrown a series of purple blobs at his canvas. 'If that's what you see, son, you need your eyes testing.' Or his head, she thought. A change of subject was called for. 'I've just seen a woman walking about and talking to herself.'

'She does,' replied James vaguely. 'She's Gilbert's mother.'

'Mrs Shawcross.' This was not a question.

'Mothers in these parts tend to be rather burdensome,' he said. 'Do you think I should put some more yellow in?'

Sadie shrugged. 'Please yourself, but I'd never hang it over my fireplace.'

James laughed. 'Ooh, you're one hell of a fierce critic.' He looked at her, looked at a face that was careworn and wonderful. Although James Templeton fooled around with his talent, he had been well taught. The trouble was that boredom had set in, causing him to go a bit abstract. But here was a subject worth painting. 'Where do you live?' he asked.

'Bolton. Emblem Street.'

He nodded, seemed pleased. 'Would you mind awfully if I asked you to sit?'

Sadie looked round, saw no bench. He had a chair, a folding thing made of cloth and metal, but there was nowhere for her. 'There's a milestone over there,' she told him. 'But you'd not hear me from that far off.'

He was still nodding. She had the most enthralling features, strong yet soft, feminine but weathered. 'I mean sit for me. Let me paint your portrait.'

Sadie looked at the purple blobs. 'Could you do me proper?' she asked, her words shaded by doubt. 'I mean, would I finish up looking like I'd been covered in gentian violet?'

'No. Mrs . . . what's your name?'

'Martindale. Sadie Martindale. And who are you?' She remembered telling their Mary not to talk to strangers, yet here she was, gabbling away to this young man.

'I'm James Templeton,' he replied.

The Templetons were real money. His mother had been in the paper, because she did a lot for crippled children. Wasn't her son lame? She glanced at the man's feet, saw the built-up shoe. 'What would I have to do?'

'Well, I'd want to see you in your own setting. I could do the sketching there, get your features right, then I would finish off in my studio.' He waved a hand towards the top of the hill where a very fine house sat above all else. 'Up there.'

Sadie swallowed. 'You want to come to ours?'

'If you don't mind.'

It was funny, but she didn't mind. And it was nothing to do with feeling sorry for him because of his leg. She'd heard about this before, or had read somewhere that upper class people and lower class folk got on really well together. According to whatever she had learnt, it was them in the middle who weren't sure of their ground. 'Number thirty-four,' she told him. 'Come on Sunday.' Mary would be out, and the lads were easy to get rid of.

His face lit up, then fell. 'Can't. Not this week. Mother is putting on some sort of a show at the house. She's experimenting with young people now. We are all to be guinea pigs.'

Sadie pondered. So that was where Mary was going. She wasn't sticking with them in the middle, then. Oh no, Mary Martindale had put her name down for the high jump, straight for the top of the blinking pile. 'Write to me,' she told James. 'And I'll let you know when it's convenient, like.'

'Promise?'

'Cross me heart and hope to die.'

'Don't die, Mrs M. Not until I've got you on canvas.'

He watched as she made her way down the moor, saw the pain in her movements. Mrs Martindale's legs were a properly matched pair, yet she suffered, too. He guessed that she worked in a mill, that she knew what it was to live from hand to mouth, from Friday to Monday, from pawnshop to grocer's. Something should be done for her, he told himself. She wasn't young, wasn't old. He judged her to be in her early fifties, yet her gait would have been cause for concern in a person of seventy or more.

James packed up his paints, struggled to his feet, folded up his little stool. When he reached the lane, he was pleased to see that Sadie was nearing the bus stop. It wasn't fair, he told himself. He'd said that to his father once, and Eric Templeton had smiled wisely, had delivered a short speech on the errors of Communism. James had no interest in politics, wouldn't have known a red from a yardbrush. All the same, it wasn't fair.

Vera sat on the back doorstep, knees up to her chin, arms wrapped around her lower legs, as if hugging the skirt close to herself. He would be here in a minute. Her heart was bouncing about in her chest like the ball in a table tennis game. Vera Hardman was not easily frightened, yet she shook uncontrollably, forced herself to hang on to her legs.

William was on guard beside her. She had thrown the ball a few times, and he had brought it back willingly, but she seemed to have gone off the whole idea now. So he stretched out full length in front of her and waited. Sooner or later, she would buck up and play with him again.

'What are we going to do?' Vera asked her companion.

He cocked his ears, listened, heard no key words. He could walk to heel, play dead, sit and fetch. He licked her hand, got no response. She needed to be quiet, then. They got like that, the two-legged ones. All the same, he kept a tawny eye on her, because she wasn't usually this miserable.

Vera closed her eyes and rocked to and fro. 'Come on, Edward,' she said under her breath. The trouble with being a mistress was always having to wait. She couldn't telephone his house from the call box outside Tonge Moor Post Office, couldn't get on a bus and knock at his door. She had to sit here and behave herself, had to hang about until he came. 'I love you,' she whispered. 'But get a bloody move on, will you?'

Sheila Foster from next door poked her head over the fence. 'You all right, Vera?'

Vera opened her eyes. 'Hiya, Sheila. I'm a bit worn out, that's all. We got a few in on their way home from the Starkie last night. They must have drunk the Starkie dry, so they came to me. They hadn't a leg to stand on between the four of them. The boss threw them out.'

'Is . . . is he coming?'

Vera nodded. Sheila Foster was the best sort of neighbour. She didn't gossip, she was genuinely concerned about her fellow man, and she had a sense of humour fit to bust the sides of a bishop. Sheila knew about Edward and Vera, but she kept her mouth shut, even when other residents of Tintern Avenue started with their questionnaires. 'He'll not be long,' said Vera.

'You're on the peaky side, love.'

In spite of everything, Vera grinned. Sheila Foster always looked peaky. She was the nearest thing to an albino that Vera had ever seen, though Sheila did not have pink eyes. Her hair was the palest ginger, while eyebrows and lashes had retained the platinum colouring with which the woman had been born. The eyes were very clear and very green, like two pretty jewels in the white-as-snow face. 'I wouldn't know if you were ill,' remarked Vera.

'You would. I go bright red. Charlie used to chuck water at me till I cooled down.'

Vera nodded. 'He was a lovely man.' Sheila's husband had died months earlier, had tumbled off a roof while tiling a new house up Breightmet way. Sheila was childless and probably lonely, but she carried on like a trooper, going to work, cleaning her house and minding her three cats.

Sheila looked at the dog. A real friend to Vera, that animal was. And the best thing about William was that he didn't bother with cats, didn't chase them, didn't run away from them. 'That's a grand animal, Vera.' There was something wrong, but Sheila Foster was not one for prying. If and when Vera needed her, she would be there. Vera had looked after her neighbour right through the inquest, the funeral and for weeks after Charlie had been buried.

'I can hear him,' said Vera as a key scraped in the front door. 'I'll perhaps see you later on, Sheila. Keep your fingers crossed for me, will you?'

Sheila crossed her eyes as a demonstration of her willingness to cross just about anything for her friend.

Vera walked into the house and closed the door. The dog would remain outside for ten minutes, because William's breed of enthusiasm could be tiresome at times like these.

Edward kissed her, felt the sudden stiffness in her thin body. 'Vera?'

'Sit down.' She urged him into a chair, then plonked herself on the sofa. 'Edward, I'm pregnant.' That was the highest hurdle cleared.

A couple of seconds ticked by while he absorbed the information. Vera was going to have his child. Soon, they would become a family. A grin broke out. 'Oh, Vera—'

'A girl up Scafell Avenue says she knows somebody who knows somebody,' said Vera. 'They're supposed to be cheap and clean. Bromwich Street, she thinks. I pretended it was for a friend, not for me. But it is for me.'

'What?' He had suddenly forgotten his manners. 'What are you talking about?'

'Getting rid,' she said.

Edward leapt up from the chair and stood over her. 'No,' he said quietly. 'There will be no need for that. Within a few weeks, I hope to be a free man. Not legally free, but at liberty to choose, at least.'

Vera nodded quickly. 'I know all about that, love.' The details were unclear, though he would be leaving his wife and his children soon. But her worries lay elsewhere. 'I'm terrified,' she mumbled.

'I'll be with you long before the baby is due.'

This was promising to be extremely difficult. How could a woman explain to a man that she wasn't normal, that the idea of motherhood was a nightmare? If she could just go to sleep, then wake up with a child, that would be fine. But it didn't happen that way. 'I can't,' she managed. 'I can't do it.'

'Can't do what?'

She leaned back and rested her head. Three children had been ripped from her sister, Audrey. When the third little creature had rested in its tiny coffin, Audrey had bled to death. Three times, Vera had been there for their Audrey, had held the screaming woman's hand, had helped the midwife to clean up the messes, had washed and dried those little bodies. On the third occasion, she had also made Audrey ready for the grave. 'I just can't do it, Edward. I don't want to die like my sister did. And I don't fancy living through the pain she suffered. It's something I never want to do. So I have to get rid of this baby.'

Edward sank to his knees. 'There's no need for you to be afraid, because medicine has come on a long way. Much of the pain can be eliminated.' She was very slender, with hips that seemed too narrow for childbirth. 'If necessary, a baby is delivered surgically while the mother has an anaesthetic.'

She stared hard at him. He seemed to want this child, and she should be grateful for that. How many women in this predicament had been abandoned by their married lovers? But the fear was so deep and so powerful that she could not reason with it.

'Wait a while,' he urged. 'See how you feel about things in a week or two.'

In spite of her reluctance, Vera was tired enough to nod her agreement. 'I'll hang on for a bit, then.' With luck, she might miscarry early. A loss after a month or two was painful, but not life-threatening. Part of her mind played with the idea of getting help without involving Edward. She could have the abortion and pretend that there had been an accident. Except that she needed money . . .

While he went to open the door to the frantic dog, Vera sniffed back her tears. What if she went through with the abortion and got pregnant again? She had always believed that she would not conceive, because her mechanism had never been regular. 'I knew,' she whispered into the empty room. 'I just knew I'd never get caught. How wrong I was.'

William licked her hand, got no answering pat.

Vera stood up, looked at Edward as he re-entered the room, announced her intention to make tea. She feared him now, feared the loving. Loving made babies.

'I'll always be here for you,' he told her.

She smiled, avoided his touch and went into her little kitchen. Finding Edward had been the happiest accident of her whole life. If she lost him, she would be as lonely as poor Sheila next door. And the thought of life without the man she loved was almost unbearable.

FIVE

It looked as if Mother had prepared to feed the five
thousand all over again, but on a scale that defied
both rationing and miracles. The dining hall, which
was seldom used these days, had white-draped tables
all round its edge. Hired waiters hovered behind
bowls of punch, bottles of wine, chicken legs, hams
and salads. James noticed a huge bowl of caviare,
wondered who on earth would eat it, because the
damned stuff was nearly as ghastly as cod liver oil.

'James.' Maude Templeton fiddled with her son's
tie. 'Now, this is all for your sake. Please have a lovely
time. We have gone to a lot of trouble on your
behalf.'

James did not trust his mother. She was a good
enough woman, and he loved her in his fashion, but
she was almost always up to something. Maude had
instigated Mrs Shawcross's diet plan, he felt sure of
that. It would be just like Mother to take it into
her head to campaign for the 'improvement' of her
unfortunate neighbour. And now, she was concentrating on the betterment of her son's lot in life. He
inhaled deeply, wished that tomorrow would arrive
quickly. 'Mother?'

'Yes, dear?'

'Would you mind telling me what this is all about?'

Maude tut-tutted. 'Why couldn't you have gone for a fitting, James? Mr Pybus was quite prepared to do a quick job for us.'

James scowled, then ordered himself to stop scowling. 'I have not cast a plate,' he informed her. 'So we don't need the blacksmith just yet.'

'Those old shoes are scuffed. No amount of polishing would get them right. Poor John Duncan worked for hours on them last night. But even John can't do the impossible.' She turned away to examine a set of beautiful crystal tumblers, picked up two of the nearest to persuade herself that the family glassware was clean enough to be out on parade.

'Mother?'

'Yes, dear?'

'You are up to something.' She was superbly dressed in a violet suit that served to bring out the colour of her magnificent eyes. For a woman of forty-seven, Maude was wearing well. He studied her, took in the flawless pearls against the flawless skin, thought about Sadie Martindale and her poor, weary legs. Mother was spoilt, as was he, as was his father. 'What is going on, Mother?' She bristled with energy and goodwill, looked like someone who was about to furnish the cat with a huge bowl of cream. This was her 'charity' mode. This was how she looked whenever she raised money for children with limited mobility and special needs.

James could be extremely disconcerting, Maude told herself. Sometimes, she felt as if he could read her mind, her soul, her sins. 'Well, you don't get out much, dear. Lately, you haven't been further than the field across the way.'

'I drive. I'm not a total cripple,' he answered.

'But you need to see more people, have more fun.'

He thought about the invited guests, ran his mind's eye over the list. The Bertrands, the Carter-Pollards, Colin Ince with the dreadful sister who could not snare a man. The Inces were horse breeders, and members of the family bore a strong likeness to the creatures they nurtured – big, yellowing teeth and sad eyes. Miranda Haverford and David Preston-Lloyd were expected, together with dozens more double-barrelled and brainless bores. 'This is not my idea of amusement,' James said. 'I would rather follow John Duncan round and watch him cleaning windows.'

Maude sighed. 'You are so ungrateful. Do you have any idea of the cost involved?'

James would have been quite happy with a bottle of lemonade and a bar of Fry's, but he held his tongue.

'And Gilbert is coming.' She paused, cleared her throat very delicately. 'With Constance.'

He heard the space between the words, noted the infinitesimal gap that said so much more than anything else. 'You don't like Connie.'

'When did I say that?' She arched the perfectly plucked eyebrows, brought them south when she remembered how easy it was to create frown-lines. A woman's face was her fortune, and she must not spend it all at once by being over-expressive in the forehead department.

'Every day for the past fifteen years, you have spoken of your intense dislike for Connie. She broke my toys, fell out of one of our trees while stealing the apples, screamed back at everyone when the house-keeper told her to go home. More recently, she has become forward, difficult, stubborn. Connie is far too modern for you, Mother. Need I continue?'

Maude was momentarily nonplussed. Then she rallied determinedly. 'Times are changing. Women are not as reticent as they once were. As you just said, Constance is merely modern, James. She's plucky, strong and willing.'

James awarded his mother a wry smile. 'Such outstanding qualities might be of interest to the Inces. You sounded as if you were describing a rather well-cultivated brood mare in need of a suitable stallion.'

Maude Templeton knew when to be quiet. Her husband was a docile man, but she had made him so by simply keeping a rein on her own opinions and wishes until the time felt right. There was a lot of Eric in James. There was also some of her own intuition and cunning, she realized.

'Are you trying to pair me off with Connie, Mother? By the way – she wants to be Connie from now on. Is that the reason for this bloody panto-mime?' He made a sweeping movement with his hand, pointed out the dimensions of Mother's latest folly. 'The engagement is announced and all that, society page of *The Times*, put the shampers on ice and book a good photographer?'

Maude took a step back. He was cleverer than she and Eric were, was younger, of a different genera-tion. Children these days were so . . . knowing.

James could feel his facial skin tightening and blanching. He loved Connie, had wanted her for years. But if he ever did get her, and he doubted that he would, he would do it off his own bat. A cold fury ran right through him, causing his pores to open and his sad, stupid leg to ache right up to the hip.

He was not a quick-tempered person. James strove to be fair and sensible at all times, because he knew only too well about life's injustices. 'Mother,' he began. 'I wish you had bothered to tell me about your intentions. Is she just another racehorse? Will she turn out to be a satisfactory dam for the Templeton bloodline?'

He was so near the mark that Maude actually blushed. 'James, I just felt that—'

'NO!' All movement in the hall stopped. Waiters froze, platters held in mid-air, their faces strained. James loosened his tie, pulled it over his head, tossed it to his mother. 'Enjoy yourself,' he said. 'I'm going out.'

The completely unflappable Maude Templeton flapped. She forgot the servants and the hired help, grabbed her son's sleeve, tried to force him to stay. 'Please. Please, James. For my sake, for Constance – do stay. Where are you going?'

He stopped, steadied himself against the door-frame. 'I am going to see a woman about a painting,' he said. 'And I shall return in the fullness of time.'

Maude wheeled round, looked at all the motion-less figures in the room. 'Get on with your work,' she snapped. Then she ran from the room and into the entrance hall. 'Eric,' she screamed. 'Do something with him. Eric? Where are you?'

James went out into the sunshine and unlocked his Morris. This time, Mother had stepped well over the line.

Sadie opened her door, felt her eyes widen. 'James? It's Sunday. You said you couldn't come today – you were supposed to be writing to me.'

He smiled apologetically. 'My foot hurts and I'm

dying of thirst. Will you please take pity on me, Mrs Martindale?'

She was a bit flustered after ironing. Tommy was in the back yard, was cursing and swearing fit to burn because he couldn't squeeze the window into the air raid shelter. Bernard had suffered yet another wash at the slopstone, had piked off towards Derby Street with his hair combed. And Mary was hobnobbing up Belmont with Teddy Shawcross's lad. Mary had put Sadie straight, had admitted to her that the party was to be held in the mansion, not at Aston Leigh. 'Aren't you supposed to be at a do? Isn't it at your house?'

'Yes,' he said.

'Why are you here, then?'

'I'll tell you in exchange for a cup of tea.'

She walked into the house, heard him hobbling along behind her. It was funny, because she wouldn't have felt comfortable with Ethel Hyatt from next door in the house, yet she felt totally unthreatened by James Templeton, whose dad was as near to royalty as Sadie could imagine. 'I bet you've never been in one of these little houses before, have you?' she asked as she brewed the tea.

'Yes,' he replied. 'My father owns quite a number of them. Not here, but in Manchester, Salford and so on. He's having some electrified as we speak.'

She stopped pouring. 'I thought it were all fields and farms that your dad owned.'

James shook his head. 'Bits of everything, really.' He looked round the room. It was roughly the size of his walk-in wardrobe at Top o' th' Moor. 'It must get a bit crowded,' he remarked.

Sadie grinned. 'You've not seen the size of our Bernard. He could fill a room on his own, my eldest.

Tommy's about average, but our Mary's tall for a lass.' She doled out milk, passed the sugar. 'She's at your house. That's why I came up on the bus. I were having a toot, see what she were letting herself in for. She met yon neighbour of yours, that Gilbert. Stepping out of her class, is my Mary.'

'She's with Gil?'

'Aye. Is he all right? I mean, will he do her any harm?'

James thought about that. 'I shouldn't think so. Though I know him as a friend, you see. We've sort of grown up together. I don't know how he is with women. But he's a jolly sort of person, and I can't see him doing any deliberate damage.'

Sadie pursed her lips. 'That's the trouble with folk pairing off. The harm's not deliberate, it just happens.' She looked at the fair-haired lad, admired his suit, wondered why he looked so frazzled. 'What's up, then?'

He drank some tea. 'Mother and her machinations, I'm afraid. She's spent hundreds of pounds on this so-called soirée, because she has picked out my bride. I imagine that she intended to create a situation in which Co— in which the young lady and I would finish up together. Games, and so on. Still. She can play her charades without one of her main characters. Perhaps this will teach her to keep her beak out.'

Sadie pondered for a few moments. 'So you've just walked out, like?'

'That's about the size of it.'

She blew on her tea, took a sip. 'Get back,' she said as she placed her cup in its cracked saucer. 'You've made your point, James. You've made her sweat. There's no road you can leave your mam swanning about among all them young folk. What'll she say when they ask where you are?'

He didn't care.

'James?'

'Mrs Martindale, I am twenty-four years of age. If it weren't for this damned leg, I'd be making something of my life. But because I remain at home, Mother treats me like a baby.'

Sadie sniffed. 'That's your fault, then. You should bugger off and get your own place. But before you do, get that tea drunk, get up off your bum and get home. Honest, lad, if you don't, you'll live to regret it. We only have one mother each, you know. No matter what she's done, you mun stand by her. And if you have to leave home to get close to her in other ways, then get gone.'

Tommy chose this moment to burst into the room. 'Bloody thing,' he said crossly. Then he noticed the company.

'Trouble?' asked James.

Tommy saw the suit, heard the accent in those two short syllables. 'I'm trying to put a window in the air raid shelter. I want to make it into a shed where I can mend bikes.'

James nodded. 'I'll send someone round tomorrow,' he said. 'Someone from my father's happy band of workers. He'll put it all together for you.' He stood up, lifted Sadie's hand and kissed it. 'That window of yours can be mended at the same time.' He waved a hand towards the boarded-up section. 'I must away now,' he declared, striking a pose. 'To cater to Mater.'

Sadie laughed, reached across the table and smacked his hand. 'Just get off with you. And mind what I said.'

Tommy Martindale lowered himself into a chair, waited until the front door closed. 'Who the hell were that?' he asked.

Sadie looked at her youngest. He was dressed in a filthy vest, torn trousers and worn-out shoes. His face was the colour of mud, except where sweat had made narrow and winding rivers of relative cleanliness. 'That, Tommy, were what you might call a gentleman.'

Tommy shrugged and grinned. 'Any more tea in that pot, Mam?'

He parked the Morris in the driveway, sat for a moment or two to consider what Sadie had said. She was a wise woman, he decided. He had made his point, but he must not alienate himself from his family. Sadie was right – a fellow did get just the one mother and, even if Mother was a nuisance, she was the one and only.

There were other cars stabled in front of the house, including two Rollers and a rather nice Bentley. He wondered whether the Inces had arrived in a horsebox, then ordered himself to behave properly. Mother was doing her best, he supposed. She had watched him through binoculars, had probably seen him mooning stupidly after Connie Shawcross.

As if conjured up by his thoughts, Connie put in an appearance. She was walking along the side of the house with Gilbert and a rather fine-looking girl. The latter was probably Sadie's daughter, and she was a stunner. James stuck his head out of the car. 'Gilbert? Look after her – her mother's a friend of mine.'

Mary approached the car. So this was the famous James Templeton, the friend about whom Gilbert had raved for an hour or so. 'I'm Mary,' she said. 'And how do you know my mam?' She should have said mother. Next time, she would try to remember to use the right words.

James tapped the side of his nose. 'Your mam is to be the subject of a painting.'

Connie hooted loudly. 'You haven't painted anything or anyone normal in months.'

'That's all right, then,' announced Mary. 'Because there's nothing normal about Mam.' What did it matter? Mam, Mother, it was all the same thing in the end. 'She's a character. Mind, if you want to know about bunions or corns, she's your woman. And she's very good at apple pudding, too. If you play your cards right, you might get a plateful.'

James got out of the car. 'Mother and I have had a slight contretemps,' he explained. 'And I buggered off for an hour. So I must away now and smooth the maternal feathers.' He limped off into the house.

Gilbert stared after his friend. 'He's got guts,' he said. 'I couldn't face Mrs Templeton if I'd had a row with her. In fact, she's terrifying even when she's in a good mood.'

Connie laughed. 'Mrs Templeton does not have rows, Gil. She probably calls them slight differences of opinion.'

'Then I should beg not to differ.' Gilbert took Mary's hand. 'Come on, I'll show you the spot where James painted the Wars of the Roses. A red flower, a white one, a bow and arrow and some dead pigeons.'

Connie hooted with laughter. 'They were doves, Mary. The doves of peace. And they weren't dead – just resting after the battles.' She followed the pair with her eyes, though she kept her feet planted on the driveway. There was something about the look in

Gil's eyes, an expression that led his sister to believe that Mary might be special. God help her if she was, Connie thought. Mother would have the vapours if and when she met Mary. Alice's son with the daughter of a common millworker? God forbid. Of course, Alice Shawcross's selective memory might well allow her to ignore the fact that she, too, had married beneath herself.

Inside the house, Connie found the party in full swing. The ongoings were noisy, while the large room felt stuffy in spite of open windows. She avoided a couple of potential suitors and headed for the library. It would be quieter there and not so hot. As she made her way towards the back of the house, she heard voices, was riveted to the spot when her name was mentioned.

'I'm sorry, Mother,' James said clearly. 'But you really shouldn't have gone to all this trouble. Connie will never marry me, no matter how many vols au vent and fruit cups you ply her with. You have wasted your money and the servants' time.'

'Nevertheless, you should show more respect for your mother.' This was Mr Templeton's voice.

'I know you are fond of the girl,' said Maude Templeton. 'And I just want you to be happy.'

'Mother!' Even from a distance, Connie heard the controlled anger in James's tone. 'She isn't a toy or a new pair of socks. Connie is a person. You can't buy her for me, you see. Sometimes, I think you imagine that all things are purchasable, that you and I will get our own way for ever just because we have money.'

'James, be careful.' Eric Templeton sounded very unlike his usual calm self.

Connie Shawcross forced her feet to move. She turned back, ran through the dining hall and into the front garden. Tears pricked her eyes and blurred her vision. Someone tried to touch her, but she swerved and carried on until she reached The Rise. The way to her own house was downhill, and she ran like the wind until she reached home. What a party that had been, she told herself once the door was firmly closed in her wake. She rubbed her eyes and walked towards the staircase.

'Constance?'

'I have a headache, Mother. I'm just going to lie down for a while.'

Alice, who had hoped for developments today, backed away. Constance was hurt, and Alice did not know how to help. She should have known. She should have known and understood her children better, ought to have made more of an effort. Was it really too late to begin now?

She sat next to the silent piano, found herself drifting backwards in time, as if going over old ground would give her an insight into the new. A perfect childhood. Golden days that had merged now into one glorious reminiscence, picnics in the fields, journeys to Wales and Scotland, holidays spent playing on beaches and basking in the sun, parents whose love had shone far brighter than the feeble light of Earth's single star.

Eleanor and Samuel Fishwick had radiated affection, had drawn their only child into the aura that always surrounded them. She had been protected, played with, cosseted and spoilt. Whatever she wanted, she got. Whatever she disliked was eliminated from her life, with the result that a succession of nannies and tutors had been dismissed on the whim of a small child.

Alice's eyes narrowed. A small child – were those

words the key? Mother and Father had doted on her, but their deepest love had been for one another. She sat up straight in her chair, was suddenly bolt upright. She had been an expression of their mutual adoration, no more than that. The beautiful child she had been must have pleased them, had probably been an ornament for display – look what we bought together, what we made together. 'I was not loved,' she whispered into the still room.

Her nose had grown large, while the blonde curls had straightened and turned a lacklustre brown. As she had matured, her parents had become closer to each other, as if clinging together in the presence of a dying dream. Their exquisite ornament had turned out to be a plaster figure from the fair, a chipped and graceless thing, a poor replacement for the Royal Doulton they had ordered.

Alice stood up and walked to the window. There had been trouble, she thought. It had been nothing to do with her, but Mother had cried a lot, while Father had taken to drinking brandy in this very room. Alone. She moved her head and looked at the buttoned leather chair where Father had sat with his Courvoisier. It was strange, but she had not remembered the trouble until now. Why? How could she have forgotten those dreadful days?

Ah yes. Love. Love had arrived at her gate, had swept her off her feet. Edward Shawcross, that handsome knight in shining armour, had offered to take care of her. Mother and Father, still quiet, had allowed their daughter to marry Edward after an engagement so brief that it had caused gossip. Then, Eleanor and Samuel Fishwick had taken a holiday, a well-earned cruise from which they had simply failed to return.

Alice had not dared to get close to her own children. She stood now in a sunlit window and pondered all the loves she had lost. First Mother and Father had deserted her, then Edward's affection had cooled to the point of refrigeration. Alice had a habit of losing love, it seemed. She was, she supposed, like a reversed magnet, one that had been placed in a position where it could merely repel or be repelled. 'What I don't love, I can't misplace,' she murmured, fighting back a river of self-pity that welled within her. 'And I have become too careful of myself.'

She realized that she did love her children, but that she had held back, had declined to express her feelings. In fact, poor Constance had been the target of some of Alice's bitterness, because Constance had remained lovely. The world would be Alice's daughter's oyster, because Alice's daughter had the power that comes from physical beauty. It was time for Alice to grow up, time for her to stop the sulking and the petulance. She walked into the hall and stood at the foot of her stairs.

Stairs were easy now, because Alice was fitter after all the walking. Yet the staircase at Aston Leigh was, at this moment, like Mount Everest. A climb of twenty steps faced her, one for each year of her daughter's life. It had taken a score of twelvemonths for Alice to reach the foothills. How could she explain to Constance? How could she justify herself, her behaviour, her neglect? The children had always been healthy, well clothed and well fed, but their souls had been starved.

With no climbing aids save guilt, Alice Shawcross placed her foot on the bottom step and walked with bated breath towards her distressed child.

*   *   *

Connie lay on the bed, her eyes closed. The voice kept on and on inside her head, 'She will never marry me, she is not for sale.' Oh, James. She didn't know whether or when she would marry, had drawn up no short-list of candidates. If only she had someone to talk to. The 'select' schools she had attended had borne no lasting friendships, because the pupils had been drawn from far and wide. There was no-one here who could comfort her, while poor James was likely to continue wallowing in his own misery. Still, James had Gilbert, at least, and she was glad about that.

Mary – what was her name? She seemed pleasant. Perhaps Mary could become a friend, then. Her stomach churned, partly because of hunger, but mostly as a reflection of her state of mind. Her body mechanism was going too fast, was urging her to be up and out of here. She needed a job, a future, a sense of self, her own place in the world.

'Constance?'

She had not heard the opening of her door. 'Mother.' She heaved herself up.

'Stay as you are.' Alice walked to the bed, then perched herself on the edge. 'You seemed upset when you came in. Would you like to talk about it?'

Connie was flabbergasted. Mother had never been one for discussing things. In fact, debate of any kind seemed to be against Alice Shawcross's religion. Mother just told people what to do, then they either did or didn't do whatever. Doing something right brought no praise, while failure to follow an order often resulted in criticism or sarcasm. 'I have a headache,' Connie said weakly and truthfully.

Alice sighed and dropped her chin. 'We have

never been close, Constance. That was always my fault, because I am the adult. In years, I am the adult. But I have never trained myself to act as a grown-up person.' No-one had trained her. No-one had helped Alice to mature.

Connie felt embarrassed in the extreme. This was turning out to be the very devil of a day. Mrs Templeton wanted to turn Connie into Mrs Templeton Junior, while Mother wanted . . . what? To be a mother? After all this time?

'You may make a poor mother, too,' Alice was saying. 'Because you have no example to follow. I cannot explain why I am as I am. I can only say that I shall try to be better.'

Connie shot upward and stared at the stranger who sat on her bed. She did not know this woman. Was Mother suffering from some terminal disorder that was prompting her to repent her shortcomings? 'Are you ill?' asked Connie, her eyes raking over Mother's face.

'No. I have not felt so well in a long time. The exercise is doing me good. And, of course, I have given up chocolate. That was a battle, but I seem to have won.'

'Yes. We rather thought you had.' Mother looked slightly better, a bit thinner, a lot less pale and sad. 'Why have you come up here? Did you and Mrs Templeton plan to marry me to James?'

Alice shook her head. 'I had hoped, I must admit. Lately, things have changed somewhat. I am changing. But Maude never will. She tends to turn her hopes and dreams into reality. What happened?'

Connie threw herself back against the pillows. 'A row. His parents are shouting at him because he went off earlier. He went off in a huff because he must have worked out what was afoot. All that trouble just to get me and James together. We're together all the time as it is. There was no need for all the pomp and circumstance, because we see each other almost every day.'

Alice thought about that. 'It's just Maude's way,' she said. 'Perhaps Maude and I have something in common. We both seem to act without consulting anyone else.'

It was fine to joke about rearing difficult parents, Connie thought. But to face the problem head on like this went far beyond a joke. Mother might be right. Connie found communication with her parents difficult because they, Mother in particular, had seldom tried to reach her verbally. 'You weren't in on the plan, then?'

'No. I had an idea about what was going on, because Maude suddenly began to sing your praises. But I dotted no i's and crossed no t's.'

'Thank you.'

Alice rose stiffly and walked to the window. She organized her thoughts, her feelings, worked on how best to say what needed to be said. 'You have little to thank me for, Constance. I am an unhappy woman, though that should not affect the way I treat you. It's a big failing of mine, this inability to face family life head on. I am sorry. You are a good daughter and I love you. And you play the piano beautifully. I mention the piano because I pick holes in your playing. It's hard to know why I do that, but I hate myself every time. Perhaps I am envious of your talents.'

Connie remained speechless, felt winded, as if she had just run in a race of some kind.

'Your grandparents will be home soon.' Alice's

bones were uneasy. The return of the Fishwicks would, she felt sure, mark the end of something and the beginning of something else. 'I don't know why,' she murmured absently. 'I don't know why they left in the first place.' She swivelled, faced her daughter. She wanted to tell Constance that the Shawcross marriage had been built on a riddle, but she could not. Constance had to be kept out of the storm. Which storm, though? Why and how did Alice sense this thickening of the atmosphere, this awful silence that heralded the first crash of thunder? 'Constance, I shall try to be a better mother.' She smiled, nodded and left the room.

For at least five minutes, Connie was rendered immobile. Where was Gil when she needed him? Probably up to his eyes in wine and that new girl of his. Was it menopause? she wondered. Was Mother going through that difficult time? Her hands shook in spite of the heat in her bedroom. Mother had finally flipped. Mother was getting ready to be trussed up in a restraining jacket and taken to the lunatic asylum.

A clock struck seven. And where was Father? He spent more time at work than he did at home. Even on Sundays, he often went out to the mill, while weekday evenings were largely devoted to council business. Anyway, there was no love lost between the parents. They simply existed side by side, went from day to day, from meal to meal, from room to room avoiding each other's eyes.

God, what a mess. Connie felt as if she stood at a crossroads whose signposts had been removed or painted out. There were no directions, no instructions. How could she have considered writing as a career when she failed to connect with those who were supposedly nearest and dearest? Her parents were almost like figures in a painting, motionless, two-dimensional and unreachable.

She got off the bed and dragged a comb through her hair. When the new dress had been put away, she left the room and went out to the landing. An unfamiliar sound reached her ears, and she stood still, waited for her brain to analyse the noise. Mother was crying.

Lottie Bowker, Aston Leigh's longest ever surviving cook, stood at the foot of the stairs. Lottie was into her third year, was a legend in her own life-time, because she had the ability to endure her mistress's taunts. 'Go to her, love,' she said. Mrs Shawcross was a very unhappy lady.

Connie nodded, saw the terrible sadness in Cook's eyes.

'She needs somebody,' said Lottie. The master of Aston Leigh had another woman, a red-haired piece from Tonge Moor. Had the gossip finally travelled to Belmont? Was Mrs Shawcross mourning the death of her marriage? Though this wasn't a marriage, not really. While she stood and pondered, Lottie re-alized that Connie was all Mrs Shawcross had in the world. Lads weren't the same, she told herself. When all came to all, a woman could depend only on female offspring.

Connie smiled at Cook. 'I'll look after her,' she mouthed.

Sheila Foster poured out two more cups of tea. Vera looked terrible, as if she had aged overnight. It was difficult for Sheila to understand her neighbour's fear, because Sheila would have given anything for a baby, a real, live, miniature part of Charlie. His sudden death had been a body-blow for Sheila, because she had existed just for him, had breathed for him. If only she had given birth to a child of his, the loneliness would have been less acute.

Vera sniffed, blew her nose for the second time in five minutes. 'I can't reason with this fear,' she said. 'I've tried telling myself I'll be all right, but it makes no difference. The fact is, I'm frightened to death.'

'You will be all right, I'm sure. It's only natural to be a bit scared the first time.'

'No.' Vera sank back into the cushions on her neighbour's sofa. 'It's as if I've always known that I couldn't be a mother. I mean, I thought I'd never get pregnant, even after I met Edward. Infertile, or so I hoped, or so I thought. And now, I've been proved wrong.'

'What does he say?'

Vera shrugged listlessly. 'He wants me to have the baby, says he'll be living with me well before it's born.'

'Did you talk to him about getting rid?' asked Sheila.

'I did. He wouldn't discuss it.'

Sheila sat down next to her friend. 'Is it only the birth that bothers you, or do you dread rearing a kiddy?'

'I won't rear it,' replied Vera. 'It'll die, or I'll die, or we'll both die.' She placed her cup on the floor, twisted the handkerchief in her hands. 'I've not enough money to get it done without Edward's help. I thought I could just have the operation, then tell him I'd lost it by miscarriage. Only I can't afford it.'

Sheila sat perfectly still, anticipated the question before it emerged from her companion's mouth.

'Have you spent all that insurance money, Sheila?'

'No.'

Vera waited for more, was disappointed. 'Will you lend me forty pounds?'

'No.' Sheila got up and walked to the fireplace. Her heart bled for Vera, yet she could not help, could not hand over money that would be used to kill a child. 'I can't, Vera. I can't.'

'Why?'

'I . . . well, you see, it's against my religion. We don't have abortions, us Catholics. And if I gave you the money, I'd be helping you to commit a murder. I'd be like what they call an accessory.'

Vera shook her head slowly. 'It's not a person, Sheila. It's just a little lump of jelly, no arms or legs, no face. It's not killing.' She paused. 'It will be killing if I go into labour. What will you think then, after I die? Will you wish you'd helped me?'

The church had been Sheila's sole consolation since the untimely death of her husband. She had not lapsed completely before Charlie's death, though her attendances at mass had been sporadic, to say the least. But Father Sheehan had nursed her through the bereavement, had sat with her well into the night on several occasions. He was her strength, her link with Charlie, the wall against which she had leaned during the early days of widowhood.

'Sheila? You're my only chance.'

Sheila stood in front of the grate with her feet planted firmly and her arms folded. There was no chance that she would consider helping to rid her neighbour of this unborn infant. What would Father Sheehan say at her next confession? All the Our Fathers, Hail Marys and Glory Bes in the world could never cleanse the soul of a deliberate killer. 'No, Vera.' Her voice was steady and clear. 'If you die –

and I'm sure you won't – then that will be God's will. If I lent you the money for an abortion, the baby's death would be through my will and yours.'

Panic rose and sat in Vera's gorge, seemed to threaten her ability to breathe. She was trapped, terrified and confused. The loving was over, no matter what happened in the future. Even if she lost this child, there could well be others, further threats to her physical and mental well-being. She jumped up, kicked the cup away in her haste, then fled from the house.

Sheila stood in the doorway of her home and watched Vera Hardman doing a disappearing act onto Tonge Moor Road. Vera was wearing fluffy blue house-slippers and a loose dressing gown, was in no fit state to be running about all over the road.

Sheila stepped outside, stepped back into the house again, rummaged through her mind in search of a solution. Annie Parsons. Annie lived three doors down, and she had a telephone because she was a midwife. Sheila snatched up her keys and ran, slamming the door behind her. If Annie Parsons was out delivering a child . . . She hammered on the knocker.

Annie opened the door. 'Sheila? Whatever's up with you?'

The visitor leaned against the door frame. 'Annie, phone Edward Shawcross at Fishwick's. Tell him to get round here straight away. Tell him I've gone after Vera, and that she's somewhere on Tonge Moor Road.'

'What's happened? . . .' Annie's voice tailed away, because Sheila was already through the gate.

Sheila ran like the wind up Tintern Avenue, stood on the corner, looked left and right along Tonge Moor Road. Vera was nowhere to be seen. A bus clattered by, then a ragman's cart and a coal lorry. Across the road, the door of the Co-op hung inward. Sheila crossed over, looked inside the shop, saw three queues of women holding Co-op points slips in readiness for the next dividend receipt, but there was no sign of Vera.

The chip shop was still closed, and the ironmonger's was empty. Sheila stumbled over a pile of buckets beneath the ironmonger's window, ran down towards the next corner. Vera was not in the newsagent's. Tonge Moor Library yielded no success, nor did Betty's dress shop. Convinced that Vera had done herself a mischief, Sheila walked homeward. All she could do now was wait for Edward Shawcross to arrive.

He came about twenty minutes later. Sheila opened her door and took him inside. 'She's scared to death of having that baby,' she told him immediately. It was too late for anything but the truth. 'She'd do anything to be rid of it. I refused to lend her money for an abortion, and she just shot off up the avenue before I could stop her. She's not dressed, Mr Shawcross. All she's got on is her nightclothes and slippers. To be honest, I think poor Vera's going crackers.'

Edward looked at Sheila, saw her distress. He failed to understand what was happening here. He was going to sort out all the problems, was intending to look after Vera and the child. 'I've told her that she and the child will be cared for,' he said. 'What more can I do?'

Sheila bit her lip. 'It's like a craziness,' she said. 'As if the thought of going into labour drives her out of her mind.' It was so hard to describe. 'I had an auntie who was feared of spiders. She used to scream every time she saw one, and she wouldn't go back into the house until somebody had got rid. We told her the spiders wouldn't hurt her, but she couldn't believe us. Even though she knew a spider wouldn't kill her, she stayed frightened. It's the same thing with Vera, only her fear's about childbirth.'

Edward stared at Sheila for a few moments, then strode out of the house. Vera could not have gone far. Why was this happening? He saw neighbours coming out of their homes to stand in whispering clutches at the gates. It wasn't supposed to be like this. Vera was the best thing in his life, the only person worth living for. Except for his children, of course. But Vera Hardman had given him joy, a new lease, reasons to continue. Soon, the mill and all its difficulties would be behind him. There was to be a child, a fresh beginning.

He ran up the main road, looked into gardens and down side streets. When he failed to find Vera, he trod up and down the back alleys, even tried calling her name a few times. Castle Hill School and the playing fields were deserted. A feeling of hopelessness overcame him. Vera, who had brought him happiness, was turning into yet another problem.

Edward walked down the road again, then remembered the off-licence. Would she have gone there? he wondered. Mr and Mrs Tattersall had been kind to Vera, especially after the death of her mother. He quickened his pace, peered into Povey's bread shop on his way. At Tattersall's, he hammered on the door. The off-licence was not yet open, but Vera might have got in through the side door leading to the living quarters.

A very harassed Bertha Tattersall opened the shop door. 'Thank God,' she said. In Bertha's opinion, God had no place in this adulterous situation, but help from any quarter was welcome at the moment. 'She's in the back.' Bertha's tone was clipped, judgemental. 'Len's with her. As far as we're concerned, Vera needs a blinking head-doctor.'

Edward lifted the counter flap and walked into the Tattersalls' living room. There, amid boxes of crisps and crates of ale, Vera sat weeping.

'We've just had a delivery,' said Bertha, anxious to explain the condition of her usually spotless home. 'And we were going to put all this away when Vera arrived. Screaming for gin, she was.'

Vera lifted her face, saw Edward, screamed with renewed gusto. 'He's going to make me have this baby.' She clung fiercely to Len Tattersall. 'He won't let me choose.'

Len patted Vera's shoulder. 'You can't get rid, love. It's a locking-up job, is that. You could finish up in prison, Vera.'

'Better than dead,' she sobbed.

Bertha Tattersall surprised everyone by smacking Vera across the face. The blow was not gentle, and the weeping woman's head shot sideways with the weight of it. Stunned by the attack, she stopped crying.

Bertha drew breath. 'Now, you listen to me, Vera Hardman. There's not a woman in England who doesn't feel what you're feeling. Three times, I went through it, worried past reason because our mam died in childbed. You're no different from anybody else, so stop making yourself so special. Get home. And no, we're not giving you a bottle of gin. Take a couple of stouts, because the iron'll buck you up, but gin is not on your menu, love.' Bertha folded her arms, then nodded stiffly to show that her speech was over.

Edward stood with his hat twisting in his hands. Where was his lover? Where was that light-hearted little woman who had made his existence worthwhile? Lumbered already with one miserable woman, he could not bear to contemplate the concept of taking on a second.

'Edward?' Vera stared up at him.

'Yes, dear?'

'I've never asked you for anything, have I? Because you're the one with the family, you see. I really, really believed that I couldn't have children, and I was glad. But this changes everything. I can't be on my own, not now, not while I'm so frightened. You'll have to find somebody to live with me.'

He lowered his chin. Who would want to look after a person who was so obviously bent on self-destruction? There was only one thing for it, he decided. As an honourable man, he must take care of Vera himself. 'I shall send you on a little holiday,' he told her. 'I'm sure that Mr and Mrs Tattersall will allow you the time off.'

The licensee and his wife nodded their heartfelt relief.

'When you return, I shall be with you.' He reached out a hand and helped Vera to her feet. 'Take a friend with you. Cornwall is very pleasant. Or Devon. Perhaps Sheila would enjoy a change of scenery? I'll get a little cottage where William will be accepted. And we can put Sheila's cats into the cattery.'

Vera stared at him and straight through him. He was bewildered and nervous, was acting not out of love, but out of a sense of fair play. It didn't matter, she told herself, because the love was over anyway.

While Edward went for the car, Vera sat as still as a rock. Her fate was sealed, it seemed. So she had better get on with it and take the consequences. But inside her heart, there remained an icy lump of dread.

SIX

Edward's discomfort was increasing daily. In the south of England, he had a deranged mistress who was expecting his child; at Aston Leigh, he shared a house with a wife whose efforts to improve herself were becoming painfully noticeable.

About Vera, he was confused. Abortion was a crime, and he could not bring himself to contemplate such a measure. Yet the woman he loved was in pain, the sort of pain he could not understand, let alone cure. His thoughts swung back and forth like a quickened pendulum, and he was losing the ability to make rational judgements about Vera.

Meanwhile, Alice had started to converse during meals, had even gone so far as to offer up several feeble jokes. Gilbert seemed slightly disconcerted, but Constance encouraged her mother's endeavours. Edward simply stumbled from day to day in a world that he failed to understand. His future had been plotted out so carefully after the arrival of the Fishwicks' letter. With his duty done, Edward was to ride off into the sunset with very little money, and with Vera as his passenger. But now, things were not so simple.

He threw down his napkin and stared at the

woman who sat opposite. She had fined down a little, and her hair was different, shorter, thicker and less severe. Her clothes had begun to hang loosely, and she had taken to wearing scarves, perfume and jewellery. Was that lipstick on her mouth? he wondered. What the devil was she up to now? Complications, riddles that rendered him perplexed. Perhaps Alice was preparing for the return of her parents, though Edward doubted that. His wife had taken no interest in her appearance for years, despite having attended, albeit unwillingly, many civic functions. Alice had been dowdy and unpleasant for as long as Edward chose to remember.

'Would you like some more cheese?' asked Alice.

'No, thank you.' Would he like some more cheese? Until lately, no such question would have arisen. The maid hovered, served, offered second helpings. If Alice was trying to create a family here, she had left it rather late.

Connie was somewhat annoyed with her father. She knew that her parents' marriage was not perfect, but could the man not make some sort of stab at meeting Mother partway? He was so distant, so cold and absent in his manner. 'How is the mill going, Father?' she asked him.

'Very well,' he replied.

'Mary's mother works for you,' said Connie.

'Mary?' He sounded as if he answered out of politeness, rather than as an interested party.

'Mary Martindale. Gilbert's friend,' said Connie.

Sadie's daughter, he said inwardly. How on earth had his son become involved with the Martindales? They were decent enough people, though their social circle was a mile away from Gilbert's usual sphere. 'Sadie works for us,' he said. 'She has terrible trouble with her feet.'

Alice placed her glass on the table. Edward knew about his employees' various problems, yet he had no idea about hers. She felt no anger, no jealousy. Had she continued to love him, she might have experienced some pain, but the distance that had grown between herself and him was too great for any bridge to span. 'Mary's a pleasant girl,' she remarked.

Gilbert gulped down a mouthful of water. This really was too much, too weird to be credible. Mother had spoken about half a dozen words to Mary, and those few syllables had been transmitted over telephone wires. The world was going crazy. Mother was a snob, had always been a snob. She liked things done correctly, and she would forgive little that fell short of perfect. The mother he remembered would not have welcomed Mary into her life. The mother he remembered would have been worried about fortune-hunters. Gilbert's gaze slid over his sister and onto his father. Had Mother married a gold digger? Was her own mistake the reason for her temperate attitude?

Edward pulled out his watch and looked at it. Twenty-five minutes after six. Vera was away and there were no meetings for him to attend. He was condemned to remain at Aston Leigh in the company of a wife he disliked and children he hardly knew. A diversion was called for, some kind of activity that might while away an hour or two. 'Would you like a game of cards?' he asked his daughter.

Connie looked at Gilbert. When had they last played cards? Three, four years ago? 'Do you fancy a hand of rummy, Gil?' she asked.

Gilbert nodded, seemed stunned. Mary was

working at the cinema tonight, so he was at a loose end. 'All right,' he said. 'But not for money.' He winked at Connie. 'Minnie the Minx cheats,' he told his father.

'Mother?' Connie held out very little hope, but she asked all the same.

'That will be very nice,' said Alice.

Edward paused, a thumb frozen momentarily in his watch pocket. He did not mind conversing with his children; in fact, they were both rather good company, but how was he going to sit in a social situation with a woman he always took pains to avoid? Alice was staring at him. The slate-grey eyes had fixed themselves on his face, but there were no questions in their depths. It was as if she already knew everything about him. Perhaps she did. Vera's exit from Tintern Avenue had been far from low-key. There had been a guard of honour lining the pavements, shoulder-to-shoulder neighbours who had come to see Vera and Sheila off on holiday. The spectators had shaken their heads sadly, because Vera had gone a bit doo-lally.

'Would you mind if I joined you?' Alice asked. She was going to know her children before they left home altogether. She planned to try to be a mother rather than a spoilt brat, and she realized that such a task would not be easy.

'No,' Edward lied.

They walked into the study, Gilbert and Connie first, then Alice, with Edward dragging his feet at the back. The game progressed without incident until Connie accused Gilbert of cheating. There followed much hilarity as Gilbert was searched by his sister, who was convinced that a full set of cards had secreted itself inside Gilbert's shirt. While the siblings wrestled, Alice watched them, and Edward watched Alice. She was smiling. The woman had never been a mother, had seldom displayed much more than a passing interest in her young.

Edward was thoroughly puzzled. The Shawcrosses had not functioned as a family for a long time. There had been seaside holidays, buckets, spades, and ice-cream cones, but Alice had simply sat and kept order. Suddenly, she was taking an interest. 'I have some paperwork to do,' he said before going out to the hall. He would find something to occupy himself, he decided.

The telephone rang. He lifted it, spoke his name, waited for several seconds.

A creaky voice answered. 'Edward? Is that you?'

'Yes.'

'Sorry. Old age. I'm a bit deaf. We are on our way now from Trinity Street Station.'

The line went dead. Had that voice belonged to Samuel Fishwick? Were they back at last?

'Who was that?' Gilbert stood behind his father, shirt-tails dangling after Connie's assault on his person.

'I think it was your grandfather.'

'Really?' Gilbert turned back and called, 'Mother? Your long-lost parents are on their way.'

Edward straightened his tie and began to ascend the stairs. At last, his exit from Aston Leigh was at hand.

Eleanor Fishwick, who had been round and pretty in youth, was now thin and as wrinkled as rotted fruit. She looked like something that had been produced out of poor hide at Walker's Tannery, Edward thought. Her husband, Samuel, was also reed-thin, though his skin was paler and yellower than his wife's.

Alice stood in the driveway with her husband and children. The mother she remembered had been fragrant, with nut-brown curls and clear blue eyes. This lady with sun-frizzled hair and leathery skin was far removed from Alice's memory. She was inexplicably terrified of these two ancient strangers.

Eleanor approached her daughter. 'How lovely to see you again, my dear,' she said vaguely before pouncing on the grandchildren she had never seen. She scrutinized Connie, found her to be beautiful if somewhat pale, then she turned her attention to Gilbert. 'Fine boy,' she proclaimed. 'Might we go inside? We were a long time on that wretched ship. And the trains were as slow as snails.' She turned to her husband. 'Come along, Samuel,' she said. There could be no doubt about the woman's position in the marriage – she was the leader, he the mere follower.

Samuel Fishwick approached Edward Shawcross slowly. The old man walked with a limp and supported himself with an ivory-handled cane. He held out a hand and grasped Edward's outstretched fingers. 'My dear boy,' he said softly, the voice scarred by age and suffering. 'I am so delighted to see you again.'

Connie watched the scene, thought it strange. Grandfather had made a beeline for Edward, had left his daughter to stand alone in second place.

'Alice,' said the old man. 'Are you well?'

'Yes, thank you.'

They could have been acquaintances or business contacts, Connie thought. She smiled dutifully at her grandfather, then followed the party into the house. Father was on pins. He kept removing the watch from his pocket, staring at the time and winding a mechanism that was already tight.

The visitors were too tired for company. They went straight to their room and promised to give out presents in the morning. Ada dashed about with trays and hot water bottles, was forced to find extra blankets.

'They will feel the cold,' Alice told her daughter.

'But it's roasting,' exclaimed Connie.

'Not as hot as Africa. Remember, they were a very long time in a hot climate.'

Connie, continuing to sense a mystery, sought her father. She found him in the study with his head in his hands. 'Father? Are you ill?'

He was a prisoner who had caught a glimpse of the world outside his cell, but he was not ill, and he said so.

'Why have they come?' asked Connie.

Edward knew now why the Fishwicks had come home. Just a glance at Samuel had said it all – the old man was dying, probably of a liver complaint. How on earth had Edward managed to pretend that Alice's father would come and take over the mill after all these years? He was nearing seventy. Edward had remembered a robust man of middle years, and that man had gone the way of all flesh towards his dotage. 'I don't know,' Edward answered. 'Perhaps they grew tired of travelling.'

Connie placed herself in the chair next to her father's desk. 'Why did they go in the first place?'

'I don't know,' he lied carefully.

'It was very sudden, I believe.'

'Yes. I suppose Sam wanted a change from the mill. When I married your mother, he decided to put the lot into my hands.'

'You were a weaver.'

'Long ago, yes.'

'And you went from weaving to being in charge?'

'Yes. Your grandfather had me trained by a chap who had managed the mill for donkey's years.'

She would get no more out of Father. Mother was the same, as tight as a clam when questioned about her parents. Yet Connie guessed that Mother was genuinely ignorant of the full truth, while Father was more likely to be the one with the guilty secret. 'Why are you so unhappy?' The question had leapt out of her mouth of its own accord, it seemed.

'Unhappy?' Edward picked up a pen and placed it in the top drawer. 'The job is tiring. And council work can be wearisome, too.' He was unhappy because he needed to run like hell for the hills, wanted to be his own man, Vera's man.

Connie studied him. He was upset, she thought. Disappointed, perhaps, and terribly lonely. 'You don't love Mother,' she whispered. 'And she doesn't love you. What happened to both of you, Father?'

What happened? 'Don't, Constance,' he said. 'Please don't.'

She rose from the chair and left the room.

What happened? Edward closed his eyes and drifted slowly back to Delta Street, his home of twenty-odd years ago. The trip was not made willingly, though Edward realized that he had to take this route. There was so much to explain, so much to justify, especially to himself.

Mam was long dead, and Dad was fading fast, existing from one drink to the next, losing control of his bodily functions and of his mind. Paul, Edward's older brother, had disappeared over the horizon, was nowhere to be found. In a filthy hovel, Edward Shawcross nursed his father to a bitter and extremely painful end.

The neighbours came round, bringing food and sympathetic words. With his father dead, Edward Shawcross was completely alone except when at the mill. So he threw himself into the work, became a master weaver at a surprisingly young age. A year or so after his father's death, Edward got rid of the house in School Hill, moved into a couple of rooms in Goldsmith Street, bought a few decent items of clothing and a pair of leather shoes.

It was a Thursday night. On Thursdays, Edward met up with a few friends from the mill and played a quiet game of darts in the King's Head on Deansgate. The landlord granted the winners an extra pint, serving them just before the towels went on, then allowing the team to hang around chatting and joking after the closing bell. By the time the party broke up, the Town Hall clock was thinking about striking half past eleven. The young men separated and made for their homes.

It all began just outside the main post office. From the side entrance, a group of three or four men ran quickly away from Deansgate and away from Edward. He listened to clogs or boots clipping the flags, wondered briefly about robbery connected with the Royal Mail. He was just about to continue homeward, when he heard a sound that was to alter dramatically the course of his life. Someone moaned. There were two choices; Edward could go home, or he could investigate. He chose the latter and took his first step towards a different future.

A bloody mess lay on the pavement. It breathed and made sounds, so it was alive. Edward bent and touched the heap of clothes. 'No police,' said the creature before lapsing into complete unconsciousness.

Edward searched pockets and a wallet that lay nearby, found a couple of handkerchieves, a receipt and some small change. Reaping no information, he turned the person over and began to wipe the face. To illuminate the subject, he lit a series of matches. Blood, black in the paltry light of tiny flames and a waning moon, was beginning to congeal on the face of . . . the face of Samuel Fishwick, owner of the mill in which Edward worked.

He sat back on his heels, removed his own coat and covered Mr Fishwick. No police. Where did the man live? Wasn't it Belmont? Fishwick's distinctive maroon Austin stood nearby, its starting handle lying in the gutter. Edward picked it up, found it to be sticky and nasty to the touch. This was the weapon, he thought. Mr Fishwick must have been preparing to drive home when the attack was launched. So, Edward was now responsible for an injured man and a motor car. Mr Fishwick needed moving. The central police station was round the corner, a mere three or four hundred yards away. He had to decide whether to obey his boss or get the law. He obeyed his boss.

Driving for the first time was difficult. Having placed Mr Fishwick in the rear seat, Edward turned the engine over, climbed into the cab and tried to remember what came next. Having been a passenger on very few occasions he had a vague idea of the principles, but no experience of the actual practice. He pressed pedals, leapt about for a while, finally managing to move the vehicle in a line that was more or less straight.

Belmont was out of the question. Edward drove past the open market in first gear, then rattled up Derby Street over cobbles and tramlines until he reached home. Fortunately, there was little traffic about, since most sensible folk were already tucked up in bed in order to face another working day.

Home was two rooms above a butcher's shop in Goldsmith Street. The rent was low, because Edward was supposed to act as night-watchman in case of burglars. He opened the side door and carried the owner of Fishwick's mill up a steep flight and into his bedroom.

What next? He surveyed the man on the bed, then sat down in a wicker chair until his breath returned properly. There was no way he could take Mr Fishwick's car back to Belmont. For a start, he couldn't drive properly, then there was the problem of finding the exact house. He searched Fishwick's pockets again, found nothing new, no diary, no address.

With warm water and a flannel, Edward washed the bloodied face. There was an open wound across the left temple, though the blood was setting into a scab. He ran inexpert fingers over the skull, came across a couple of bumps and another sticky patch. The arms were still the right shape, and there was nothing unusual about the legs, so the man was probably out cold as a result of blows to his head.

'Who are you?'

Edward dropped the flannel. 'Shawcross, sir. I found you in the alley at the side of the post office.'

Fishwick grunted. 'My head hurts.'

'You've been attacked. Shall I get the police?'

'No.' There was a surprising amount of energy behind the syllable.

'A doctor?' suggested Edward.

Samuel Fishwick drifted back to sleep. He snored loudly, but his breathing seemed even enough. Spittle and blood dribbled slowly from a corner of his mouth, while his whole body twitched as if some invisible puppeteer had started to pull strings.

Edward waited. After an hour or so, he nodded off in the chair, his own arm acting as a very uncomfortable cushion. Pins and needles woke him. It was five-thirty; the alarm clock would sound in half an hour. He decided to leave the clock to run its course, as it might wake Fishwick, too.

The man on the bed was still. His skin was waxy, but at least he had survived the night. It occurred to Edward that he might very well be accused of murder or manslaughter if Fishwick died. Ten to six. He crept out to the kitchen and sat at the scarred and stained table. He could hang because of the man in the other room. A recognizable car stood outside; Edward had no way of protecting himself from the barbs of fate. His future lay in the hands of an unconscious person in the next room, a man whose brain had possibly been damaged during the attack.

The alarm sounded. Edward rose from the table, took a deep breath, then walked into the bedroom.

'Bloody hell,' cursed Fishwick. 'Stop that blasted noise, will you?'

Edward complied, then waited for further instructions.

'Who are you?' asked Fishwick again.

'Shawcross, sir. I'm a weaver in your mill. We had a game of darts at the King's Head last night, and I found you on my way home. You were outside the post office. So I brought you here, because I don't know where you live.'

Samuel Fishwick struggled into a sitting position and swung his legs over the side of the bed. 'Where's the bathroom?' He swayed ominously.

'There isn't one, Mr Fishwick. There's a lavatory in the yard, just down those stairs and turn—'

'Thank you,' snapped the visitor. 'Stay here,' he ordered as Edward moved to offer his help. 'Do you hear me? I want you to remain here while I think this through.'

Edward stayed. He sat for about five minutes, listened while Samuel Fishwick returned from the yard and climbed the stairs very unsteadily, waited until the man had seated himself on the bed once more.

'Go to the mill,' he ordered. 'Tell them my car has broken down and that you are going to get help. Then take the tram to Belmont. You'll have to walk the last bit, because the tram stops at the bottom, and my house is on The Rise – about halfway up – it's called Aston Leigh. Mrs Fishwick will be worried, so just tell her that I've had a slight accident and that she must send Dr Wilkinson. Is that clear?'

Edward nodded, made for the door.

'Shawcross?'

'Yes, Mr Fishwick?'

'Not a word about this. Not a whisper about last night. Do you understand?'

Edward nodded again, took his cap from a peg on the door, then went to do his master's bidding.

When he finally reached Aston Leigh, the door was opened not by a maid, but by a plumpish young woman in a grey dress. It was plain that she had been crying. 'May I help you?' she asked anxiously.

Edward removed his cap. 'I have to talk to Mrs Fishwick,' he said. 'Mr Fishwick sent me. My name is . . .' He found himself talking to no-one at all.

'Mother!' shouted the girl. 'It's a man to see you. Father sent him, so he must be well.' She remembered Edward, turned on her heel and came back to him. A maid appeared with a handkerchief covering the lower part of her face. She, too, had been weeping. 'Is Mr Fishwick all right, Miss Alice?' It was clear that the whole house had descended into disorder because of the missing man.

Miss Alice smiled upon the unexpected guest. 'Do come in.' She led him through the hall and into a small library with a baby grand near the French window. In a large leather chair sat a substantial woman with reddened eyes. 'I was just about to send for the police,' she wailed. 'Where is he?'

'In my rooms, ma'am,' Edward managed. 'He has had a bit of an accident, so I took him to my place, because I'd no idea where he lived. He wants Dr Wilkinson. He won't let the police come, Mrs Fishwick.'

The younger woman came to stand in front of Edward. She was not comely, but she was pleasant enough. 'Did you save my father's life?'

Edward shrugged and kept his eyes on Mrs Fishwick, who was trembling visibly in the leather chair. 'He's going to be all right, Mrs Fishwick,' said Edward.

'How did it happen?' asked Miss Alice Fishwick.

Edward opened his mouth, closed it immediately. The boss wanted him to keep quiet, so he would. 'I looked after him as best I could,' he said carefully. 'Cleaned him up and put him to bed. I had to drive his car, and I hope I've done no damage. It was making some funny noises. I've never driven a car before.'

Eleanor Fishwick stood up. She mopped her tear-stained face, then walked across to Edward, placing a hand on each of his shoulders when she reached him. 'My dear boy,' she said softly. 'I shall never be able to repay you for your kindness.' She turned to her daughter. 'Alice, send someone for Dr Wilkinson immediately. He must be told that this is an emergency.' Eleanor returned her attention to Edward. 'The doctor will take you home in his motor car. I shall come with you, of course.'

While arrangements were made, Edward was plied with tea, toast, eggs and bacon. He ate ravenously, suddenly realizing how hungry he had been. As he polished off the food, Alice Fishwick stared at him with adoration lighting up the plain face. The way she looked at him was embarrassing, so he talked to her once his plate was empty.

'You're a hero,' she said more than once.

Edward, blushing and inept, kept shaking his head. 'Anybody would have done the same,' he told her, though he kept the details to himself. He valued his job too highly to risk dismissal through carelessness.

The doctor, a tall man in black, drove Edward and Mrs Fishwick to Goldsmith Street. They entered by a side door, thereby avoiding the prying eyes of the butcher and his early customers.

Edward stayed in the kitchen while the doctor examined his patient. Mrs Fishwick gave a little scream when she saw her husband's injuries, but she quietened when the doctor reassured her. 'Where's Shawcross?' This was Mr Fishwick's voice.

Summoned by his master, Edward put in a reluctant bedside appearance. 'Yes, sir?'

Fishwick stared grimly at his saviour. 'Go to work,'

he ordered. 'Mrs Fishwick will arrange to have my car removed. It broke down outside here last night. Do you understand? It failed here, just outside the shop.'

'Yes, Mr Fishwick.' Edward felt like a naughty schoolboy awaiting punishment.

'I shall have to remain here until my face clears up,' said Samuel Fishwick. 'There's no point in making myself the subject of gossip among servants and mill-workers.'

Edward's jaw dropped. After the opulence of Aston Leigh, the Goldsmith Street bedroom was a slum dwelling. 'As you like, sir,' he replied. He had the feeling that Samuel Fishwick was hiding, probably from those who had attacked him. He could have gone home in the motor car without attracting attention, yet he was choosing to remain here. The man was frightened, Edward decided.

Eleanor came to Edward's side. 'We do not need to stress that discretion is of the utmost importance, do we?'

'No,' replied Edward. What the hell was going on? The boss had been battered, yet he was cowering here like a common criminal whose choices of residence had been removed by the need to conceal himself. 'Shall I go now, Mr Fishwick?'

Eleanor did not share her husband's view of Edward's immediate future. 'He must remain here, dear,' she said. 'You will need attention, food and so on. There is no telephone. Mr Shawcross will run your errands and keep you comfortable.'

The subject of Edward's welfare was not on the agenda, it seemed. Where was he going to sleep? The wicker chair was not cut out to be a bed, a fact to which Edward's bones continued to attest. He was young, but he needed a mattress.

As if reading their host's mind, Eleanor spoke up. 'After dark, I shall send a pallet round. We have two or three of those in the attic. Then you will be able to stretch out next to Samuel and keep watch over him.'

'Thank you.' He didn't know what to do or say next, so he returned to the kitchen and placed the kettle on his gas ring. How could he cook for this man? Fish and chips from the local shop were all very well, but they were hardly smoked salmon and caviare. And he was confused, totally bewildered by the chain of events. Why couldn't the man go home?

The doctor passed Edward on his way out. 'I shall wait in the car for Mrs Fishwick,' he said. 'The wound looks worse than it is. If he lapses into unconsciousness, get him to the hospital as quickly as possible. However, I am confident that he will recover without further treatment.'

Edward sat on a backless chair and waited for the kettle to boil. In spite of the quietness of their voices, he heard every word of a mystifying conversation.

'Will you be safe?' she asked.

'Here, I will. But what about you, what about the house?'

'They won't come there, surely, Samuel?'

'After last night, I would be surprised at nothing. Tell the gardener to move in, make him sleep in the hall. He's as big as a tank, so no-one will get past him. I'll sort something out. As soon as I feel a bit better, I'll make sure the Turnbulls stay clear. But I need time to think.'

A short silence followed. 'Alice and I could go away, I suppose,' said Mrs Fishwick. 'Though I would much rather stay near you.'

Samuel coughed, complained about his headache. 'I'm sorry, Ellie,' he said.

'We all make mistakes,' she answered. 'But how are we to guarantee our safety? We have no way of knowing when they will strike out again.' She paused. 'You gave them the money?'

'Yes.'

'Do they want more? Are we to become the victims of blackmail?'

Even from the kitchen, Edward could feel the tension. There was a silence of about twenty seconds, then Samuel spoke up again. 'She died, Ellie. Yesterday morning at about ten o'clock.'

'Oh, my God.' A chair scraped. Edward heard Mrs Fishwick pacing to and fro, could almost touch her panic. Finally, she was still. 'The child?'

'Alive, as far as I know.'

Edward sat perfectly still. When Mrs Fishwick poked her head into the kitchen, he jumped. But she said nothing; she simply looked straight through him, her eyes swimming in pain and misery. But after a second or two, her expression changed, hardened. Edward shivered. There was something so cold about Mrs Fishwick, as if she were making plans or plotting revenge of some kind.

He brewed the tea, took some enamel mugs from a shelf, found milk that had not quite turned, a bag of sugar and some plain biscuits.

Samuel Fishwick ate and drank ravenously, the colour returning to his cheeks after a second mug of tea. 'That was grand, lad,' he said, the Bolton accent deliberately exaggerated. He smiled at his wife. 'I like this boy, Ellie,' he said.

Eleanor touched Edward's arm. 'You will be amply compensated for your trouble, young man.'

'There's no need,' replied Edward.

'See?' In spite of his situation, Samuel managed a smile. 'I get the feeling we could trust him with our lives.'

They dwelt for several days in close confinement. Edward travelled to and from Belmont for clothing, shoes and food. Each time he visited, Alice's delight was obvious. She held him back, made him late while she questioned him about her father, about his own almost non-existent family, his work.

In the dingy flat over a butcher's shop, Edward and Samuel became unlikely friends. They told jokes, played endless games of cards, battled over a chessboard brought by Edward from Aston Leigh. After three days, Samuel threw the towel into the ring. 'I've taught you too well,' he said when Edward beat him at his own game for a second time. 'You took a risk with that bishop, but it paid off, by God.'

Edward found that Mr Fishwick's taste in food was very like his own. They dined like kings on salmon of the tinned variety, ate tripe and onions, masses of chips soaked liberally in brown vinegar, consumed a fair amount of bottled beer. While in his cups one night, Samuel Fishwick decided that he had taken a thorough liking to his host. He swept aside the chessmen and penned a letter on Edward's cheap notepaper. 'Tomorrow morning,' he mumbled drunkenly, 'You take this to Ernie Atkins. We shall get you sorted, son, get you a proper career in cotton.'

Ernie Atkins arrived on the fourth evening of Samuel's stay. He was second-in-command at Fishwick's, had been the boss's right hand man for years. Stooped and grizzled, he sat in Edward

Shawcross's kitchen and made no comment about Samuel's scars or his present address.

Samuel patted the old man's veined hand. 'See this lad?' he asked.

'Aye, I do,' replied Ernie.

'Well, he's a good one. Ernie, you'll not last for ever. You must train him up, because anybody who can learn chess in two days can run a mill. When you go, I want somebody I can rely on.'

Ernie sucked his teeth and looked Edward up and down. 'Right,' he said. 'He's strong enough, so I reckon he might fettle. You've to keep on top of the buggers,' he told Edward. 'Once they know who's in charge, they buckle down and get on with it.' He spoke again to his employer. 'I'll start on him when he comes back, then. When you're sorted out, like.' He made no reference to his employer's reasons for lodging in Goldsmith Street, was obviously Mr Fishwick's trusted servant.

The subject of their conversation was bemused, to say the least. He was a weaver by trade and he could read, write and count as well as the next man, but he had never considered himself to be management material.

Ernie Atkins, having heard and absorbed his instructions, left the two men to pursue their battles with chess and cards. Edward carried on feeding the boss, continued to report daily to Mrs Fishwick at Aston Leigh. He took letters back to Goldsmith Street, did all the shopping and cooking, made sure that Mr Fishwick's wound was continuing to mend.

At the end of six days, the owner of Fishwick's mill was stronger. The scar was fading, and he was beginning to plan his future. He opened a letter from his wife, frowned, read the message several times. 'Our

Alice has taken to you as well,' he commented in a casual tone. 'Do you like my daughter?'

Edward pondered for a few moments. He hadn't given a great deal of thought to Alice Fishwick, hadn't really formed an opinion on the subject. 'Yes,' he answered politely. 'She seems to be a very nice young lady.'

'Good.' Samuel wrote his reply. 'Take this up tomorrow,' he said. 'And here.' He took a wad of notes from an envelope. 'Get yourself a suit, son. Something in a nice dark blue. And you have my permission to walk out with Alice.' Expecting neither comment nor question, Samuel Fishwick picked up a newspaper and buried himself in the crossword.

That night, Edward Shawcross slept fitfully. He realized what was being asked of him, was forced to face several dilemmas. Could he be like Ernie Atkins? Could he shield the boss from the barbs of misfortune, could he become a faithful and un-questioning slave? As he tossed about on his pallet, the size of his decision became apparent. He could walk out with Miss Alice Fishwick. Permission had been granted for him to court and marry the boss's daughter. Why? Why now and why him?

She was all right, he supposed. She giggled a bit and was on the plump side, but she wasn't a bad sort. There was a kind of sadness in her voice and in her eyes when she spoke about her parents, as if they hadn't loved her enough, hadn't done enough for her. But all Edward could see was a huge house with a garden, domestic staff and enough to eat. She should have been grateful for all that, he told himself. Ample food on the table was an attractive concept. Edward had dragged himself up by his wits, had experienced many hungry days. The dread of returning to total poverty was strong.

He got up quietly at about half past three, all thoughts of sleep abandoned. There was a feeling of disquiet in his heart, a sensation that caused his stomach to crave food. Food was love. Food was the staff of life, and very few had chosen to break their bread for Edward Shawcross. He ate three scones with butter, drank a cup of milk. No more hungry days. All he needed was to be nice to Alice Fishwick, marry her, live with her and work for Samuel Fishwick. Mr Fishwick was in some trouble, but he still had the power to pave Edward's future with gold.

The following morning, a Mr Maurice Dyson arrived at the Goldsmith Street rooms. He talked quietly with Samuel in the bedroom, then came into the kitchen and handed Edward an envelope. 'The address is on the front,' Mr Dyson said. 'Make sure that these people know that you are a mere emissary, then you will be safe.'

Edward stared at the envelope, stared at the visitor.

'I am Mr Fishwick's lawyer,' said the man. 'If you meet with trouble, come to my office in Mealhouse Lane.' He all but clicked his heels before walking out.

Edward fingered the envelope, raised his head and saw Samuel Fishwick in the doorway. 'Shall I go now?' Edward asked.

'Hang on a minute.' Samuel lowered himself into a chair, invited Edward to sit opposite him. 'Lad,' he began. 'The best thing that's happened to me just lately is you. It could have been any bugger walking past that night, but it was you. I believe in fate, you see. Now, the way I look at it is this.' He clasped his hands in front of him, looked for all the world like a man at some sort of ordinary, everyday committee meeting. 'I need you and you need me. Am I right?'

Edward squashed a thousand questions in his mind and nodded hesitantly.

'Have you had days when there was no silver lining, no grub and no fire lit?'

'Yes.' That query, at least, was easily answered.

'I can mend all that,' said Samuel Fishwick. 'Years back, I should have looked for somebody to help Ernie Atkins. He's a damned good manager, and I'd not hear a word to the contrary. But he's old, Edward. Now, what Ernie doesn't know about cotton would fit on a postage stamp. More to the point, he knows how to deal with folk. So, I've found another I can trust. That's you. I've just got a feeling about you. So are you with me?'

Edward inclined his head again.

The millowner lit a cigarette, narrowing his eyes against the first rise of smoke. 'I've made a mistake,' he said softly. 'A bloody big one. My wife – God love her – is the perfect woman, and she has forgiven me.' He tapped ash into a cracked saucer. 'My daughter, Alice, must never hear about what I have done. Is that understood?'

'Yes, sir.'

Samuel got up and walked to the window. 'That envelope. It's addressed to a Mr Turnbull from Halliwell Road. He's the person you must see. His daughter, Molly Turnbull, was my . . . fancy piece, I suppose you might say. She had a baby, a boy, a few days ago. She called him Peter, or so I'm told.' He paused, dragged hard on the tobacco. 'Molly died. Her brothers beat me up the night you found me. So there's a lot of money in there,' he waved a hand towards the envelope, 'and the deeds of the house they live in. I need to put a stop to their blackmail.'

Edward swallowed. Would this offering really put an end to the threats, or would the Turnbull family continue to demand money with menaces?

'I'd have liked a son,' said Samuel. 'A legitimate son, but it wasn't to be.' He returned to the table. 'Life's a bugger, you know. I've enough money, a good home and a lovely wife. My daughter – well – she's been a grand lass – she's not what you might call a raving beauty. But there's no harm in her.' He coughed, drew again on the cigarette. 'I need to have her wed. And I need her to marry somebody I can depend on. Do you get my drift?'

'Yes, Mr Fishwick.' Edward's head felt as if it was swimming. Money, management, marriage . . . what next?

'So take that to the Turnbulls. And promise me you'll never say a word to Alice about that baby.'

'I promise.'

The older man's eyes narrowed. 'She could find out, I suppose. But there's a fair sum put aside for the Turnbulls. They'll get a weekly income out of the mill, enough to keep my by-blow and all the rest of the family in near luxury. As long as they keep their damned mouths shut.'

Edward still lingered, waited for more information.

'I suppose you're wondering why I've stayed here? Well, it's me they're after, not my family. So, even if they had gone up to the house – and thank God, they haven't – I wouldn't have been there. They're tough men, the Turnbulls, but they'd not hurt Ellie. Or Alice.' Alice sounded very much like an after-thought. 'I imposed on you while those house deeds were sorted and while my solicitor negotiated and arranged for maintenance payments.' He paused, and then said wearily, 'I think I'll have a rest now, because I'm exhausted.'

When Samuel Fishwick was safely in bed, Edward plucked his cap from the hook and set forth for Halliwell Road. The bulky envelope seemed to burn his chest when he placed it inside his clothes for safe keeping. There were hundreds of pounds in the package, he felt sure. He could just disappear and set himself up somewhere else – Preston, Lancaster – even London. Knowing himself to be an honourable man, Edward Shawcross carried on towards trouble.

The house was a two up and two down on Halliwell Road. It looked decent enough, with a nicely stoned step, clean curtains and a newly painted front door. Edward hesitated, then forced himself to knock. A woman answered. She was grey before her time, and a mewling baby nestled in her arms. 'Yes?' she asked.

She could not have been much more than forty-five, thought Edward. The remains of youth showed in her eyes, yet the faded hair made an old woman of her. 'Is Mr Turnbull in?' he asked.

'Which one? There's four of them. My husband's Norman, then there's our Derek, our Ron and our Micky.'

'Your husband, I think.'

She stepped back. 'Come in. He's just having his dinner.'

Norman Turnbull was in the back kitchen. Crutches leaned against the wall next to him, and he was sitting in a wheelchair. 'Who's this, then, Tess?' he asked.

'I'm . . . I'm just a messenger.' Edward pulled at his collar, was suddenly hot. 'From Mr Fishwick.'

Norman Turnbull dropped his fork. He sat for a few seconds with anger on his face, then fought to control himself. 'How is he? My lads knocked seven shades out of him last week. I told them to leave him alone, because he's not worth hanging for, only after our Molly died . . .' He pushed himself away from the table. 'It's not right, you know. What Fishwick did to our lass was bloody terrible. I suppose he's recovered, eh? I suppose he's come up smelling of roses as per usual?'

Edward nodded, felt the colour rising in his cheeks when Tess Turnbull ran from the room. 'His face was a mess,' he managed.

'Aye, well, our Molly's dead and buried, so happen he should carry scars for life. And yon babby's what killed my girl. It's Fishwick's child.'

Edward felt as if he were the sinner. Mr Turnbull, confined for much of the time to a wheelchair, was still a man of great dignity. Yet his incapacity rendered him unable to control his sons, while his daughter had died giving birth to an illegitimate child. 'I'm sorry,' Edward muttered. 'I've just brought this.' He placed the envelope on the table. 'It's the deeds to your house, some money and information about a weekly income as . . . compensation.'

Norman Turnbull nodded. 'Aye, it's as well my lads are out at work. Not that I'm blaming you, mind. You had nowt to do with the death of our Molly. If I could get back on my feet and earn a living, I'd tell Fishwick where to shove his promises. Any road, the lads'll keep quiet from now on, I hope. It were just their reaction when our Molly died.'

The man wheeled himself away from the table, then approached the visitor. 'Her mam helped her through the birth, like. Doctor came, said our Molly was going to be all right. Only she had a haemorrhage later on, and we couldn't get her to hospital quick enough. So we lost her.' He sniffed back the grief. 'Bled to death upstairs, she did. No money can ever make up for that. No money can fetch her back and give my grandson a mother.'

Edward felt his eyes pricking ominously. How could Mr Fishwick have done such a thing? 'I'll . . . I'd best be getting back,' he said.

'Aye well, tell him I'll try to keep the lads away, but they're a bit awkward after a drink.' He wheeled himself towards the front room. 'Are you working for him, son?'

Edward inclined his head. 'Yes.' He had the feeling that he wasn't just working for Fishwick. The suspicion that he had been bought, body and soul, was at the forefront of his mind. Yet even that was better than poverty.

SEVEN

He woke with a start when his arm slipped off the edge of the chair. It had been some time since he had slept in a chair. In Goldsmith Street, there had been a cane seat painted blue, a bed with frayed blankets, one of those small iron grates in a corner. With no money for coal, Edward had often gone to bed immediately after coming in from work, as bed was the warmest place for a poor man. Then, along had come Samuel Fishwick Esquire, with his problems and his promises.

Edward glanced at the clock, discovered the time to be four-thirty in the morning. It was as if he had travelled back twenty-odd years to relive the beginning, to explain to himself the mechanism that had led him to Aston Leigh, to Alice, to the mill and into chronic unhappiness. Now, he had problems of his own, and those troubles mirrored Samuel's torments too closely for Edward's comfort. How he had pitied the Turnbulls; how he had blamed Alice's father for the death of that young woman. 'Life never changes,' he muttered to himself. Vera was in Devonshire with her neighbour. Vera was on the brink of nervous collapse because Edward Shawcross had impregnated her. He should have been more careful, should have learned from the mistakes and cruelties of his father-in-law.

He rose and poured himself a small brandy, returning to the desk to sit with the globe cupped in his hands. He and Alice had been married within weeks of their first meeting. She had doted on him completely, had derived great pleasure from buying his clothes and turning him into the prince of her dreams. Her father had bought her dream, had paid for it, had continued to fend off the Turnbulls with cash. Even today, Samuel Fishwick's mill supported his bastard son.

Edward sipped the warming fluid, told himself that he would be fit for nothing in the morning. This was morning. This was the darkest hour when worries ballooned out of all proportion, when a wakeful man knew that he was the only soul in the world condemned to wait for the sky to lighten.

The exit to Africa had been Eleanor's idea, he thought. That sad, devoted, yet cunning wife had sought to remove her man from the scene of his crime, had wanted to create a different life in a new setting, where Samuel's rebirth could take place without witnesses. So Edward had been left to tackle the Turnbulls. He had used his discretion when responding to their demands, had made sure that their lips had been as sealed as he could make them. And now, the original sinner had returned to die.

With the glass emptied, Edward closed his eyes, heard the noise of the mill, saw old Ernie Atkins demonstrating the spinning process. Edward could almost hear the voice of that long-dead man explaining the ins and outs, poring over ledgers and order books in Mr Fishwick's office. Edward had been judged a ready learner, sufficiently competent to be left in nominal charge as soon as the ink had dried on the marriage certificate. Fortunately, Ernie had survived long enough to train Edward to a standard that had proved adequate, just about. For more than twenty years, Edward Shawcross had been master of Fishwick's mill.

His eyelids flew open. Did he want that mill? Was he going to need it? After all, Vera was supposedly the centre of his existence, had become the means by which he would escape the ball and chain that bound him to Alice and to Fishwick's. Was Vera going to be there for him, or was she just another unsuitable woman?

Guilt sat on his tongue like rotted meat, made him want to spit away the unpalatable taste of his own dishonour. For a long time, he had travelled in a vehicle that had taken him through life effortlessly and surely. The steering had been easy, because a route map had been prepared for him. He had lived here in relative luxury, had allowed the mill to continue along its own tracks. The future promised to be difficult, at least. Relative poverty would not worry him unduly, he insisted inwardly. But Vera's unhappy state did not bode well for the days to come. He felt powerless and sad.

It occurred to Edward that he was one of life's natural passengers, because Samuel Fishwick had made him so. Everything had been handed to him on a plate – status, money, then his position on the council. He had been voted in, but colleagues in Edward's civic life had been keen to promote him to alderman. Unresisting, Edward had allowed himself to be put wherever his fellow man had wanted to place him. It had all been too easy, too soft. At forty-four, he was still a relatively young man. Wasn't it time for him to plot his own course? And could he do that without a co-pilot?

The sun opened a lazy eye and peeped over the horizon. An area of pale turquoise spread itself across the morning sky like a newly dyed length of cotton sheeting. Another day. Edward picked up a pen, doodled on his blotter. Samuel was home. The man who had taught him chess, who had eaten cold tripe and stale bread, was here to collect . . . what? His property, his pound of flesh? The old chap was unfit, too sick to take over the mill, too frail to face the Turnbulls and demand his money back. Over the years, a certain family on Halliwell Road had bled hundreds, even thousands of pounds away from Samuel Fishwick's mill. No, that blood money would never be retrieved.

'What do I want?' Edward asked an early bird. 'I haven't built my own nest, haven't hunted and fed my young, not really, not off my own bat.' There was a restlessness in him, an urge to take responsibility for himself, for Vera and the child. Yet alongside that feeling ran another of equal weight, a terror of failure. He had never failed, because he had not needed to try since 1927. Edward Shawcross decided that he was a weak man, but forgivably so. Anyone who had suffered hunger would know how easy it was to ape the behaviour of a successful man. All the spadework had been done by earlier Fishwicks. Samuel had left an easy task, though the road ahead was becoming unclear of late. British cotton was threatened by cheap Eastern competitors. Bolton was no match for India, because the rules of the game had changed.

He watched the blackbirds scurrying about, listened to their singing and to their raucous quarrels. It was strange that such a tuneful bird was capable of creating cacophony. Like Alice, he thought, though she no longer screamed at him. The quarrels had ceased long ago, because all feelings between them had died of neglect.

Alice had started off demure, sweet, almost lovable. Her plainness had been acceptable, because her nature had been pleasant. But he had disappointed her. He had not managed to compensate for the loss of her parents' affection. At the age of eleven or so, poor Alice had ceased to be the pretty product of their love. A bitter woman, she had sulked and moaned, had killed the last vestiges of her husband's already dwindling respect.

No doubt there were things to be done. Samuel had returned a physically broken man, so he would probably want to tidy up after himself. There would be a will, bank accounts to close or transfer, bequests of certain items to be planned. And he, Edward Shawcross, would be the runner of messages, he supposed. It would be like going back to the beginning again, bring me, fetch me, carry me, except these would not be simple errands involving cod and peas or fresh Eccles cakes.

The door opened. 'Edward?' It was Alice. She stepped into the room and pulled the dressing gown tightly across her body. She was thinner, seemed taller. He grunted a good morning, waited for her to sit. 'What are you doing so early?' he asked eventually, expecting that the answer would doubtless hold little interest for him.

'Father's very ill,' she said. She didn't know who to talk to. Gilbert and Constance were too young to be troubled. 'I think he's going to die,' she said. 'He's a terrible colour and so dreadfully thin. Without the stick, he can't walk.'

Edward suddenly felt pity for her. The pretty child who had become his plain bride was now a middle-aged woman with no company save his. He should have been a better husband, should have played fair. It wasn't Alice's fault, he said inwardly. Alice had been spoilt for a decade, then had been excluded from the lives of two very selfish people once her amusement value had declined. Her insecurities came from the old couple upstairs, egocentric to the last. 'He certainly looks sick,' said Edward. 'But it's hard to tell. Perhaps the hot weather made him ill.'

Alice was surprised by her husband's tone. For once, he seemed to be actually talking to her, talking and listening. 'We should never have married, you and I,' she told him in a moment of weakness that seemed strangely brave.

He nodded. 'We scarcely knew one another.'

'Then my parents went away so unexpectedly. I thought they had perhaps had second thoughts about us. But they liked you. I was the disappoint-ment, not you.' She stared hard at him. 'It was almost as if they wanted to get rid of me in order to go abroad. As if I needed to be tidied away.'

That was the truth of it. Edward lowered his gaze, tried to think of something to say. It was so long since he and Alice had conversed, that he hardly knew how to treat her. 'We'll have to get young Dr Wilkinson,' he said. 'Young' Dr Wilkinson, a man now in his late forties, had succeeded his father, the one who had ministered to Samuel Fishwick in Goldsmith Street. 'Get him to give Samuel the once-over.'

'My father will probably need to go into hospital,' said Alice. 'From his colour, I'd say he has a liver complaint.'

'Yes.' The birds continued to sing joyfully, as if

making further mockery of this sham of a marriage. A mental image of Vera screaming in terror shot into his mind. He had a son, a daughter, a wife who was going to need some help while her father lay dying. Vera was hundreds of miles away, was sitting staring at the sea for endless hours. Sheila had written, had told Edward that Vera was still in a state of shock. Soon, Alice would know. Edward's presence in Tintern Avenue had been noticeable, especially after Vera's outburst. 'Shall we send for some tea?' he asked.

Alice glanced at the clock. 'Ada will be up and about soon.' She walked to the door. 'I'll go and dress,' she said absently. All she could do was to carry on as before, wash, clean her teeth, get dressed. These were the rituals that kept mankind sane during the most terrifying hours.

Edward walked to the window, watched the sun establishing its position in a faultless sky, listened to an overture that promised a grand day. God, what a total bloody mess. Alice needed help and sympathy, Vera needed the same. And he was just one man, just one pair of eyes, one set of limbs, one heart.

His garden was magnificent, with a splendid display of roses, but it wasn't his garden. He had borrowed it for a while, no more than that. Sometimes, he had the feeling that he had sold his soul to the devil, though Samuel Fishwick was hardly qualified to be a Satan. But would poverty have been as bad as this? Edward wondered as the sun warmed the soil. Probably. He had made his choice, and must suffer the consequences.

George Wilkinson placed his bag of tricks on a hall table. Behind him, Alice Shawcross waited stolidly, her hands folded at the waistline, her chin set as if preparing to cope with the worst news. Mother and Father had returned yesterday, yet neither had spoken properly to their daughter.

The doctor sighed, turned to face her. 'He has weeks, a couple of months at the most. Palliative treatment will be made available. We can treat the pain, but not the cancer.'

Alice blinked, but her body remained rigidly still.

'Would you like a second opinion, Mrs Shawcross?'

'No.'

George Wilkinson had known the Shawcrosses for ages. After his father's death, he had taken over the practice. Even before the demise of Charles Wilkinson, George had been present as his father's apprentice at the births of Gilbert and Constance. Since then, he had treated the whole family for various disorders. Alice was a depressive type. He had watched her sinking beneath the weight of an unfortunate marriage, had witnessed her swift arrival at middle age. 'Are you thinner?' he asked.

She nodded. 'Deliberately so. I've given up chocolate and started walking.'

'Good.' He picked up his bag. 'I'll be back later to give him an injection. Just keep him comfortable. If he wants to eat, that's fine, but don't be surprised if he refuses food. Your mother has my prescription for morphine.' He smiled at Alice, collected his hat from the stand, then left the house.

Alice felt cold. The day was fine and bright, yet her bones were chilled and she needed someone to talk to. Constance was upstairs being dazzled by tales of far-away places. Mother was in good form, was rattling on about elephants and tigers while Father lay dying. Mother had got used to the idea of Father dying, Alice supposed. Gilbert had gone out to play tennis, while Edward was absent as usual.

The time had come, Alice informed herself firmly. She must set forth and make a friend, must find someone in whom she might confide her worries. There was only Maude Templeton. Alice stood on the threshold of Aston Leigh and wondered whether she was finally going crazy. How on earth could she consider confiding in Maude? Maude was well known for her acerbic tongue and rigid views. The Templetons were landed, were of a different social class. Nevertheless, Alice walked off in the direction of Top o' th' Moor. It had to be Maude, because there was no-one else.

James was annoyed. He was not given to tantrums, had been a good baby, an easy child. But he was cross, to say the least of it. Mother had been poking about in his room. She had unearthed all manner of things, from half-finished poems to his diaries of the past two years. Mother had read his innermost thoughts, his dreams and his desires. And James had caught her red-handed. 'Why?' he asked now.

Maude sat very still, hands folded in her lap, legs drawn to one side in the manner she had been taught as a girl. She would not raise her voice or her temperature, because she was a lady. 'We never talk,' she advised her son. 'Sometimes, I feel that I scarcely know you. It may all seem rather amusing to you, but I have always blamed myself for your affliction. I needed to discover how you really feel about yourself and about life. Drawing those silly pictures of forceps wrapped around your head is all very well, James, but have you ever considered my feelings?

And having that wretched instrument painted and hanging over your bed is hardly likely to ease my conscience. I want to know you, and that is the truth.'

James was not in the mood to be cajoled or comforted. He was twenty-four years old, a graduate from Manchester College of Art, a laughing depressive who eased his own pain by amusing others. The deep feelings, those private emotions too raw for open expression, had been couched in verse or in painting. His diary was private, for no-one's eyes but his own. 'I am no longer a child,' he said. 'I am an adult and I deserve the consideration you would show to any other person living in your house. There is no need for you to search my soul, Mother. I am a separate entity now. The umbilicus was cut some years ago.'

The beating of Maude's heart belied the cool exterior. She loved her son and wanted his happiness. He deserved to be happy after all the pain he had endured, all the stretching and pulling and fitting of clumsy boots. James loved Constance Shawcross. This fact was written in his diary, in his poems and all over his face whenever the girl was near him. 'I am sorry,' she said stiffly. Maude was unused to apologizing.

'That's easy to say,' he replied.

It hadn't been easy, though Maude continued serene on the surface. 'Would you like a holiday?' she asked.

James nodded pensively. 'Yes, I rather think I should like to get away. But on a more permanent basis, Mother.' The time to fly the nest had come.

'You are considering leaving home?' In spite of her resolve, Maude's voice raised itself. 'Where will you go?'

James knew where he was going, had known since the moment he had caught Mother going through his things. His immediate reaction had been to get out of the house, and he had wandered about Bolton for the whole of the previous day, had found somewhere to live. 'I'm going away to paint,' he told her now.

'You can paint here.'

He shook his head slowly. 'No. I've gone through all my little phases, and now I want to do some meaningful work, something that might outlive me. Even if nothing sells, I'd like to leave my view of the world for someone – anyone who might be interested.'

Maude took a look at her watch. Eric would not be back for hours, but husbands were seldom around when needed. Eric would talk sense to James, would reach him on a level that was denied to mere females. 'Talk to your father first,' she said. 'He'll be back this afternoon.'

James picked up an orange and left the room, tossing and catching the fruit as he went.

A maid entered. 'Mrs Shawcross to see you, madam. Shall I show her in?'

Maude was in no mood for visitors. However, she would receive poor Alice. Poor Alice was having a dreadful struggle with her weight, and her parents had arrived from Africa. 'Show her in,' she said.

Alice refused coffee, sat herself in a comfortable chair next to a fireplace of Italian marble. She studied Maude for a while, answered questions about the return of her parents, wondered whether she might really confide in this woman. 'Maude, my father is very ill. In fact, I have just been told by Dr Wilkinson that he is dying.'

Maude Templeton was very sorry. 'All those years

183

without seeing him, and now . . . Oh dear. I am so very sad to hear that, Alice. Are you sure about the coffee?'

Alice was sure. 'There is something strange about my life,' she began tentatively.

Maude wore an encouraging expression. 'Strange? In what way?'

'Well, I've always wondered why they went off so abruptly, why they encouraged Edward to marry me. You know, they just passed me on to him like a package, as if they considered me to be part and parcel of Aston Leigh. Edward has been caretaker of the business, of me and of the house.' She paused. It suddenly didn't matter. Whatever Maude made of this, Alice had to let it all out. 'He doesn't love me, never has loved me. And there is something going on. There has always been something going on. Soon, I shall know whatever it was, and I am afraid of the answers to all the questions I have never asked.'

The mistress of Top o' th' Moor eased herself back in her chair. Alice Shawcross's life had been so small, so narrow. She had failed to use her husband's civic status to her own advantage, had seldom left the confines of Aston Leigh. She shopped occasionally, went for dress fittings, travelled to Manchester when she needed a department store, put in a very rare appearance at Bolton Town Hall. But Alice had become a bitter woman with a face that echoed all her inner rancour. Lately, though, she had seemed to be improving. 'What is happening, Alice?'

'It's an end,' replied Alice thoughtfully. 'I feel that a line is going to be drawn across the page, but I don't know how to start the next paragraph. Am I being silly, Maude?'

For some strange reason which remained inaccessible, Maude Templeton was flattered. Few people had confided in her thus far, because she and her husband were 'top drawer' in the district, landed gentry who did not need to work for a living. 'No, Alice,' she said seriously. 'I am a great believer in instinct. You know, when James was born, I knew in here that something would go wrong.' She pressed a hand against the 'here', right in the centre of her perfectly proportioned upper body. 'He is being difficult, so I do sympathize, my dear. Families can be such a trial.' She paused for a moment. 'Is there anything I might do?'

Alice shook her head. 'Be kind enough to listen, that's all I ask. You know, my parents have hardly spoken two words to me. It would be easy for a stranger to think that Edward was their son and I the mere daughter-in-law.'

'That is terrible.'

Alice closed her eyes and leaned against a feather-filled cushion. She was suddenly exhausted and afraid. 'I was a pretty child,' she said quietly. 'A glorious mass of blonde curls, quite a little Shirley Temple in my time. I was a toy, an amusing item that reminded them of their love for one another.' Her eyes opened. 'Then I grew up and was not as pleasing on the eye. Their love was the most important thing in their lives. Once I ceased to be entertaining, I was cast aside like a worn-out shoe. They did not have many friends, because each needed the other to the exclusion of anyone and everyone. It was a lonely place for me, that house.' It remained lonely, would always be a bleak setting.

Maude could think of nothing to say as consolation, so she remained silent.

'I've been a terrible mother,' continued Alice.

'Now there, I must disagree.'

Alice smiled sadly. 'You don't live with us, Maude. My resentment for Constance has been shameful. She is so beautiful, so perfect. In fact, I have apologized to her. You have already helped me just by listening, and by advising me about my diet. Perhaps if I can get into shape and learn to like myself, then I might become a better person and a better mother.'

Maude jumped out of her chair with an alacrity that was startling. 'Excuse me,' she said hurriedly, her eyes fixed on a point outside the window. She ran from the room. 'James?' she shouted. 'James, what are you doing?'

In response to his employer's raised voice, John Duncan, the manservant at Top o' th' Moor, scurried through from the back of the house. Maude Templeton was not a shouter. He stopped in his tracks to witness the unusual sight of Maude running towards the main door.

Alice got up and walked into the hall, saw Maude rushing along, noticed that John Duncan was now hot on her heels.

Outside, James was putting cases and painting equipment into his car. Maude, all thoughts of gentility abandoned, was gripping the arm of her only child. 'Please, James. Wait until Eric comes. You must not go off without talking to your father. How can you do this? How can you be so cruel?'

John Duncan stood by helplessly while James kissed his mother.

Alice arrived at Maude's side. 'He'll be back,' she said in a tone that was meant to encourage.

Maude drew herself up and took Alice's hand for

support while James climbed into the driving seat. The unshakeable Maude Templeton was trembling like a leaf, and her ague seemed to travel right through her neighbour's body, too.

'Things are happening to both of us,' said Maude through gritted teeth. Her faith in instinct was sharpened in this moment. Alice had known where to come, had probably sensed within herself that she and Maude would be needing each other. 'I only read his poems,' she said tearfully as James's car pulled away. 'I was trying to find out about him, about how that leg really affects him. And he resents me so much.' She pulled herself together, because the servants were gathering. 'Go back to your work,' she told John.

The two women returned to the small drawing room. 'I had hoped that he would marry your daughter,' Maude said. 'In my mind, I had the whole thing settled.'

'Don't,' said Alice softly.

'He loves her,' replied Maude.

Alice stared down at her hands, saw the wedding band twisting loosely on her thinner finger. The ring was ready to drop off at any time. 'Arranged marriages do not work,' she told her new-found ally. 'And I should know, shouldn't I?'

Connie sat on her milestone. She was restless, had been made so by listening to Grandmother's tales of far-away countries and exotic animals. The atmosphere at home was stranger than ever. Gilbert had done his usual disappearing act, leaving Connie with no confidante, no ready ear. The grandparents had taken no interest at all in Mother. She might just as well have gone to the moon for all they cared.

Having met the Fishwicks, Connie was beginning to understand her mother's aloof attitude.

James hove into view, the windows of his car wide open to allow easels and canvases to poke their various angles into the lane. He slowed down when he saw Connie.

'Are you leaving the country?' she asked. The thought of life without James was not palatable. He made her laugh, made her think. She squashed the realization that she was rather too fond of this difficult man.

'I am leaving my mother,' he replied. 'She has driven me out by driving me mad, so I'm driving myself off into a better life.'

Connie's heart gave a disappointed lurch. This was her best friend in the whole world. 'Traitor,' she said. 'How the hell am I supposed to carry on without you? The grandparents have finally arrived, and they're gruesome but interesting. Well, she is. He lies down all the time. Dying, probably, poor old soul. There'll be no-one to talk to if you go. Gilbert's tied up with tennis and Mary Martindale.'

He opened the door. 'Come with me. Just jump in and wave good-bye to the past. We can live in sin, or we can marry at your earliest convenience. Though we're not keen on marriage, are we? What with your lot not talking to each other and my lot being civilized. If I ever show symptoms of civilization, will you warn me?'

'I shan't be there to warn you. I shall be here in this bloody miserable house. You are a rotter, James Templeton. Anyway, enough of the banter. Where are you going?'

'To a prefab,' he replied proudly. 'My own little tin house on Eldon Street. No-one else will live in it

– the place leaks and is subsiding. It was going to be pulled down as unsafe, because the council could not afford to shore it up. So I'm doing the necessary renovations and saving the prefab from being removed from the landscape. In return, I am to be allowed to rent it for a year or so.'

Connie could not manage to picture James in a prefab. He had spent all his life in a house twice the size of Aston Leigh. 'Those prefabs cover about the same area as your greenhouse,' she told him. 'They're roasting in summer and freezing in winter. My father and his cronies are trying to get them condemned.'

James's face wore an expression of deep inner hurt. 'They've only been up for a few years,' he said. 'People are needing them, which is why they were built in the first place. And no-one is pulling down my little house. Tell the alderman to mind his own business. I shall start a "preserve the prefab" campaign.'

Connie poked her head into the car. 'What on earth is that?' She pointed to an object on the passenger seat.

'A miner's helmet,' he informed her. 'I shall need it for my work. Damned hazardous places, the pits.'

She stuck out her tongue. 'You can't be a miner.'

'Why not?'

'It's dangerous.'

'And I'm a cripple?'

'I didn't say that.'

He nodded sagely. 'No, but you thought it. Aren't you going to wish me well?'

Connie planted a soggy kiss on his cheek. 'I shall visit you,' she promised. 'Just to make sure that you haven't faded away.'

He wiped his face with a paint-spattered handkerchief, thrust the gear lever into first. 'One day,' he foretold with great solemnity, 'you will marry me, Miss Constance Shawcross. No-one else could possibly tolerate such a messy kisser.'

She watched the car getting smaller as it rushed towards the bottom of The Rise. It was going to be awful without James, especially now, with Gilbert all lovelorn and threatening to leave university to be with Mary.

'Hello, Constance.'

Connie turned and inhaled deeply. 'Mother,' she began carefully. 'Could you do me the most tremendous favour? Would you call me Connie from now on?'

'Yes, dear. Was that James?'

Connie was awestruck. Yes, dear? Only weeks earlier, Alice would have insisted on avoiding the shortened version of the name. 'Yes. He's got a miner's helmet, says he's going to work down the pits.'

Alice shook her head. 'Never mind,' she said vaguely. 'James does some very peculiar things. It's because he's an artist, I suppose.'

When Mother had walked off, Connie re-established her right to the milestone. A milestone, she told herself, was a thing of great significance. She should sit here while making up her mind about the rest of her life. After ten minutes, she was getting nowhere and getting bored. But she would do something, anything. Otherwise, without James, she might go stark, raving mad.

Sadie Martindale had a fridge, a daughter who was walking out with a boss's son, the luxury of a part-time only job, and she also had their Tommy and their Bernard. Though the two sons seemed restless and ready to fly the nest, which fact did not please Sadie at all. So she threw herself into her cooking with gusto.

The whole of Daubhill and Deane knew about the fridge, because Sadie often bought extra sausages, black pudding and tripe to put in her refrigerator. It was a big fridge, so she awarded it its full title whenever neighbours were within earshot.

Their Mary was in a funny sort of category, really. Sadie didn't know whether to brag or keep her mouth shut, because it could all fall through once the lad went back to university in London. Anyway, she had the feeling that their Mary was reaching for the stars, so Sadie kept quietish about the relationship between Mary and Gilbert, though she harped on a fair bit about Mary's managerial post. Sadie's own part-time job was something she aired every day while donkeying the step and polishing the windows. With Mary being in management, Sadie had come up in the world, though she still had to get down to her own scrubbing.

Bernard Martindale was another kettle of fish altogether. He was fed up with the pit and had declared his intention to rejoin the forces. Having missed the war because of being too young, Bernard had survived national service, just about, and he suddenly wanted to go back. The reason for wanting to go back was called Eileen Lonsdale. Eileen was an ugly girl with hard, pebbly eyes and a waxy skin. She lived with her widowed mother in a filthy house up Derby Street, and she saw Bernard as her ticket out of squalor.

Sadie stared at her older son. 'Have you been messing about with her?'

Bernard opened his mouth in a 'no' shape, then shut it when he saw his mother's no-nonsense expression. Since getting her fridge, Sadie had become more positive in her views. He took a step back and waited for the inevitable.

'Is she in the family way, Bernard?'

'I don't think so.'

'So you have been messing with her, you daft bugger.'

Bernard sighed heavily. Eileen Lonsdale had been giving away her favours for about ten years, ever since leaving junior school. She was one of those people who could make anybody do anything she required. It was her eyes – evil, they were. And she had a way of talking so sensibly that a man got confused and forgot the madness in the face. 'Mam, I'm going back in the army. I've signed up, so that's an end of it.' The army was hard, but it was better than the pit. Anything at all would be better than the pit.

'They could send you to Germany.'

'I know.'

'There's Germans in Germany.'

'Aye, there would be.'

'You know what I mean. I don't want you mixing with foreigners, they've got queer ways.' She sniffed. 'Still, I suppose you'll have to keep clean in the army.' Their Tommy would be able to have a bedroom to himself. If he stayed, that was. Sadie had a bit of a bone to pick with Tommy, but she was saving that for later. One way and another, kids were a bother.

Any road, Bernard took up a lot of space in the tiny house. 'I'll miss you,' she told him truthfully. 'And stay away from that bloody Eileen. I've heard as how she's got her claws into a binman, so let him put up with her crazy ways. She'll end up in a lunatic asylum, that one.'

Bernard sat at the table and made his way through half a loaf and most of the jam. He wasn't going to be the one to tell Mam about their Tommy. Tommy, at twenty-one, was courting a girl from Noble Street, and the affair was serious enough for Tommy to have given the girl his army tags. So there would be just Mam and Mary, Bernard reckoned. As for Eileen Lonsdale – she could take a running jump, because everybody had cut a slice off her. Bernard would be better off out of it, because Loony Lonsdale had taken a shine to him. And best of all, the mine would become a nasty memory.

Mary came in. It was one of her nights off, so she didn't have to go putting on her uniform and polishing her torch. She gazed at Bernard. 'You look like the cat just after he's eaten the cream.'

Bernard grinned. 'I'm back in the army. Corporal and all, I am. So watch how you talk to me, I'm a man of substance.'

Mary clouted him with her purse, then sat down to wait for her tea. It was stew tonight. Mam's stews were legendary, because they could contain anything at all that was edible, yet they always turned out grand.

Sadie plonked two bowls on the table and glared at Bernard. 'You won't have bread and jam before meals in the army, lad.' How were they going to manage without his money? Mary had got the domestic finances worked out perfectly, but did Bernard eat more than he paid in? Probably. He'd put himself outside the best part of two white loaves since yesterday. 'What are you doing tonight?' she asked Mary.

'Gilbert's taking me to meet his grandmother. They've just got back from Africa.'

'Africa?' Sadie frowned. 'I don't know why folk want to be messing about in foreign parts, it's not natural.' Bernard was halfway through the stew already. He seemed to inhale food like other people breathed oxygen. 'So will they be piking off again to Africa?' She made the last word sound like poison.

'The grandfather's dying,' said Mary. She studied her brother. 'That Eileen's been looking for you,' she said. 'If you don't want her, she's going to marry the poor binman.'

'I don't want her,' said Bernard.

'Neither does the bloody binman,' snapped Sadie. 'Aye, you'd best get gone to the army, lad. Even the Germans is better than Eileen Lonsdale.'

Tommy came in. He hung up his cap, rubbed his hands together in expectation. 'Back in the army, then, our kid?' he said to his brother.

Sadie paused, ladle in hand. 'Tommy, I've had Ethel Hyatt spitting down my neck all day. What's all this about you and a girl messing about at the back of Kippax's?' She was losing her children. She stood in her crowded kitchen doling out stew, and she could almost feel them all pulling away from her. Mary was doing well in her job, Bernard was off to serve king and country. Even little Tommy was on his way out. He was a serious lad. He wouldn't go chasing a girl round the houses just for a bit of slap and tickle. 'Who is she?'

Tommy's face was as red as beetroot. 'Dorothy Ingram from Noble Street.'

Sadie breathed a sigh of relief. The Ingrams were decent folk, not like some she had mentioned several times already. 'Fetch her home, then. I don't want Ethel Hyatt coming round here telling me about you breathing heavy in a mill yard.'

Bernard choked on his stew, got a good thumping on the back from his brother.

Sadie, her face set determinedly, carried on feeding her adult brood. Inside, her heart felt as if it would break. She was going to be surplus to requirements, on the scrap heap. There was no chance of her working full time, not with her feet. She promised herself a good cry later, once this lot had cleared off for the evening.

Someone hammered on the door. Sadie hobbled off and flung it open, found Eileen Lonsdale standing outside with her arms folded. 'What do you want?' asked Sadie.

'Fer t' see your Bernard. I'm going fer t' sue 'im fer breach o' promise.'

Sadie put her head on one side. 'What did our Bernard promise, Eileen?'

'Fer t' wed me.'

Sadie nodded wisely. 'He's not been well, love. You're the fifth girl to knock on my door this week. It's a terrible illness he's got. Doctor says it's called marry-me-tosis or something along them lines. So he's going away for the sake of his health, is our Bernard. No use suing him, love. He's got a medical certificate to do with his condition, so he's what they call exempt.'

Eileen was floundering beneath the weight of Sadie Martindale's oratory. From the gist, she managed to glean the information that Bernard was not well enough to get married. 'All right, then,' she said amiably enough. 'I'll see yer, Mrs Martindale.' She ran off, presumably to find her binman.

Mary was in hysterics when Sadie returned. She

threw her arms round her mother's neck and kissed her. 'Mam, please stay in my corner, will you?' Mary calmed down eventually and lectured her brothers. 'This is what you might call a mam in a million,' she told them. 'And don't you ever forget it, either of you.'

Samuel Fishwick was a doomed man and he knew it. The pain was getting stronger, while he grew weaker by the hour. Eleanor had done her best for him, had spent many recent months dragging him round hospitals and specialists all over North Africa. In Cairo, he had learned the worst. His liver was a mess and it wasn't going to improve. So he had left the Nile to come home to this freezing house. He'd forgotten how cold England was, how icy Aston Leigh could be. And this was summer, he reminded himself. Still, he would not survive to battle through an English winter.

Eleanor hadn't said much, but they had never needed words to communicate. She understood him perfectly, had shown no surprise when he had asked her to go and find the boy. Peter Turnbull. He would be about the same age as Gilbert, Alice's boy, except for a year or so. So Gilbert and Constance had an uncle who was hardly older than they were.

Gilbert was a university student. In Samuel's opinion, universities turned out nancy boys who weren't fit to run a sack race, let alone a mill. He remembered Edward and that little place he'd rented over a butcher's somewhere up Daubhill. Edward hadn't been to college, hadn't needed rolls of paper and a daft hat. They had played chess while dining on fish and chips. A back yard lavatory, a mucky old table with the *Bolton Evening News* masquerading as a cloth, the flat cap hanging on the kitchen door. Rummy, they had played. Perhaps Peter Turnbull would turn out to be another Edward, and perhaps he wouldn't. Whatever, Samuel prayed that all the other Turnbulls had moved away or passed on.

Molly. Poor little Molly had bled to death with Samuel's son in her arms. Eleanor had been so understanding. She had never blamed her husband, had always maintained that the other woman was usually the culpable party. And he would see Alice right, too, would make provision for her and Edward. Anyway, the Turnbull lad might not be interested in helping Edward and Gilbert run the factory. But it was worth a try, and it would ease Samuel's conscience. Eleanor had better hurry, because time was running out.

She came in and sat next to the bed. Her hand on his brow was so gentle and sweet-smelling. 'Find him,' he begged.

'I will.'

'Soon?'

'Today.' Eleanor was becoming perturbed. If Samuel got hold of Peter Turnbull, he might just decide to leave some money to the bastard. 'Rest,' she whispered. 'Rest and get well.' He would never get well.

Eleanor gazed into space, tried to care, failed. He had betrayed her. How well she had taken the news of his infidelity; how supportive of her man she had been. A clock ticked, reminded her of all the years she had spent in the company of her 'beloved' husband. He had played about with a Molly Turnbull, a worthless creature from the back streets. He had lain down with her, had copulated with her, had pleasured himself.

Eleanor's hands tightened until the knuckles were white. She had played the game, had played it so well. In fact, she could have made her fortune on the stage or in films. She looked down now upon her sleeping spouse. 'I, too, had my moments, dearest. And now, your time is running out.' The passage of years had done little to assuage Eleanor Fishwick's fury. For an endless age, she had acted the part of a wonderfully supportive wife, and her reward was coming. When Samuel died, she would begin a new life.

After he had drifted into a drugged sleep, Eleanor went to the wardrobe and took out the dark grey coat she had bought in Manchester just days earlier. It seemed suitably sombre as garb for a woman about to watch the death of her husband.

She walked slowly downstairs, saw Alice pottering about with geraniums. Alice seemed to have a way with plants. And now, Alice's mother was supposed to bring a half-brother into the life of the daughter she had abandoned over twenty years ago. It was a mess, must not be allowed to get messier. Peter Turnbull was probably just another feckless piece of human dross. He was disposable, unimportant. Alice looked tired and as unbeautiful as ever.

'Going out, Mother?'

'Yes. There's someone I have to see. Look in on your father, will you?'

'Of course.'

Eleanor paused. 'He's been talking nonsense,' she said carefully. 'About people from long ago, a Peter, a Robert – workers from the mill, I suppose. Just humour him, dear.' She walked down the path, turned the corner and found Edward waiting in the lane. 'Did you never tell Alice about the Turnbulls?' she asked.

'No. As far as I know, she's unaware of the man's existence.'

Eleanor was relieved. Alice seemed to have drifted through life in a state of total unawareness. 'Let's go,' she told her son-in-law. 'I only want to see where he lives. After all, a proportion of Samuel's money has gone to Halliwell Road for some considerable time.' She had to think, had to concentrate. Peter Turnbull must not be allowed to stand in her way. No-one should stand in her way . . .

EIGHT

'Tell me about him.' Eleanor Fishwick surveyed the Belmont she had left behind for more than two decades. An estate of tacky little houses had sprung up at the bottom of The Rise, and the moors appeared to be smaller, but few major changes had taken place during her prolonged absence. 'What sort of a person is this Peter Turnbull? From what I have gathered in the past, his family certainly left a lot to be desired.'

Edward groaned inwardly. Why did he have to do all this? He had carried the mill, paid the workers, had kept the Fishwick wheels turning. He had also taken care of Samuel's bastard. The lad received money every week, was the outright owner of his cottage, spent his time lazing around, visiting cinemas, drinking in pubs and generally making a thorough nuisance of himself. 'He's a layabout,' said Edward. 'And I do hope Samuel's not thinking of mentioning Turnbull in his will. After all, there are two legitimate grandchildren.'

Eleanor, who had kept her husband happy for many years, had trained herself to know when to close her mouth and when to speak up. This, she felt, was a time for her to appear frank and open. 'There is a problem, Edward. Samuel wants to meet his son. Of course, I have supported my husband these last few days – just as I always have, but I agree with you. Samuel is not himself. He is not well enough to make decisions, Edward. In fact, his mind is showing a distinct tendency towards wandering.'

'The poor man's dying,' said Edward bluntly. 'We are complying with a deathbed wish. But I'm certain that Peter Turnbull will take full advantage of these circumstances. He's had everything paid for him, so he's never kept a job for more than a few months. His grandfather died many years ago of some wasting illness – he was in a wheelchair when Peter was born. Tess Turnbull raised Peter, but she also died young. The three uncles bled us for a while, then two were killed in action. I paid Uncle Micky off about four years ago, got him to sign a document pledging secrecy in return for a cash sum. He went off down south somewhere, so Peter's on his own.'

Eleanor nodded. 'Do many people know that Turnbull is Samuel's son?'

'I think not,' replied Edward. 'They were a cunning lot, though the grandparents seemed decent enough. Peter's had far too much to lose, so he wouldn't spoil his own game by being indiscreet. His Uncle Micky probably lost interest in Peter. Micky set himself up in a small business, a garage, I think. The situation is not universal knowledge by any means. There is, I think, a neighbour who knows the truth, but she is reputed to be a good soul.'

'Stop the car, please.' When Edward pulled into the kerb, his mother-in-law turned and looked at him. 'We have to tell a lie,' she said. 'Poor Alice and her children must be considered, as must you. I remember when I first met you, just after you saved

Samuel's life. Had he stayed outside that night, he might have perished. You looked after him. You made sure that he was safe and that no-one knew about his little peccadillo.'

Edward, whose own little peccadillo mirrored so closely the mistake of his father-in-law, pushed a finger down his collar to loosen it. The day was hot and the shirt was on the small side. 'What can we do?'

'Play for time,' she answered. 'We must fail to find Peter Turnbull. He could be away on holiday, could be visiting his uncle. Or perhaps he is doing national service.'

Edward shook his head. 'Too old. Gilbert's twenty-two, so this fellow must be more than a year older. As for national service, he side-stepped that due to flat feet and poor eyesight. I don't know about the fallen arches, but I believe he sees well enough to play a reasonable game of darts.' He shook his head slowly. 'This is a difficult business,' he concluded unnecessarily.

Eleanor stared at the Town Hall clock in the distance, wondered what on earth could be done. 'You know, I think Samuel's interest arises from the fact that Molly Turnbull's child is male. Samuel may be very ill, but his mind has not collapsed completely, not quite. It would not surprise me if he gave away the lot to a young man with the ability to adopt the name of Fishwick. He wanted a son. I failed to provide him with one.'

He considered Eleanor's statement. Eleanor had not failed her husband; the one she had failed was Alice. Edward was beginning to understand Alice. She was a lost and lonely soul whose isolation had turned into bitterness. He thought about Eleanor, about how cool she seemed now, at a time when the man she supposedly adored lay at death's door. In her younger days, during her daughter's childhood, this woman had pleased herself, had pleased her husband, had excluded all else from her life. Even today, she was calculating how best to serve her own interests.

'I failed,' she repeated.

Edward maintained his silence for a few more seconds. If Eleanor Fishwick wanted sympathy, she could look elsewhere. 'I understood from Samuel that Peter Turnbull's birth certificate has the word unknown under the paternal section. The man can prove nothing,' he said.

'Samuel can, while he's alive,' she answered quickly. 'So we must stop him. Edward, he has weeks to live at the most. The drugs will be increased soon, and he will be aware of very little. So we must lie.'

Edward shivered. The sun was beating down on the car and turning it into an oven. Yet his marrow seemed to be screaming for the sort of heat that was not radiated. He was sitting in a car with a woman of ice. This was a female who had not loved her child. She had rejected her one and only daughter, because that daughter had been judged unworthy. Eleanor's statement about doses of drugs raced around in his head, making him dizzy. He wanted to run, to put space between himself and this creature who seemed to be contemplating . . . Edward swallowed. The word murder was not sitting happily in his consciousness. Or would it be a mercy killing? Was Eleanor capable of mercy?

'There must be no meeting,' she said firmly.

No wonder she had shown no reaction when Samuel had wandered from the path of righteousness. She hadn't cared. All that love, all the hugging and kissing and worrying over her beloved husband – had that been an act, a lifelong performance? Now, Eleanor Fishwick was thinner, rawer, as if the flesh she had lost had been a mantle covering her true self. 'He wants to meet Peter Turnbull,' insisted Edward. 'And he will become upset if we deny him the chance.'

'No,' she muttered. 'Cancer requires a lot of morphine. He will forget his so-called son. We must make excuses for a while, that is all. Your children, your wife and yourself – why should you be cut off now, after all your years of work?'

Her real concern was herself. Perhaps she envisaged a scenario in which her weakened husband would cling to his son and wipe everyone else from his mind and from his will. 'Do as you wish,' he said. 'I shall go along with whatever you decide.' After all, what was the alternative? To bring a bloodsucker to Samuel's bedside? To create a situation that might impoverish Gilbert and Constance?

'I knew you would see my point,' said Eleanor. 'Now, after you've shown me this ghastly man's house, could we visit the Co-op, do you think? One of the things I missed was English bacon and real Cheddar cheese. And there's a wonderful shop on Deansgate – they sell marvellous tomato sausages, or so I'm told by Cook.'

With her dying husband wiped from her thoughts, a happy Eleanor Fishwick went shopping for food.

Gilbert and Mary wandered hand in hand through the garden of Aston Leigh. Mary was smitten, while Gilbert was head over heels in love and in shock. He had not been in love before. There had been women, mostly at university, whose charms he had enjoyed, but this was different. He was happy, sad, brave and terrified all at once. Words were useless. If he pored through a dictionary, he would find nothing to describe his emotions.

He clung tightly to her hand. With Mary, he was happy; apart from her, he felt cold and lonely. London was two hundred miles away. Soon, he would have to go away again, would be forced to separate himself from the girl he adored.

Mary sensed his unease. It had been a wonderful time for her, too, but she was afraid of becoming too dependent on a man who had allowed her to look through a window at a lifestyle that was not her own. It could be difficult to stop wanting the things she had seen. She was a mere spectator, had no chance of becoming a participant. And there was a need for independence, a desire to get somewhere on her own, not as a passenger in another person's vehicle. In Mary's opinion, there were two ways to success; she could create a future of her own, or she could marry into someone else's. Mary preferred the first option.

'I'm not going back,' he told her again.

She slapped his arm playfully. 'Yes, you are. I don't want you blaming me because you're one degree under.'

'Don't mock,' he said. 'It isn't funny. And I'm only going to step into Father's shoes, anyway, so what's the point of studying for a degree?'

She didn't know. But he had been so full of university at the start, had told her all kinds of schoolboy-style yarns about midnight parties and rag stunts. 'University's an opportunity, Gil. You would miss your friends.'

'I would miss you more.'

She pulled away from him. 'Gil, I don't want you to stay. Go back, then see how you feel in a few months. I'll still be here. I'm not going anywhere.'

She didn't love him, he decided. Had she loved him, she would have begged him to stay by her side for ever. Mary was not a usual type of girl. She was beautiful, yet her looks seemed unimportant to her. Most women of Gil's acquaintance would have used all their charms to snare a man, thereby ensuring a modicum of security for the future. Mary talked about owning a business, about a restaurant with music and decent food, a place where respectable people could have a pleasant meal away from hardened drinkers. 'I have money,' he said tentatively.

'Good. You'll need it.' Mary had money, too. In the Bolton Savings Bank, there were ninety-seven pounds and four shillings. There had been over a hundred, but she had bought Mam some comfortable shoes in soft kid. She stopped, drew him to a standstill. 'I don't want your money, Gil. I've not gone out with you to better myself. I like you. You make me laugh. Don't start coming over all serious, will you?'

'I only mentioned money in case you needed investors in your restaurant,' he said. Then he took the plunge, 'I think I'm in love with you,' he whispered.

'Yes, and I used to think Father Christmas came down our chimney every December, but I grew out of it.'

He stumbled deliberately, a hand to his chest. 'You mean there's no Santa Claus?'

She laughed. 'It's a bugger when somebody makes you grow up. Still, never mind. Let's go and find the fairies at the bottom of your garden.'

'Gilbert?' Alice was waving from the French window.

He left Mary and walked back to the house. Grandfather wanted to see him. 'Shan't be long,' he called to Mary before going inside.

Alice wandered down the path, tried to appear casual while studying her son's loved one. The boy was very much involved, had been off his food, had taken to sitting alone while waiting to see Mary again. It was so sweet to watch, yet so painful. Had Alice ever felt like this about Edward? Had Edward ever loved his wife? And would poor Gilbert suffer after returning to his studies?

'Is Mr Fishwick no better?' asked Mary.

'No, I'm sad to say,' replied Alice. 'He has lived in some difficult climates – India, South Africa and so forth. After the war, they settled in Morocco and his health deteriorated. Mother took him to Cairo where there was a better hospital. Quite apart from the odd bout of malaria, Father liked a drink, I'm afraid. So his liver's in very serious trouble.'

'My brother drinks,' said Mary, anxious to have a conversation with Gil's mother. Alice Shawcross seemed shy, as if she wasn't used to seeing many people. 'He's going back in the army, and Mam says he'll spend his pay on beer.'

'Your mother works at Fishwick's?'

Mary nodded. 'Only part time, Mrs Shawcross. She has terrible feet, so she can't be standing up for too long. Anyway, she's very grateful to Mr Shawcross for letting her cut down on her hours.'

Mary had a definite Lancashire accent, yet her speech was not lazy. This was an intelligent girl with a tremendous amount of energy. Alice was training herself, slowly and deliberately, towards a more open mind. Only weeks earlier, she would have been aghast to find her son keeping company with a girl from the meaner streets of Bolton. 'Gilbert seems reluctant to return to his studies in London,' said Alice.

'I know. He should go back,' replied Mary. 'I mean, his dad doesn't need him at the mill, so he'd be better off finishing what he started. Half a degree's no use, is it?'

'I suppose not. But Gilbert seems to be very fond of you. Perhaps he doesn't want to leave you?'

'It's too soon for that sort of thing,' answered Mary readily. 'We've only just met. If I'd been looking where I was going that night, I wouldn't have bumped into him. Please don't think it's anything to do with me, Mrs Shawcross. I've not asked him to leave university.'

Alice inclined her head thoughtfully. 'He's not a true academic. I suppose university is the male equivalent of a girls' finishing school. We pack off our boys in the hope that someone will turn them into adults.' She raised her chin and looked Mary in the eye. 'That would be a difficult task with Gilbert, he's so young at heart. Well, I shall leave the decision to him. Now, shall we go inside? Cook has made some lovely lemon barley.'

Mary followed her hostess inside, sat in a house the like of which she had only seen in magazine pictures. There were paintings, crystal decanters in a little wooden frame, beautiful carpets, real leather chairs. 'I love your house,' she told Alice. 'It's beautiful. So many lovely things.'

Alice, who didn't love Aston Leigh, smiled at Mary, then went to fetch Constance. Beauty, she mused, was in the eye of the beholder. This house was an unhappy place, well decorated, but without a soul. And Alice had a strange feeling that her days here were numbered. But she shook herself and carried on with the task of finding Constance and entertaining Mary Martindale.

The man in the bed was reminiscent of a shrivelled bird. A beak-like nose was the predominant feature, while the eyes had sunk back into their sockets, hazel irises pale in a yellowing surround. He seemed to be yellow all over, though his hair had remained brown and thick, with just a hint of grey above the ears.

'Grandfather,' said Gilbert. 'How are you today?'

Samuel looked at the boy. He was a good-looking lad, tall, with bright blue eyes and a shock of dark hair. 'Peter,' he said, the voice thinned by age and pain.

Gilbert understood that his grandfather was dying. His mind seemed to be suffering, which was only to be expected, especially since the morphine injections had been introduced. Grandmother was in charge of the drugs. A wicked-looking needle lay on a bedside cupboard in a blue-rimmed enamel kidney bowl. Gilbert could not have stuck the thing into anybody, not for a king's ransom.

'Peter,' repeated Samuel. 'There's not much time.'

'It's Gilbert.' He sat on the chair next to the old man's head. 'Would you like me to read to you?' There was a terrible smell in the room, one that Gilbert had never encountered before. It was similar to the stench of stored paper, as if a million old books had been left in a damp attic to rot away over the years. 'The *Evening News* is here.' He scanned the headline. 'I see we're sending troops to Korea to help the Yanks.'

'Bugger Korea.' There was energy in the tone. Samuel's eyes seemed to burn suddenly, as if his temperature had climbed dramatically. 'You are my son.'

'Grandson,' said Gilbert politely. He folded the newspaper and placed it on the floor. 'I'm your grandson.'

The eyelids, loose and orange-streaked in the creases, lowered themselves. 'Molly died,' whispered Samuel. 'Ellie forgave me, of course, but I damaged your mother, Peter. I killed her. Will you forgive me?'

Gilbert decided to play along. 'Of course I will.'

'So many things to say,' mumbled the sick man. 'Edward has been good to me, looking after Alice and the business. He has a lad, you know. University, so I'm told. What bloody use is a university when there's cotton needing spinning?'

'My view exactly,' agreed Gilbert.

Samuel smiled, creating a death mask on the white pillow. 'It's in that brown case over there.' A claw raised itself. 'Get it now, Peter, before Ellie comes back. Edward and Alice have enough – I've made sure of that. But you have been deprived, my son. So it's to be equal shares from now on.'

Gilbert remained where he was.

'Go,' hissed Samuel. 'Get it. Ellie doesn't know about it. I had it witnessed in Egypt. You must take it to a solicitor, dear boy. Make sure that it will stand up in Britain. Oh Molly, poor Molly.'

Gilbert decided that he must humour the dying man, so he crossed the room and found a small attaché case. He could feel those feverish eyes following his every move.

'Pocket. Inside,' wheezed Samuel. 'Take the envelope, Peter. Take it now.'

Gilbert lifted out the manila envelope. The name on the front read Peter Turnbull. He carried it to the bed, smiled when he saw relief invading the ravaged features. 'I have it,' he said.

'Good. Make sure you hang onto it.'

'I shall.' Gilbert remained where he was until his grandfather fell asleep, then he rose quietly and placed the envelope in his pocket.

'Give that to me.'

Gilbert swivelled, saw his grandmother in the doorway. 'I beg your pardon?'

'Give it to me.' Eleanor tiptoed across the room. 'He keeps doing this, Gilbert,' she explained, her voice low and steady. 'There have been at least three others who have been given bits of paper. He's rambling.'

Gilbert did not like the expression on Eleanor's face. She was so controlled, yet the small movements of her eyes and a twitch near the upper lip betrayed a level of nervousness. 'Then my keeping this will do no harm,' he reasoned.

'It will also make no sense,' she replied. 'He is asleep, so he won't know that you have given it to me.'

Alice had raised two polite young people. She had not spent a great deal of time with them, had not managed to nurture their souls, but their manners had been drummed home thoroughly. Nevertheless, Gilbert made one last effort. 'Grandfather was not confused yesterday,' he said. 'In fact, he was telling me all about the pyramids and your trip to India to see the Taj. So he was lucid enough then.'

Eleanor Fishwick closed the door, then stood with her arms folded. She said nothing, yet her very posture seemed threatening.

Her grandson looked at the small woman who had once been large, saw grim determination in her stance. 'Who is Peter Turnbull?' he asked softly.

Eleanor raised an eyebrow. 'God knows. I certainly don't.'

'Then why do you want me to hand this over?'

'There could be something of mine in it, or photographs that will be special once your grandfather is dead.'

Gilbert turned and looked at Samuel Fishwick. Death was near, was hovering in the air and waiting to pounce on this brittle, almost transparent person. Something had happened in the last twenty-four hours. Morphine was a strong painkiller, but surely it could not act so swiftly? Only yesterday, Samuel had waxed lyrical about the beauty of Egypt, the magnificence of India, the wonderful pride of a huge country that had recently evicted its white slave-drivers.

'Give it to me, Gilbert.'

He swivelled round. 'Here you are, Grandmother.'

Eleanor seemed to shudder as she took the envelope. 'Thank you,' she said.

Gilbert left the room.

His grandmother breathed out an enormous stream of relief and sat on the commode chair. Her hands trembled as if this were the middle of the coldest winter in England's long history of unstable climatic performances. That had been a near one, far too close for comfort. She slipped the envelope into a nearby drawer, then fixed her gaze on the man she had married almost fifty years earlier. Should he survive, the golden wedding would be celebrated in a month. Of course, he would not live to enjoy that.

Mary Martindale and Connie Shawcross got on like the proverbial burning house. Each had a well-developed sense of humour and that particular breed of mischievous energy which creates constant banter. Connie was tickled pink about Gil and Mary. This was the sort of girl who would keep Gil's feet on the ground. He was a bit on the silly side, was inclined to take life rather too easily. Thus far, his student days had been wasted in riotous living, and Connie could not imagine her brother emerging from Imperial with a good level of honours. Mary was right for him, she thought. Mary would encourage him to make the best of himself, whether he stayed at home or went back to London.

The two girls were enjoying cold lemon barley with ice cubes clinking in the tumblers. Halfway through her drink, Mary exploded with unseemly laughter, spilling a mouthful onto her blouse.

'What now?' asked Connie.

'Sorry. I was just thinking about my mam's fridge,' replied Mary when the bout of coughing ended. 'She polishes it every day like a precious ornament. All the neighbours queue up waiting for ice cubes and lollies. She's taken to remembering her aitches. The trouble is, she can't remember where the aitches should go, so she's giving hice cubes away to 'er from next door.' She mopped at her blouse with a handkerchief. 'It's a riot.'

Alice jogged past the window. 'There goes my mother,' sighed Connie. 'Training for the Holympics.'

Mary clouted her friend with the soggy handkerchief. 'Don't you start,' she said. 'There's enough with me having a funny mother.'

'Funny?' Connie arched her eyebrows. 'You know nothing, girl. See her?' She pointed to Alice, whose gait had slowed to a brisk walk. 'She's never spoken to us since 1940, except to tell us when we were doing wrong. Now, all of a sudden and without written warning, she's gone reasonable. I spoke to James Templeton on the subject just the other day, and he reckons we should sue. People have no right to make alterations without planning permission. My father's an alderman, so we know all the rules.'

'She was nice to me,' observed Mary.

'You see? She's got no right to be nice. We used to know exactly where we stood in this household. Now, out of the blue, we are in receipt of praise when we expect abuse.' She nodded thoughtfully. 'Poor Mother. It's a damned shame. We've been living with a very lonely woman.' Her tone was becoming serious. 'Father's always been agreeable, but absent. It's easy to be nice when you're never there. He's the one who should be blamed, I think.'

'They like him at the mill.'

Connie smiled. 'Oh, yes, he's wonderful to work for. I love my dad, Mary. He's really solid, like a rock, but a rock that's miles away at the seaside. He needs a good talking-to.'

'Are you going to do it?'

'Of course,' answered Connie. 'The fact is that women always have to do the talkings-to. Mother's done it for years, then Father has breezed in with sweets and toys, all smiles and pretty words. So it's about time somebody had a word with him.'

Mary agreed, but she kept her thoughts to herself.

Men were all right, but they weren't much cop when it came to sorting out a family. They were always at work, in the pub, stuffing their faces at the table, or snoring in a chair, the *Bolton Evening News* wafting over their faces with each noisy breath. 'Gil's a long time,' she said.

'Talking to Grandfather. He's probably reading the paper for him. The poor old chap can't even sit up any more.'

Mary placed her glass on a silver coaster.

'Mother is very uncomfortable with her parents in the house.'

The visitor said nothing, as she knew little about the Shawcross family.

'I don't like my grandmother. She's very strange,' mused Connie.

'You can say that again.' Gil strode into the room. He picked up the jug, poured an iced drink for himself, then downed it in five thirsty seconds. 'I wouldn't like to get on the wrong side of her,' he declared. 'There's no warmth in her at all – she reminds me of a snake, cold-blooded and wicked.'

Gil was not one for damning people without evidence. 'What happened?' asked his sister.

Uneasy with his thoughts, Gil decided to keep them to himself. What would be the point in distributing his discomfort? 'Nothing much,' he lied. 'It's just the way she looked at me – and at her husband.'

'Must be in the genes,' remarked Connie. 'An absence of love breeds an absence of love. We'll probably be terrible parents, too.'

Gil shook himself out of his gloom. 'Last one to the milestone's an idiot,' he yelled, giving himself a headstart. As he ran through the grounds of Aston Leigh and onto The Rise, he saw Mother making her way down to the main road. Like him, she was getting away. He sat on the grass verge and stared at the window behind which Grandfather Fishwick waited for death. The house seemed uglier than ever. Gil shuddered slightly, then laughed as Connie and Mary dashed over to thump him. It was a lovely day, so he shook off his cares and enjoyed himself.

Eleanor Fishwick picked up the newly acquired phials. There were four of them, each marked off in doses printed on the glass. She congratulated herself on her earlier performance at the doctor's surgery. 'So careless of me,' she had cried. 'Three full containers of morphine lost when I crushed the bottles underfoot.' She had presented George Wilkinson with a few shards of glass. 'So I shall have to ask for more, I'm afraid.' The 'spilled' fluid was in a hip flask behind the chest of drawers in Samuel's bedroom. She had emptied out the drug before smashing its containers. With over twice as much morphine as prescribed, Eleanor was well prepared for the unpleasant but necessary task.

She sat next to Samuel and stroked his hair. It was dirty, matted with the sweat of several days. Although he had been washed regularly, he was too ill for a thorough shampooing. Everything about him smelled terrible, his breath, his skin, his sheets and pyjamas.

He was suffering, she told herself. He was suffering now just as she had suffered all those years ago when he had mated with a trollop. How supportive Eleanor had been, how saintly and forgiving. Inside, she had bled as profusely as the proverbial stuck pig, but the wounds had not been allowed to show themselves on the surface. Like a

Trojan, she had weathered the storm, and now, more than twenty years on, she was supposed to act the faithful wife all over again while Samuel gave away her inheritance to a bastard.

Well, that she could not do. She allowed her mind to travel along a route that had taken over two decades, through India, China, the African continent. They had dined with the best, had supped in the same rooms as princes. She had kept an eye on him for so long that it had become a habit, a part of her daily routine. Women had always loved him, had always clustered round Samuel. Where were they now, those coiffured heads, those bodies clad in oriental silks? Where were they now, while the man lay stinking in his own illness, skin as yellow as a spring crocus, eyes rolled back, crusty talons decorating hands that had once been elegant?

He had not strayed again. They had tried, those cunning females, those determined remnants of an Empire soon to fall. But Eleanor had decided not to suffer any more, so she had changed herself, had become thinner, quicker in body and mind. This man was hers. She had bought him, had paid in full with sleepless nights and tear-filled days, with the effort she had made to placate and entertain this jaundiced, breathing corpse.

She rose and took the boiled hypodermic from its bowl. It occurred to her that the needle was unnecessarily sterile, because its job would be not to preserve, but to terminate life. With steady hands, Eleanor Fishwick drew the first double dose, dabbed spirit on her husband's sagging flesh, plunged sharp metal into muscle. The doctor had trained her to deliver the morphine, how to ease her beloved's passage through these final days.

When Samuel's eyes opened, she smiled at him. 'Sleep, my precious,' she whispered.

He looked adoringly on his wife. 'Thank you,' he mouthed.

In another hour or so, she would repeat the procedure. It was for Alice's sake, too, of course. And there were the children to consider, Constance and . . . Gilbert. The boy would forget, she insisted. Old people did become confused, especially towards the end. Peter Turnbull might easily have been someone from abroad, someone who had resembled Gilbert.

Samuel was so peaceful now. The creases were smoothing themselves, as if a Godly hand had reached down to iron out the cares of seventy years. But the hand was not God's; it was hers. Finally and justifiably, she had become the instrument which would plan the end of this long partnership.

The clock ticked gently, each movement marking the passing of one more second. Sixty times sixty, then the injection would be repeated. He would feel nothing, would suffer no more. What joys were left to him, anyway? He could not eat, could not walk in the sun or read or drink his favourite brandy. This was a kindness, Eleanor reminded what remained of her deliberately dulled conscience. Dogs and horses were put down when life became too onerous. Even cats and other vermin were destroyed in order to curtail their pain.

She moved to the window, placed her watch on a small table and prepared to wait. Outside on the grass, her grandchildren played rounders with the girl called Mary. Their voices were young and vibrant, and they drowned the quiet snores of the man in the bed. In the rocking chair, Eleanor moved gently back and forth, back and forth, soothing herself with the gentle motion. Under her breath, she hummed Brahms' 'Lullaby', her eyes fixed on life while her trusting lover drifted peacefully towards his Maker.

James Templeton was inordinately proud of his little tin box. Erected hurriedly towards the end of the war, these detached prefabricated houses were considered by many to be the ultimate luxury, because they had gardens, nice fireplaces and fitted kitchens with fridges and cookers built in.

He stood at his front door and looked into the little hall. To his left were two bedrooms, the larger of which contained his work. Directly opposite, there was a bathroom, while the living room, on his right, led into a nice little kitchen. No mother, he kept telling himself gleefully. No servants, no interruptions, no complaints if he skipped shaving for a couple of days.

James's prefab had sunk a bit, had drifted apart from its foundations, and the roof was not reliable. He had paid twenty pounds to have the house steadied, and ten pounds to a roofer who had made a lot of noise, mostly while slurping tea in the kitchen. This was James's own place. He could go out, stay in, do absolutely nothing, or paint and write for hours on end. He could choose whether and when to answer the door. He was even experimenting with photography. It was absolute bliss.

The neighbours were interesting. While attempting to turn his Anderson shelter into a darkroom, James had listened to the Robinsons. Bob Robinson had returned from the war with one arm and a stammer. Edith, his wife, a large woman who worked in a huge, town centre bakery, was not blessed with a high degree of patience. She had a tendency to finish off her husband's fractured sentences, and her interpretation of Bob's intended messages was not always accurate.

Poor Bob's misfortune was further aggravated by identical twin daughters named Patricia and Pamela – Pat and Pam for short. When Bob started to call a name, both girls disappeared like magic before the word was fully birthed.

James's investigation into photography had been short-lived, as he had developed nothing beyond hiccups while in the air raid shelter. Bob, doing his best to tell Edith that the coal had been delivered, had been prompted so many times that the cat, the cooker and the corporation had all played a part in the almost one-sided discussion. After five minutes, James had emerged from his hide and fled into the house as fast as his bad leg had allowed.

The other side housed an Irish family surnamed Murphy. Danny, as big and loud as a bull, worked in a Westhoughton pit. Mona Murphy, at four feet and eleven inches in her shoes, was a tartar. Her two sons were totally subservient, while Danny was completely under a thumb the size of a child's little finger.

Living in close proximity to others brought a new dimension into the life of James Templeton. He was learning how privileged, yet how deprived he had been. There was a whole way of life he had never glimpsed before. People worried about things that had never occurred to him, like clothes wearing out and rent money falling short of the required mark. They lived loudly, too, were not concerned with the opinions of others, did not hide their feelings or worry about niceties.

He closed his door and walked into his living

room. No ornaments cluttered the place, no bits of brass, pottery or silver. Having spent a lifetime trying to avoid collision with Mother's precious oddments, James was enjoying a very unelaborate style of living. There was a sofa, a chair and a table with two stools. A small wireless stood on the sideboard, and his own paintings covered various stains on dirty cream walls.

This was a new beginning. He stared up at his mauve and yellow cow/elephant and told himself that the indulgent phase had ended. A restlessness was invading his soul, an urge to paint and write something meaningful. There were no rules now, no bells to announce meals, no hovering servants. He ate when hungry, slept when tired, worked when motivated. It was time for him to start earning a living.

Having haunted the offices of the local press for two days, he realized that he was not going to become a journalist. Everyone at Tillotson's seemed to work on the run, a sandwich in one hand and a pencil in the other. With his game leg, he was hardly built for chasing an exclusive, though his car might have been useful. The editor had been gloriously unimpressed by James Templeton's degree in art, so James Templeton was thinking again.

He didn't need to work, of course. There was money in the bank, and Mother would no doubt send supplies once she discovered where her fledgeling had settled. James scanned the room, imagined the look of horror on Maude's face when she eventually saw this prefab. She would probably order a weekly hamper from Fortnum's and a fatted calf from Joseph Barton's shop.

What could he do? It would have to be a more-or-less sitting down job with no counting involved. He had gained a school cert pass in maths, but numeracy was not James's strong point. Most clerical posts seemed out of the question, then. As for typing, he would challenge anyone to a duel as long as they used no more than two fingers. He picked up the newspaper, glanced idly through the advertisements. Then he saw it, a gem of a job, the reason why he had been born.

He laughed out loud, roared with glee when he conjured up his mother's face. Her son an insurance man? Her James going into people's houses collecting funeral pennies? 'It's work and it's honest,' he told his absent parents. Tomorrow, he would join the ranks of Wesleyan and General and his new life could begin.

Eleanor tiptoed round the bed and looked at him. His chest still moved up and down, and his colour seemed to have improved. How much of the damned stuff was it going to take? Perhaps she had gone far enough. All she needed was for him to remain asleep and unable to ask questions about his bastard son.

It was midnight. She would have to start on the third phial soon. Dr Wilkinson had called, had expressed his satisfaction with Samuel's degree of comfort. 'It won't be long now,' he had told the would-be widow. Not long? Samuel was looking better, had even opened his eyes once or twice, had taken a dribble of water between the shrivelled lips. Was he going to talk again?

She began to pace back and forth, eyes fixed on her husband, hands twisting nervously beneath the thin bosom. What if this had all been a mistake? Perhaps two or three doctors were capable of similar misdiagnosis. There had been miracles, too, cases of terminally ill cancer victims who had suddenly improved sufficiently to live a normal life again. A normal life? Was it normal for a man to bequeath a part of his wealth to a so-called son he had never seen, never known?

Samuel opened his eyes, seemed not to focus for a while. Then he noticed his wife, smiled for a split second before allowing a dull pain to register on his face. She had been such a good companion, such a faithful spouse. Even now, she was ministering to him, was drawing up that pale fluid, the elixir that wiped out thought and eliminated pain. 'Peter?' he managed.

Eleanor nodded, turned him over, rubbed alcohol on sagging skin. It was now or never. She could not continue like this, could not stand guard day in and day out in order to keep the family at bay. In her hand, a massive dose of morphine sat beneath the needle. She tapped out a bubble, plunged the steel into his buttock. The muscle stiffened, relaxed as the hypodermic was removed. This injection would almost certainly be his last.

Eleanor sat near the window and began her vigil. For three whole nights, she had dozed in a chair, had forced herself to remain alert. The sounds of the old house were re-establishing themselves in her mind, were pulling on the cords of memory. The thud of the front door, a creaking board just outside the main bathroom, the whisper of wind in the poplars.

It was not a happy house. Alice and Edward slept in separate rooms, while the children, grown and well nourished, seemed ill at ease, as if waiting for a bell or a siren that would mark their exit from Aston Leigh. Eleanor's feelings for the old place were mixed. It was hers, she supposed, yet it did not seem to be home. What would she do after Samuel's death? Would she stay here, travel again, start a new life in another part of England?

She fell asleep, her head lying sideways against the chair's shoulder. The music in her dream was wonderful, a string quartet playing Bach, white table-cloths spread beneath cedars, a gentle breeze lifting their skirts and fanning its way across a pool of blue water. Men in long white garments walked along the road, their mules laden with carpets for the tourist market. Dazzling diamonds on women's fingers, pitchers of cool wine, a black-tied waiter bearing silver goblets on a silver tray. Native girls with pitchers on their heads, the smell of— She woke with a start.

The smell of death hovered in the room, and she rose quickly to throw open the window. An ominous silence drummed against her ears, an absence of sound louder than cacophony. He was dead. There was no need to go to the bed, no need to look for the rise and fall of his fleshless ribs, the beat of a heart in a wrist. She wiped her face on a damp cloth, ran more water into the basin. In the mirror, a dark ghost stared back at her, a hollow-eyed creature with thinning hair and wrinkled skin. She had aged more in the last seventy-two hours than in the past five years.

She washed her face and hands, dried them on a soft towel. In a moment, she would go and look at him. It had been a long night and a long, long life. Samuel had never known her anger, had never been allowed to feel the depth of her hurt. For as long as she could remember, Eleanor had been an actress who had played her part well. The travelling had made her sacrifice worthwhile, because she had seen all the places she had dreamed of in her youth. But Samuel had not paid the full price. Until now.

Slowly, the widow walked to the bed and smiled upon her husband's corpse. How many lovers had she taken in those twenty years? Ten, a dozen? While Samuel Fishwick had played cards and roulette, his doting wife had paid him back a hundredfold. In the arms of a series of men, Samuel's loyal Ellie had taken some of her revenge.

Laughter bubbled in her throat, but she squashed the threat of hysteria. How much she had achieved. She must not spoil it now. 'Remember all you did,' she whispered. From an overweight young woman, Eleanor had turned herself into an attractive temptress. Her skin had been good, had settled back firmly after stretching across layers of lingering puppy-fat. Since her early thirties, Eleanor had managed her weight by denying her stomach.

Abroad, she had taken a lover in many ports of call, sometimes two when the stay had been lengthy. Many had pleased her; Samuel had seldom managed that. Although her heart was cold, Eleanor's flesh was far from frigid, and she had appreciated those men whose performances had been better than adequate. The secret was to avoid falling in love; love meant pain, diminution of self, the surrendering of power. Samuel had been her one and only love. His betrayal had taught her never to love again, had primed her to skirt the edge of passion's flame without getting burnt.

She kissed her fingers, then pressed them against the icy, waxen lips of her dead partner. He should not have betrayed her. Revenge served cold was sweet indeed, and this man was very, very cold. It was important to look sad, she reminded herself. With her gaze still fixed on the figure in the bed, she reached into the cabinet for smelling salts. Sal volatile was a wonderful maker of tears.

The sky was lightening perceptibly. A few birds began to tune vocal cords in preparation for their dawn performance. From the woods, the sound of a cuckoo clashed with the final hoot of a homeward bound owl. She had done it. She had helped him through his misery, had smoothed the lines of anguish from his brow. She had freed him, had freed herself, had thwarted the chances of a bastard opportunist.

There was nothing wrong in what she had done. A man who suffered the agony of terminal cancer needed a push into the next life. Alice should be grateful, as should those children of hers. No vestige of guilt was allowed to dwell in Eleanor's mind. She had done her best, no more and no less than that.

Eleanor breathed in the salts, rubbed her eyes, walked to the door. She would wake Alice first, would weep and wail, would drag her daughter to this bed of death. Funeral arrangements must be made, she reminded herself, and she would need to buy a suit in black. After the pomp and ceremony of the burial, she could begin her life anew.

On the landing, a thought popped into her head. Edward must stop making payments to Turnbull. Let the man starve, let him work for his living if he wanted to eat. Edward had done well. He had kept the mill running, had sent money to Samuel, had reared a family. Perhaps Edward's usefulness was coming to an end? Ah well, she would deal with everything in time.

NINE

'You can't just go barging in there!' Sheila Foster's usually colourless face was red with exertion. She was worn out after her supposed holiday in Devon. Keeping an eye on Vera had not been easy; even William had been a bit of a pest, chasing about all over the place, jumping in boats and messing about with half-dead fish and furious crabs.

Vera, wild-eyed and with her flame-coloured hair bushed out around her face, looked for all the world like the kind of person who had been locked away out of sight by a Mr Rochester. She wasn't making sense any more, wasn't trying to appear normal. And now, she was steaming up the path of Aston Leigh and into the arms of trouble.

'Vera!' shouted Sheila again. 'Will you stand still and listen to me? Vera!'

Vera would stand still for nobody. Edward Shawcross would do nothing for her, so perhaps his wife might. Alice wasn't likely to want a wrong-side-of-the-blanket baby on her Christmas list. Alice might give Vera the money for an abortion, then everything could get back to the sort of normal that was so difficult to remember these days.

Sheila ground to a halt and stood back helplessly

while Vera Hardman rattled the brass doorknocker hard enough to waken the dead. If the ground had opened, Sheila Foster would have jumped voluntarily into the void, because she had never been so embarrassed and shown up in all her life. Well, that wasn't quite true. Trying to stop Vera jumping off cliffs had been no tea-party, either. Vera had walked into the sea fully clothed, had marched into a Dartmouth doctor's surgery and demanded to have the baby removed there and then without anaesthetic and without fuss. She had been dragged from the sea by a fisherman, had been heaved out of the doctor's surgery by police and two male patients.

No-one answered the door. Vera stood back, surveyed the house, banged again. She was in no mood for being ignored. If they didn't come to the door soon, she might just decide to break one of the bay windows.

There were few signs of improvement in Sheila's neighbour. She had travelled north on the train in the guard's van with her dog, and Sheila had journeyed in the same comfortless compartment. A huge sliding door had needed watching, so poor Sheila had ended up guarding the guard's van. William had howled for about two hundred miles, had finally fallen asleep in his locked travelling basket. But Vera had remained very alert. Vera didn't sleep any more. All day and all night she rocked in a chair or paced about the floor. The whole thing was becoming too much for Sheila. In spite of her beliefs, she had come dangerously close to drawing on poor Charlie's insurance money to put Vera out of her misery.

'There's nobody in,' said Vera sadly.

'I've told you,' answered Sheila, relief showing in

the tone of her voice. 'They'll be at the funeral. Even the servants will have gone to the graveyard. Important family, the Fishwicks.'

'Whose funeral?'

Sheila looked up to heaven and hung onto her patience grimly. Vera wasn't herself. Vera was somebody else altogether, was nothing like the neighbour Sheila knew and loved. 'Her dad died. I read it out loud from the *Evening News*. Don't you remember? I kept telling you on the bus that there'd be nobody in.' She sat down on the step and had a good look at Vera. She appeared crackers, that was a fact. Her cardigan was fastened in all the wrong holes, and the stockings were odd, one in a pale fawn, the other in a nasty shade of tan. Still, at least the shoes were a pair this time, so that was a bit of an improvement.

'I'm not budging,' spat Vera. 'I shall wait.'

Sheila was suddenly more than weary. If she didn't watch herself, she'd be going on holiday with Vera again, this time to a padded cell with a bucket in a corner. 'I'm sorry, love,' she said quietly. 'I can do no more for you. This is all beyond me.' Leaving Vera here on the doorstep of Aston Leigh was probably criminal, but Sheila was well past caring. She needed sleep, a good wash and a few strong cuppas with several sugars. 'I'm going home,' she said. 'Because I'm worn out and I've had more than enough.'

Vera Hardman put her head on one side. 'Leaving me? Leaving me here on me own?'

'Yes.'

'Why? How can you do that? I'm not well.'

Vera's next-door neighbour and ally lifted her shoulders. 'You are as well as you want to be, that's a fact. Can't you get a grip? Can't you just take life as it comes? Because you'll get nowhere as long as you carry on this road.'

Edward Shawcross's mistress sat down on his doorstep next to her friend. 'I'm trapped,' she said. 'I'm in prison, Sheila. And the jailer's just a little blob of jelly. I can't break out, because I can't see the bloody enemy. So I'm going crazy.'

Sheila nodded. 'That's the first sensible thing you've said in weeks, Vera Hardman. You are going round the bend and taking me with you. So you've two choices now, lass. You can get up off your bum and catch the bus with me. Or you can stop here and upset a woman who's just buried her father.' She sniffed, picked up her handbag and rose to her feet. 'Please your bloody self,' she said. 'I'm off home to see to my cats.'

She stalked down the path towards the gate, her ears straining for the sound of following footsteps. Turning into The Rise, she deliberately refrained from looking back. Somebody had to get Vera back on course. It had been a long few weeks. Dartmouth was probably a lovely place, though all Sheila remembered was combing tea-rooms and cobbled streets every time Vera and William had gone missing.

She stopped, listened, heard nothing but birds, then a coal lorry dragging its bulk along Belmont Road. If she ever returned to Devon, she would steer clear of Dartmouth, and especially clear of the Royal Castle Hotel, because she felt too ashamed to face those lovely, soft-spoken people ever again. In the Royal Castle, she had been left with William while Vera went to the toilet. Vera had gone to the toilet for twenty-two whole minutes. The dog had created mayhem, while every chambermaid, porter and waiter had scoured the hotel from top to bottom.

Sheila glanced back, saw no-one emerging from the grounds of Aston Leigh. At the Royal Castle, Vera had finally been discovered in a linen cupboard, where, after a fortnight's insomnia, she had nodded off on a pile of monogrammed bath towels. The doctor's surgery had been the next port of call, and that had caused considerable trouble, not only to the local police force, but also to several innocent patients who had probably felt a damned sight worse after that particular visit to their doctor.

It could not go on, Sheila told herself firmly. Vera had to get better, because Vera was, deep down, a truly decent woman. She was scared witless by the prospect of childbirth, but that did not make her a bad person. Slowed by guilt, Sheila came to a halt. She would have to go back for her. She would have to walk all the way up this damned hill again.

'Sheila?'

The exhausted woman swivelled round. 'Thank God,' she murmured. With the odd, concertina-ed stockings and the baggy cardigan, Vera resembled a neglected schoolchild. 'Look, I'll phone him later on. I promise, Vee. When we've had a sit down and a cuppa, I'll wander up to the phone box with William. Mr Shawcross's dad-in-law's funeral should be over and done with by teatime, eh? Then I'll tell him to get round to your house.' She would tell him more than that, a lot more. Vera wanted watching full time, twenty-four hours a day until the pregnancy's end.

Vera managed a watery smile. 'I'm sorry, Sheila. I can't help it.' What use would Edward be? she wondered. He couldn't wave a magic wand, wouldn't pay for an operation. She didn't really want to see him any more, but she couldn't think of any other course of action.

Sheila took her friend's hand, guided her like a child towards the main road. 'I know you can't help it, love.' But Sheila couldn't help it, either. Dragging Vera Hardman on and off buses was not Sheila's idea of fun. Somebody else would have to take over, because Sheila had done her stint. Yes. It was time for Edward Shawcross to shoulder his responsibilities.

Gilbert Shawcross stared across the gaping grave and into the pale eyes of his maternal grandmother. She had shed no tears today, had simply sat during the service, had knelt to pray, was just about to throw a handful of dirt onto a box containing her husband of fifty years.

An echo in Gil's head kept forming the name Peter. Peter Turnbull, he seemed to remember. How quickly the old man had deteriorated after mistaking Gil for this Peter fellow. Grandmother had been in charge of Samuel Fishwick's comfort, had ministered to him, had doled out the painkilling drugs. Uncomfortable with his thoughts, Gil took his turn to throw a few crumbs of soil into the grave. For a few very brief minutes during recent days, he and Connie had known a grandfather.

Edward was genuinely sad. He had quite liked Samuel, though he had not seen him for many years. Their correspondence had been conducted via the business, yet many letters had contained comments and questions of a more personal nature. Samuel had been a father figure, while Edward had taken the place of a son. But now, there was a son. Undoubtedly, Eleanor was bent on keeping Peter

Turnbull well out of the picture, but Edward still managed to worry. Peter Turnbull, along with most other Boltonians, would have read the announcement in the local press. Samuel Fishwick was dead, and Peter Turnbull was a greedy, idle young man. It would only be a matter of time before he turned up with his begging bowl polished and primed for use.

Alice sighed. It was a very sad day, because she had just said goodbye to a stranger. Daddy had been a card in his youth. She remembered all the laughter, the parties, Mummy and other ladies floating round in layers of chiffon and lace. Champagne on high days, sherry before meals, a sip for her if she smiled sweetly enough. But the sweet smiles had stopped, had been replaced by a dumpling face above a dumpling body, and Daddy had abandoned his ugly daughter and his business.

Connie took her mother's arm. 'Come on,' she urged gently. 'Let's go home and eat Cook's lovely sandwiches. She made some specially for you, salmon and cucumber.'

Alice smiled. Constance was turning out to be a good girl. Constance couldn't help being excessively beautiful any more than Alice might have helped becoming unattractive.

Connie was watching Gil too. He was staring at Grandmother again. It seemed rather rude, she thought, the way her brother was keeping his eyes fixed so firmly on a seventy-year-old widow. Gil didn't like his grandmother, but that was hardly a reason for such infantile behaviour. She left her mother and sauntered across to Gil. 'What are you up to?' she asked between gritted teeth.

'Nothing much. I'm attending a funeral,' he replied.

'And trying to upset the old lady?' Connie sent a sweet smile in the direction of Eleanor Fishwick.

Gil pushed his hands into his pockets, looked down at the earth. 'Is that better?' he asked.

'What has she done to you?' asked Connie.

'What did she do to Grandfather?' was Gil's response.

Connie dug him in the ribs. 'Don't talk like that, especially next to the grave,' she whispered.

Gil muttered something about morphine.

Connie wheeled round, pulled Gil with her, pretended to look at the wreaths that waited to be placed on the grave after it had been filled in. 'Gil, behave yourself.'

He wiped his hands on a handkerchief to remove the last remnants of soil. 'There's somebody called Peter,' he said quietly. 'The old man wanted to talk to him. He thought I was Peter, and he asked me to take an envelope from a briefcase. A new will, he said, a will made in Africa. I was supposed to have it verified.' He paused, looked over his shoulder. Grandmother was on her way back to the cars. 'As far as I know, Grandfather never spoke again after that. She was in the doorway.'

'Grandmother?'

He nodded. 'Listening. She dragged the envelope from me, made me hand it over there and then.' He gazed down at a formal arrangement in yellow and white, read the words attached to a small card. 'TO MY DARLING HUSBAND'. 'She kept him very well sedated after that, Connie. I tried to visit him, but she prevented that, said he needed to rest. Even Mother got turned away from the deathbed.'

Connie's flesh crawled. She, too, had been refused admittance to her grandfather's bedroom. 'Who is this Peter? I'm sure he's never been mentioned before.'

Gil shrugged. 'I don't know.' He swivelled, watched the old woman stooping to get into the first car, the vehicle that was supposed to contain the deceased's nearest and dearest. 'But she knows, Connie. I'll swear she does. And now, with Grandfather dead, she probably feels safe.' He paused, pondered. 'But I'm going to find the man, Connie. Turnbull. Peter Turnbull.'

Connie dragged Gil away from the graveside. This was no way to behave on such a sad day, she told herself. But Gil hadn't a nasty bone in his body. He had been a terrific brother, a good friend, an ally whenever Mother had been in one of her moods. Gil wasn't the sort to go about making up tales about people. And Grandmother did have the coldest face.

Edward sat next to his wife in the second car. She had not wept, had not even looked unhappy during the funeral. Strangely, he understood exactly how she felt, because his own parents had been less than adequate. Was this the reason for the Shawcross's deficiencies as rearers of young? he wondered.

Gil and Connie had joined them. 'Grandmother has taken it well,' commented Gil. The old dear was riding home in splendid isolation, had ordered the rest of the family to follow on together in the second car.

'He was a very sick man,' said Alice. She stared ahead through the windscreen, saw the back of her mother's head in the leading vehicle. It had always been like that, Alice told herself. Mother and Father together, everyone else several paces behind. Although now, there was no Father. 'He came home just to die,' Alice told her children.

That was not the truth, thought Gil, though he entertained this opinion in silence. Samuel Fishwick had returned to England in order to pursue unfinished business. In spite of the lack of proof, Gil felt certain that Eleanor Fishwick had ensured that any such transaction had remained incomplete.

Edward had no idea of what to do. Even the dog was quiet, as if it had been sedated. 'Has William eaten?' he asked Sheila.

Sheila closed her eyes and leaned back in the chair. The ability to close her eyes was a luxury, and she did not bother to raise the lids while she made her reply. 'I don't know. God alone can tell what's going on in Vera's mind. I kept her and the dog fed while we were away, but I'm telling you now, I've had enough. I've never been so tired in my life.'

Vera gazed at Edward Shawcross. He had got her into this terrible mess, yet he was unwilling to do anything about it. Oh, he had carried on about how he would support her and the child, about how he would leave his wife and live with her, William and the little stranger in her belly. But she didn't want Edward, not any more. She wanted the house to herself. The dog could stay, because he was no trouble, but Edward was a man. Men got women pregnant – that was how life carried on. Well, it could carry on without her. 'Go home,' she told him now.

He sat with his arms folded, wondered how the hell poor Sheila Foster had coped on that so-called holiday. There was a wildness in Vera's eyes, an expression that spoke volumes. It was plain that she had become unpredictable, that she might just run out of the house at any minute and jump under a bus or a train.

Sheila opened an eye. 'There's some scraps in the meatsafe,' she said. 'Bits of pie and some sausage and black pudding. Give them to the dog.' It occurred to her that she was giving orders to a boss, but she was well past caring. Let somebody else manage, let somebody else be accountable for a change.

Edward rose, took the animal into the kitchen. The place was a mess, cups and saucers piled in the sink, dirty clothes on a chair, grease all over the cooker. He fed the dog, noticed how ravenously the poor thing ate. If Vera could not care for a dog, she would be useless with a child. She was in a dreadful state. Her hair looked as if it hadn't been washed for a week, and the skin on her face had darkened, particularly round the eyes. Vera was not sleeping, was not eating properly, was failing to keep herself clean. Where was the lively woman who had made love on the floor in front of the fireplace? He stood in a filthy kitchen with a dog for company and wondered what the hell he was going to do.

The dog went outside, cocked a leg, dug up a bit of soil and worried a rubber bone. Edward leaned on the door jamb, knew that he could not leave Vera alone tonight. Sheila had done more than her fair share. Sheila Foster needed to get back to her own house for a decent night's sleep. He ran a hand through his hair, felt the dampness of his own sweat. It had been a long day, a day that had contained a funeral, a buffet meal for family and guests, then, to top it all, a phone call from Sheila. According to Vera's neighbour, Vera was out of order. Well, he had seen that for himself now. What must he do?

It was eight o'clock. The sun was thinking about doing its famous disappearing act, and the dog wanted to come back inside. Edward allowed

William to pass him, lingered for a few moments in the kitchen. There had to be someone who could move in and look after Vera for a day or two. Who, though? Who could he trust with this situation?

For a few seconds, he was back in Delta Street. A beautiful girl with bouncy, dark brown curls ran along the pavement, her arms outstretched, tears staining the pink cheeks. 'Eeh, Teddy,' she wept. 'Your poor mam, God love her. Come on to our house. We'll make you a nice butty and get you washed.' Sadie. Sadie Evans, whose father was the local ragman, whose mother worked at Kershaw's mill, had come to rescue him and Paul from their house. Teddy took the girl's hand and went with her to a nice, warm house with nice, warm people. His own dad was in the pub, of course. Mam was dead, and Dad was dead drunk, as ever.

The Evans family talked in hushed tones while Teddy ate his roast ham sandwich and Sadie went out to find his brother Paul. Their Paul was an adventurer, was always up to his neck in water or staggering about at the top of a mill chimney. Mam had just died of drink. Dad would probably die of it, too. Teddy and Paul, both skeletally slim, had survived thus far because of neighbours such as these. The Evanses, the Cromptons and the Warburtons had kept the two lads alive.

'Mr Shawcross?'

Edward shook himself into the present day.

'You were miles away,' said Sheila.

'And years away.' Gilbert was spending time with Sadie Martindale's daughter. Sadie Evans-as-was no longer had bouncy brown locks. Sadie had bad feet, grey hair and the heart of a lioness. He could talk to her, because she was still the woman who had cared for him during that other bad time.

'What are we going to do?' asked Sheila.

'I'm sorry,' he mumbled. 'You should not have been expected to cope.' He took a wallet from his inside pocket. 'Would twenty pounds be adequate compensation for your pain?'

Sheila Foster, who had a complexion pale enough to make a bleached pillowcase appear dirty, was suddenly beetroot red. She breathed in, steadied herself against the meatsafe, glared at Edward Shawcross. 'Don't you dare,' she whispered, the words strangled on their way out. 'I don't want your bloody money. You're all the same, you rich folk. Some things have no price, Mr Shawcross. Friendship is one of them.'

It was Edward's turn to blush. 'I didn't mean—'

'I need a rest, that's all,' she said. 'And some help when she starts acting daft. Don't you dare offer me money. You couldn't afford to pay for any of it, you ignorant sod.' She straightened, craned her neck towards him. 'I feel sorry for you,' she said. 'Because all the riches you have are in the damned bank. Apart from brass, you've got nowt.'

He tried to speak, but she rattled on. 'I'll see to her when I'm rested. Till then, get her sorted. She needs a doctor who'll talk to her about this baby. Not a pill-pusher, somebody who'll sit down and listen to her proper.' She nodded curtly. 'It's been a long month, Mr Shawcross. I'll see you soon.'

Edward followed Sheila into the living room. 'This is a great deal to ask, Mrs Foster, especially after all you've done, but could you stay a little longer? I need to go and find someone to take your place.'

Sheila, her feet planted on the front doormat, folded her arms. Her skin had returned to its proper shade of paleness. 'Aren't you stopping with her, then?' An invisible eyebrow was raised above a startlingly green iris. 'We thought you'd be moving in.'

'He's not,' snapped Vera.

Edward glanced back into the room at his lover. She was curled up like a frail autumn leaf, a dry, brittle thing with no hope for the future, no chance of survival. 'Vera,' he said softly. 'You are doing yourself harm.'

Vera, whose eyes were of a green softer than Sheila's, simply stared blankly at the man she supposedly loved. She wanted him to go away. If he would just bugger off, she might manage to forget her predicament for a minute or two. 'It's all over,' she mumbled finally. 'This one will likely kill me. If it doesn't, then I'll keep it and bring it up myself. If I come out of the mess in one piece, I don't want any more.' She looked him up and down, ran an eye over him as if assessing his value as a saleable or purchasable item. 'Just get gone,' she said wearily.

He staggered back as if he had been punched in the chest, steadied himself against the door frame. It occurred to him at that moment how much Vera had meant to him. She had cared for him, had cared about him, had been there simply for him. And now, he was alone once more. She had been his ticket, his hope for a better life in years to come. 'Why?' he asked.

Vera simply lowered her head and scowled.

Edward returned to Sheila. 'There's nothing else for it,' he said. 'I'll have to get . . . get someone to do the operation.'

Sheila maintained her rigid stance. 'You do as you please,' she answered calmly. 'But you'd best be ready to go to prison.' She nodded in Vera's direction. 'See her now? Well, that's nothing to what she'll be like after getting rid. If it's not blood poisoning, it'll be a nervous breakdown. She'll talk, I'm warning you. She'll say enough to have you locked up – and whoever does the abortion'll be keeping you company, too. So put that in your pipe and set fire to it, Mr Shawcross.'

He picked up his keys and walked to the door, standing perfectly still until Sheila moved to clear his path. Vera said nothing; she simply sat in her chair and stared at the floor.

Edward Shawcross walked slowly up Tintern Avenue. For discretion's sake, his car was parked on Tonge Moor Road, just a hundred or so yards away from Vera's house. But his progress was marked by the twitching of curtains and the sudden opening of doors. He was a marked man.

The journey to Sadie's house seemed endless. He drove through the town centre, slowed as the car nudged its way along Derby Street. There was no-one else; there was only Sadie Martindale.

Sadie was cleaning her Frigidaire with bicarbonate of soda and a few drops of white vinegar. Ethel Hyatt had got herself into a right dudgeon over Sadie's fridge. Ethel wanted one; poor Denis was doing all kinds of odd jobs to provide his wife with the means to keep up with the Martindales.

Sadie sighed, carried on cleaning. Bernard Martindale would be leaving home again in a matter of hours. He was at the pub, was saying a beery farewell to all his motley crew of mates. Tommy, bless him, had taken Dorothy Ingram to the Queen's Cinema where, no doubt, Mary would make sure they got plenty of ice-cream and popcorn.

Sadie sat down with the cloth in her hands. Everything seemed to be sorting itself out where her children were concerned. Bernard would get a career in the army, and Tommy was probably on the verge of settling down with young Dorothy. Mary, the unknown quantity, appeared happy enough to be a manager for the retired Mr and Mrs Smith. But Mary was ambitious. She saved every penny, was in full charge of her own destiny, it seemed. Gilbert Shawcross had received his marching orders from Mary; Mary had almost convinced the young man that she wouldn't be interested in anybody who left a job half done. So the unhappy lad would probably be on his way back to London when summer ended.

A frantic knocking forced Sadie to abandon her task and her daydreaming. Before she could reach the front door, it burst inward to reveal the sweaty face of Sadie Martindale's least favourite person in the whole world. 'Ethel?' Sadie managed. Was the kitchen tidy? Had she put the clean pots away?

Waiting for no invitation, Ethel Hyatt marched into Sadie's house, her eyes redder than her face.

'Ethel?' Sadie had never seen her next-door neighbour in such a state. 'Sit down. Shall I make a brew?'

Ethel shook her head.

'Something to eat?' She wouldn't mention the fridge, not this time. She'd a set orange jelly and a nice blancmange in the Frigidaire, but Ethel needed no more goading.

Sadie sat down opposite her neighbour. 'Ethel?' she said yet again.

A huge sigh travelled right through the large woman, causing various bumps and bulges to quiver with emotion. 'Have you seen him?' she asked.

'Eh?' Sadie thought for a moment. 'Who?'

'My Denis. He's gone.'

'Gone?' Sadie felt like a stupid parrot, but she couldn't seem to help herself. Denis had never gone anywhere without a special dispensation from his wife. A small and wiry man, Denis Hyatt went to work, came home after his shift, peeled spuds and veg, washed dishes, battered rugs in the back yard. Ethel did most of the outside chores, like windows and step, because she wanted the street to admire her handiwork. But everyone knew that she was the boss, while her husband did exactly as she ordered.

Ethel rolled her piggy eyes. 'I don't know what I've done to deserve this, Sadie.'

Sadie knew, though she set her mouth firmly in the closed position. Even a worm turned at the finish. Even a man as browbeaten as poor Denis Hyatt had a modicum of self-respect in his puny breast. 'Has he gone shopping?' asked Sadie. 'Happen he ran out of something.'

'Don't talk daft.' Ethel wiped a tear from a rounded cheek. 'It's past closing. There's only the outdoor licence open, and I sent him up for no beer and toffees, did I?' She sniffed back a few more drops of grief. 'And he wouldn't need his suit and all his shirts to go shopping, would he?'

Sadie tried to think of a reply, found no suitable words.

'He's left me, Sadie.' These words were delivered with very heavy drama. 'He's gone and left me. And,' she sat up suddenly, as if she had received a double dose of some medicine that provoked anger, 'he's took half my knives and forks, some plates, cups, sheets and blankets. Best towels and all.'

'How did he carry that lot?' Sadie was practical, as

always. Then she remembered. 'Did you go to the market today?'

Ethel nodded. 'I got some nice cod fillets and some lovely new spuds. And he weren't even there to bloody eat them. Why?'

'Well, there were a horse and cart in the back street. I thought it must have been a ragman giving the animal a drink, 'cos it were there a while. Your gate opened and closed a couple of times, but I put that down to you filling the bucket for the horse and fetching rags for the cart. You must have been at the market then, only I thought you'd come back. There was somebody in your house at about half past three, Ethel. And I never gave it a thought, honest. Wasn't Denis at work?'

Ethel nodded. 'Aye, he were. Well, he were supposed to be at work.'

'Then he's took time off.' Sadie paused for thought. 'You'll have to go round to Swan Lane tomorrow, Ethel. You could happen catch him after his shift finishes.' In spite of her sympathy for the escaped man, Sadie entertained a feeling of pity for Ethel, too. Ethel Hyatt looked as if she'd been clocked across the face with half a housebrick. 'You should have a cuppa, love,' said Sadie. 'With sugar for shock.'

Ethel placed a hand on her heaving bosom. 'I couldn't swallow to save my life, Sadie. What am I going to do?'

'Go round to the mill tomorrow and—'

'If he won't come back, what'll I do?' Ethel had managed not to work since the birth of her first son. During the war, she'd been drafted to clean at the munitions factory, but, apart from that, Ethel had kept house while Denis had gone out to earn the money. 'Me kids is all gone with families of their own. I've nobody.'

Ethel Hyatt's children had disappeared over the horizon like bats out of hell at the first opportunity. She'd been a very strict mother, had often chastised her offspring physically. In fact, one or two of the poor little buggers had been marked from time to time. 'Happen he'll be back tomorrow,' suggested Sadie.

'No.' Ethel Hyatt dragged herself to the edge of her seat. 'He's took all that stuff because he's found another woman. He'll be setting up house with some bloody floozy he's met.'

Sadie could not imagine Denis with a floozy, no matter how hard she tried. She couldn't imagine him with a life of his own, either.

'I'm not showing meself up,' insisted Ethel. 'Crawling round to the mill and begging him to come home.' The rubbery lower lip quivered again. 'But how am I going to pay me rent? I can't. I'll have to move in with one of me children.'

Sadie Martindale kept quiet. Nobody would take Ethel in, especially anyone who knew her well. She was too loud, too bossy and too nosey. 'Bernard's going in the army tomorrow,' she said eventually, making a feeble effort to change the subject.

Tear-reddened eyes looked up at Sadie. 'Ooh, I couldn't, love.'

'Eh?' Had Sadie missed something?

'Well, there's still only the two bedrooms, even with your Bernard gone. Mind, we've all took turns sleeping downstairs, haven't we? I know me and Denis had the parlour when the kids were young. I'll think about it. Ta for offering.'

Sadie backtracked her way through the conversation. She hadn't offered anything. She certainly didn't want Ethel Hyatt moving in. Hurriedly, she invented a relative in Liverpool. 'She might be moving in,' said the hostess mournfully. 'Since her husband died, she's been that miserable—'

'What did you say her name was?'

'Our . . . Margaret. She's a second cousin. I said I'd take her in if she felt like a change.' This was terrible. She should not be telling lies, though the truth would have been far more painful. 'Try and get your Denis back, Ethel. I can't imagine how he'll carry on without you.'

Ethel blew her nose on a rag. Nobody used best handkerchieves except for special occasions, and Ethel was no exception to this rule. 'I suppose I'd best go home.' The lip trembled again. 'It's not like home without him, Sadie. I know he's not much, but he's me husband. There's no way I can sleep on me own. I've never slept on me own for years.'

Sadie raised her eyes to heaven. Here she was with Ethel weeping all over the place and now there was somebody else battering a fist against the door. Tonight, the Martindales' house was like the Blackpool platform at Trinity Street Station during Bolton holidays. She abandoned Ethel and walked down the narrow lobby.

Edward smiled hesitantly when the door opened. 'Sadie?'

She frowned, glanced over her shoulder. 'I've somebody here,' she whispered.

'I'm desperate,' he replied.

'So's my neighbour. Her husband's done a disappearing act after thirty-odd years.' She didn't know what to do. Even nuisances like Ethel Hyatt needed help occasionally. 'You'll have to go in the parlour.' She grabbed his arm, dragged him inside and shoved him into the front room. 'All we want now is a brass band and the Hallelujah chorus,' she muttered on her way back to the kitchen.

'Who were that?' Ethel was just closing the fridge door.

'Nobody.'

'But I heard a knock. Is it Denis?'

'No.'

Ethel gathered up her nose-rag and what remained of her dignity. 'Sorry I troubled you, Sadie,' she said. 'Will you go with me to Swan Lane tomorrow?'

Sadie promised that she would think about it, then ushered Ethel Hyatt out of the house. In the lobby, she leaned against the wall for a second or two, wishing with all her heart that Teddy Shawcross, Ethel Hyatt, Uncle Tom Cobleigh and any others would just bugger off and leave her alone. She'd been ironing Bernard's bits and pieces for hours, and then—

'Sadie?'

'I'm coming.' He had stuck his head out of the parlour door. 'Go in the kitchen,' she told him.

He sat at the table and remembered another occasion when a man had needed help. There had been a chessboard and a pack of cards, fish and chip suppers, a doctor and a lawyer. This situation was similar, because it involved an illicit relationship. 'I'm in a mess,' he said bluntly. 'A real pickle.'

Sadie sighed resignedly and sat opposite him.

'It's difficult,' he continued, 'because your daughter and my son have been . . . seeing a great deal of one another.' If Sadie helped, she would need to be discreet. He remembered the twitching curtains, knew that his secret would be out in the open soon enough. But the thought of Gilbert discussing any of this with Sadie's daughter made him less than comfortable.

Sadie's spine was suddenly poker-straight. 'Eh? What's me daughter been up to?' Surely Mary wasn't in any trouble?

'Oh, it's not Mary,' he said quickly. 'And it's not Gilbert, either. I'm the culprit.'

She stared at him quizzically, clasping her hands on the green velveteen cloth. 'Spit it out, Teddy. I've a lad going in the army tomorrow, so there's a few things needs doing.'

Spit it out? He wasn't looking forward to the sound of it, the taste of it. Here he sat with a woman who had recently been carpeted for smoking at work, and he had no choice but to beg for her help. 'I've never forgotten, Sadie,' he said.

'I know that, lad.'

'Outside work, we're still old friends, I hope.'

She gave him an encouraging smile. 'Do you want a cuppa? I'm having one, because I'm fair clemmed.' She got up, rattled the kettle, stuck it on the fire. 'I'll brew in here so we can keep an eye on the kettle. Gas ring's through there.' She waved a hand in the direction of the scullery. 'But I'm old-fashioned, I like the taste of smoky water.' She sat down again. 'Come on, I've not all night, you know. Our Bernard's packing still wants finishing.'

Edward inhaled deeply. 'Sadie, I'm in dreadful trouble. More to the point, my lady friend is in trouble. And I don't know where to turn, because she's gone strange.'

Sadie blinked a couple of times. 'In the head?'

He nodded. 'A neighbour's been seeing to her. I sent them away for the best part of a month, hoped

248

the air in Devonshire would buck her up. But it didn't. She seems to have some terrible fears, the sort that can't be reasoned with.' He paused, closed his eyes, caught a mental picture of Vera's face. 'She wanted an abortion, but I couldn't risk that. And I want . . . I wanted . . .'

'You wanted the kiddy?'

He opened his eyes. 'Yes. I wanted her, too.' He stood up, began to pace about the room. 'My marriage hasn't been . . . perfect. It's not Alice's fault. It was the way things were with her parents – oh, ages ago. That's all water under the bridge, but we're not happy, Alice and I. So I found this other life, this—'

'This other woman, you mean.'

'Yes. She was everything I wanted, warm, humorous, energetic, intelligent.' He shrugged.

'So she were all them things, and now she's none of them.'

'Nail on the head, Sadie.' He stood at the window and looked at Sadie's yard, a tiny place with an air raid shelter taking up more than its fair share of space. 'I am at my wits' end. She—' He turned, looked at Sadie. Sadie was tired to the point of exhaustion. What was he doing here? This woman had troubles enough of her own.

'Go on,' she urged gently.

There was nothing else for it. He would have to telephone Alice and say that he was staying out for the night. Lying was just a skill he needed to work on. 'I'm sorry,' he said. 'I shouldn't have come.'

'Course you should. It'll go no further.'

'I know that.'

She tapped on the table with her fingers. 'What do you want me to do?'

249

Edward considered the question. He wanted her to have eyes in the back of her head, needed someone who could stay awake twenty-four hours a day until . . . until when? Until he moved out of Aston Leigh and into Tintern Avenue? The idea made his stomach churn. Vera wasn't Vera any more. She was empty, like a house that had been deserted by its tenants. 'I don't know, Sadie.' He returned to the table and sat down. 'My father-in-law was buried this morning. Things are up in the air. There'll be a will to sort out, the business, my children.'

'And your wife.'

He nodded.

'And are you planning on setting up home with this lady friend of yours?'

He wasn't planning anything, not now. He was just trying to keep Vera safe, because if anything happened to her, that would be his fault, and he would probably live with the guilt for the rest of his days. 'That was the idea.'

'But you've changed your mind.'

Edward had not changed his mind; Vera had made all the changes. 'Things are different now. She is terrified of giving birth. Her sister lost several babies, then she died after the last one was stillborn. Vera has got it into her head that she will not survive. She's not well, not her normal self.'

'So you're looking for a nurse? Why don't you hire a proper one?' He could afford it, after all. He was a boss, owner of a mill, he was— A sudden thought bombarded her mind. 'You don't own Fishwick's, do you?'

'No.'

Sadie lit a Woodbine, inhaled deeply, coughed. 'Teddy, you're not sure how you're going to be placed, I suppose. I mean, it's not likely you'll be bag and baggaged out of the house, but things could be different, like, depending on old Mr Fishwick's will. So there might be no money for a nurse.' She took another drag of tobacco smoke. 'You'd have been a lot worse off if you'd moved in with this woman.'

He lowered his head. 'I loved her, Sadie. I still love the Vera I remember. And I've saved. When I look back, I did quite a good job, because I kept the mill going, kept the workers paid, kept my family, kept Samuel and Eleanor in the style to which they had become accustomed.' He raised his chin, looked at his companion. 'I was going to walk out, Sadie. I was going to take my own clothes and my bank book, and I intended to live with Vera in a council house up Tonge Moor.'

She swallowed. 'What about being an alderman?'

'Bugger that. She was . . . she was magnificent.'

'Then she still is.'

He shook his head sadly. 'No, Sadie. She thought she couldn't have children. She's been . . . irregular. She felt safe, because she had convinced herself that she'd never become pregnant. This has changed her. Even if she lost this baby, she would continue to live in dread of a repeat performance. So would I.'

Sadie was looking at a beaten man. Teddy Shawcross had taken life by the horns over twenty years earlier, had thrown himself headlong into his work, had lived in a loveless marriage, had become an important local figure. 'Why don't you just go home, lad? Let this woman take care of herself. You've two lovely children. Our Mary thinks the world of that boy, and she's not easy pleased. And you owe your wife something, don't you?'

He shrugged listlessly. 'I can't let Vera kill herself.

The relationship is an open secret, anyway. I'm sure Alice has heard the rumours. There is no way I can deny Vera. She is my responsibility.'

'I can't help you tonight, love. But you can pick me up at dinner time tomorrow, and I'll stop with her till you get sorted. Leave worrying about our Mary to me, I'll do the explaining.' She smiled encouragingly. 'And keep me little job open, Mr Shawcross.' He was Teddy, he was Mr Shawcross and he was Alderman Shawcross. He was also dangerously close to becoming a broken man.

TEN

Maurice Dyson, now as shrivelled as a very pale prune, was still a practising lawyer. He was the one who had sent Edward on an errand some twenty-three years earlier; he was the one who had arranged for the Turnbull family to be placated after the death of Molly. He cleared his throat, turned over a leaf of rich vellum, then peered over his spectacles at the family.

Mr Dyson knew the contents of this old will by heart. The document would leave Edward Shawcross at the mercy of Samuel Fishwick's widow. Apart from four separate bequests, each valued at one thousand pounds, the whole property had been left to Eleanor. Maurice Dyson, who had met some characters in his long life, had never been at ease in the presence of Eleanor Fishwick. She had been rather too supportive back in 1927, too determinedly unmoved by her husband's folly.

Eleanor glanced at her watch. 'We're waiting, Mr Dyson,' she said coolly.

The solicitor read out the boring bits, the jargon that was supposed to reassure the reader of the testator's sanity, then he got down to business. Four thousand pounds had been set aside for Edward,

Alice, Constance and Gilbert. '"The bulk of my estate, including the property known as Aston Leigh and the factory trading as Fishwick's, is for my wife, Eleanor Fishwick",' intoned Mr Dyson.

Eleanor tightened her lips to prevent a smile from escaping. She had done it. She had made sure that Samuel had left nothing to the by-blow. 'So that's that,' she said, a manicured hand patting the front of her hair. She looked around, nodded at Edward, Alice and the children. 'We shall talk later,' she told them. 'Of course, there will be no changes at the house. I think we can all manage to co-exist for the time being. And I shall certainly not ask you to leave Aston Leigh, as it is your home.'

Gilbert was suddenly almost glad about university. He had not wanted to return to London, still dreaded leaving Mary, but his need to separate himself from Grandmother Fishwick was horribly strong. She was a strange woman, one who did not allow emotion to stain her face. She was, he felt sure, quite capable of feathering her own nest with no regard for anyone else. Was she a murderess? Had she killed her husband?

Connie nudged him. He was staring again, was sitting with his eyes fixed on the old woman. Gil had been quite annoying lately, had been chattering on about this Peter Turnbull fellow, had been wondering where to look for him. It was all of no consequence, because poor old Grandfather, whose mind had probably deteriorated towards the end, was now dead and buried.

Edward yawned behind a hand. Two nights with Vera had rendered him almost immobile. She had ranted and wept, she had rocked to and fro in a chair for hours at a time, had escaped twice from the house.

Sadie Martindale was minding Vera today, then Sheila Foster had volunteered to do a few nights. No-one had mentioned Edward's absence from home. It seemed that he had not been missed at all.

Alice had noticed, though she continued to say nothing. He had begun to leave. She had expected it to be sudden, but her husband was absconding a little at a time, was building up to the grand exit, she supposed. The woman was red-haired and as thin as a twig. She lived just off Tonge Moor Road in a shoebox of a house with a handkerchief sized garden at the front. The private detective had been well worth the forty pounds.

'Mother?'

'Yes, Connie?'

'Would you like a cup of tea in Tognarelli's?'

Tognarelli's. How long was it since Alice had been there? Situated at the top of a building on Mealhouse Lane, Tognarelli's offered knicker-bocker glories, banana splits, milkshakes, hot or cold Vimto, ice-creams in all flavours. It was a place for children, somewhere to go when a day trip to Blackpool was out of the question, or when infants needed coaxing on those dreary shopping-for-school days. 'If you'll try some shoes on, I'll take you to Tognarelli's,' mothers would promise.

'Mother? Tognarelli's?'

'That would be lovely,' said Alice. Had the detective really been worth his money? What difference did knowing Vera Hardman's name make? Edward didn't love his wife, had never loved her. Alice's parents had simply wanted to be rid of their daughter, had even been willing to pass her on to a man with no education. 'Are you coming with us, Mother?' Alice asked Eleanor.

'Certainly not. The place will be full of young people and noise. Mr Dyson will drive me home.' She sounded so imperious, had obviously been thoroughly ruined by her long sojourn in foreign lands.

Edward was holding the door open while Mr Dyson gathered up papers. Alice would not invite her husband to join them. Gilbert was coming, though. Perhaps this was the opportunity, Alice thought. If they could find a quietish corner, she might be able to talk to her children about . . . about an idea that had begun to shape itself in her mind. It was frightening. Alice chased out the fear, pushed herself out of the lawyer's offices. Tognarelli's was just two doors away, its open doorway displaying a wide flight of stairs. It was quite a climb, but Alice was fit for it.

Connie gazed into her dish. Heaven must be a place like Tognarelli's, she mused ecstatically. Manna from above, ambrosia, nectar and all the rest of those poetic edibles could surely hold no candle to the magnificence of Mr Tognarelli's splits. There was a bit of melted vanilla in her dish, so she picked up the long-handled spoon and chased it about. 'I used to lick it when I was little,' she said to no-one in particular.

'Do it,' said Alice. Licking out a dish in public was nothing compared to Alice's half-formed plan. From whence had this odd idea arisen? she wondered. And why was it sticking in her brain like a gramophone record with a blunt needle wedged in the scratched groove?

The junior Shawcrosses looked hard at their mother. She had gone peculiar, was thinner, sharper, rather less than conventional. Getting used to a newborn mother was extremely confusing and difficult. They had always known what to expect – wipe your nose, straighten your tie, stand up properly or you'll grow deformed. Connie was the first to speak. 'Grandmother can throw us all out now,' she said.

Alice shrugged lightly. 'She won't. Mind, if we stay, I want the whole place redecorated. It's so gloomy. But the mill will go,' she told her children. 'British cotton's on the decline anyway. In her place, I would certainly off-load the business. Once the loose ends are tied, Mother will go hot-foot down to London to find herself a rich widower.'

Gil's jaw dropped. 'He'd have to be blind, or stupid, or both.'

Alice's mouth twitched. 'Then pray that she does find a blind and certified lunatic, because she'll go through every last shilling if she doesn't marry again. Mother likes the good life.'

Connie thought about the awesome concept of poverty. 'Well, I'll have to get a proper job now.'

'We shall see,' said Alice vaguely, her eyes fixed on a young man who was ladling ice-cream into a tall glass.

'Just have a small one,' suggested Gil.

Alice shook her head. 'I need to lose another couple of stones, because my life has been somewhat less than active.' She inhaled deeply. 'Starting a new business is going to require an enormous amount of energy.'

Connie dropped her spoon. 'You're going to work?'

Alice nodded. 'We are all going to work.' She grinned at Gil. 'It's young Mary's fault,' she said jokingly. 'I seem to have caught your lady friend's disease, the need for a business of my own.' She pondered for a split second. 'A business of our own,' she amended. 'For all of us.'

Gil finished off his ice-cream, mopped his lip with a handkerchief and wondered whether his mother had finally flipped her lid. The best thing would be to humour her, he decided. 'A shop? Is that the sort of business you envisage?' He knew that Mary was keen on retail.

Alice fixed cool grey eyes on her son. He was a decorative boy, quite suitable for what she had in mind. 'You each have a thousand pounds,' she said. 'I have several thousand, because my grandparents left me some stocks and so forth. There is a property on Deansgate that used to house offices and small shops. Enquiries are being made on our behalf.'

Connie and Gil noticed the 'our' again, waited for more.

'That friend of yours,' continued Alice, her attention awarded now to Gil. 'Mary. She has a few ideas in her head about a restaurant. But my plans are rather larger than that.' She took a deep breath. 'We should open a department store, nothing too grand, but with some good fashions, shoes, accessories, a section for men's clothing, too. There is ample space on the ground floor for kitchen and restaurant. Those American chainstores are all very well, based on penny bazaars and so forth. But a family concern is always a good thing. We would not be faceless creatures in some New York or London boardroom.'

One day, Gil thought, a man might walk on the moon. There were all kinds of crazy notions about space travel, comics that fired the imagination of lively boys. There was more chance of man living on

Mars than of Mother serving at a shop counter. 'We've no experience,' he said.

Alice inclined her head. 'When cotton started to come into Lancashire, no-one had experience of it. Crofters bought spinning wheels and looms, taught themselves how to spin and weave. If you would care to count the chimneys in this town, you would find dozens, Gilbert. Lack of experience did not stop the growth of that particular industry. All we need is confidence, some financial advice and a few books. Oh, and a visit to Harrods and Fortnum's would not come amiss.'

Connie grinned broadly. 'Mother, what on earth is Father going to say?'

'What does he ever say?' was Alice's response.

'Nothing,' replied Gil. 'Well, very little.'

Alice picked up her handbag. 'Exactly. And I think you'll find that he'll be saying even less in a month or so from now.' She stood up. 'Right. Come along, troops. We shall take a stroll, and I'll show you the building I have in mind.'

Maurice Dyson's car turned into the driveway of Aston Leigh. He got out, walked round to the passenger side and opened the door. Eleanor Fishwick placed a hand on his, swung her legs onto terra firma, alighted with elegance. 'Thank you,' she said vaguely. 'You will telephone me, of course, when someone makes an offer for the factory.'

This was not a question; it was an order from a superior being to one of her minions. 'Of course, Mrs Fishwick.' He managed not to touch his forelock as she waved coolly in his direction.

To underline the dismissal, she awarded him a nod, then walked up to the front door and let herself in. The house was as quiet as the grave. Lottie Bowker, cook to the Shawcross family, had been given the day off, while little Ada Dobson was out shopping. Disgruntled by the lack of attendants, Eleanor made her way upstairs. Tognarelli's, indeed. What on earth was Alice thinking of?

The doorbell sounded. Eleanor sat down at the dressing table, removed her hat, pouted at herself in the mirror. The face was lined, but she had seen worse. When the visitor rang the bell again, she rose impatiently and went to answer. She was unused to doing things for herself. For many years, she had even had a dresser, a little woman who had washed, ironed, sewn, altered clothes and waited on Eleanor Fishwick in exchange for meals and a few pennies for her family. But all that was in the past.

'Mrs Fishwick?' The young man was tall and thin with dark hair and hazel eyes. He had chosen his moment carefully, had waited on the lane occasionally since Samuel's death, had finally found the widow on her own. 'I'm Peter Turnbull.'

Eleanor staggered back, a hand to her throat. The nightmare had arrived, had spoilt the new dream of wealth and freedom. 'What do you want?' she asked, the words emerging in a whisper.

'Just my due,' he replied.

She allowed him to enter the hall before any passing person caught sight of him. 'You have been provided for,' she said eventually. There was a slackness round his jaw, while a small paunch advertised his liking for beer. 'You have been supported by my family since—'

'Since I was born. Since my mother died. And now, your husband is dead,' said Peter Turnbull. 'My father is dead.'

Eleanor tut-tutted, her head moving slowly from side to side in a gesture of denial. 'Your father? My husband was not your father.'

'Can you prove that?' His upper lip curled in a sneer.

'The onus is on you,' she said. 'Can you prove that Samuel was your father?'

Turnbull nodded, dragged an envelope from his jacket. 'This came about two months ago. From Cairo. He wrote to me, told me that he had changed his will and that I was to come into the business and get a share of profits. He has admitted on paper that he's my father.'

Eleanor sat down suddenly in a Chippendale corner chair, her hands grasping the curved edges of its arms. 'That's impossible,' she gasped. 'He was too ill to write.'

'But he managed, Mrs Fishwick.'

Eleanor rallied determinedly. This young man was not quite what she had expected. He talked reasonably well, seemed sure of himself, was definitely not without brains. 'Is his name on your birth certificate?'

'No.'

'Then he is not your father.'

Peter Turnbull gazed around the entrance hall, saw valuable pieces of furniture and porcelain, paintings on the walls, a tapestry halfway up the stairs. 'Your husband gave the house I live in to my grandfather,' he said. 'As compensation, or so I was told. I can prove that I've had an income from Edward Shawcross, and my uncle, who has moved south, knows the whole story. So smoke that, Mrs Fishwick.'

She concentrated on breathing steadily, ordered her brain to click into gear. This man's face had hardened, and she caught a glimpse of the rapscallion described by Edward. If only Samuel had not written that damned letter. Without the letter, she might have managed to deny this man's claims. She fought for calm, remained still and silent for a few seconds.

'Well?' sneered the intruder.

The possibility of Peter Turnbull putting in an appearance after Samuel's death had been strong, but, in the absence of tangible proof, the man's assertions could have been dismissed. Perhaps Samuel had, out of the goodness of his heart, kept the Turnbull family ticking over after the various tragedies they had endured; perhaps Edward, too, had handed over money. After all, charity was to be praised, and hadn't the grandfather been crippled? Hadn't this young man's mother died tragically? But now, there appeared to be actual proof of Samuel's paternity. Now, her whole future was suddenly threatened.

'Are you all right, missus?' Sarcasm hemmed the words.

'Of course.' She forced a smile to pay a brief visit to her face. 'May I see that for a moment?' She reached for the letter.

'No.' He removed a sheet of paper from the manila envelope, held it a distance away from her face. 'You're not getting your hands on this, Mrs Fishwick. Not unless you pay for it. But look, that's his signature – and here – "I have altered my will and have expressed a wish for you to be employed in the mill in some suitable capacity . . . and you shall, therefore, have a share in the profits, such sums to be paid to you on a quarterly basis . . . if the mill is sold, you will benefit from the sale."' He folded the page, replaced it in its envelope, thrust the whole thing into his pocket. 'A lawyer will make a good case out of that.'

Eleanor shrugged. 'Do as you please. We shall fight you, of course. And how will you afford the legal fees?'

He nodded wisely. 'I've a house I can sell, Mrs Fishwick.'

She tapped her fingernails against polished oak. 'Very well,' she said. 'But things are up in the air just now, Mr Turnbull. I am selling Fishwick's mill. Of course, the price will not be good, as cotton mills are not very profitable just now.'

'I can't wait for that,' he said. 'I'm broke now.'

Eleanor was a seventy-year-old woman who was suddenly aware of her age. Here she sat, having reached the frailer side of life, having released her poor husband from unbearable pain, having left behind a wonderful lifestyle, only to find that a healthy young man was threatening her security. 'I shall meet you,' she said carefully. Her mind raced. 'Just let us recover from the funeral first. My daughter is very upset and—'

'My half-sister, you mean.'

Determinedly, Eleanor forged ahead. 'And any hint of this could make Alice ill. Perhaps I could visit your home in a few weeks?'

He didn't want her in his house. She was a tight-faced old hag with wily eyes. 'No,' he replied. She was clever, far too clever for his liking. 'Somewhere else.'

Eleanor attempted a smile. 'I shall send some money to your address by registered post. Immediately, of course. Then . . . three weeks from today shall we say? In a place of your choosing, naturally.'

'Why not now?' he asked. 'What difference will a few weeks make?'

Eleanor found herself gabbling, as if trying to overtake the speed at which her frantic mind was working. 'The executors have things to do, papers to sign, properties to transfer. Nothing can happen overnight.'

He paced up and down for a few moments. 'Three weeks tonight, then,' he decided. 'And I'll come here after dark.'

'You must not come to Aston Leigh,' said Eleanor.

'Right. I'll be in that field across the road, then. And the cash you're sending – fifty quid'll do for now. In three weeks, I'll be wanting a letter from you. You can write it all down.'

'Write what?'

'That I'm his son, that the mill's partly mine.'

'Very well.' Her thoughts were all over the place. 'But not near the house, please. Go up to the top of The Rise, past the big house and to the woods. No-one must see us.'

'Three weeks tonight,' he snapped. 'Be there.'

She plastered an expression of grief across her face. 'This house is in mourning, Mr Turnbull. I shall tell my daughter and grandchildren about you only when they have recovered from the shock of Samuel's death. You must stay well away from Aston Leigh . . . Peter.' The name almost choked her. 'I'll be at the edge of the woods as soon as possible after dusk.' She nodded quickly. 'I shall write the letter you require, and a cheque for a further one thousand pounds. That should keep you in funds until the factory is sold. In return, you will give me that letter from Samuel.'

'Eh? I'm not parting with this.'

'Oh for goodness' sake,' she said. 'You will have the same statement from me. I just want my husband's letter back. You will have no need of it, not when you have my admission on paper. I promise that you will come out of this very handsomely, Peter.'

He didn't trust her. But what could an old woman possibly do to him? She was the wrong side of seventy, looked as if a puff of wind could bowl her over. 'All right,' he said. 'But no funny stuff.'

Eleanor sat perfectly still while the young man made his exit. For how much longer must she continue paying for her husband's indiscretion? The Turnbull family had taken a large amount of money over the years, money that should have come to Eleanor.

Ada Dobson entered by the front door, stopped in her tracks when she saw Eleanor Fishwick sitting in the hall. 'Who were that?' she asked innocently. 'He passed me on the drive.'

Eleanor jumped to her feet with an alacrity that was enviable in a woman of her years. 'How dare you?' she shrieked. 'How dare you enter my house by the main door? You are a servant, girl. You do not enter except by the rear porch. Do you understand?'

Ada's lip quivered. Things had started to get so much better, because the mistress seemed to have improved of late. But now, there was this old horror to contend with.

'Are you heeding me?'

'Yes, Mrs Fishwick.'

'Then take your parcels and your baskets and get out of here. Go through the front door, then walk round to the kitchen. Remember your place. This is my house, mine.'

Ada wept buckets as she made her way along the side of Aston Leigh. Mrs Shawcross had never bothered about which door got used. Of course, Ada would not have entered that way if company had been in the house, but there had been no company. Just that nasty old woman, that was all.

The nasty old woman poured herself a sherry. It was early for alcohol, but she deserved it. Her heart settled down as the drink hit the spot, and she sat in the drawing room with her fingers tapping the side of the glass. Peter Turnbull had to be eliminated. Getting rid of Samuel had been easy, necessary. Poor Samuel's pain had been dreadful, she kept reminding herself. She had done him a service, had eased his way out.

This was a different matter altogether. Turnbull was young and robust, might easily overpower her. However, he was not immortal, and she had twenty-one days during which she could make plans. Bullets felled most things; even elephants dropped to their knees when targeted by the right calibre. Samuel's handgun was upstairs, was still packed away at the bottom of a cabin trunk. Tonight, she would find it, clean it, load it. In a few weeks, she would use it.

Bodies were messy things. They were not easy to shift, were very heavy, especially once they had stiffened with rigor. But there were plenty of trees, plenty of hiding places. Few people went into those woods, because the ground was so rough, so uneven. Alice had been forbidden to play in the woods, because getting lost would have been so easy. A pretty child, she had been once.

What about the sound? Would anyone hear the firing of the gun? Even if somebody did hear, poachers would be blamed. Would anyone miss

Turnbull? She thought the problem through, realized that she had no choice. Alive, he was definitely dangerous. Dead, he would not blackmail her, would not speak up for himself. And who would possibly suspect an old lady of murder?

Eleanor poured a second sherry and waited for her family to return from town. She had their interests at heart as well as her own. For everyone's sake, she must shoot Peter Turnbull in exactly three weeks from today.

'What do you think?' Alice Shawcross swung the key in her hand, allowing its string holder to wind around her fingers.

'It's big, Mother,' replied Connie.

Gil was still at the head-scratching stage. Unlike Connie, he had been privy to few of Alice's thoughts in recent weeks. But the picture was here for him to see, now. Mother was a couple of inches smaller all round, a couple of slates short on the roof. 'How?' he managed at last. 'How do we fill it?'

Alice wheeled round slowly and smiled at her son. 'With dreams, Gilbert,' she said softly. 'We fill this place with dreams.'

Almost convinced that his mother needed a doctor, Gil kept his counsel, decided to humour her for now.

It was a big shop that had once been several small shops, that had recently been a warehouse-cum-offices. The outside of the building was quaint, the two upper storeys in that black-and-white effect copied from Tudor times. There were several doors, some large windows, a few smallish ones, and steps here and there where the ground floor changed levels.

'Hats,' mused Alice aloud. 'To a woman, a hat is a statement. She can change who she is simply by wearing a different hat. Tailor-made dresses and costumes, tailor-made suits for men. Fabrics for those who prefer to make their clothes at home. Handbags, gloves, scarves, ready-made clothes. China, lovely ornaments and dishes at the lowest prices we can manage.'

'Mother.' Gil cleared his throat. 'You're talking about a department store. Owners of those are millionaires who can afford to buy in bulk and keep the stuff in warehouses. We're not in that category.'

'Nor do we want to be,' replied Alice smartly. 'Select but affordable is the ground we shall cover.'

Connie knew little about business, yet she managed to be excited. There was a separate part on the ground floor, an area with its own door leading onto Deansgate. 'Mary's restaurant, Gil,' she said. 'Over there, through that door. There's even room for a little dance floor in the middle.'

Gilbert Shawcross had a suspicion that both his female relatives had taken leave of their senses. The war was not long over; there were still shortages, and one of those shortages was money. 'Who will buy?' he asked.

Alice smiled at him. 'In the corner of most women's purses, there are what I call dream pennies. Those pennies are saved by . . . by buying less bleach or a cheaper cut of meat. We shall have club cards, Gilbert. Customers can buy outright, or they may want to pay a certain sum from time to time as savings towards a purchase. We shall keep those things set aside upstairs. Their money will be in our account gaining a little interest. No-one loses.'

Connie was developing a great admiration for

Mother. At the age of forty-three, Alice Shawcross was showing signs of self-respect. 'We have to try this,' Connie told her brother.

'Oh, indeed we do,' added Alice. 'I need your money,' she told both of them. 'Gilbert, you are not going to become a scientist. Carry on at university if you wish, because education is seldom wasted, but I feel that you would be happier here doing a real job, meeting people, working towards a new family business.' She straightened her shoulders. Straightening her back made her thinner, taller, more confident. 'Your grandmother will sell the mill. So we shall simply find something else to do.'

'What about Father?' asked Connie.

Alice looked at the floor, wondered about carpeting, parquet, linoleum. 'Your father has his own plans, perhaps. He will tell you in time, I'm sure. But Edward will not be interested in this.'

They walked through the whole building, found two further floors with an office, toilets for staff, storerooms. 'The ground and first floors will be sales areas,' said Alice. 'And the top will be for offices and the storage of small items. Yes. We shall do very well here.' Interested in life at last, Alice Shawcross led her children homeward.

Sadie Martindale had achieved the impossible; she had managed to get the better of Vera Hardman. It seemed that Vera had finally met her match, because Sadie stood for no nonsense whatsoever. Two new locks had been fitted, one each to the front and back doors. The keys to Vera's domain were now hanging on a long piece of string round Sadie Martindale's neck. She wore this rather non-decorative item inside her clothing, allowed it to mix with whalebone, elastic and cotton somewhere near her equator.

Vera was bucking up very slightly. The notion that she might survive the birth had arrived with the lessening of nausea and the victory of Sadie Martindale. 'It's one of them things that happens,' Sadie explained wisely. 'You get stuff in your blood when you're pregnant.'

'Stuff?'

Sadie nodded. 'Aye. Your bones gets stronger and you start feeling happy.'

'I'm not happy,' insisted the expectant mother.

'No, but you're better than you were.'

Vera considered the statement. She had arrived at a place where life or death didn't seem to matter. She was simply riding with the flow, was taking each day as it came. 'I'm not going through this again, though,' she told her companion.

Sadie unplugged the iron from the light fitting, then replaced the lamp. 'You don't have to. You can get yourself doctored, just tell them you're in pain and all that. A woman up Swan Lane had it done for growths in her womb, fibroids, I think. Aye, get neutered. Or there's things you can use – not that I know much about all that carry-on. Neutered would be safest.' Contraception didn't always work, mused Sadie. Vera was one of the few who needed to unload their equipment for the sake of sanity.

'Shall I book in at the vet's, then?' asked Vera.

'Please yourself.' It wasn't a bad job. Sadie arrived at nine o'clock every morning, left at six. A nice woman called Sheila Foster did the nights, and Edward Shawcross called in at least once a day. Sadie got all her meals and a few quid at the end of every week. Saturdays and Sundays, she swapped with

Sheila, staying at home during the day and in Vera's spare bedroom at night. 'Shall I make a brew?'

Vera nodded, dropped a stitch, cursed loudly. 'I can't be doing with this thin wool,' she said. 'And I hate lemon. Why does everything have to be lemon and white?' Sadie's idea of occupational therapy did not suit Vera, but Sadie was one of those people who couldn't seem to take no as an answer.

At least she was trying, Sadie told herself as she went to make the tea. It had been hard going for the first few weeks, because Vera had even refused to wash and dress, but she was clean at last, was eating occasionally.

'I don't want him here any more,' called Vera from the living room.

Sadie retraced her steps. 'You what?'

'I've gone off him. I don't want you to let him in.'

'Oh.' Sadie dried her palms on the flowered apron, stepped into the room, managed not to fall over the dog. 'But he's paying me, Vera. He's the one who's keeping you going.'

'He's the one who got me in this mess.' Vera threw down a half-finished bootee. 'I know I've been ill, Sadie. I know I've been out of my mind. But I'm not as bad as that any more. I've just . . . like I said, I've gone off him.'

'It took two of you to make this baby, love. I've known Teddy Shawcross since he were born, and he's no more a sinner than anybody else.' Teddy was on the weak side, Sadie thought. A nice bloke, but not a strong one. And no wonder, the way he'd had to drag himself up as a child.

Vera didn't know what she meant to say, could find no words to express her feelings. 'It's just the way I feel,' she said. 'I don't want to see him, Sadie.

When he comes, will you tell him that?'

'No, I won't. You can tell him your bloody self, Vera Hardman. It's time you grew up. We can't be doing everything for you, me and Sheila. We don't mind cleaning up and keeping you company, but that's as far as it goes.'

Vera sank back into her chair and picked up *Gone with the Wind*. At least she could absent herself for a while, immerse herself in the American Civil War instead of knitting stupid little bits for a child she had never wanted.

When Edward walked in, she closed the book and placed it on the chair arm. She looked him over, decided that he was quite nice-looking and that she definitely didn't need to see him again. 'I want my keys back.' Sadie had given him copies of the new keys, and he had owned copies of the older keys for months. 'I want you to stay away,' she said clearly. 'You can pay Sadie and Sheila, because I'm not fit to be left here on my own, but I don't want you to carry on visiting.'

He looked at Vera, glanced at Sadie who was hovering in the kitchen doorway. His life was sliding away from beneath his feet like a rug on a polished floor. He knew that Eleanor Fishwick would sell the mill. At the will-reading a few weeks ago, the old woman had looked like a cat who had swallowed a lot more than the cream. There would be his family to think of. Leaving Alice in a reasonable degree of comfort might have been all right, but he would not happily subject her and the children to a life of relative poverty.

'Put them keys down,' advised Vera.

Had Eleanor and Samuel remained abroad, Edward would have handed over the business to a manager, would have placed the financial reins in Alice's hands. But if the mill got sold . . . What had he expected long-term? he asked himself now. Had he hoped that Eleanor would die first, that Samuel would act more fairly? And what about Peter Turnbull?

He stared at the woman he loved, the woman for whose sake he had been willing to change his own lifestyle. Hunched in her chair, Vera looked almost as old as Eleanor. Vera was less frantic than she had been, was making a stab at reading and knitting, but she wasn't really Vera. Vera was warm, funny, affectionate. The husk that housed his child was a stranger.

'Take no notice,' snapped Sadie. 'She doesn't know what she wants.'

'Oh, but I do,' said Vera. 'I want my life back. I want to go and work at the outdoor licence like I used to. I want to take my dog for a walk without people following me to see if I've jumped under a train. I want to be by myself, no baby, no nursemaid and no bloody man.' She glared at Edward.

He tossed the keys onto a chair, swivelled on his heel and walked out of the house. In the street, he stood for a few moments and breathed in some fresh air. Vera had died; he had killed her. The spirit of the woman he had loved no longer existed. All that lingered was a bag of bones, a dried-up shell that mocked him and cared nothing for him.

On Tonge Moor Road, Edward sat in his car. For the time being, he had an income and the use of a house. Eleanor had said several times that things at Aston Leigh would remain the same. But very soon, the whole world would know about Edward Shawcross and Vera Hardman. Curtains twitched, tongues wagged and gossips ran round the town like wildfire. Samuel Fishwick's love-child had remained a fairly well-kept secret, but this was a different age, a different matter altogether.

Alice already knew. Although she had said nothing, Edward felt in his bones that Alice was fully aware of the situation. Time was slipping away from him, was another strip of carpet on another waxed floor. The sadness he felt about losing Vera was almost unbearable. There had been somewhere to go, something to look forward to. Now, there was nothing.

He began to understand Vera's panic. She had not wanted to live, because the world had not suited her. The phobia about childbirth had pushed her towards instability, but the sadness had probably been there already. Vera had nursed her sister and her mother, had watched both die. Beneath that laughing surface, the depression squatted permanently, its tentacles spreading quickly each time the woman's frail veneer was pierced.

Edward watched people going about their business, some arriving home from work, others doing last minute shopping, baskets swinging, feet flying along the pavements.

Sadie's shift would end soon. Should he wait and offer her a lift, should he talk to her? Could that wise lady suggest any solution, any answer? No. Sadie could do and say nothing that would alter the circumstances. He was on his own, had always been alone. Tears threatened, but he sniffed them away. Self-pity must not be allowed. Self-pity was one of the least attractive of human failings.

With his heart empty, Edward Shawcross made his way home. It was over. Soon, he would be forced to move on towards a future for which he had no map.

Connie threw down her coat and ran round the little house, in and out of bedroom, studio, bathroom, living room, kitchen. 'James, James, it's wonderful!' she screamed. 'Oh, what fun. Everything's so compact.'

'Small,' he said.

She stood still and looked at him. 'What's the matter with you?' He had dark smudges under his eyes, looked as if he hadn't slept for a month.

'I have been down the pit,' he explained. 'And I need another bath. I was drawing. They smuggled me down in this cage thing.' He leaned against the wall to ease his leg. 'Connie, I have never been so terrified in my whole life. It's weird, eerie. There's a whole different world down there – they're like a separate human species, crawling about on their hands and knees, shovelling coal hour after hour. Under our feet, there is a culture.'

Connie glanced at the floor. 'A sub-culture, I suppose. Under here? Now?'

'Possibly. They dig down, then they spread out for miles. Water drips. If no-one's working that particular section, the water's as loud as the Town Hall clock. Every day, somebody saves somebody's life. They take it for granted. You save me today, I'll return the favour tomorrow. The only time I saw a miner in a flap was when this huge chap opened his lunchbox and found cheese sandwiches. "Bloody cheese again," he roared. Other than that, there was no trouble. They know that any day could be their last.'

He was really fired up, more alive than Connie had seen him in ages. 'How did you paint in the dark?'

275

'With the lamp on my hat and with a few others borrowed from another shift. And I didn't paint – I just sketched. You should see the work, Connie. I don't know whether it's good or bad, but it says something.'

She allowed herself to be dragged back into the studio. A large canvas on the easel had been compiled from charcoal drawings around the walls. Coal-streaked men with rippling muscles laboured with picks and shovels. Props held up the 'ceiling', lengths of wood that supported the earth and everything on its surface. 'There could be a house on top of that lot,' she remarked. 'Or a train, or a river. It's like Atlas, isn't it? Condemned to take the weight of the globe for ever.'

James nodded excitedly. She understood. Somebody understood. 'The lads think I'm crackers,' he told her. '"Why don't you paint fields and flowers like everybody else?" But they are underneath all the flowers, Connie. They're buried alive. The whole bloody lot could collapse at any moment. Yet they sit there with their sandwiches and billy cans, all eating more coal dust than food, and they tell jokes. One lot played cards for ten minutes, but the cards got covered in dust and they couldn't tell a knave from a king. The only light they had was on their helmets. So they gave up and cracked jokes instead.'

'So brave,' she said.

'So desperate,' said James. 'They must need work badly to go down there every day. And, of course, what happens when all the coal's gone? There are holes everywhere. Will we sink because the earth's lost its belly?'

She couldn't bear to think of that. 'What else are you doing?'

'Poetry, photography and collecting insurance for Wesleyan and General.'

'Your mother will be pleased.'

He laughed. 'My mother's OK, Connie. I know I make fun of her and the We Hate Our Mothers group, but I do love her. She's as tough as a miner's boots. Old Maude will get over my misdeeds, I'm sure.'

'Has she found you yet?'

James chortled again. 'Is the pope a Catholic? Of course she has. I now have eight tins of salmon, a bowl of fruit and enough biscuits to feed a small nation. Cup of tea?'

'Please.' She walked into the living room and sat on a sofa that had seen better days, probably in an earlier century. The minimalist style seemed to suit James. Apart from a lump of coal whose shape bore a strong resemblance to a man's face, there were few ornaments. He had a wireless, an easy chair and a dining table with two stools. There was lino on the floor, and a horrible rug in brown lay in front of the fireplace.

He appeared with Crown Derby cups and saucers. 'Mother's,' he said. 'She's decided that I'm gifted and eccentric, but she insists on the best china even for reprobates like me.' James studied the girl of his dreams. 'Right,' he said. 'Out with it. What sort of a life have you been enjoying?'

Connie took a mouthful of tea. 'Strange, James. A couple of weeks ago, we had the will-reading. After that, Mother took us to Tognarelli's, then to a soon-to-be department store. Mother is going to become a magnate.'

'My God.'

She shook her head vigorously. 'I don't know what the world's coming to, James. The landed gentry ends up down a mine with cheese sandwiches and some drawing paper; Grandmother tells us that we may continue to live at Aston Leigh, but that the mill will be sold; we are then taken down to Deansgate to view a property that might make a restaurant and a department store; Gil believes that Grandmother killed Grandfather, and—'

'What did you say, Connie?'

'You heard me, James. There's a complication called Peter. This Peter person was meant to be included in Grandfather's new will. But Grandmother made sure that the new will did not see the light of day. My brother thinks Eleanor murdered Samuel.'

'How?'

'Morphine. She was in charge of it. For the last day or so of Grandfather's life, no-one was allowed into the bedroom.'

James thought about that. 'But the doctor would need to account for all the drugs, Connie. Pharmacies don't dole out morphine like aspirin. There shouldn't have been sufficient to kill him. She would have been issued with enough for one day at a time, then—'

'Gil says she might have saved it up.'

'Well, there's only one way to find out.' James stirred his tea with a penknife. 'He'll have to be dug up.'

'Don't be silly, James. You're as bad as Gil. Who's going to invade Heaton Cemetery with picks and shovels?'

He shrugged. There were plenty of those on the

coal face. 'I could hire a gang of miners.' This was no joking matter. 'Connie, who is this Peter?'

'Probably an illegitimate relative. Somewhere, there's a chap called Peter Turnbull who is really a Fishwick. But Grandfather was beginning to wander in his mind, you know. Peter Turnbull could have been a figment of a senile imagination. Though Granny Smarty-pants was keen enough to wrench the will from Gil's hands.'

'He held it?'

'Yes.'

'Did he read it?'

'No. He never got the chance to look at it. Grandmother tore it out of his hands and ordered him out of the room. Something fishy is going on, James.'

'Fish-wick-y, you mean.' James drained his cup. 'You know, we haven't had ordinary families, you and I. My dad's a good enough sort, but he's a cold and distant man – something to do with the way he was raised, I suppose. Your father's no nearer to you than mine is to me.'

Connie took up the theme. 'My mother's gone radical. She's had her hair cut and she's talking about starting a business. I get the feeling that Father is sliding out of the picture. And your mother is . . . brittle. She's so abrupt, yet I can tell she's a kind soul underneath.' Connie sighed dramatically. 'Taken all round, we've turned out quite well, James. Make another cuppa and bring out the biscuits.'

He limped towards the door. 'You're one up on us, though. It must be really exciting to have a possible murderer in the family. Imagine the mileage you could get out of that. "My Grandmother is a Murderer" plastered all across the front page of the less reputable newspapers. Could I press you to a cream bun? Or a couple of digestives?'

Connie threw a cushion at him and demanded two cream buns. After all, it wasn't every day that one's family became interesting.

ELEVEN

'I am going to bed,' announced Eleanor Fishwick. 'And I trust that I shan't be disturbed.' She was genuinely tired, yet she could not afford to be. Since the previous month, when she had become a rich widow at the reading of the will, life had been hectic and full of chatter. There was a buzz in the air at Aston Leigh, something connected with visits to London and whether to sell small items of furniture. Tonight, with so much on her mind, Eleanor could take little interest in the plans of her daughter and her grandchildren. Tomorrow, perhaps. Tomorrow, after . . . after Peter Turnbull's exit from the scene.

She sat on the edge of the bed in which Samuel had died, stared through the window, watched Ada Dobson wobbling homeward on a rickety bicycle. Lottie Bowker was already in her little room under the eaves, as she rose early to do the master's breakfast. Everyone else, with the exception of Edward Shawcross, was in the drawing room talking a lot of silly nonsense about opening a new shop in the centre of Bolton. Well, Alice wouldn't get far, not with a paltry few thousand. And Eleanor had no intention of squandering her own cash on a project of such obvious foolishness.

The gun was wrapped in a small towel inside a crocodile handbag. A cheque was already written, along with an unsigned and rather inconclusive letter, just in case anything should go badly wrong. This was going to be a long, long night, because the disposal of the man was merely the first step. The concept of murder did not trouble Eleanor Fishwick unduly, but the threat of prison or worse was rather disconcerting. She would remain outwardly serene, just as she had for well over two decades. With luck and good management, she would survive.

She waited, watched the clock, listened to each rhythmic second as, simultaneously, it marked its own brief life and its own demise. Dressed from head to toe in black, Eleanor let herself out of the room, locked the door, then made her way down the back stairs of Aston Leigh. These uncarpeted steps were for the use of servants, and Eleanor's progress was marked by creaking sounds, though there was no-one near enough to hear the noise.

Outside, she took a spare back door key from beneath a flowerpot, then made her way along the side of the house towards The Rise. The sun was waving a final and rather dull goodbye when Eleanor passed Top o' th' Moor. Fortunately, the Templetons' house was well shielded by hedges and trees. Anyone peering through an upstairs window might have seen a shadowy figure, but identification could prove difficult. Although Eric Templeton owned the Top o' th' Moor woods, he was not much of a gamekeeper where the copse was concerned. People went into the woods, emerged with rabbits, were never confronted or scolded by the Templetons. So if Eleanor did get noticed she would probably be ignored, as would any report from a firearm.

She no longer allowed herself the luxury of feeling consciously terrified. Her mind was empty and cold, and she had gone well past the point of no return. The money was hers. She had worked for it, had stayed for a lifetime with a man who had betrayed her. Never, never would she forget what Samuel had done all those years ago. No amount of compensation would satisfy Eleanor, though she certainly intended to grab what she could.

The woods were not yet completely dark at the edge, though the dense centre looked fiercely black. Eleanor sat on a stump and waited, listened to the rustle of birds as they returned home for the night, heard the low call of a stirring owl. The man would arrive shortly. He would appear out of nowhere, would be sent back into nowhere.

'You came, then.'

Eleanor jumped. He was behind her. 'Hand it over,' he ordered without ceremony. This was a creepy place and he wanted to be out of it. 'The cheque and the letter.'

She rose to her feet, swung round, placed a finger on her lips. 'Go further in,' she whispered. 'I think I saw someone coming over the field.' She pushed her way into the woods, felt a branch scraping her face.

He grabbed her shoulder. 'That's far enough,' he snarled. 'Get on with it.' The woods scared him, though he would not have admitted that aloud in a million years.

Eleanor got on with it. She plunged her hand into the bag, pushed the index finger into position, raised the bag, fired.

Peter Turnbull dropped like a stone, lay in a crumpled heap not much more than two yards away from her. Thrown backwards by the recoil, Eleanor steadied herself against a tree trunk. Smoke streamed out of the remains of the crocodile bag. The report had been loud, yet no-one would come, surely? Men with families to feed often took pot shots at rabbits in the Belmont district.

She breathed in the smell of cordite, coughed against its unpleasant odour. The bag was in shreds. It had been a perfectly good bag, too. Strangely, she experienced no reaction, no racing of the heart. For a few moments, she remained in contact with the tree, then she stepped forward and felt Peter Turnbull's wrist. There was no pulse. The bullet seemed to have lodged inside his chest, and death must have been instantaneous, as very little blood had seeped through the shirt.

Slowly and carefully, Eleanor Fishwick removed the gun from its shredded cover of crocodile hide, wiped it on a white handkerchief, then placed it on the ground with her ruined bag. A part of her mind questioned this action, as she would be disposing of the evidence later and at comparative leisure. But she quickly realized that she had simply been postponing the inevitable. On the floor of the copse, a body lay. And she had to get rid of it.

Tut-tutting beneath her breath, Eleanor gazed around, commanding her eyes to work as best they could in the dimness. She was too close to the edge here. If Turnbull had followed her into a deeper part of the woods, she would have found ample cover, but now, she was forced to use her depleted resources to drag this dead weight to the nearest safe location.

First, she raided the pockets, found the letter from Samuel and the keys to Turnbull's house. When these were safely deposited about her person, she began the task of hiding Peter Turnbull's body.

Fortunately, an adequately suitable place was only yards away. A little at a time, she moved the remains further into the trees, her progress slowed by uneven land and thick foliage. Finally, exhausted by her efforts, she pushed the corpse into a hole at the base of a very large tree, then covered the aperture with branches, leaves and clumps of moss. He was gone, it was finished, she was free.

After a few seconds' consideration, she retrieved the gun and the bag, then pushed them behind the branches and into Peter Turnbull's makeshift grave. Sometimes, it made sense to keep all the eggs in one basket. Now, there was just one hiding place, one burial ground.

But something made her ponder. Carrying the gun home was dangerous, yet she dared not leave it here. 'Just leave it for a day or two,' she whispered aloud. 'Come back for it.'

An inner voice ordered her to pick up the weapon and the shattered bag. She would not return to these woods, could not imagine herself ferreting about around a rotting corpse. The weather was warm; he would soon begin to moulder. After a second or two, she pushed her hand into the hole and dragged out her property. Twigs scraped at the skin of her arm. She almost screamed when she touched him again. He was still warm. Shuddering, she backed away.

Eleanor began to retrace her steps. When she reached the clearing at the top of The Rise, she stood silently and peered around. No-one must see her. The night was clear, the sky a deep French blue studded with sequins. But Eleanor Fishwick had no time to muse on the fabric of nature; she had work to do, work that might well take the rest of the night to accomplish.

She slid like a ghost past Top o' th' Moor, past Aston Leigh and down the hill until she reached a clump of houses whose occupants, in Eleanor's book, were nouveau riche and not quite the thing. She hid the gun and the bag at the edge of a field, reminded herself that she must pick them up later, on her way back. If she got stopped, or if the car broke down, she would be in the company of no murder weapon. The job was only half done, she said mentally. There was much to do before she could rest. Breathing more easily, she arrived on Belmont Road and found the car parked exactly as instructed. With the spare keys in her pocket, she was ready for the next stage.

Under her breath, she thanked the motor industry for push-button ignition. She could not have swung a starting handle to save her life. This little Austin was her gift to Gilbert, who had developed a habit of staring at his grandmother. Brand new, the car had been delivered earlier by a young man from a garage in Bolton. 'Leave it on Belmont Road,' Eleanor had advised. 'Just before the turning into The Rise. I don't want him to see it until tomorrow. Surprises are so much nicer over breakfast, don't you think?'

The salesman had not thought. He had simply pocketed his commission and done the old woman's bidding. In Eleanor's room, a solid gold bangle worth hundreds of pounds nestled in a box of blue velvet. If Gilbert could have a car, then Constance, too, should receive a valuable gift. Everything had been worked out, right down to the finest detail.

She drove to Halliwell Road, parked the car in a side street, then waited until the road was reasonably clear. It was almost ten o'clock, so most people were either at home or inside a public house. She locked the car, walked down the road and found the house she had looked at with Edward. The key was a perfect fit. She slid inside, closed the door, leaned on it for a while until her eyes adjusted to interior darkness.

It was an ordinary two-up-two-down, a staircase rising out of the kitchen and a small lean-to scullery attached at the back. She walked through the down-stairs rooms, inhaled the smells of rancid fat and stale washing. Peter Turnbull had not been a clean-living young man, it seemed.

From the pocket of her coat, Eleanor took Samuel's gold-plated lighter and illuminated the immediate environment. It was a pigsty. Dirty washing was draped over chairs, table and a huge Victorian dresser. A slopstone in the scullery was crammed full of dirty dishes, the sickly-sweet smell of mould rising from filthy crockery produced by at least half a dozen meals.

It took about two hours to search the house thor-oughly. Impeded somewhat by kid gloves, Eleanor made her way through drawers, boxes, cupboards. She shifted Peter Turnbull's mattress, almost gagging at the odour of unwashed human flesh. She rolled back rugs and mats, sought loose floorboards, prised them up, fiddled around between joists.

There was nothing. She dared not illuminate the rooms fully, because someone might knock at the door in order to speak to Turnbull, but the lighter and a candle offered a modicum of help. Satisfied that there was no evidence of Turnbull's connection with Samuel, she sat on a chair, carefully placing a sheet of newspaper on the seat first. The house was probably full of fleas and germs, but she had to remain, had to hang on until the dead of night. Used to biding her time, the old woman slept fitfully in the house that belonged now to a dead man.

During the drive home, Eleanor experienced an uncomfortable feeling, a notion that she had forgotten something, that she had left something undone. But tiredness was confusing her, was clouding her mind, so she simply carried on homeward. When the car had been returned to its space on Belmont Road, she made a final effort and dragged her weary bones up The Rise, picking up the pistol and the wrecked crocodile bag as she passed the field. Aston Leigh was in darkness. She slipped round to the back, used the spare key, then returned it to its hide beneath the flowerpot. Tomorrow, someone might be chided for neglecting to secure the house properly.

The rear stairs creaked again, but she was too tired to notice. Silently, she unlocked her bedroom door, went inside, replaced the key in the inner lock. When the letter from Samuel to Turnbull was shredded, she placed it in the grate, adding to it the document she had made out for Turnbull. When the cheque was torn up and thrown into the fireplace, she rooted in her pocket for Samuel's lighter. It was not there.

Panic fluttered in her breast, but she calmed herself deliberately. The gold-plated lighter was engraved with Samuel's initials, but how many people had the initials SF? Quite a few, she supposed. Anyway, the thing could be anywhere. It might have been dropped in the street, in the car, in . . . in the dead man's house. Yes, she had used it there. With a trembling hand, she lit a match and set fire to the papers in the grate. Everything would be fine, she kept telling herself. She had done well, had achieved her goal. That lighter, if it turned up in Turnbull's house, could have been stolen by him, could have been given to him. She could not go back, could not search his home again.

She lifted a bedside rug, used a brass letter opener to prise up a board. When the murder weapon and its container were hidden, Eleanor allowed herself the luxury of a relieved sigh. It was over, it was finished, she was safe. A ghastly smell rose from her clothing, a mixture of all the odours she had encountered in that dreadful little hovel. She tore off her outer garments and tossed them into the bottom of her wardrobe.

In the bathroom, Eleanor stared at her image. The mirror reflected her face, and her face had a mark down the right cheek, a stripe where over-hanging branches had broken her skin's surface. That was a bloody nuisance, she told herself. It was two o'clock in the morning, and she had been 'in bed' since nine o'clock. How on earth might she have injured herself in the bedroom?

Oh well, she had to be up early anyway, because she was going to fetch Gilbert's new car from Belmont Road before breakfast. She could have a fall on her way there, could report the accident on her return.

At half past two, she was bathed and ready for bed. At six, she would need to be up and about in order to have her little mishap. She set her alarm, put her head on the pillow and slept immediately.

Vera Hardman lay wide awake, her hands clasped over her abdomen. Inside, in a dark and comfort-able place, Edward Shawcross's baby was cradled. It didn't worry, didn't care about the host from which it took its nourishment. This was August 1950, and the doctor reckoned that Vera was three months pregnant. In February, she would have to go through all the pain of giving birth to a creature in whose father she seemed to have lost all interest.

Why? she asked herself. Everything had been so wonderful. She remembered him coming into the shop for all kinds of strange things, remembered how he had looked at her, how he had sounded. He had been a piece of magic, because he had awakened in Vera a capacity for love, for physical passion. She had not expected to be loved, had not looked for a partner. But he had walked into the shop and into her heart, and now, she had erased him.

William missed him. The dog had grown used to Edward's pattern, had taken to lying behind the front door at about six o'clock each evening. Edward brought bones and meat for the dog. Even now, he often left parcels on the doorstep. William, sensing Edward's presence, usually scraped at the door in a frantic effort to reach him. But the man no longer stayed, because he was no longer welcome.

Vera wondered whether she was going crackers. It was difficult to understand how and why she had loved a man one day, only to reject him the next. Perhaps she had depended too much, yet she had been so careful about keeping her distance, had taken what was on offer, had asked for no more. She had not demanded that he leave his wife and family, had not expected that.

She turned onto her side, drew up her knees and wept silently. He had not been magic enough. Edward had not taken away the fear, the terrible dread of childbirth. He had not taken away the baby, had not cared enough to help her. Even now, after a gap of several years, she could hear her sister's screams, those dreadful animal sounds that had emerged when each dead baby had been ripped away.

There was no help for Vera. She had settled to her fate, was taking each day as it came. Were all people like this? When Death crooked his bony finger and beckoned, did everyone grow used to his ugly presence? For much of the time, she was peaceful, almost lethargic. It was as if a very deep part of her soul had accepted the inevitable. In six months, she would die.

Her stomach churned, rested, rolled again. A fluttering, quivering movement made her hold her breath. This was not indigestion, she informed herself. Like a summer shower, the tears were suddenly dried away in the heat of a sensation akin to excitement. Inside her belly, life had just made its first movement. Rolling onto her back again, she placed her fingers on the slight swell, imagined that she felt him moving again. He was so small, so gentle. He was frail. Perhaps it was only wind in her stomach. Perhaps the baby hadn't really moved yet. But that didn't matter, because now, she suddenly wanted, needed this child.

She threw back the covers and jumped out of bed. Yes, yes, she was crazy. Laughing and crying simultaneously, Vera ran from her bedroom and into the room where Sheila slept. 'Sheila!' she yelled. 'Wake up, wake up!'

Sheila sat bolt upright. 'What the bloody hell—?'

'He moved, Sheila.' She stretched herself out next to her neighbour, tried to breathe evenly, made an effort to quieten herself. 'It's so strange,' she whispered. 'It's another person wriggling about under my skin. Feel.' She grabbed Sheila's hand, held it against the small bulge.

'Vera, I was asleep.'

'He's not asleep,' replied Vera. 'He's playing.'

Sheila felt a flutter. 'Could be wind,' she pronounced. 'They don't start their acrobatics till about four months. Aye, that'll be your cheese on toast.'

'It's not, it's not. That's my baby, Sheila. That's my son or daughter.'

There was no understanding some folk, Sheila thought. One minute, Vera wanted rid. The next minute, she was leaping about at God only knew what time in the morning just because of a bit of wind. 'They don't move till well gone four months,' she repeated sleepily. 'It'll be that cheese you had at supper time. I told you not to eat cheese so late.'

Disappointed, Vera got up and left the room. Downstairs, she sat on the sofa with William. Her mood and her attitude were changing yet again, it seemed. There had to be somebody somewhere who would share in this. She felt like running about, singing and dancing because there was hope. Hope had arrived in the form of a tiny, fluttering creature who was defenceless, vulnerable and utterly dependent.

William scratched an ear, waited for his mistress to speak. She had been quiet of late, had not given him much attention. When her hand touched his head, he grinned, the pink tongue lolling from the side of his mouth.

The baby had a father. He would need that father. If Vera died, who would take care of the tiny soul inside her belly? Who would take care of William? It had to be Edward. Edward would understand the almost unaccountable joy she was feeling. So this was motherhood. There was the fear, the pain and the screaming, but there was also the love. Vera sat in the chair and waited for morning. Tomorrow, she would begin her life all over again.

'I bought it just for you, dear.' Eleanor beamed at the grandson who did not trust her.

'Thank you,' Gil said carefully. 'It's absolutely marvellous, Grandmother. Borrowing Dad's car was difficult, because he uses it so often.' He steeled himself, planted a quick kiss on a papery, wrinkled cheek. There was a red weal down her face, a scratch she had reputedly acquired before breakfast while walking down The Rise to pick up the Austin. She had fallen into a hedge. Gil felt uncomfortable.

'You will have your freedom now,' said Eleanor. She had bought him. From now on, he would be nicer to her, would be grateful.

He was uncomfortable because the wound was dry, crusting over. This accident had not happened in the past hour; the scratch on Eleanor Fishwick's face was definitely not newborn. 'Your face seems to be healing already,' he said lightly.

'Good skin, good blood,' she replied quickly. She cursed herself. Had she been thinking straight, she would have peeled back the scab and opened the wound to obtain fresh blood.

Connie was twisting a beautiful bracelet round her wrist. She was not a great lover of jewellery, but this was an exceptional item, solid, heavy, wonderfully engraved. 'This is lovely, too,' she told her grand-mother. 'Thank you.' Like Gil, she played the dutiful grandchild. Eleanor Fishwick was strange, but interesting. There was a coldness about her, a look in her eyes that spoke of confidence, even arrogance.

Gil walked round the car, was genuinely happy to

receive such a gift. Today, he would go to visit Mary in the Market Hall, would tell her about Mother's grand plans for the future. He would not be returning to Imperial College, because he, his sister and his mother intended to start a business in Bolton. What about Father? What would he do after the sale of the mill? Gil would speak to Mother again. She was always vague when questioned about her husband, often making statements about Father being busy with plans of his own.

Edward emerged from the house, exclaimed over the car, looked at Constance's bracelet. Oh well, they deserved some compensation, he supposed, because the old woman was about to whip the rug from under them by off-loading the mill.

'You look dreadful,' remarked Eleanor.

He felt dreadful. He had sat in his office for half the night drinking whisky, had waited for sobriety to arrive before returning home for a change of clothes. Yet a flicker of hope had been kindled in his breast, because Vera had telephoned him just moments earlier. She seemed well again, wanted to see him.

Gil's eyes were fixed on Eleanor Fishwick once more. Nobody developed scabs as quickly as that, he told himself. Was she an alcoholic? Had she been knocking back the booze in her room, had she fallen during the night? No. She was too cool, too calm and certain of herself. Alcoholics did not have Eleanor's apparent serenity. What had she perpetrated now? He bit down on his lip, swallowed the questions.

Connie dug her brother in the ribs. 'You're doing it again,' she said, the words sliding softly from a corner of her mouth. 'Stop staring, will you?'

He could not help it. The nasty suspicion that

Eleanor had helped Samuel into the hereafter remained in Gil's mind. She had done something else, too. She had done something during last night.

'I didn't sleep very well,' announced Eleanor.

With that statement, Gil concurred inwardly.

'I think I shall return to my room for a nap.'

Gil kept his eyes on her, did not flinch when their gazes met. Peter Turnbull. He had to find Peter Turnbull.

'You are pleased with my choice, Gilbert?' Eleanor's tone was modulated, controlled.

'Very much so,' he answered. 'It's an excellent car, one of the best on the market.'

The rhythm of Eleanor Fishwick's heart quickened, returned to normal within two seconds. The boy knew something. There was an unspoken accusation in his face. Had he followed her, had he been a witness to the killing of Samuel's bastard? Not likely. He would have alerted Scotland Yard and Buckingham Palace by now. She had done them all a favour, she insisted inwardly. She had removed a threat, a parasite who would have fed endlessly on Fishwick money.

'Goodbye,' called Edward. He walked to his car, opened the door.

Eleanor held her grandson's stare. She would have to go away rather earlier than planned, though she needed to remain in England until the business was sold. Why was he gaping so? What on earth did he imagine? Samuel had been ill, confused, dying. Surely Gilbert was not suspicious? She had arrived at the bedroom door in time to see Gilbert taking the will from the case. What had Samuel told him? She shuddered slightly, turned as smartly as her years allowed and went inside the house.

'That's a wonderful car,' said Connie.

'Yes.' Gil waved to his father as he left for work.

'You don't sound too pleased,' remarked Connie.

'She's paying us,' he mumbled. 'She's trying to get us on her side, because . . .' Because of what?

'Don't be silly.'

Gil shrugged. 'Perhaps I am being silly,' he said. 'But she is up to something, Connie. Mark my words – our grandmother is no sweet old lady.'

Connie punched him playfully. 'Let's go for a drive,' she suggested. 'Try out your new car.'

They bowled over the moors, took hairpin bends at breakneck speed, drove to Rivington and all around Horwich. Connie, who was not of a nervous disposition, was slightly worried by her brother's driving. 'Slow down,' she said a couple of times.

He parked the car, sat in silence for a few seconds. 'She did it with morphine,' he said. 'She saw Grandfather off, I'm sure.'

'It was a kindness if she did.'

Gil shook his head. 'No. He was talking to me and he had to be stopped. And Connie, I'll swear she's done something else as well.'

'What?'

'I don't know. She was up to no good in the night, I think. That scratch on her face was not from a fall she might have had this morning. It was healing, drying up. It looks as if she was hit with something sharp that scraped her cheek from top to bottom.'

'She went into the hedge, Gil.'

'Quite possibly. But she didn't do it this morning. I wonder if she found Peter Turnbull before I did?'

Connie wriggled in her seat. The idea of a criminal grandmother was not attractive. 'I thought I was the one with the overactive imagination. Gil, you can't go on like this.'

Gil raised his shoulders. 'True. I might be the next item on her hit-list.'

Connie laughed, though the sound had a hollow quality. 'How does an old woman kill a grown man? That's assuming, of course, that this Peter Turnbull exists and is not a child or another old person. She's seventy, Gil. She hasn't the strength for killing people. She certainly couldn't tackle you. Anyway, she's our grandmother. Grandparents don't wipe out their children's children.'

He lowered his head, pondered. 'Murder requires organization, mental skill and cunning. It's nothing to do with physical stamina, Con. It's planning, careful strategy. There's poison – that's a favourite with females. And there are weapons that can be used by anybody. All you need is a strong finger.'

'Guns?'

'Yes.'

Connie thought about that. 'We haven't any guns, Gil. Father won't have them in the house, not since we brought that dying rabbit home. Remember? The poor thing had been shot? Well, Father got rid of his shotguns then, after our little funeral in the back garden. You don't seriously believe that Grandmother has been running round in the night with a gun?'

'She might have brought one back from Africa.'

'An elephant gun, I suppose.'

Gil turned sideways and looked at his sister. 'Mock if you like. They went on safari several times in Kenya. Grandfather killed that rug in our hall and sent it home. She went with him and she probably knows about guns.'

Connie tut-tutted. 'And who was her victim last night?'

'Peter Turnbull.'

'Rubbish,' said Connie. 'Utter tripe. The old man was more than a little confused when he said that name. There's probably no such person.'

Gil pressed the starter button. He was about to drive away when another car appeared and overtook them. 'Isn't that Father?' he asked.

Connie stared ahead, watched the car slowing to a stop. There were two people inside the vehicle. It was definitely her father's car, and her father was definitely with a woman. 'Good grief,' she exclaimed. 'Who is that?'

Gil could have hazarded a guess, could have said that this was probably Father's mistress, but he kept quiet. Mother and Father had never been close, so Father had found someone else. Although the logic was plain, Gil felt an ache around his heart. Poor Mother.

Connie opened her door.

'Con? Where are you going?'

'To talk to my father,' she snapped. 'To find out what's going on. I wonder if Mother knows?'

'Of course she does. Mother always knows everything – isn't that a favourite saying of yours? Don't do it, Con.' If Connie spoke to Father and the woman, things might get out of hand. As long as no-one confronted the situation head on, Father might come to his senses and stay at home. 'Leave it, Con.'

Connie was not listening. She slammed the door and marched up the hill towards her father's car.

She lowered her head, looked through the driver's window, past her father and studied Edward Shawcross's passenger. A thin, red-haired woman was talking animatedly, was waving her hands about and chattering. Connie tapped on the glass.

Shocked and suddenly red-faced, Edward flung open his door and stepped into the road. 'Constance,' he began uncertainly. 'What are you doing here?'

'That is exactly the question I was planning to ask you,' she replied. 'You have some sort of explanation for this, I suppose?'

He ran a hand through his hair. 'This is my . . . friend,' he managed. 'You must try to understand, Constance, that your mother and I have not been . . . together for many years.' He stood between his daughter and the vehicle, tried to keep the two women apart.

Connie backed away and walked round to the passenger side. She stared into Vera Hardman's green eyes, took a step away when the stranger wound down her window. 'Who are you?' Connie asked.

'Vera. Vera Hardman.'

Connie nodded. 'I see. Are you in the habit of going for drives in my father's car?'

Unable to frame an answer, Vera closed her mouth and waited for Edward to sort out the situation. The morning had begun so well, had been so promising. She had walked with Sheila up to the telephone box, had spoken to Edward, had dashed home to tell Sadie that things had started to look better. But now, everything was spoilt.

Edward joined his daughter on the grass verge. 'Constance, I was going to tell your mother soon, very soon, that I intend to . . . to begin a new life.'

Connie gazed at the man who was her father. 'It's all Mother's fault, I suppose?' From the corner of her eye, she saw Gil approaching. 'You were never there. You were always out at the mill or doing council things. We have never mattered at all to you.'

'That is not fair,' said Edward. 'You don't understand—'

'I don't understand?' Connie's voice was raised in anger. 'How on earth can you know what I do or don't understand? You have not talked to me properly in ages.' She turned her attention to Vera. 'He will ignore you, too,' she said clearly. 'And perhaps he will leave you when he grows tired of you.'

Gil grabbed his sister's arm, tried to drag her away. 'Connie, come on,' he urged.

She shook him off, shook a finger at Edward. 'Don't patronize me, Father. Don't you dare. I'm no longer a child, so don't start preaching about understanding and starting a new life away from my mother.' She waved her hand at her father's car. In spite of herself, she spat out a mouthful of anger. 'Are you blind?' she asked. 'Have you looked at that woman in your car? She's . . . she's common. She looks as if she's been starving in a slum, as if she's never had a decent meal.'

Edward inhaled deeply. 'No, Constance. I am the one from the slums. I am the one who lived on his wits because there was no food in the house. Don't make the mistake of categorizing people, dear. We are all human beings, all the same.'

Tears leapt to Connie's eyes and spilled down her face. Blindly, she turned from her father and leapt into the road. For an endless, frozen second, she heard the screech of brakes, caught sight of a huge shape, experienced a stab of pure terror. Pain overwhelmed her, dragged her down into its dark and unforgiving maw.

The driver of the lorry was catapulted forward, his head smashing the windscreen, his body impaled on the steering shaft. He died instantly, was killed by his desperate attempt to stop before hitting the girl.

Edward and Gil ran forward, saw that Connie was trapped beneath the vehicle's wheel. The back of her head, which had made sharp contact with the road, was bleeding. 'Lift,' screamed Edward. 'Gilbert, lift the damned thing.' Incredibly, the two men managed to raise the lorry. 'Vera!' yelled Edward.

Vera, who had climbed out of Edward's car after hearing the screech of brakes, ran forward and dragged Connie from beneath the large vehicle's wheel. The lorry was dropped immediately, and both men stood panting for a few seconds.

'We shouldn't move her any more,' said Vera. 'Get an ambulance.' She knelt beside Connie and burst into tears. This was all her fault. If she hadn't phoned Edward, if she hadn't ever met him in the first place, if she hadn't been expecting his child, if she hadn't gone crazy, none of this would have happened. 'Go on,' she screamed. 'Find help, hurry up!'

Gil dashed off, jumped into his new car and went in search of a phone.

Edward, white-faced, tore off his tie and twisted it around Connie's leg. The bleeding from her head was slow, but she was losing a great deal of blood from the shattered remnants of her right leg. He panted with exertion as he tightened the tourniquet. Had he told this sweet child how much he loved her? Had he spoken the words, had he listened to her troubles, had he smoothed her path? Angry with himself, he wept silently, hardly noticing the sobbing female at his side.

'I can't bear it,' wailed Vera.

Vera didn't have to bear it. He looked at her, remembered that she was here. 'This is my fault, not yours,' he said. Tears ran down his face and into his beard. 'She's my daughter, Vera. She's hurt because she fled from me. Oh God, send that ambulance.'

Vera Hardman backed away, terrified by the vision of Connie lying unconscious in the roadway. She raised her head, caught sight of the lorry driver's face. It was smashed and bloody, the mouth twisted for all eternity, the eyes widened in an expression of fear and disbelief. She had been so selfish, so self-absorbed. Everyone suffered. Everyone carried a cup of grief, sometimes full, infrequently empty, often half-filled by memories of loves lost. She could do nothing for Edward's daughter, nothing for the poor driver of the lorry. Somewhere, the man's family would be carrying on as always, living life, brewing tea, working, sleeping. And into that ordinary world, a policeman would walk, a bringer of tidings so awful that the family would cease to function for a while.

She dropped down to the verge, pulled her skirt down over trembling knees. The man she had loved, the man she had planned to love again, was fighting to save the life of a beloved daughter. Alice Shawcross could be taking her morning coffee at this moment. She might be reading or listening to the wireless or having a wash. Alice's daughter lay bleeding, and Alice didn't know. The bearer of tidings in this case would be the police, or Edward, or the boy.

The ambulance arrived, Gil in hot pursuit behind it. Vera watched while Connie was placed on a stretcher, while Edward climbed into the vehicle with his daughter, while the ambulance shot away with its bell clanging. Someone touched her arm. She turned, gazed into the face of Edward's son.

'Shall I take you home?' he asked.

Vera shook her head. 'No, love. Go to your mam and tell her before the police do it. Take your mam to the hospital. Don't be worrying over me, now.'

He drove away, leaving Vera sitting on the verge.

The child seemed to move again, and Vera bled inside for Alice. The blob was not a blob any more. It had little hands and feet that moved and played. It had a little heart, a soul. Alice's blob was now a beautiful girl with a crushed skull and a smashed leg. Vera suddenly knew about motherhood, how it felt, what it meant. It meant laying down your life, if necessary, so that the young would survive. Since the foetus had seemed to move, Vera had been a mother. If she died, it didn't matter, as long as the infant got a chance of life.

Could she take Edward Shawcross away from his family now? Would he want to come? After all, his love for Vera had caused an accident bad enough to kill his daughter. Oh, how she hoped and prayed that the girl would live.

Police arrived just after the ambulance bell had died away. Vera, who had carefully averted her head, looked once more at the poor, dead driver. She and Edward had killed him, too. His kith and kin would be told that he had died while trying to preserve the life of a young woman, but Vera knew better. That man had lost his life because of her and Edward.

She was questioned, prompted to give the details of the incident, then she was driven home in a black police car. Inside her house, she flung herself at Sadie Martindale and wept copiously. 'Lock me in,' she sobbed. 'Lock me in again, Sadie. I've just killed a man and Edward's daughter. She might not be dead yet, but . . .' The words were swallowed.

Sadie patted Vera's back and made there-there sounds. Vera had been doing so well, had been coming along a treat in the nerves department. 'Who's dead?' she asked.

'The driver.'

'What driver?'

'Lorry.' Vera pulled away, blew her nose, folded herself into a chair. 'His daughter ran out. She saw me and she ran out and the driver stopped so fast his face was all smashed.'

Sadie cottoned on at last and sat down. 'Teddy Shawcross's girl?'

Vera nodded. 'Ambulance took her to hospital. Her poor mam, Sadie, her poor mam.'

Sadie swallowed, tried to imagine how she would feel if their Mary ever got run over. She didn't know what to say to Vera, didn't know how to comfort her. Sadie was not judgemental by nature, except in the case of Ethel Hyatt from next door on Emblem Street. And even Ethel had her problems. The fact that Teddy Shawcross had committed adultery with this sobbing woman was no business of Sadie's. Teddy and Vera would answer in time to their Maker, as would every other soul on earth. But Sadie didn't blame them, didn't criticize. Yet the fact remained that Teddy's girl had been injured because of the affair. 'So young Constance saw you together, was that what happened?'

Vera nodded.

'And she weren't best pleased, I take it.'

'Upset. Very upset. Edward tried to calm her down, but she ran off and . . . and it happened.'

Calmer now, Vera scrubbed her nose with a mangled handkerchief. 'I'd just made my mind up about this baby. I'd just started to feel as if everything might work out. It moves about, you know. It's a real little person. But he already has two children, and one of them is shifting out of the way to make room for mine. It's not right, Sadie.'

'Nowt's never been fair, love.'

'Her head was bleeding. One of her legs is all crushed. She ended up under a bloody truck.'

'I know.'

'What shall I do?'

Sadie considered the question. 'Nowt. Just stop here and look after yourself and that baby. Vera, for God's sake, don't start slipping back again. I know it's terrible, this accident, and I know you feel guilty. But you can't do anything to mend it.'

Vera breathed in deeply, the air shuddering its way into her lungs. 'That's right,' she said softly. 'I'll sit and wait. There's not a lot else I can do, is there?'

Alice Shawcross sat on a hard chair in a bleak cream and brown corridor. At the other side of some double doors, hospital staff were fighting to save the life of her daughter. The stench of human misery seemed to hang in the dull air alongside a pot pourri of Lanry bleach and pine disinfectant. To her right, a man in a brown overall pushed a bucket along, sloshing water here and there, spreading it out, wiping it up in an unenthusiastic manner. She wanted to scream at him, wanted to make him stop. Constance was injured, and nothing should continue as before.

Gil was seated opposite his mother. He leaned forward, elbows on knees, his chin resting on curled hands. The full horror of the day's events was finally hitting him. Until now, he had been too busy running for the ambulance, dashing home for Mother, driving to the hospital. Now, with his head spinning and his stomach heaving, he was beginning to relive the accident. He saw Connie's blood on the road, her hair stained dark red, the huge wheel resting on her leg. Her leg. Oh God, had that really been one of his lovely sister's limbs? Splinters of bone, raw flesh . . . Gil's stomach deposited its sparse contents on the floor.

'That's all right, young man.' The mopper-up galloped to Gil's side. 'I'll see to it, so don't you be worrying.'

Alice stayed where she was. The weight of her sorrow and anxiety was so great that she could not move to help her son. 'Gilbert?' she enquired faintly.

'I'll be all right, Mother.' He wiped his face.

'Water?' asked the cleaner.

'No. No, thank you.' Gil knew that even water would choke him.

The double doors opened, and Edward stumbled into the corridor. 'They won't let me stay,' he said. He gave the doors a black look, as if these inanimate objects were to blame for his expulsion.

Alice nodded. Doctors and nurses were not keen on members of families hanging around when the patient was in a mess. 'How is she?' Alice asked.

'Unconscious.' Edward glanced at Gil, wondered whether the lad had told Alice the full truth. 'They think her skull is fractured.'

'And her leg?' asked Alice. Gilbert had said something about Constance's leg being broken.

'A mess,' said Edward bluntly. 'Their main

concern is her head, but they are working hard to save the leg, too.'

Alice's spine was suddenly ramrod straight. 'Save it? Gilbert said it was broken, but—'

'It's very damaged,' said Edward. He sat down next to Gil, watched the cleaner scooping up vomit. 'Gilbert?'

Gil pulled himself away from his father. 'I'm fine,' he snapped. 'Worry about Con, not about me.'

Edward leaned back against the wall and closed his eyes. He could not bear to look at Alice. Alice had never done anybody real harm. She had grown embittered by her parents' neglect, had allowed middle age to creep up on her prematurely, had tried, of late, to improve herself. He was the sinner. He had married for money, for security, had lived to regret the mistake.

'Edward?'

'Yes?' He still kept his eyes closed.

'What happened?'

What happened? He had happened. He had driven out to the countryside with his mistress, had been seen by his children, had caused Constance to run into the road and—

'Father's too tired now,' said Gil evenly. 'Perhaps later, when . . . when Con comes round.'

Gratitude filled Edward's chest until he thought he would burst. It welled up into his throat, poured out of his eyes, leaked from under closed lids, streaked its way down into the beard.

Alice stared at him, her face devoid of expression. She could not remember an occasion on which he had wept. But she was too tense to comment, too anxious to care. Let him cry. Let them all cry, because Constance was hurt.

Edward blew his nose, stood up, walked along the corridor to the end, stared through a window, walked back again. Gil remained motionless, Alice fiddled with handbag and gloves. Her watch informed her that she had sat here for a mere twenty minutes, yet she felt as if she had spent a lifetime in this grim hospital corridor.

The double doors opened with a flourish, spat out a small man with glasses and a thin moustache. 'Your daughter regained consciousness for a few seconds,' he said happily. He smiled benignly upon the seated mother, flashed a smile at the father and the brother. 'With luck, she'll come out of the coma quite quickly,' he added. 'No sign of any more bleeding under the skull.' He sat in the chair next to Alice, turned slightly so that he could make real contact. 'The leg will be a job,' he said.

'Can you save it?' asked Edward.

The doctor nodded. 'We certainly hope so. She's young, healthy and tough, Mr Shawcross. There will be scars, of course, and she could lose some bone. She'll need therapy afterwards. For quite a long time afterwards, because she is going to be immobile for the foreseeable future.'

Alice looked into the young doctor's pale blue eyes. 'She might have one leg shorter than the other. Like poor James Templeton,' she whispered. The tears came, and the doctor held her gently in his arms. A stranger was comforting her. Gilbert was too sick to offer succour, but Edward continued his usual pattern by staying well away from her.

She pulled herself together, allowed the doctor to dry her eyes. 'Might I see her?' she asked.

'Let us work on the leg,' he suggested. 'Go home and rest. Telephone in an hour or so. She is in very good hands, Mrs Shawcross. Sitting here won't do any good. For your own sake and for your daughter's, go home and get some rest.'

Alice managed a weak smile. 'Yes,' she replied. 'I know you'll do your best.'

TWELVE

Sheila Foster and Sadie Martindale were as unalike as cheese and chalk. Sheila was vigilant up to a point, but she drew the line where lost sleep was concerned, especially since the disastrous holiday in Devon. But Sadie seemed to sleep with one eye open, and she always kept the new doorkeys about her person, usually attached by a very long piece of string. Sheila, who did not relish the concept of turning over in bed and impaling herself on two inches of metal, left the keys on a wicker bedside chair.

Vera sat up well into the night, photographs of the injured girl and the dead man imprinted on the insides of her eyelids. With her eyes wide open, she read a bit, watched William sleeping, did some knitting. Sleeplessness was becoming a habit; since the accident, Vera had managed just a few daytime catnaps.

She passed the slipped stitch over, purled two together, swapped the needles, knitted one row. Apart from short flashbacks when she blinked, she was strangely calm. Her prime goal in life had become the protection of her sitting tenant. She wondered how she had managed to become so frightened, wondered how on earth she had suddenly stopped being petrified by thoughts of childbirth. According to Sadie, this peacefulness was all a part of God's plan for women.

At about three in the morning, Vera made her decision. She pulled from a sideboard drawer a pad of thin, lined writing paper and penned a letter to Edward. He had opened a little bank account for Vera and the unborn, and he could continue to support them by making weekly or monthly donations into the bank. With her tongue poking from a corner of her mouth, Vera wrote slowly, determined to make sure that the message was clearly expressed.

She raised her head, looked at William, felt the wetness of guilt welling in her eyes.

Please look after William, she penned. *He is a grand dog, but he can't come with me. Don't try to find me. If anything goes wrong, or if I need more help or money, I will write to you.*

I can't tell you how sorry I am about what happened, because there aren't enough words in a dictionary. But when I saw your daughter getting run over because of you and me, because of us, I knew that she must be as important to her parents as my little bulge is to me.

At least I got the chance to tell you that I am feeling better about the baby. Please take care of your family, especially your daughter. I shall be in touch.

Vera chewed at the pen, wondered how to sign the letter. With love? With all her love? Faithfully, sincerely? In the end, she just put 'Vera' before shoving the page into an envelope.

After a couple of hours' thinking time, Vera still had no idea of where she was going, but, as dawn's fingers stroked the room, she collected necessities quietly, taking underwear from the kitchen rail, a pile of ironing from a chair. Sheila was snoring and snorting in the spare bedroom. Vera picked up the keys, packed a few belongings from her own room, then went downstairs.

William stood in the doorway, needful eyes fixed on his mistress, the tail held uncertainly at half-mast. Would she take him? Would he be accompanying her, or must he stay here with the other people? The two women were very nice, but they weren't his. Vera was his. The tail descended when he saw the expression on her face. He was to be left.

Vera packed her case, sat down with the dog. 'It's a grand house,' she told him. 'Gardens, a wood full of rabbits. Two shakes, and you'll be running daft on the moors. I will see you again. I promise, William. If I come out of this lot OK, you'll be on the visiting list.' Like the little creature in her belly, William existed only by the whim of humanity. He was allowed no decisions, was curbed by the so-called civilization into which man had dragged him. 'You should be howling at the moon,' she told him. 'Hunting to feed your young, chasing wild things.' She squatted down next to him. 'Worst night's work you ever did was warming yourself at yon caveman's fire. Anyway, Edward will look after you.'

She opened the door silently, pushed her bags outside, wiped a tear from her eye. William would be all right, she insisted determinedly. If Edward didn't take him, Sheila would, because he was very good with cats.

Vera got on the first bus to town, sat for an hour on Trinity Street Station, wondered which train to catch. It didn't matter, she supposed. Where she went was not important. But going was.

*   *   *

Eleanor Fishwick was worried. At the base of a very old tree in the copse, a body was hidden. Had Peter Turnbull been beneath a few feet of soil, she might have been happier. Under the floor of her bedroom lay a ruined bag, the murder weapon and a handkerchief. The missing lighter was not on the agenda, as that was probably at a different scene. She could not risk going back to Turnbull's house, but she must return to the woods and make sure that the dead man was not readily noticeable.

The granddaughter had been run over. Except for the servants, Aston Leigh was empty, because everyone was lingering at the hospital. Eleanor thought about Constance, who had seemed to be a pleasant enough child. It was a great pity, she supposed, but the girl should have been more careful.

The front door opened. 'Mother?' It was Alice. The old lady stayed where she was, did not speak until Gilbert and Alice reached the drawing room. 'How is she?' The dutiful question was coated appropriately with a small serving of concern and tenderness.

'They are working very hard to save her leg,' replied Alice. 'And she was unconscious again for a while. We were told to come home, just as we were yesterday.' For seven or eight hours, surgeons had laboured over Connie's leg. And now, today, they were operating again.

Gilbert sniffed. He was not fooled by Eleanor, not for one second. She had not accompanied Mother, had shown no desire to visit her injured grandchild. She was completely selfish and uncaring about her family.

'I'm sure she will make a complete recovery,' said Eleanor.

'How are you sure?' asked Gil. 'You didn't see the accident, and you weren't at the hospital.'

Eleanor changed the subject deftly. 'Where's Edward?' she asked.

'He had to go off on business,' said Alice. 'He has probably called in at the hospital, too. I think I shall go and lie down.' She left the room and dragged her worry-worn body upstairs.

'Does your new car run well?' asked Eleanor.

'Yes, thank you.' He could not be bothered with her. A part of him wanted to scream at her, wanted to demand to be told about Peter Turnbull, wanted to ask why she had spent money on a car and a bracelet, but Connie was stricken and he could not think straight. He turned to leave the room.

'Why don't you like me?'

He stopped dead in his tracks. 'Because you are cold,' he answered without thinking.

'Cold?'

'Calculating, self-absorbed,' he said.

'Turn round when you speak to me, boy,' Eleanor demanded loudly.

Gil wheeled in the doorway, faced the female dragon. 'I am not a servant who sleeps in a mud hut at the bottom of the garden,' he said softly. He tried to imagine how she would have treated her attendants, shuddered at the idea of her cruelty. 'I'm not here to polish your silver and cook your food. My name is Gilbert; I do not answer to "boy".' He shook his head at her. 'My sister is fighting for her life in Bolton Royal Infirmary, yet you sit here concerned with the fact that I don't like you. Nobody likes you. You treat our staff like dirt and you ignore my mother. You never bothered to contact me or Connie during your long holiday abroad. Why should we care about you?'

Eleanor gazed levelly at her grandson. He knew too much. He probably knew all about Samuel's bastard, all about that long-ago affair between Samuel and the slut. 'You are extremely insolent,' she snapped.

'Thank you, Grandmother. Your opinion is much valued.' He stamped out of the house and went off to fume quietly in the rear garden.

Eleanor Fishwick breathed with difficulty, felt as if she had a huge lump of food stuck in her gullet. With her eyes closed, she tempered her inhalations, fought to regain a sensible rhythm. How dared the boy talk to her like that? She had done nothing wrong, had sought only to clear the way for Alice, Edward, Constance and Gilbert.

Alice. She remembered a beautiful child with hair the colour of corn, eyes of smoky grey, body lithe and strong. Within a dozen years, the hair had faded to brown. The eyes had been overshadowed by an over-large nose, and the rest of Eleanor's daughter had been covered in layers of lard. That dumpy and unattractive young woman had been pleased enough to marry a handsome man called Edward Shawcross.

Eleanor's eyelids flew open. Had Edward told Alice about the Turnbulls? No, she insisted confidently. Edward was a dependable man, one who would never hurt Alice deliberately. Yet there was a space between them, an uneasy peace. Still, Edward must have grown disappointed and disillusioned. Alice had made no effort, had turned into a frump, a miserable-faced housewife with no personality of her own. No, no, Alice knew nothing about her father's past, not from Edward, at least.

The body. Few people went into the woods unless they were looking for rabbits. It was a densely populated thicket, full of untended hawthorn, holly and other prickly items. She put a hand to her cheek, felt the scar. Would the corpse be smelly? How could she approach the decaying man, how would she manage to reassure herself that he had not been discovered or dragged out of his hide by an animal? This was summer. All meat went off in summer. She wished that she had dug a hole and buried him properly, but wishful thinking was a waste of time.

Edward came in, bade her good afternoon, poured a sherry for her and a scotch for himself.

She thanked him, sipped the mediocre amontillado. 'Constance will be fine, I hope?'

He nodded, nursed his glass, perched on the edge of a chair.

'Did she recover consciousness?'

'Briefly.' Edward swallowed the spirit in one gulp.

'Where did it happen?'

'Near Horwich. I was passing through and we . . . I saw it happen.'

'Dreadful for you.'

He raised his head, looked at her. 'Worse for my daughter, worse for my son. He was with her. They had gone for a drive in his new car.'

'Yes.'

He jumped up, refuelled his tumbler.

'Are you ill?' Eleanor asked.

'Shocked, I suppose,' he replied after a pause. 'It was a very unpleasant business.' He could not tell Eleanor about Vera. There was a pecking order in these situations, and Alice should be allowed to hear the sorry tale first.

'You will return later to the hospital?'

He nodded, then left the room.

Eleanor finished the sherry and settled down for

a short nap. She was too old for all this, far too old to think of moving a body in order to bury it. Could she burn the dead man? The woods would not catch fire, as the sun-starved ground was always damp. Even in hot weather, the copse remained moist. With petrol, she could perhaps dispose of Turnbull. No-one would notice, especially at night.

This idea was dismissed immediately. If just one person in the Templeton's house was wakeful, he or she might notice the flames and the rising smoke. The dead man would have to remain where he was, she supposed.

As for Gilbert, he would, she hoped, be totally absorbed for the time being in the recovery or otherwise of his sister. There would be time enough to worry about him later, after all the fuss about Constance had died down. The silly girl should have looked where she was going. Only an idiot stepped into the path of a large, oncoming vehicle.

The evening newspaper was pushed through the letterbox. Eleanor heard the brass flap as it sprang back into position, waited for Ada Dobson to fetch it. Of course, Ada and Lottie Bowker were probably weeping and wailing all over the salad in the kitchen. Exasperated, Eleanor went to pick up the *Bolton Evening News.*

There was nothing in it. She flicked past a column whose subject was her granddaughter's accident, but that was of no interest. Feverishly, she scanned each page, found no mention of the missing Peter Turnbull. It was not surprising, she thought, because the young man had been far from clean. No-one with such filthy personal habits could collect a lot of friends. She remembered the stench of his house, the litter and the dust. He would not be missed, because mankind did not need his sort.

She sat for a while, tried to plan her future. After the sale of the mill, she would give Edward and Alice the house and some money to live on. Then she would take off, make for London, get in touch with people she had met on her travels. Perhaps she would go abroad again, see Europe, return to Africa. India was no longer attractive, because the foolish British government had opened its fingers and allowed India to trickle away.

The clock chimed. From the dining room, sounds of preparation could be heard, the chinkings of glassware and silver. Good. Her appetite remained healthy and robust. Peter Turnbull could rest undisturbed until after dark.

James Templeton glowered at his mother, as if he blamed the bringer of such sad tidings. 'Are you sure?'

Maude sighed. 'Would I make up a story like this one, James? Mrs Ainsworth has been our housekeeper for many years, and she is completely dependable. She had it straight from the mouth of Lottie Bowker. Lottie Bowker would not tell lies about Constance – she is far too fond of the Shawcross family. Constance is in hospital.' Maude paused for a second. 'She ran out into the road and was knocked down by a lorry. Her leg is shattered. When she gets better, she may . . . she may have a limp.' Maude had called at Aston Leigh, only to be told each time that Alice was at the hospital or resting in her room. 'I still haven't managed to talk to Alice. The poor woman must be dreadfully upset.'

James sat down abruptly, his hip jarring against such sudden movement. From infancy, he had limped. Even now, at the age of twenty-four, he remembered learning to walk with the aid of leg-irons and parallel bars. While others had attended nurseries and infant schools, James Templeton had struggled to become upright, had striven for endless, sweaty hours to fit in with the rest of the human race before making his debut at the age of five and a half.

'James, I understand that you are fond of her.'

He cleared his throat, tried to steady his voice. 'I love her,' he said softly.

'I know,' replied Maude.

He raised his head. Mother looked so sad, so hurt. 'Perhaps she will have me now,' he murmured. 'We shall be like book-ends, a set, a pair.' The tears hovered. 'It's more than just a leg, Mother. It's a whole way of life, a difference that makes us notice-able for all the wrong reasons. Pity in people's faces, a change in their tone when they talk to us. They mouth their words very carefully in case we are as stupid in our heads as we are in our limbs.'

Maude sat beside her son on the lumpy sofa. 'James, I am so sorry.'

He put an arm across her shoulders. 'Not your fault,' he said, the words split by the threat of sobs. Not Connie, no, no! 'I am not your fault. I am the fault of those who should have delivered me prop-erly, surgically.' He paused, drew breath. 'Whose fault is Connie?'

'The driver died. He did his best. One can hardly blame the poor soul.'

James dried his few tears, rubbed at his face with the cuff of a paint-spattered shirt. 'Connie is a bit wild,' he said. 'But she wouldn't run out into the path of a vehicle. There must be more to this. Why did she do it?'

Maude lifted her shoulders. 'Goodness knows. She was out with Gilbert. His grandmother has bought him a car and they were giving it its first outing. Mrs Ainsworth thought the accident had happened near Horwich and that Mr Shawcross saw it.'

'Was he with them?'

'Yes, he was there when it happened.'

'In Gil's new car?'

'No, no. He was in his own car.'

'In Horwich?'

'I suppose so,' replied Maude.

'And no-one else was injured?'

'Just Constance. And the driver of the lorry. He is thought to have died instantly.'

James stood up and gazed through the window of his tiny metal home. Visiting hours at Bolton Royal were ridiculously rigid. During several attempts to improve his leg, James had enjoyed the questionable luxury of a private, single room in the same hospital. He had been so lonely between visits, so isolated from the world. 'Is she allowed visitors?' he asked.

'Just family for the time being, I should think.'

He reached out and touched his mother's shoulder. 'For a pain in the neck, you're not too bad as a mother,' he told her. 'Perhaps I could mark you up and sell you on, make a profit.'

Maude grimaced. 'James, I do so love your compliments.' She loved him, too, loved him with that passionately protective love that accompanies so many single offspring. 'Come home,' she pleaded, her face colouring. Maude Templeton was unused to begging. 'It will be so much easier to get news if you come home.' She admitted freely to herself that she would have done or said just about anything to get him back to Top o' th' Moor. 'This place is so grim. Have a rest for a while. You look tired.'

James shook his head slowly. Maude had been as good a mother as she could manage. She was a bright, lively lady with rather too much time on her hands. 'Did you hear about Mrs Shawcross's idea, Mother? About some kind of department store?' For a few seconds, James forced himself to stop thinking about Connie, made his mind concentrate on the woman who had raised him. 'Mother, you should join her. Do something. Use your brain.'

Maude stared at him. 'You mean I should work?' This was a completely new concept, one she had never considered.

'Everyone should work,' he told her. 'Everyone has something to offer. You would be excellent in business, and I think you and Mrs Shawcross should get along splendidly.' A shop would give Connie, too, something to aim for, a reason to get better, to walk, to be strong, to find hope for the future.

'Well.' Maude pondered. 'What would your father say?'

James Templeton's father was a man of great wisdom and forbearance. 'Father would give you your head. He would also advise you. Ask. There's no harm in asking.'

'Will you come home if I do go into business?'

'No.'

Maude rose, picked up her handbag and the keys to her car. 'I miss you,' she said.

'And I miss you,' James answered. 'But I'm a big boy, Mother. You can't carry on protecting me and planning my life.'

'But we could find you somewhere better to live.'

He didn't want a 'better' place, because this prefab was ideal. He was within reach of mills and factories, was in the centre of his Wesleyan and General Insurance round. He was painting in spinning rooms, weaving sheds, customers' houses. He was sketching in mines and on street corners. 'This is right for now,' he said gently. 'For what I'm doing at the moment.'

'Collecting insurance?' The perfectly shaped eyebrows were raised.

'I am meeting people, Mother. I'm painting and writing and, until today, I was happy.'

'She will survive, James.'

He walked with her to the door. 'Thank you,' he said.

'For what?'

'For being a brilliant person.' He waved her off, closed the door and leaned on it. For five or so minutes, he cried like a baby. Then he returned to his little studio and carried on painting, applying to the canvas a mixture of oily daubs and grief.

Connie stared at the ceiling. This hobby was not pursued by choice, but out of necessity, as her neck was in a vice-like contraption, while her right leg was suspended in the air by means of pulleys and straps. The room stank of medicines and disinfectant, and the ceiling was an unpleasant shade of pale sepia.

She ached all over, was probably bruised from stem to stern. It was strange, because she could see that lorry as plain as day when she closed her eyes, yet it had been a mere shape at the time of the accident.

Her leg was a mess, or so she had been informed. She had been forbidden to move, and she wondered how on earth she might manage to disobey such an order. Her left heel was sore after constant contact with the mattress, so she bent the leg at the knee and placed the bottom of her foot against the sheet. She had moved; she had accomplished the impossible, had disobeyed the Terrible Blue Witch.

The Blue Witch was a ward sister of uncertain temperament. She had sat for a while with Connie and chatted away about matters mundane, yet she could be as sour as the grapes of wrath when the mood took her. She was horrible to the younger nurses – Connie had heard one of them crying after Sister Blue Witch had yelled at her in the corridor.

Connie wanted to go home. She wanted to rip the plaster of Paris from her leg and run away. But she couldn't. And had she been able to free herself from the bondage, there would still have been nowhere to go.

Home had been Mother, Father and Gilbert. Father's interests lay elsewhere now. He had always been absorbed by the business, but he had also found himself a woman, a thin, red-haired creature who went with him for little drives in the countryside. Connie could not remember when Father had last taken Mother out. There was no time for family, because the mill, the council and the woman left Aston Leigh off the list, out of the picture.

She was trapped. She could not even look out of the window, because her torturers were trying to keep her spine in a nice, straight line after its trauma. The worst bloody trauma of all was being forced to lie here like a vegetable. For the first couple of days, she had drifted in and out of sleep, but the unconsciousness had lasted only a few hours. She had woken in the operating theatre, only to be knocked out again while her leg got set. And now, at nine o'clock in the evening, she was about to spend her third night in hospital.

The door creaked. 'Feeling better, are we?' It was the Blue Witch.

The bits of Connie that were free twitched. 'Go away,' she said. 'Go and bully someone else. You only talked to me because they thought I might be comatose. All that nice chat was to keep me in the land of the living.'

'Now, now, I—'

'Now, now, you're a bully. There was a nurse crying outside my door earlier. But I'm not afraid of you, so don't waste your energies.'

Sister Margaret Peacock picked up Connie's chart and wrote on it. There was no brain damage, thank God. But there was another point that needed clarifying. 'Miss Shawcross – were you trying to kill yourself?'

Connie gritted her teeth. 'Is that any business of yours?'

'Not particularly,' replied Sister Peacock. 'But the psychiatrist needs to know.'

'Well, just tell him to keep his distance, please. There is nothing wrong with my mind. I had an accident.'

Margaret Peacock sat in a chair next to Connie's head. 'Your brother told us that you just dashed out. The road was quiet, yet you threw yourself under the only moving vehicle. Why?'

'That's my affair, not yours.'

The nurse stood up and put her face over the patient's. 'Listen to me,' she said, her tone quiet and conversational. 'We've put in a lot of effort here.' She decided to pull no punches, to shock the young madam into talking. 'That leg of yours looked like something off Bolton market, something skinned and ready for the stewpot. Eight hours. Eight hours in total of theatre time was spent on you, Miss Shawcross. We couldn't knock you right out in case we induced a deeper coma, so we pussy-footed about with our breath held. That's a beautiful job.' She pointed to the strapped-up limb.

'Thank you so much.' The sarcasm in Connie's tone was clear.

'Right, then.' A long, blue-sleeved arm reached out and clutched the iron bedstead. 'If you are going to kill yourself, we won't bother. If a child keeps breaking a toy, its mother might as well give up on the repairs. Why should we concentrate on restoring you to health if you're going to do this all over again?'

Connie looked up into a pair of warm brown eyes that seemed strangely divorced from the rest of this skinny, bossy woman. 'I had a shock,' she replied quietly. 'A family matter. The shock made me run. The lorry came and I went under it.'

Sister Peacock nodded just once. 'Right, that's all I wanted to know.' This girl had not been told about the lorry driver's fate. She was perky – even cheeky, but there was a frailty about her, a vulnerability behind the beautiful face. 'We have informed your parents of your progress. They will visit again tomorrow.'

Connie blinked rapidly. 'Not my father,' she said. 'Just Mother and Gilbert.'

The nurse looked hard at Connie. Twice, this young woman had refused to receive Edward Shawcross. 'As you wish,' she said.

Connie pondered. 'No,' she said thoughtfully. 'If my father comes separately, you may send him in.' There were things she wanted to say to him, but she needed him to be alone. 'But if there's anybody with him, try to send him away.'

'Would you like something to drink?'

Connie sighed. She had to drink from a spouted cup, because she could not sit up properly, could not be a human being. 'Please.' She took the thick china cup and sipped some water. 'How long will I be here?' she asked.

'Weeks, certainly.' Sister Peacock placed the cup on the bedside locker. 'Your head is fine, but the leg . . . well, we'll have to take that very slowly.'

When the door closed behind the Blue Witch, Connie allowed her tears full rein. She thought about James Templeton, the man who loved her, the man who had limped since . . . since for ever. He had always been so aware of his difference, his separateness from whole people. If her leg didn't heal, she would be in the same boat. The limb throbbed terribly. The painkillers were scarcely touching this dreadful agony. She could not move, was unable to ease the stiffness and soreness in the rest of her body.

The door opened again. 'Go away!' she shouted, a sob crashing through the words.

'Shut up.' The door closed.

Connie gasped, knew who it was. 'Who let you in?'

James leaned over the bed. He was wearing a white coat, a bright smile and a ridiculous false moustache fastened to a pair of joke spectacles. A stethoscope dangled down his chest. 'Dr Ebenezer Templeton at your service, ma'am. MB, BSc, DFC and Bar, specialist in ingrowing toenails and cat-spaying.' He swung the stethoscope. 'What seems to be the problem?'

She could not help smiling. 'Where did you get the white coat and the instrument?'

'Stolen, m'lud. Forty-seven other offences to be

taken into consideration.' He produced a bag of fruit. 'Have a grape.'

Connie chewed on fruit that was forbidden because its bearer was trespassing. She spat out the seeds, placed them on a proffered sheet of newspaper. 'What happened to the driver?' she asked.

James hesitated. 'He died.' There was nothing to be gained from lying.

The last vestiges of colour drained from her face. 'My fault.' She closed her eyes.

'Was it?'

'Of course it was, James. I ran into him and he tried to avoid running into me.'

James removed the foliage from beneath his nose. 'But why did you run?'

Connie opened her eyes, because hiding behind the eyelids had not worked, would never work, not while the film kept running inside her head. 'Father was with a woman,' she said. '*The* woman, probably. He was so stupid and pathetic, trying to explain why and so forth. And I suddenly couldn't listen. I know Mother can be a misery, but she doesn't deserve that, James.' She breathed deeply. 'I ran. I didn't hear the lorry, hardly saw it. The next moment, I was in hospital. And that poor man died.'

He stroked her hair. 'You would never hurt a living thing. I know you. I've known you for a long time, Connie. It's not as if you deliberately set out to murder someone.'

A mental picture of Grandmother's face was quickly chased away. 'Find his wife or his mother. Go to see them. Tell them that I'll help all I can.'

'I will.' He continued to smooth her hair. 'I'll find them for you. Please concentrate on getting well.'

Connie looked deep into his eyes, saw the boy

from next door, the lad in whose company she and her brother had taken so much pleasure. He had always been of an inventive turn of mind, had been an expert at trouble. 'Remember when we got into Colonel Manson's greenhouse and you took the blame?'

James nodded.

'Well, you can't do that this time. When we pinched apples and rounded up pheasants to save them from being shot, you always volunteered to take the punishment.'

He shrugged. 'Nobody hits a cripple.' The words were no sooner out of his mouth than he wanted to bite them back.

'I may well find out about that for myself,' Connie whispered after a short silence.

He attempted a retrieval of Connie's chosen subject. 'Those bloody pheasants,' he said. 'We shoved them into an empty stable – remember? And the horses on each side were clinically insane for months. The birds weren't a bit grateful. I bet we all have the scars to this day.'

Connie smiled weakly. 'James, you are so kind. You have always been so good to me.'

He blinked to mop some moisture from his eyes. 'Look, you have a chance of coming out in one piece and without a game leg. Just do as they tell you. It's 1950, and all kinds of things are available to the boffins these days.'

She didn't care about that. Perhaps she deserved to be marked, because she had taken away the life of an innocent working man. Lying motionless was part of the punishment, too, since Connie had never been still in her life. 'You'd better go,' she advised seriously. 'Before you get charged with impersonating a doctor. They'll probably lock you up for life.'

James patted her head before removing his hand. 'No, Connie. It's the doctors who should be arrested for impersonating humanity. But as long as you behave like a slightly disordered piece of meat, the medics will do you proud.' He bent, kissed her brow. 'Be good,' he whispered. 'No Morris dancing, no climbing trees. See you soon.' Inside, the words 'I love you' demanded to be released, but he held them back. Connie had enough trouble without being mithered by a lunatic 'doctor'.

When James had left, Connie closed her eyes again and let the pictures happen. She could not see the driver's face, but a loud screeching sound advertised his attempt to avoid a collision with a stupid girl. He was dead. What about his dependants? Did he have a wife, children, old parents in need of care? Had he suffered, had he died quickly?

She grasped the cord on her pillow, pushed hard against the bell button. A young nurse came in, possibly the one who had been crying earlier. 'Is something the matter?'

'Come here, please.' Connie smiled up into the bright, happy face. This one hadn't cried in a while. 'Would you ask the Blue Witch to do something for me?'

The eyebrows arched themselves. 'Pardon, miss?'

'The Terrible Blue Witch. Sister Peacock.'

Loud laughter filled the small room. 'Oh God,' said the nurse. 'Wait till I tell the others.' She sobered, waited for Connie to continue.

'I want to help the family of the lorry driver who died,' she said. She had asked James, but there was no harm in using belt and braces to be sure. 'It's very important.'

The merriment ceased. 'All right. Don't you be worrying, we'll find out what we can. I'll be back in a bit with the bed bath trolley. If you need a bedpan, just give us another buzz.'

Connie carried on staring at the ceiling. It had been a very long few days, a time that had begun with a whole Constance Shawcross, a time that was ending with a broken Connie. The pain would keep her awake tonight, and the guilt might render her sleepless for some considerable time to come.

Alice Shawcross stood at the drawing room window, though nothing was registering in the sparse light of evening. Behind her, Edward Shawcross leaned against the mantel, his eyes fixed on the marble hearth. It had not been easy, but he had done it. He had told Alice about Vera, and Alice was probably preparing her reply.

She did not turn round. 'Tintern Avenue,' she said eventually. 'A very thin woman with rusty hair. I have known for quite a while, but thank you for telling me.'

She had already been aware, yet she had said nothing. 'How?' he asked.

Alice shrugged lightly. 'I had you followed. You married me for my family's money, so I do like to know exactly where it is being spent.'

'Alice, I—'

'Oh, do be quiet.' At last, she turned to face him. 'I have wondered over the years why my father chose you.' She nodded thoughtfully. 'Because you were chosen. Was he grateful because you saved his life? Was I the prize?'

'No,' he answered. 'It wasn't like that.'

'How was it, then?'

Edward pushed a hand through his hair. He had been afraid of poverty, afraid of alone-ness. Samuel Fishwick had offered the world on a plate, and Edward had grabbed for it. The price he had paid was marriage to a woman he had not loved enough. 'I don't know,' he answered after a few seconds.

'There is something you are holding back,' she insisted.

Edward was holding back Alice's half-brother, a man who was scarcely older than Gilbert. But he had made a promise, so he could say no more.

Alice crossed the room unhurriedly and stood in front of the man she had married, the man who had fathered her children. With deliberate slowness, she raised a hand, drew it back, then delivered a hefty blow to his cheek. 'You will go upstairs now, Edward, and you will collect from your room enough clothes to fill one suitcase of average size. The rest of your belongings will be given to the Salvation Army in Bolton. I want you out of this house now, this evening.'

He did not flinch. 'There is more,' he said. 'Constance saw me with my . . . with Vera. She was hurt because she was running from me. She ran straight into that lorry.' He hated himself, wanted to die. But death would have been too easy. Edward Shawcross was condemned to live with the knowledge that he had caused great pain and suffering to Constance.

Alice steadied herself by placing a hand on the back of an armchair. 'So,' she said breathlessly. 'You have been the cause of my daughter's terrible injury. Get out,' she snapped. 'Before I change my mind about that one suitcase. Don't come back. Don't go near Constance or Gilbert, don't contact me. As for the mill – stay out of there, too. I'm sure we can find someone to run it until it is sold.' Her voice was rising in pitch. 'You are a despicable man,' she screamed. 'A weak and stupid lump of nothing!'

He left the room, listened to her sobs.

Alice sat down, imagined that terrible morning's scene, saw Constance backing away from the unpalatable truth and into the path of the lorry. A coldness entered her breast, an icy numbness beneath which her temper bubbled. She must be calm, must be deliberate and careful. Mother was in the house . . . Or was she? The less Alice saw of Eleanor, the better. Mother was not exactly a source of comfort. Mother was not a person who should be allowed to see Alice weeping.

Edward was a damned fool of a man. Alice knew that she had been less than perfect as a wife, but he should have talked to her, should have discussed things. Instead of which he had ignored her, had invested his energies in business and civic life. While she, Alice Shawcross, had sulked like a child and stuffed her face with chocolates. 'I'm as bad as he is,' she whispered.

Gilbert came in. 'Mother?'

She dried her eyes hastily. 'Your father is leaving,' she said softly. 'Tonight.'

He was not surprised, though the confirmation sickened him, seemed to cut right into his chest. 'Don't cry,' he said. 'I'll still be here. So will Con, when she gets out of hospital.'

Alice tried to smile, failed. 'Will she walk again, Gilbert?'

'As long as she stays away from strong magnets,' he replied, trying to make things sound a little less serious. 'She could well become attractive to magnets, as they've bolted her together with bits of metal. The doctor seemed very hopeful, Mother. Don't cross the bridge. We haven't arrived at it yet. And I'll do all I can. You don't know how pleased I am about the shop, because I'm not cut out for university.'

'And Connie wants something to do,' added Alice. The tears dried. 'Let's get it ready, Gilbert. Let's make something for Constance, something for her to step into.'

Gil grinned as cheerfully as he could manage. 'That's the spirit.' He sat down and watched his mother making her weary way out of the room. Father was going. He was going off to live with an unremarkable and terribly thin female who looked as if she had just been rescued from a Nazi concentration camp.

The young man didn't know what to think, how to feel. He was angry with his father, yet he understood the need for love and warmth. Mother was not a demonstrative type, so Father had looked elsewhere. And what had he found? A breathing skeleton. If the woman had hidden charms, they were very carefully concealed within that slight frame.

How would life be from now on? Grandmother was about to sell the mill, Father was about to disappear, Mother was going to invent a department store. And Connie, who was worth ten of any other Shawcross, including himself, was stretched out on a rack of torture in the infirmary.

Where was Grandmother? he wondered. She had walked through the front gate some fifteen minutes ago, had wandered off towards the woods. Gil hoped with all his heart that Eleanor Fishwick would move on once the mill was sold. He didn't like her, didn't want to share living space with her.

He heard his father in the hall, chose not to move. The front door opened and closed, then a car engine was turned over. This was the end of something and the start of something else. Gil sat as still as stone while his father drove away. The clock chimed ten times, settled to rest its little hammers until the next quarter. At ten o'clock on a warm summer night, everyone's life was altered.

Eleanor Fishwick stood at the edge of the woods and heaved the contents of her stomach onto the earth. Her hands shook, while her legs seemed to have gone on strike, because they would not take her weight. She sat down, leaned against the bole of a tree. In her capacious bag, a few scraps of crocodile lay wrapped in a handkerchief. She had taken up the floorboard, had realized that bits of material were missing. Returning to Turnbull's grave had become a necessity, because the crocodile handbag had all but exploded when the bullet had made its exit.

A shot was fired. In the woods, people were looking for rabbits. It was a dangerous place, she reminded herself. A person could be killed by accident. She raised her head, breathed deeply, wondered about accidents. The single bullet that had felled Turnbull was from a high calibre pistol, not a shotgun. Most of the opportunists who looked for food carried shotguns, but who was to say that a pistol had never been fired in those trees? She bucked up, inhaled, exhaled regularly through her mouth to stem the nausea. There could be no bits of crocodile leather left with him now, surely?

He had become a soft, boneless thing whose shape changed when prodded with a branch. The weather had been mercilessly hot, and Peter Turnbull had rotted quickly. Eleanor shivered as she recalled the thick, black cloud of flies that had risen in response to her probings. A purple hand had been disturbed, had slithered from the hole, maggots crawling out of cracked, festering flesh. Eleanor had seen death before, but this had been her first encounter with decay. Abroad, the dead had been buried quickly in order to win the race against decomposition.

It was done, anyway. She had the bits of her bag, and her gun was well hidden, so no-one would ever connect her with the death of Peter Turnbull. Edward might put two and two together, but he would never speak up. Wasn't there an uncle? Yes. He had gone south, would perhaps remain there. With any degree of luck, Eleanor would be out of the picture before the body was discovered.

She had forced him deeper into the hole beneath the tree's ancient, exposed roots, had rammed him repeatedly until he had disappeared into that makeshift sepulchre. But now, she must get home quickly before anyone missed her.

The nausea lessened, and Eleanor Fishwick walked back to Aston Leigh. She did not notice a figure at an upstairs window, was unaware of her grandson's watchful eye. With a tremendous feeling of relief, she went upstairs for a bath.

THIRTEEN

Sadie threw open the door, felt Sheila's anxious, hot breath on the back of her neck. Sheila Foster had committed an unforgivable sin; Sheila had allowed Vera to escape like a thief in the night. 'Oh,' said Sadie, her whole body seeming to deflate. 'It's you.'

Edward Shawcross nodded. 'I want to speak to Vera, please.' He had neglected Vera, had been too concerned about his daughter. Constance had not wanted to see him, and he understood why. In spite of that, he had haunted the Bolton Royal Infirmary for hours on end.

Sadie stood back, pushed Sheila against the wall to allow Edward access into the tiny hallway. 'You want to speak to her? So do I. Only she's not here. She's took her knitting and a load of clothes, just buggered off without a please or a thank you or a kiss my backside, if you'll pardon the expression.'

Edward pardoned it with a jerk of his head, ran a hand through his hair. 'Last night?' This couldn't be true. Vera was pregnant, was in no fit state to go wandering off.

Sadie nodded vigorously. 'She were upset, like, hadn't been sleeping proper, just nodded off in the chair sometimes. After what happened to your girl.

I think she took all the blame on herself. Any road, me and Sheila thought Vera might have gone somewhere with you, or that you'd found her a house. Mind, she would have told us, I suppose. Did she not talk to you, then? We thought she might have telephoned.'

'She didn't.'

'How is your daughter?' asked Sheila.

Edward walked into the living room and sat down. 'She's in hospital, but the wound to her head was not as bad as it seemed. However, her right leg took the full weight of the lorry. They've hung it up in some sort of contraption.'

'But she'll be all right?'

Edward smiled gratefully at Sheila Foster. 'I hope so. Thanks for your concern.' He turned to Sadie. 'Vera seemed to have recovered from all that . . . other business. But, as you said just now, the events of the other day must have sent her off course again. Did she leave a note?'

Sadie reached up and took the letter from the mantelpiece. 'I think she left this for posting, but your name's on it, so take it now. That's the only clue we've got, only we didn't like the idea of opening it, 'cos it's not got our names on.'

Edward tore at the envelope, pulled out the single sheet. 'It tells us nothing,' he said. 'Except that we are forbidden to go out searching for her.'

Sheila sank into a chair. 'In the cottage down Dartmouth, she locked herself in a bathroom for over an hour. I had to get the next-door neighbour to break the door down, because she'd put the bolt on. She were just sitting on a stool with a blank look on her face. Bloody terrifying.'

'She's over all that,' said Sadie. 'Since the baby

started shifting about a bit, she's been a lot better. No. This is different. She happen thinks she should leave you to look after your daughter, Mr Shawcross.'

'She does.' He waved the letter. 'Of course, I shall put money into the bank for her, because she'll need to live somewhere.' He gazed into the empty grate. 'She won't have gone far, I suppose. And she has left William, or so she says in the note.'

Sadie nodded. 'Aye, William's in the back garden. He's been yelling and howling, so I put him out. He knows she's gone. He knows she's not coming back. Funny things, dogs. They sense what's in the wind, don't they?'

Edward scratched his head. He had lost his home, his mistress, and the respect of his children. Soon, he would lose his job, too. Even if he did go into the mill against Alice's wishes, it would only be a matter of time before Eleanor Fishwick sold the business.

On top of all of which he seemed to have acquired an alsatian dog of unusually huge proportions. Vera had always said that William must have had a St Bernard somewhere along the branches of his family toilet. She had been amusing before the pregnancy. 'They don't have family trees like us,' she had said. 'To a dog, a tree is a lavatory' . . . and she was gone. The laughter had just started again, too. Yesterday, in the car, Vera had been choosing names for the baby, had gone from Adam to Zachariah, from Annie to Zoe before settling on Michael Edward or Susan Joan. She didn't want another Vera, because she'd always considered Veronica to be a burdensome Christian name.

'Are you all right?' asked Sadie. Teddy Shawcross wasn't looking very healthy today.

'I'm homeless,' he answered bluntly. 'My wife

338

ordered me out, my children don't want to know me, and Vera has disappeared. I have probably lost my job and my self-respect but, apart from all the above, I am very well, thank you.'

'Bloody hell,' said Sadie. 'Would you like a cuppa, a bit of toast or a few biscuits?'

Edward shook his head. It would take more than a brew of Horniman's to set him to rights.

'Stop here,' suggested Sheila. 'The rent's paid, so you might as well stay. There's beds upstairs.' She blushed slightly, the pale cream skin acquiring a faint colour for a few moments. He would know about the beds, because Vera had been his mistress, his bit on the side.

He managed a grim smile. 'The lace curtains on Tintern Avenue would be shredded by the weekend. Anyway, my name is not on the rent book.'

Sadie's jaw hung for a second as a thought struck. 'What about the corporation? What about you being an alderman? They'll not be thrilled about you getting chucked out of your house, will they? Oh, what a bloody mess.'

Edward nodded his agreement with Sadie's sentiments. 'I'll resign,' he said.

This was terrible. Sadie had always been rather pleased about little Teddy Shawcross, because he had made good. In spite of having been born in a slum and to feckless parents, Teddy had done all right. But now, he was losing everything. She felt as if this human good luck charm was being melted down before her very eyes. 'Is there owt at all we can do, lad?'

'No, Sadie,' he replied. 'But thanks for caring. I really do appreciate your concern.'

Sheila provided her contribution. 'What about

the dog? He's a nice one, but I don't think I could cope with him, not with my cats to feed as well. And the trouble is, he'd keep dashing back here looking for Vera. If she's done a bunk, William should move somewhere else.'

Edward sighed resignedly. 'I'll take him, but not yet. Will you stay on here for now?' he asked Sadie. 'Just for a short while. There are things I need to sort out.'

'Course I'll stop,' she answered. 'My lot can take care of theirselves for a bit, do them good. Any road, there has to be somebody in this house in case Vera takes it into her head to come back home. So I'll stop on and see to the dog till you've got yourself settled.'

Edward thanked the two women, then left the house. Outside, he felt as if a thousand eyes were fixed on him, but it didn't matter any more. He had to get to the hospital to make sure that Constance was still improving, then he needed to find somewhere to live.

As he drove towards town, he allowed his mind free rein, thought about those little rooms in Goldsmith Street, about the chess games and the meals eaten from newspaper. He was back to square one, except that he had no little home above a butcher's shop. But that was the least of his worries, because he had an injured daughter and a missing lover. Later, he would sort out somewhere to lay his head. For now, he must concentrate on Constance and Vera.

Vera Hardman dragged her case from the luggage rack and heaved it and herself out of the carriage. Dust and smoke hung in the air, suspended like bits of fog in the heat of summer. She coughed, stood on the platform while a writhing mass of humanity edged its way towards the promised land. This was Blackpool; this was Mecca for those who had escaped for two weeks from the vice-like grips of cotton and coal.

Vera found a bench and sat down. She had four pounds, sixteen shillings and fivepence in her purse, a bank book in her handbag and a small case filled with clothes. Tucked away in her little account, there was almost enough for the abortion she had craved, but she didn't want the operation any more. All Vera needed was somewhere to live until her baby was born.

Until four days ago, the future had seemed hopeful. Edward had been prepared to leave his wife, had sat in the car, had chatted on about a little house in Harwood or Bromley Cross, somewhere away from the smoke and dirt of Bolton. Then that poor girl had come along, had seen Vera, had dashed away from the truth and towards the lorry. Edward had commitments. As long as he paid in a bit of money every week, Vera would see to herself while he looked after that hurt girl. It was only fair, Vera told herself firmly. Constance needed her dad more than Vera needed her lover. She closed her eyes, crossed her fingers and wished for Constance Shawcross's full recovery.

She carted her case along to Left Luggage, put it in store, placed the ticket stub in her purse. Her main aim now was to find a room. Following the crowd, she made her way through to the promenade, stood and watched while families cavorted on the yellow sands. Behind her, the famous metal tower overlooked the proceedings, while horses clopped along with the better-off holidaymakers in glossy open carriages.

Children screamed, threw water, dug holes, built castles and forts. A large man in a vest, rolled-up trousers and straw hat wobbled out of the sea, threw himself into a deckchair, cursed when the seat collapsed beneath him. A fat woman who must have been his wife was doubled over with glee, her howls climbing above all the other sounds that floated up from the beach.

Vera found herself smiling. It must be lovely to be part of a family, a proper family with sandwiches wrapped in greaseproof and a jug of tea bought from a nearby vendor. Little brown limbs flew all over the place, perfect arms and legs attached to beautiful, happy, sun-kissed children. In a year or so, perhaps Vera would be here with a tiny child, bucket, spade and paper flags. Her son or daughter might sit right here, opposite Blackpool Tower where the largest crowds always gathered. He or she could learn to build sand-pies and castles, could splash at the edge of the water, practise throwing and catching a ball.

She turned and looked along the Golden Mile, took in the penny arcades, the rock shops, the sellers of ice-creams and candy floss. There were fortune tellers, fish and chip shops, barrows overflowing with beach toys and brightly coloured postcards. Silly people wore silly hats with KISS ME QUICK and FAST SHOOTER printed across the fronts. Miners and spinners had let their hair down, had allowed their faces and bodies to be reddened by repeated overdoses of sunshine. In a week or so, they would return to loom and seam, but the memory of Blackpool would sustain them until Christmas, the next distraction.

Vera liked Blackpool. She remembered coming with Mam, when Mam had been young and fairly strong. They had walked the length of a pier, had been photographed by a man with a big, clumsy camera. Would Bolton corporation let the Tintern Avenue house to someone else? she wondered. What about all her little bits of memories? That photo of her and Mam was in a silver frame on the bedroom tallboy. She ordered herself not to dwell on such unimportant details. She had done the right thing, had freed her lover to care for his real family.

Determinedly, Vera set forth to find a room for herself in one of the many streets that ran off the prom. The task was not an easy one, since many Lancastrians were holidaying, as was half of Glasgow, or so it seemed. She recalled Mam telling her that the Glasgow people loved Blackpool.

After searching fruitlessly for an hour, Vera began to worry. The words NO VACANCIES seemed to have burnt themselves into her brain. She needed to rest, needed to find a little place where she could lock herself away and think.

At last, she found a house that was dingier than its neighbours. MON REPOS was a grey-fronted, middle-of-terrace boarding house. The paint was parting company with the door, and the brass letter flap had not seen polish since Preston Guild, Vera reckoned. Lace curtains were darned in places, and could have benefited from a seeing-to with Dolly Cream, but Vera was past caring. She entered Mon Repos and clattered a bell on the hall table.

A wondrous sight hove into view, laboured breathing accompanying the shuffling gait. 'Any experience?' asked the vision.

'What?' Vera forgot her manners in the face of such a creature. The woman was immensely fat, with at least three chins and shiny, bulging cheeks. She wore a flowered wrap-around apron that must have been cobbled together out of several similar items, brown slippers, concertina-ed stockings and a heavy frown. 'It's two quid a week, room and board thrown in.'

The light dawned. Vera had been mistaken for a job applicant. 'What are the duties?' she asked.

Lardy hands raised themselves, the index finger of one counting on the digits of the other hand. 'Breakfasts, set, make, dish up and wash up. Dinners, set, serve and wash up. Teas, set, serve and wash up. I see to the suppers meself. You can have a bath on a Monday night at seven o'clock, buy your own soap. No men in your room, no cooking in your room, no pots in your room, no noise.'

Vera nodded.

'Are you interested?'

'I'll give it a go.'

Piggy eyes peered through layers of lard and swept over Vera's sparse frame. 'Are you strong?'

'Yes.'

'You look like a puff of wind'd see you off. Still, I suppose you won't eat much. Move in as soon as you like, start in two days. I had to sack the last one. She was a bit too free with the marge and marmalade.'

Vera waited to be shown the room, stammered her request to see it when the woman made no move.

'Attic. The one at the back. I don't go upstairs no more. I've a woman comes in and sees to the rooms and washing sheets. Go up. Move in when you're ready.'

'I don't know your name.'

The woman sniffed. 'Maisie Cunningham. Missus. I'm a widow.'

'Sorry to hear it.'

Mrs Cunningham sniffed again. 'He weren't much use, but he kept the place painted, I suppose. Are you moving in today?'

'If that's all right.'

'Aye. It is all right. I'll have to go now, I've spuds cooking.' She ambled off towards the rear of the house.

Vera climbed the stairs. A narrow runner covered the steps, the pattern long forgotten beneath years of plodding feet. The walls were coffee-coloured, with miserable Victorian prints punctuating the various marks and stains. On the first landing, there was an umbrella stand, a coat rack and a large list of rules. Breakfast was at seven-thirty till eight, dinner twelve to one. Tea was served between four and five, with an optional supper (cocoa and two biscuits) at ten o'clock. Doors were locked at ten-thirty. Use of cruet cost fourpence per week or sevenpence per fortnight. Baths, at fivepence each, could be booked with at least twenty-four hours notice.

The second landing carried a similar list, with NO JUMPING ON THE BEDS and RUBBER SHEETS FOR BEDWETTERS AVAILABLE ON REQUEST added at the bottom. The house was deadly silent, would probably have been just as quiet in bad weather, as the Mrs Cunninghams of this world liked their places to be empty except at mealtimes. 'It's like bloody Dotheboys Hall,' muttered Vera to herself. 'And folk come here for pleasure? Prison sentence, more like.'

Right at the top of Mon Repos, Vera found her room. It was unexpectedly bright, with a large window set into the roof and washed-out orange-striped curtains drawn back to let in the sun. There was a bed, a dressing table, a stool and a small wardrobe. It would do for now, she decided. When she stood in the dormer window, she could see the tower poking its metal girders towards the sky. There was something very durable about Blackpool Tower. It was not a thing of particular beauty, but it was there, would probably remain in situ for ever.

She lay on the lumpy mattress and thought about Edward. He was possibly visiting his daughter down at the infirmary. Would Alice forgive him? she wondered. He wasn't a bad man, wasn't a particularly strong one. In spite of his weakness, Vera had loved him. The baby kicked. She placed her hands over her abdomen, felt the tiny limbs moving. The fear had gone, thank God. She would work here for the summer, would save every penny, would leave when the job ended. Relieved to have found somewhere to stay, Vera snoozed away the afternoon.

Alice walked down the corridor, her hand resting on Gil's arm. Constance was doing very well. Although no-one knew quite how her leg would turn out, she was not going to lose it.

Edward stepped round a corner, stopped when he saw his wife. He didn't know whether to continue or retreat, so he simply froze until the pair reached him. 'How is she?' he asked.

'She's better,' answered Gil. 'Well enough to complain. She wants them to take her leg out of the contraption, but they can't.'

Alice said nothing. She stared levelly at her husband, her face expressionless.

'I'll . . . I'll go along and see her,' said Edward. He carried on, his feet dragging as he neared Connie's room. Alice had been angry, justifiably so. Guilt rose into his throat, threatened to choke him.

He opened the door, stepped inside.

'Who let you in?' asked Connie immediately. 'I told them to watch out for you, because I didn't want you here at the same time as Mother.'

'Your mother has gone,' he said. 'I saw her leaving. And I've been trying to visit you for days.'

Connie eyed him as levelly as she could from her disadvantaged situation. 'How could you?' she asked at last. 'How could you keep company with another woman?'

He inhaled, let out a long sigh. 'It just happened. It wasn't a planned thing.'

Connie wished that she could jump up and slap him. He was so stupid, so foolish. 'So you have left home. Gil told me. Mother didn't want me to hear it, but Gil and I have few secrets.'

Edward sat down on a hard chair next to the bed. 'Alice asked me to go – well – ordered me to leave.'

'So you've gone to that skinny red-head?'

He sighed heavily. 'Vera has disappeared. She wrote me a letter telling me to look after my family, then she simply left. No-one knows where she is.'

Connie had no idea how to feel. She loved her father, felt desperately sorry for him, yet she remained furious. 'So where are you living?'

'Don't worry about me,' he replied. 'Concentrate on getting better.' He gazed at her, saw a few lines of pain on her forehead. 'This is my fault,' he said.

Connie said nothing.

'The accident would not have happened if you hadn't seen me.'

'And we would not be here if God had not created man,' answered Constance snappily. 'Everything has its ifs. I should have been more careful.'

No matter what she said, no matter what anyone

said, Edward would always know that he had put his daughter into hospital. 'Would you rather I had stayed away today?'

She blinked slowly, thought about that. 'At first, I never wanted to see you again. But you are my father and I love you, even though I'm furious with you. Then I decided that I couldn't bear it if you visited with Mother. I imagined you standing here with her, thought you would carry on pretending that everything was normal. After all, you must have been doing that for a while. But as you have told Mother about . . . about whatever her name is, I suppose it's all above board.'

He could have wept, but he held back. Constance was a good woman, a very direct and honest person. Alice, too, was a decent sort. He should never have married her. He should have ignored Samuel Fishwick's invitation to walk out with Alice, should have overcome his fear of poverty.

'Did you ever love Mother?' asked Connie.

'I don't know.' He had liked Alice before marrying her. She had been a gentle soul searching for love and security. The two of them had been in similar positions, each having been denied the affection of parents, each looking forward to a cold future. Like a pair of fledgelings recently fallen from the nest, they had come together to share a brief warmth whose inventor had been necessity.

'I could never marry for less than love,' said Connie haughtily.

Love had been a luxury, something beyond the reach of Edward and Alice. His parents had died, his brother had emigrated. Alice, who had grown up less than pretty, had ceased to amuse her strange family. Two wrongs had certainly failed to make a right in this instance. 'We all make mistakes,' he said lamely. 'Sometimes, people have to take whatever happens to be there, because choices can be limited by circumstance.'

'Then you should have stayed single.'

Constance, laid low by injury, was claiming the moral high ground. Edward looked at his lovely daughter and hoped that she would find her dream, that she would never settle for second, third, or fourth best. 'One thing my dad used to say has always stuck in my mind, Constance. Drunk or sober, he was always saying, "Life's a bugger, then you die." Living isn't simple. Many of us make the most terrible mistakes without realizing exactly what we are doing. If I could wind back the clock, I could wipe out your accident. I could wipe out my whole life, I suppose. But there is no magic, and I am very sorry that you are in this mess. I cannot undo what I did to you, to your mother. We just have to carry on as best we can.'

Connie blinked rapidly. Her female instincts were on red alert, because this foolish man needed caring for. He was her father, and she loved him, but there was nothing she could do for him. 'Where will you go?' she asked.

'I'll find somewhere.'

'And how will you earn a living?'

He shrugged. 'I'm forty-four, a mere stripling. I have a great deal of experience in business, so some good soul should employ me. Think only about yourself. Get strong and get out of here as quickly as possible.'

'We're opening a shop.'

He nodded.

'Mother says that Maude Templeton is interested.'

'Good,' replied Edward. 'It's time Maude

Templeton found something to do.' He smiled grimly. 'Mind, I'd not want to be employed by Maude. She's so fierce.'

A nurse bustled in with a rattling trolley. 'Time for your bed bath,' she announced meaningfully.

Edward rose, gazed at Connie for several seconds. He would not come again. He would telephone to check on his daughter's progress, but he could play no useful part in her life. ''Bye, Constance,' he said. He walked out of the hospital and through the grounds until he reached his car. He would see to William, get him settled, then he might just follow the example of his mistress. This was as good a time as any to do a disappearing act.

The meeting was convened in the drawing room of Aston Leigh. Those present were asked to give their full names so that Maude Templeton could fill in a page marked Those Present. She had attended a lot of minor conferences in her time, so she was well primed with regard to protocol.

Alice looked remarkably sane for a wife who had been abandoned three days ago, for a woman whose only daughter was in hospital. She was thinner, her hair was properly done and she had even bought some smaller clothes.

Mary Martindale sat between Gilbert and a bemused Sadie. Sadie had no idea why she had been sent for. Her feet were mortallious, and she had been dragged away from Vera Hardman's house by Mary with very little warning. What if Vera came back? Sheila was there, right next door, but Sheila had proved only too well that her mind wasn't always properly on the job.

James sat apart from everyone else. He had come

when summoned because he wanted to watch Mother performing. She was in her element when organizing.

'Full name, James?' asked Maude jokingly.

'You had me christened, so you stick the result on your paper,' answered James. She always went that little bit too far when doing things correctly. Had Connie been here, this could have been the most tremendous fun.

'Right, there we are,' said Maude, obviously very pleased with herself. 'As you are all aware, we have come together to hear Mrs Shawcross speak on the concept of a rather select department store in Bolton.'

Sadie mumbled something about knowing nothing about anything, but Mary held her back.

'Alice?' beamed Maude.

Alice Shawcross stood up and smiled at her small audience. 'The mill is to be sold,' she announced. 'My mother, as sole owner of Fishwick's, has chosen to let it go. I suppose we could sit around and do very little, just live on our savings, but I have a notion that we might enjoy a new venture.' She directed her gaze towards her son. 'Gilbert is not particularly keen on university, and Constance, when she recovers, will want to do something useful. So I have taken a property on Deansgate.'

Sadie eased off her shoes, knew that she would regret this rash move later on. Squeezing her bunions back, even into the softest kid leather, was never easy.

'Mary, Gilbert's friend, has managerial experience,' continued the hostess.

Mary, whose experience might have been listed on a postage stamp with room to spare, smiled weakly.

'She has an idea about a restaurant, a place where people can buy a decent meal and enjoy a bottle of wine. That would be a separate concern, as it would open not only during the day for shoppers, but also in the evenings. Mrs Martindale might care to help her daughter in that side of the business.'

Sadie nodded. As long as she could sit down during some jobs, she wouldn't mind cooking for a living.

'Mrs Templeton is interested in fashion and hair-dressing. Gilbert is willing to try his hand at supervising the whole store in conjunction with myself and Constance. There are many facets to consider, but we will be able to offer jobs to suitable people as our departments develop. James?'

James, who had come only as an amused spectator, raised an eyebrow.

'We should like you to take charge of porcelain, prints and general home decor.'

James Templeton's other eyebrow lifted itself and joined its twin. 'Have you seen my prefab, Mrs Shawcross? It's not exactly Lancashire Life. I haven't the slightest interest in items ornamental.'

'No,' replied Alice. 'I have not had the pleasure of viewing your new home.'

James snorted and folded his arms. He did not see himself as an interior decorator.

Maude placed a hand on Alice's arm. 'Allow me,' she whispered. 'James, you are a superb judge of colour and texture. We thought you might enjoy a sort of art gallery where the exhibits can be bought. Home decor could be loosely attached and in the hands of someone else. But you could perhaps sell some of your own work.'

James thought about his multi-coloured cow.

'Bolton may not be ready for me just yet,' he said carefully. Working with Connie might be wonderful.

'Bugger Bolton,' said Gil unexpectedly. He blushed, realized that he had uttered a swear word in the presence of ladies. 'You could have exhibitions, bring some chaps in from other cities – London, even. And you're not the only budding Rembrandt in these parts.'

James would think about it. He rather enjoyed being a collecting agent for the Wesleyan and General. That line of work took him into some interesting places where he was being allowed to sketch. 'I'll take the matter under consideration,' he promised, a hint of laughter behind the manufactured sobriety. 'But I want to carry on with my other interests.'

Maude sniffed quietly. Her son's other interests involved collecting funeral pennies and the odd shilling for endowment policies. He was also drawing pictures in mine shafts, cotton mills and iron foundries. An art gallery would be so much nicer.

Ada Dobson put in an unexpected appearance. Her face was flushed and she was breathing heavily. 'Sorry to interrupt,' she babbled. 'Only I don't know what to do with it.'

'I beg your pardon?' Alice had never seen Ada in such a flap.

'It's ate a full pound of pork sausage raw, just grabbed the lot off the table. Mr Shawcross said I had to take it and give it to Master Gilbert. I said the master had happen better talk to you, but he just shoved the thing in the back door and went off. I think it's supposed to be a present,' she told Gil.

Alice shook her head to demonstrate her confusion.

Lottie Bowker, cook and housekeeper to the Shawcross family, made an entrance that was rather swifter than planned. Preceding her on a leather lead, a dog of sturdy proportions panted, the long, pink tongue quivering with the rhythm of its excited breathing.

'What is this?' asked Alice.

'A dog,' answered James.

'We can see that,' said Maude. 'But whose is it?'

'Master Gil's,' said Lottie. 'Mr Shawcross wouldn't stay. I told him you were all having a meeting, so he just left the dog and went away. It's called William.'

William chose this unfortunate moment to fall in love with Maude Templeton. He dragged Lottie Bowker across the floor and deposited a very wet nose in Maude's lap.

'I think he likes you, Mother,' laughed James.

Maude had a way with animals. She told them what to do and they did it. 'Sit,' she commanded.

William jumped up and placed a huge paw on each of Maude's shoulders. She was about the right size and shape, was a reasonable replica of his erstwhile owner. He licked off a portion of Max Factor, smiled at the nice lady.

'Sit,' she repeated.

Sadie started to guffaw, tears filling her eyes as she watched Maude Templeton 'taking charge' of the extra-large alsatian. Mary Martindale's shoulders shook with repressed glee, while Gilbert simply roared with laughter. James smiled benevolently upon the scene. It would, he thought, have made a lovely subject for one of those gushingly horrible Victorian romantics, a picture of family bliss entitled 'The Prodigal's Return'.

William, pleased about the impression he was

making, dragged Lottie round and introduced himself to the whole company. Maude, freed from the tender mercies of William's affections, giggled like a schoolgirl. James watched his mother's laughter and liked what he saw.

'Whose is that?'

The laughter stopped. Eleanor Fishwick, elegant in black, stood in the doorway.

'It's mine, Grandmother.' There was an icy edge to Gil's tone.

'Then keep it away from me,' ordered the old woman.

Gil stood up and took the lead from a grateful Lottie. 'William chooses his friends very carefully,' he said. 'And he has decided that Mrs Templeton is his flavour of the moment.'

Eleanor stared hard at Gil, read the undisguised challenge in his eyes before leaving the room.

'Gilbert, don't be rude to your grandmother,' said Alice. She wiped her face, ordered herself to stop chuckling.

Maude rose from her seat. 'Shall we have some tea, Alice?' she asked.

Alice turned to Lottie and Ada. 'Tea would be lovely,' she said.

Lottie Bowker collected her thoughts. 'There'll be no sausage in the morning,' she announced. 'Yon dog's had it all.' She left the room wondering why her statement had caused the rebirth of so much merriment.

'It's nicer without the master,' Ada Dobson told the cook.

Lottie clouted Ada with a teacloth. 'Shush,' she ordered. 'Somebody might hear you.' But as she set out biscuits and little cakes, Lottie found herself humming a tune. It was a long time since Mrs Shawcross had laughed like that. Yes, a very long time.

Edward Shawcross had taken a little flat above a baker's shop on Darwen Road, just a sitting room, kitchen, bathroom and bedroom. It was a sight cosier than Goldsmith Street had been, but it was poky. He could not have kept William here. William wanted company and somewhere to run. William wanted Vera, but Vera had gone off without bothering to say a proper goodbye.

The ex-manager of Fishwick's Cotton Company Limited sat at a small table writing his letter of resignation to Bolton Council. He could no longer pretend that he was a good-living family man with an important position in the town. He was not a husband, was hardly a father, could not be considered to be a cog in the wheels of cotton manufacturing. Jobless and loveless, Edward signed the letter, placed it inside a prepared envelope, went out to post it.

Bromley Cross was a small village with a few shops and several rows of stone-built cottages. There were a couple of public houses and one or two places of worship, but the population remained small. Not for much longer, though, thought Edward as he posted his letter. Some of the land hereabout was to be designated for building, as much of Bolton's housing needed pulling down. Soon, council and private estates would arrive to eradicate acres of green made lush by Lancashire's notoriously wet weather.

He bought two chops, some vegetables and the *Bolton Evening News*. For the first time ever, he needed to look at the Jobs Vacant section. Back in his flat, he put his chops to cook beneath a gas grill with an explosive temperament, then sat to read the paper. But he got no further than the front page. Halfway down and with a very small headline, Edward found the announcement, 'BOLTON MAN MISSING'. He read on, learned that Peter Turnbull was the person in question.

For a reason he could not explain to himself, Edward's pores opened. He remembered driving along Halliwell Road with Eleanor by his side. She had looked at the Turnbull house, had complained about the family who had taken money from the Fishwick coffers, had then gone shopping for cheese.

No, no, he chided himself inwardly. An old lady could not cause a young man to disappear. She was in her seventies, was hardly at the peak of physical fitness. Perhaps Peter Turnbull had simply gone off on holiday. But a neighbour was quoted. 'He wouldn't have gone away without telling us. He visited his uncle once for a week and he told us to keep an eye on the house.'

Edward shivered, put down the paper, went to rescue his meal from the fire-breathing dragon next to the sink. Samuel had deteriorated very quickly. He had been a sick man, yet he had talked for a while at first, had sat up in bed between bouts of pain, had even occupied a chair near the window once or twice. Samuel. Had he wanted to compensate Molly's son? Had Eleanor felt threatened, had she done away with her husband and with her husband's love-child? Surely not? For a split second, Edward was back on Halliwell Road with Eleanor. She had mentioned drugs, had said that her husband would soon be needing morphine. Had she . . . ?

In Goldsmith Street all those years ago, the younger Eleanor had looked so sad, so concerned about her husband. Yet Edward remembered an occasion in that miserable little kitchen when he had caught sight of an expression on her face, a hard, cold look that had disappeared as soon as she had noticed his attention.

His appetite for food disappeared. Which was just as well, as the meat was singed black on the outside, red-raw on the inside. He threw away the chops and made a pot of tea. Where on earth would Peter Turnbull go? He was a man of regular habits, always frequented the same group of pubs, the greyhound stadium on Manchester Road, a local flea-pit of a cinema.

Restless now, Edward jumped up and began to pace the floor. A deep unease had settled in his bones, forbidding him to be still. Life was such a bloody mess. Wherever he turned, there were problems and mysteries. Where was Vera, where was Turnbull, why had Eleanor taken the death of her husband so well, so calmly? Her smile on the day of the funeral had been so smug, so satisfied. Edward found himself hoping that living alone was not going to make him fanciful.

Sunlight played on the moors, the rays skipping between clouds to make stripes on carpets of green. In the road below, children kicked a ball and shouted to each other. An old man sauntered past with a geriatric whippet on a lead, while the lady from the newsagency dragged a desultory chamois across the shop window. Life carried on as normal, yet Edward knew that there were many things wrong, out of step, out of tune.

The bakery door slammed. Tomorrow, at five in the morning, ovens would be stoked and pans would clatter. Edward had always been a good sleeper, but there were things on his mind. He could not even set his thoughts in order, because his brain was over-crowded, populated by a million worries. Perhaps the bakery noise would wake him, though he would not mind. The sounds of normal life were a comfort.

He turned from the window, picked up the evening paper and found the jobs page. From some-where, he had to find a way of keeping himself occupied. Otherwise, he might just go insane.

The job was a nightmare, yet Vera threw herself into it wholeheartedly. Maisie Cunningham was a slave-driver. According to the woman who cleaned Mon Repos, Maisie went through assistants like other women went through nylons. She wore them till they were threadbare, then she threw them out.

Vera needed hard work, and she certainly got it. She cooked porridge by the gallon, performed scrambled miracles with cracked eggs, made the best of poor bacon cuts and stale bread. Up with the lark, she set twelve tables, brewed enormous amounts of tea, served breakfasts, cleared up, washed dishes.

Maisie Cunningham thought her ship had finally come in. This stick-insect of a woman was as strong as a horse, had a less than normal appetite and seemed to thrive on hard labour. The large woman sat at the kitchen table through Vera's first few breakfasts, her piggy eyes glinting at the sight of her new maid doing the work of two or three people. 'Don't give two slices of toast unless they ask for more,' she advised. 'And keep topping up the teapots. Them buggers out there think tea grows on

359

trees. If they ask for fresh, say we're waiting for a delivery.'

Vera did nothing of the sort. She served her customers well, was delighted to find the odd three-penny bit under a saucer or a plate, made sure that the paying guests of Mon Repos were content with the food, at least. She baked cakes and scones, produced home-made soup from the sparse contents of Maisie's larder, threw together the odd trifle.

Maisie waited to discover Vera's Achilles' heel, was almost despondent when no flaw came to light. Confrontational by nature, Maisie was being deprived of the pleasure of complaining about her staff. In the end, she resigned herself to the awesome prospect of being satisfied, then left Vera to get on with it.

The residents of Mon Repos were a sturdy lot of grim-faced folk who took holidays, along with the rest of life, very seriously. Determined to have a good time or to die in the pursuit of pleasure, they seldom smiled, while dining room conversation was limited to comments about the weather and the vagaries of the human digestive system.

Table eight was dyspepsia, table three heartburn. A woman at table four had endured a close encounter with some bad whelks, and Mr Grimes at table ten was a martyr to his bowels. At mealtimes, this happy gang of revellers sat, chewed, swallowed, broke wind, slurped tea, measured the remaining salt in a cruet set. A conversation did break out once, the topic of discussion being a mix-up between tables two and three's salt pots, plus a suspicion that somebody had been at somebody's brown sauce.

Vera loved watching the clientele. Her only regret

was that she had no time to follow them beyond the boundary lines of Mon Repos, because she was always busy or asleep. Her days off were spent in bed, as she was literally run off her feet by Mrs Cunningham. But she would have loved to witness the compulsory pleasures of these holidaymakers. She tried to imagine them on the big wheel or the swing boats, on the beach, in the Tower Ballroom. There were no children among the guests; Maisie Cunningham bracketed children with cockroaches and other vermin. The notice about jumping on beds had probably been directed at the younger end of the market, and the younger end had learned to stay away from Mon Repos.

In her spare time, when she was awake, Vera read. There was a shelf of tatty volumes in the dining room, and Vera managed, at last, to finish *Gone with the Wind*. She then ploughed through *The Three Musketeers* and *Stamp Collecting for Beginners*.

When she needed fresh air, she walked in the evening down to the prom and breathed in the smell of saline. She liked Blackpool. It was vulgar, loud and real. Hard work kept her mind off herself and ensured that she maintained a level of physical fitness. All in all, she was content with her lot for the immediate future.

The job would not last for ever. At the end of the summer, Mon Repos would close down except for Mrs Cunningham's bed-sitting room next to the kitchen. But Vera did not look forward. She concentrated on cooking and serving, kept her thoughts to herself, put her wage in the bank each Friday afternoon. The payments from Edward Shawcross continued. For now, Vera was secure.

FOURTEEN

James Templeton was working on an idea of his own. He had produced a series of pictures, had named the group 'Lancashire Life'. There were images of people down the pits, in the spinning and weaving sheds, in streets, in their homes and on the various parks scattered around Bolton. Quite a collection of Lancashire paintings was propped around the walls of his little prefabricated studio, a couple of items completed, others halfway there, several still at the rough sketch stage.

But James wanted a fuller picture, so he answered a sudden whim, handed over his insurance round for a few days and set off for the seaside. After fifty weeks of hard slog, the Bolton folk took themselves to Blackpool, Southport, Morecambe or Rhyl, and James intended to follow some of them.

Connie was improving all the time, and James was quite content to leave her to the tender mercies of the hospital. He called in to visit her on his way to the coast, cracked a few jokes with the woman he loved, then, after dropping a bag of grapes onto her bed, he sallied forth towards his next adventure.

Blackpool was burgeoning. Along the front itself, the larger hotels prospered, paintwork clean and fresh, tubs of hardy annuals gracing forecourts, the more elegant and affluent holidaymakers climbing down from horse-drawn carriages just in time for tea. But James didn't want to stay in a hotel. He was looking for the miners, the foundry and cotton workers, men and women who had escaped drudgery for a blessed fortnight. The hotels on the sea-front would be filled with plumbers, butchers, grocers with fat wallets, fat wives and chubby, over-indulged children.

He nosed his car into side streets, found the stories he was looking for. A family dragged itself along the pavement, Dad wearing the bottom half of an old suit, braces, sandals, a flat cap and a collarless shirt. The man puffed on a thin, hand-rolled cigarette and walked a few paces ahead of the rest, as if under-lining his place as leader of the pack.

Mother carried two baskets, a baby and a large black handbag. Two female children dragged spades along metal railings that topped the boundary walls of large terraced houses. The woman stopped, turned, shouted at the girls. Her face was red from sun and exertion, yet she made no attempt to unburden herself by asking her husband to carry his share. Men worked, women worried.

James parked his car, saw a pair of lovers quar-relling. She stamped her foot, drew attention to a pair of red plastic sandals that finished off legs as white as milk. Romeo shrugged, turned as if to walk away. 'Don't you bloody dare, Jimmy Eckersley,' yelled Juliet. 'Me mam'd flay me if she knew I were here with you. And me dad'd kill you as soon as look at you. He's never liked you, me dad. Right from the off, he said as how you were a right bloody Mary Ellen.'

The boy stopped, scratched his head.

A plastic sandal made contact with a grey-trousered leg. She was livid with rage. She had probably bought a two-bob wedding ring from Woolworth's, had more than likely bartered her virginity for a few days by the sea with the lout of her dreams. Her face was a picture of abject misery, forehead creased, mouth setting in a narrow, furious line. In a few years, she would look exactly the same, just a little older, a lot wiser, wrinkles round her eyes and a couple of children in tow. They never learned, never altered, still carried on marrying, breeding, complaining. It was a pattern, mused James. Perhaps in a few years, these girls would learn not to set such store by the men in their lives, not to follow their mothers into marriage and poverty. And how boring life would be for a painter when that happened, he thought.

Romeo rubbed his shins and muttered something inaudible.

Juliet burst into tears. There was no balcony, no moon, no nurse to whom she might turn in her darkest hour. She sobbed until the awkward youth placed his arms about her shoulders.

James picked up his pad and sketched furiously. With a couple of dozen strokes, he built a house, a lamppost and a gate. The girl came next, defiance in her spine, hopelessness in her profile. Romeo, with sharp elbows and an inane grin, was wrapped around the weeping girl. This was their fun; this was the holiday for which they had saved for fifty weeks.

In the distance, the disappearing family won a small space in the drawing, then the artist's attention was given to an old lady who pushed a beloved burden in a wheelchair. Darby and Joan had possibly visited Blackpool for the last forty years. The man in the chair had a twisted face, the result of a stroke or an accident. His wife's lips moved constantly, because she had to do the talking for both parties. James stopped for a while and sat on his sadness. He wanted to capture the old couple, yet he held back until the woman's face was clearly in view.

With his upper teeth grasping the lower lip as he concentrated, James translated her expression, her tiredness, her beauty. This had been an exceptionally lovely face in its time. Threads of silver hair disappeared into a scarf, while a dab of rouge on each cheek screamed a defiance that was typical of ageing glamour. As he committed the pair to paper, James wondered what they had been, where they had lived. A now familiar excitement buzzed in his chest, a fever that seemed to have accompanied this whole project.

It had not started as a planned enterprise. James had set out to draw and paint a few real things, some normal people who were not Laughing Cavaliers, Mona Lisas, King Charles the First or Second. But now, the cart was driving the horse, was pushing him along towards some sort of climax, some great expression of his true relationship with his environment.

They had stopped. The old lady knew that she and her husband were the centre of attention, was fully aware that the young man in the car was drawing them. Preening slightly and displaying twin rows of porcelain dentures, she applied the chair's brake and walked to the car. 'You doing a picture of me?' she asked.

He nodded. 'Do you mind?'

The woman laughed. 'Eeh, love, it's no skin off my nose. Are you one of them painters?'

'Yes.'

'Do you live in an attic?'

'A prefab,' he replied.

'Takes all sorts, I suppose,' she said. She folded her arms. 'Now, you have to be poor to be a good artist. They were all poor, you know. One daft ha'porth cut his ear off and all.' She looked over her shoulder at her husband. 'Were it Van Gogh?' she asked the man in the chair.

Her husband muttered something unintelligible.

'That's right,' she told James. 'It were Van Gogh. Then there were an Italian bloke what cut dead bodies up to see what they were made of. Come in for a right load of trouble, he did, got it in the neck from the church. I'm nearly ninety.'

'Are you really?' She looked about seventy-five.

She nodded merrily. 'It's Blackpool what's kept us going. Ernie's ninety-four, had a bit of a turn last month, but we've still come. Two weeks every year, we have. Course, money's scarce, but we manage. Can't afford a decent place these days, so we stop here.' She waved a hand at a weary-looking house. 'Miserable trout runs it, but she's cheap.'

'Mon Repos?' asked James. The place looked as if it had been at 'repos' for some considerable time. In fact, Rigor Mortis might have been a more suitable name.

'Aye, that's our guesthouse,' the old lady replied. 'Food's come on no end since they got a new woman in. Are you stopping round here?'

'I may do that.'

She pushed her head into the car and looked at the work. 'Well, that's all right, I suppose,' she said.

'You've got my Ernie to a T. Will you be colouring it in, like?'

James nodded.

'Aye, it'll happen look better coloured in. I'll go now, love. We have to get in round the back because of the chair.' She returned to her husband and wheeled him along the street, her back bent with the effort.

James heaved himself out of the car and limped up the steps. Inside Mon Repos he found an enormous woman with a breathing problem and a cat. The cat hung over his owner's shoulder and cast a baleful eye over the newcomer.

'Want a room?' asked Maisie Cunningham.

'Yes, please.'

'How long are you stopping?'

'Three nights.'

She stared meaningfully at the surgical boot. 'Can you get upstairs?'

'Usually.'

Maisie put down the cat and opened a large, black book on a counter that bore a bell, a list of house rules and an empty teacup. She took down his details and produced a room key. 'Number nine. Not much of a view, but it's cosy. Don't be stopping out till all hours,' she warned. 'I'm not one for high living. No women in your room, no bringing fish and chips in. It's bad enough getting the smell of food out of the dining room curtains without having the ones upstairs stinking of chip fat.'

James accepted the key and went out for his case. This promised to be a brilliant idea. He would go tomorrow to the beach, would sketch holiday-makers, donkeys, Punch and Judy, ice-cream carts.

The young lovers were still arguing. James opened

367

the boot of his car, listened to the angry words.

'What if I'm pregnant?' she shouted, clearly oblivious to anything within earshot.

'I'll marry you.' The gangly youth tried to calm his lover. 'I will, honest.'

She pushed him away. 'You're only saying that. You want all your own road, you do.' An angry finger was wagged beneath the boy's nose. 'That bloody bolster gets pushed down the middle of yon bed tonight, and you can stop on your own side.' She stamped her foot. 'Any road, you snore. You sound like a bloody pig, you do, all snorting and blowing. I wish I'd never come. I wish I'd gone to Morecambe with me mam and dad.'

The lad shook his head sadly and turned away.

'And where the bloody hell do you think you're sloping off to?' yelled the young lady. 'Don't you dare leave me here stood on me own in Blackpool.' She grabbed the boy's arm and tottered off with him.

James lifted out his luggage and walked up the short path of Mon Repos. One way and another, Blackpool was beginning to look very interesting.

The van slowed to a halt at the bottom of The Rise, then its sole occupant turned off the engine and sat back to wait. It was almost six-o'clock, so Shawcross would be on his way home by now.

Micky Turnbull was a short, bull-necked man with dark hair, brown eyes and a scar on his chin. As the last surviving Turnbull of his generation, he had left Luton to travel north on hearing that his nephew had gone missing. Peter had been on an easy wicket, because his mother had died in childbed and his father's family had paid for silence. Now, Peter's father was also dead, and Micky had come to get to the bottom of things.

He sucked on a mint imperial and shaved dirt from under his nails with a penknife. As a garage owner, he was usually mucky, but he did not want to be at too great a disadvantage when facing the boss of Fishwick's mill. With his manicure completed, he dragged a broken comb through his hair, spat on a rag and wiped his mouth and chin.

Where was Peter? It wasn't like him to bugger off like this without talking to anybody. The woman next door had written to Micky to inform him that his nephew had done a bunk. And would Edward Shawcross know about Peter's whereabouts? There was no-one else he could ask, because Peter's mates at the pubs knew nothing.

This was all a bloody nuisance, because business was booming in Luton. He'd landed a contract to service a fleet of coal lorries only last week, and here he was, sitting on Belmont Road waiting to see a bloke who probably had no answers.

Micky knew he had to be careful. If he breathed one word about his nephew's parentage, Peter's income could dry up as quickly as a summer puddle. Also, Micky's own business had been built on two things – Shawcross's money and Micky's promised diplomacy. So, he could talk only to Edward Shawcross. Papers had been signed, legal documents connected with the garage and demanding Micky's discretion. Would Shawcross sue him if he spoke up? Oh well, there was no danger of Micky spreading the news. He knew which side of his bread was buttered, so he wasn't going to go mouthing off about their Molly and Samuel Fishwick.

All the same, Peter was missing and Peter was

Micky's sole surviving relative. Mam and Dad were long gone, his brothers had been killed in action, and little Molly had died shortly after Peter's birth. The police had been noncommittal earlier on, had expressed the opinion that the young man would turn up in time. Micky did not agree. There was a deep unease in his chest, a feeling that he could not describe or justify rationally. Something had happened, something bad.

The evening wore on. Micky Turnbull relieved himself behind a hedge, kept his eyes on the road, continued to wait for Edward Shawcross. A few vehicles passed him and entered The Rise, but none contained the man he sought. It was late. All the mills would have switched to evening shift an hour ago. Was Shawcross still at his desk?

He lingered near the van, was about to give up on Shawcross when a young woman hove into view. She was swinging a little handbag, had obviously got herself all dressed up for an evening out. Micky approached her. 'I wonder if you can help me,' he began hesitantly.

Ada Dobson looked over her shoulder before replying, hoped that someone would walk down the lane soon. She had been educated by her mother not to speak to strange men. 'What do you want?' she asked. 'I'm in a bit of a hurry.'

'I'm looking for Mr Shawcross,' he replied. 'He was a friend of my dad's years back. I'm visiting, see, just for a day or two, because I live down south now. Is it that big house halfway along the hill? I thought I'd look him up.'

Ada shrugged. 'Look all you want, because you'll not find him, not round here.'

'Eh?'

'He doesn't live up here any more.' The moment these words were out, she wished that she could unsay them.

'Have they moved?'

Ada was usually the soul of discretion. This man could be a burglar or a murderer or a rapist. 'She's not on her own,' she snapped. 'Master Gilbert's a big lad now. He's living at home, because he's left university.'

'Do you work for them?'

'None of your business.' She wasn't going to tell this chap that she was the Shawcross family's housemaid. She had said too much as it was, didn't intend to divulge any further details about those who sheltered and employed her.

'But—'

Ada stepped round the stranger. 'Somebody's waiting for me,' she lied. 'I've got to go.' She flew past Micky Turnbull and ran down Belmont Road.

Micky got back into his van. What the heck was going on here? First Peter had disappeared, now Shawcross was off the scene. He started the engine and made for Halliwell Road. The next-door neighbour had supplied him with a spare key, so he would be staying at his nephew's house.

As he drove towards the town, he saw the girl waiting at a bus stop. Should he offer a lift? he wondered, slowing down the pace. No. She seemed a bit on the hysterical side, and he didn't want to draw attention to himself.

A thought struck him and he made for Deane Road. He would go to the mill and ask for Shawcross. Even if he wasn't there tonight, the workers might have an idea of where he could be found. The market was closed, its little wooden stalls stripped bare until next Saturday. He drove past the ropewalk and turned left into Fishwick's yard.

A man was making a mockery of sweeping up. He leaned on his brush, then lowered his head to look at the visitor. Glad of a distraction, he waited for the man to speak.

'Is Mr Shawcross here?' Micky asked.

'Gone,' replied the sweeper-up. 'And if you want to look round, you'll have to come back tomorrow.'

'So Mr Shawcross has gone home?' Micky opened the car window fully and poked his head out.

'Doesn't come any more. We don't know what's going on. Colin Critchley's took over and he'll have gone home for the day. So if you're thinking of buying, come back in the morning. That's when they show folk round, see.'

What was happening? 'What's going on?'

The man shrugged carelessly. 'Don't ask me. Workers is allers the last to find out. I mean, you slave for nigh on half a century, then the old boss comes home and pops his clogs, Shawcross takes his hook and we're up for sale.' He took a closer look at the man. 'You're not after buying the place, are you?'

'No, I'm not.'

The sweeper-up lit a Woodbine. 'Missus come back and all, you know. From abroad, like.'

'Whose missus?'

'The old feller's. Fishwick's wife. She brought him back from Africa or some such place, and they moved in with Mr and Mrs Shawcross. Next news, the old man's six feet under and our jobs is threatened because Mrs F wants to sell up.'

Micky scratched his nose. 'But what about Mr Shawcross? He's run this place for years. What's happened to him?'

'Dunno,' replied the cleaner. 'Just went, like.' He glanced surreptitiously over his shoulder, as if he expected an audience. 'There's been talk,' he muttered. 'A lot of gossip – you know what folk are like, specially women. From what my old girl says, it seems they might have split up.'

'Shawcross and his wife?'

'Aye. I even heard as how he's give his notice to the corporation. He were an alderman, very high thought of and all. But nobody's seen hide nor hair for days – weeks, more like.'

Micky had no time for all this. In Luton, half a dozen lorries were being serviced by a workforce that needed watching and prompting. 'Thanks, anyway,' he said before putting the gear lever into reverse.

'Who are you?' asked the sweeper-up.

'Nobody,' replied Micky. 'Nobody at all.'

James stood at the window of his room and watched the woman pegging out tea towels. She was very thin, but she was blessed with an excellent bone structure and she made the most marvellous scrambled eggs. So, here was another worker, one who catered to the holidaying masses from inland. Even recreation implied toil for somebody.

Using charcoal, he outlined the almost geometrical shape of her body, used the pad of his thumb to shade the clothing. She moved quickly, efficiently, was plainly used to housework. Her hair was reddish gold, was made even brighter by the rays of a strong sun. At nine-thirty in the morning, the day already promised to be a real stinker.

His door was pushed inward by the daily cleaner, a woman of indeterminate years with slightly crossed eyes, a mop and a bucket. James fished a florin from his pocket. 'Don't bother doing my room,' he told her as she grabbed the coin.

'You're supposed to go out after breakfast,' she informed the wardrobe.

James answered for the inanimate object. 'I'm lame.'

'Oh.' Her attention seemed to shift towards the dressing table. 'Him with the funny foot?'

'That's me.'

She smiled. 'Aye, well, you can stop in if you want. Mrs Cunningham says as how you're special, what with talking proper and having the affliction.' This last word was delivered with great import and in hushed tones. 'She caters for the afflicted,' added the cross-eyed char.

'Excellent.'

The intruder gave the fireplace the questionable pleasure of her smile, which was gap-toothed and heavily stained by nicotine. She clattered her accoutrements and left the scene.

James looked through the window and saw an empty yard. But he remembered enough, so he carried on with his sketch. Would it work? he wondered. If he joined Mother and Mrs Shawcross in this mad scheme to open up an art and decor department, would people really want to see this sort of thing?

He reverted to yesterday's piece, smiled as he remembered Juliet's anger. With a fine piece of charcoal, he gave the old lady a few more wisps of hair before setting to work on the man in the wheelchair. He had met them again at breakfast, had sat fascinated while the stroke victim had been fed by his loving wife. She was so tender, so patient and loving.

In just a couple of weeks, James Templeton had

learnt a lot about life. Women ran the domestic side of the world, it seemed. On Eldon Street, the households on each side of him laboured under matriarchy, and all seemed quite happy with the situation. But the power of females was not limited to the working classes. At home, Mother ruled the roost. Eric Templeton wrote cheques and kept the money rolling in, yet all decisions in the household were made by Maude. Father was a sort of House of Lords, an out-of-date institution whose function was simply to agree with the main parliament's suggestions.

Yesterday, when the family had walked past, the woman had borne all the burdens. She had probably decided that her husband, who toiled for fifty weeks a year, should have a rest. That pathetic vision of a poor female carrying baby and bags was likely to be the boss at home. Like one of Magee's brewery horses, her breadwinner was allowed a break in order to build up strength enough to labour for the remainder of the year.

James picked up a sketch pad, some pencils and charcoal, then set off towards his next subject. Excitement bubbled in his chest as he followed a route mapped out by a tattered carpet runner, along the landing and down some stairs. Not since college had he been so interested in his painting.

The thin woman was visible through the open door of the dining room. She was clearing tables and re-setting them for lunchtime. James hesitated before entering the room. 'No rest for the wicked?' he ventured.

She laughed. 'Oh, I don't mind. I'd sooner be busy than idle.'

Her accent was familiar. 'You're not from Blackpool, then?'

'No.'

'Me neither.' He placed his equipment on a chair. 'Would you mind if I did a sketch of you?'

'Not at all. But don't do it in Mrs Cunningham's time.'

He nodded in agreement. 'She seems to be a hard taskmaster. Though I am allowed to stay in if I wish because of my disability.'

'Her bark's worse than her bite,' said Vera. 'Anyway, I'll let you know when I have some time off, then you can draw me if you want. Mind, I'm no oil painting.'

'But you will be exactly that,' James told her. 'Or a watercolour. Whatever, you have excellent bones.' With that, he left the house and pursued the pleasure-seekers.

Eleanor scanned the newspaper, cast it aside. Peter Turnbull continued 'missing'. He was as 'missing' as anyone could ever be, because he was just about half-buried beneath the exposed roots of a very old tree.

Few people went into the woods. Those who did venture towards its darkness were opportunists who usually bore arms in the search for free food. A body with a gunshot wound could easily have been shot accidentally. Eleanor yawned. It was all a bit of a bore, really. If only the mill could be sold, she would be out of here like lightning. Cotton was stagnating. A great deal of money needed spending on the dark, Satanic institutions thrown up during and since the Industrial Revolution. She would have to lower the price.

Lowering the price would mean the lowering of her sights. There would be no world cruise, that was certain. But London was within easy reach, Eleanor supposed. If she could just sell the damned mill and get out of this miserable place.

She yawned, studied her nails, decided that she needed a manicure. Life was so tedious. The girl had thrown herself in front of a lorry, an act of foolishness that had been unduly dramatic in the circumstances. The boy was proving difficult. He was handsomely constructed and would have done very well as a temporary escort for his grandmother, but he had no fondness for Eleanor. In fact, he probably hated his mother's mother. Ah well, that was no matter. Soon, Eleanor would be beyond the reach of that particular young man's judgement.

Alice herself was always at the infirmary. When she wasn't visiting Constance, she was telephoning all over the place and looking at photographs in catalogues. A family-owned department store? That would never work.

Edward had gone off, and Eleanor found it difficult to blame him. Alice had started to become plain in her teens, was still a very ordinary woman. She was exercising, was losing weight, but she remained unremarkable. Eleanor recalled her own long-term battle with the too solid flesh, smiled wryly at the idea of anyone else suffering as she had. Weight was not often easy to shift. However, Eleanor had been comely, at least, so her own efforts had been worthwhile.

The dog was the biggest bloody nuisance of all. Gilbert had taken to the beast – even Alice led the creature out for walks, though William seemed to do most of the leading, often dragging Alice to the top of the moor so that he might catch a glimpse of his latest true love. William's fondness for Maude Templeton was the cause of much hilarity, though

Eleanor failed to see the funny side. Dogs should be kept outside, preferably chained and muzzled. She could imagine no situation in which a canine might be necessary or even tolerable.

That man was outside again. He had been walking up and down for most of the afternoon, was plainly seeking somebody. A slight feeling of discomfort stirred in the region of Eleanor's stomach, but she shrugged it off determinedly. The man was just another poacher, she supposed.

On The Rise, Micky Turnbull stared at Aston Leigh as if an answer to his questions might be found in the face of this Victorian pile. He had failed to find his nephew, had failed to discover the whereabouts of Edward Shawcross. Going round and round in circles was a waste of time. He needed to return to his business, wanted to get away as quickly as possible.

He sighed, shook his head and walked in the direction of Belmont Road. After a bite to eat and forty winks in Peter's house, he would drive back to Luton. The woman next door would keep him informed, as should the police. The guardians of the law seemed relatively unmoved by Peter's disappearance. It seemed that Peter was known to them, because he had been involved in several drunken disturbances and petty thefts in the Halliwell area. The lad was probably listed as a work-shy layabout who was not worth time or effort.

Micky drove back to Halliwell Road, parked his van and let himself into the miserable little cottage. He closed the tattered curtains, switched on the light and went to make a brew. Every local pub had been searched and all acquaintances of Peter's had been questioned. Micky was beginning to suspect that he could go round in circles for ever if he stayed. Like a dog chasing its own tail, he was getting nowhere. It was time to go home, time to get on with his own life.

As he lowered himself into a fireside chair, Micky saw a glint of yellow metal at the edge of the rug. He moved the opposite chair and picked up a lighter. It was heavy, solid, gold-plated. He turned the wheel and ignited the wick, stroked the sleek sides of this attractive object. When the flame was extinguished, Micky examined the item. In a curly script, the letters S and F had been engraved into the casing. This was probably another of Peter's little stolen toys. Micky decided that he might as well keep the lighter as a memento. After all, he had no way of guessing whether or when he might see his nephew again.

When the cup was drained, Micky Turnbull placed it on the floor, closed his eyes and nodded off. Having done all in his power, he prepared himself to return to his home and his business in the south.

'How did you find me?' Edward stood back to allow Gil into his flat.

'Followed your car,' replied Gil. He looked around the sparsely furnished room, decided that Dad and James Templeton had both chosen the spartan life. 'What are you going to do?' asked Gil. 'Are you planning on working at something or other?'

Edward sat down. 'I'm buying the bakery. Mr Gregson is due to retire, so I'm taking over.'

As far as Gil knew, his father had never been the architect of a jam sandwich, let alone batches of cakes and bread. 'But you don't cook,' he said.

'The cook cooks,' answered Edward patiently. 'And she comes with the shop.' He had scraped together enough for the lease and three months' rent. This was make or break time.

Gil looked round again, his eyes seeking evidence of female occupation. 'You're alone?'

Edward nodded.

'But—'

'But she has disappeared. I'm paying the rent on her house in the hope that she'll come back, though Vera's a tough woman once her decisions are made.' He cleared his throat before spitting out the truth. 'I am not good enough for her, it seems. To be perfectly honest, Gilbert, I'm probably good enough for nobody.'

'Nonsense,' said Gil.

'Hear me out.' Edward waited until his son was seated. 'I do hope you are made of sterner stuff, son. I'm a weak man who stepped into a gilt-edged lifestyle simply because it was on offer. There were circumstances, factors best left undiscussed. But I took the easy option, Gilbert. I have done that all my life. Now, I am reaping the benefits of my foolishness, as is your mother. None of this is of her doing, you must remember that, because she will be needing your help and support.'

Gil reckoned that a weak man would not deride himself so thoroughly, though he made no effort to interrupt at this point.

'What happened to your sister was my fault. I should have left Alice years ago, should have found the courage. Now, I am forced to begin again. This is just another happening, you see. The tide flows and ebbs, and I just ride it like flotsam.' He stared hard at Gil. 'Your mother is the strength. Stay with her, encourage her to go for that store. Like Samuel, Alice is tough.'

Gil leaned back in the chair and braced himself against the storm he was about to cause. 'Things are difficult enough for you, yet I must talk to someone. Connie's not at home, of course, and I couldn't tell Mother how I feel . . .' He closed his eyes for a moment, saw the damped-down triumph in Eleanor Fishwick's expression when her husband was finally placed in that deep, dark hole.

'Gilbert?'

The startlingly blue eyes opened. 'You referred just now to circumstances best left undiscussed. The time has come, I believe, to talk about those circumstances.' He inhaled deeply. 'I think Grandmother finished off Grandfather.'

'Never,' cried Edward. 'They were love's young dream right until the end.' Yet hadn't he wondered . . . ?

Gil reined in his impatience. 'Grandfather spoke to me about a man called Peter Turnbull. In fact, he mistook me for him, asked me to take his new will from a document case in the bedroom. She was listening. She grabbed the envelope and said that Grandfather was talking nonsense.'

Edward found nothing to say.

'He spoke no more nonsense after that, because he was dead within a day. She killed him, I'm sure.'

'Natural causes,' replied Edward, his voice faltering. 'On the death certificate—'

'There was morphine.'

'Yes, but—'

'She killed him, Father.'

Edward shifted uneasily in his seat. She was a chilling old crone, he supposed, yet she had stood by her husband all those years ago when his mistress had died in childbirth. At least, she had done all the right things. But was it possible that Eleanor had never forgiven Samuel? Had she bided her time until . . . ? God, surely not? 'Gilbert, be extremely careful, now. You can't go about making wild accusations about your grandmother.'

'Peter Turnbull has been missing for some time. You must have read about it in the *Evening News*.'

Edward remembered reading something about Turnbull, but he had been worried about Constance, about Vera and about finding somewhere to live. Now, he was up to his eyes in negotiations regarding the purchase of a bakery. 'Of course,' he replied eventually. 'So he didn't turn up? I wonder where he's hidden himself.'

Gil raised his shoulders. 'God knows. The woman next door reported it eventually to the police. It was in the newspaper.'

Edward remembered sitting on Halliwell Road with Eleanor. She had seemed angry, but not agitated. Had she said something about putting an end to all those payments? Hadn't she been more interested in going to the dairy shop on Deansgate?

'Father?'

Edward blinked. 'What are you implying, Gilbert?'

'That two men are dead.'

Icy fingers made their way the length of Edward's spine. 'For goodness' sake! She's seventy.'

'She's clever.'

'Perhaps so. But a murderess? Come on, please, this is your mother's mother. And she did stand by Samuel in 1927 when—'

'When what, Father?'

'There was . . . there were some difficulties.'

Gil waited for more, was disappointed. In spite of that, he waded right in, because he had guessed the truth weeks ago. 'In 1927, when Peter Turnbull was born, there was trouble.' He paused for a split second. 'Peter Turnbull is my grandfather's son, I take it?'

Edward inclined his head in reluctant, tacit agreement.

'And my grandfather was considering including Peter in his will.'

The older man maintained his silence.

'So Grandmother hastened her husband's inevitable death. Then, she killed Peter Turnbull. My mother has – or had – a half-brother who was only slightly older than I am. And she never knew him.'

'Alice is not missing much,' replied Edward quickly. 'The man's a ne'er-do-well, a parasite. The bad penny will turn up in time, no doubt.'

'No.' Gil's tone was firm. 'I've looked at Grandmother, studied her. Connie accused me of staring at her, and she was right. There's a terrifying absence of feeling in Eleanor Fishwick. She seems to be bent on pleasing herself and only herself. When she bought the car for me and the jewellery for Connie, she was paying us to like her. Well, Connie can make up her own mind, but I don't enjoy sharing a house with my grandmother.'

Edward lifted his hands palms upward in a gesture of near-despair. 'Look, Peter Turnbull's a strong enough chap.'

'Connie's words exactly. And my answer to you is similar to the one I gave to Connie. It's the power of the mind that breeds murder. A man in a wheelchair can wield a weapon as long as his arms aren't paralysed. A dying person is able to use a gun. She is a very intelligent and devious woman. Nothing would stop her. She sees what she wants and goes for it. If she steps on a few people, then that's just a minor irritation.'

Edward folded his arms. Was it possible? Had Eleanor murdered Samuel Fishwick and Peter Turnbull? 'We know where Samuel's body is,' he said. 'But what about the other one? How could she conceal it? Dead people are very heavy, difficult to shift. Where did she kill him? When? How?'

Gil nodded pensively. 'You and I lifted the wheel of that lorry in order to save Connie. We did that because it was necessary and because we loved her enough to produce that sudden strength. Grandmother loves herself, would be able to do almost anything to save herself from danger. She has killed him and she has hidden his body. Every time I look at her, I know what she has done. I just know it absolutely, Father.'

Edward jumped up and paced about the room. 'What are you going to do about all this?'

Gil shrugged. 'Not much. There's Mother to think of. I assume that she knows nothing about Peter Turnbull?'

Alice had supposedly been unaware of Vera's existence, yet she had taken pains to find out. 'Your mother is very deep, Gilbert. It's difficult to say what goes on in her head. But knowing her character as well as anyone might, I am fairly certain that she hasn't an inkling about her father's by-blow.'

The younger man's eyes followed his father's pacings. 'Sit down,' he begged. 'This place is too small for all that movement.' He waited until Edward had reclaimed his seat. 'So those were the circumstances. You kept Grandfather's secret, and my mother was the prize.'

It sounded so cold, so terrible. 'You are on the

right lines,' admitted Edward hesitantly. 'Without trying for one moment to excuse myself, I must tell you that poverty is terrifying. My parents were drinkers. We were fed by neighbours. My brother escaped to the other side of the world by working his passage. I was alone, young, frightened. This . . . happened and I saw my chance. Unforgivable, I know, but those are the facts and the reasons.'

Gil had not come visiting in order to judge his father. He stood up, approached Edward and placed a hand on his shoulder. 'We all do it wrong some of the time,' he said.

Edward nodded, patted Gil's hand. 'But what on earth should we do about your grandmother? If she has killed—'

'She has,' insisted Gil.

'And if she realizes that you suspect her, how safe are you?'

Gil had not thought about this. 'Oh, she wouldn't try it on me, surely?'

An anger bubbled inside Edward's breast. It frothed its way upward until it spilled from his mouth. 'If she touches you or Constance, I'll kill her,' he spat.

'Please don't do anything rash,' begged Gil.

Edward wiped his brow with a handkerchief. 'Gilbert, I am the cause of all this trouble. Poor Constance can't stand the sight of me, so I am following her progress from a distance and by telephone. Your mother is a disappointed woman who deserved a better man. And because I promised silence in exchange for security, you are now unsafe.'

Gil was relieved to find that his father was taking notice, that Edward was willing to consider the possibility that Eleanor Fishwick was a scheming and dangerous woman. 'I have spoken to no-one except you and Connie. She thinks I'm mad.'

Edward didn't care what anyone thought. If there was the remotest possibility that his children were threatened, he would act. He had never been a brave man, had never pretended to be the stuff from which heroes were cut.

'Father?'

'Yes?'

'What are you thinking about?'

'Nothing,' lied Edward. 'Come to see me again in a day or so.' His vision seemed to clear as he smiled sadly at the handsome young man who was his son. 'By the way, sorry about lumbering you with William. There was nothing else I could do, nowhere else where I could leave him.' A coward again, he had been unwilling to face Constance, Maude and other visitors.

'He's an amazing dog,' answered Gil. 'He is head over tail in love with Mrs Templeton.'

Edward found himself almost laughing. 'Then he is an unusual animal,' he said.

'And Grandmother hates him.'

The older man regained his sobriety immediately. 'There's a lot wrong with a person who dislikes dogs,' he said quietly. 'Unless, of course, the hatred is a result of an attack or a bad experience in childhood.' He nodded slowly. 'You are probably right, Gilbert. She's a bad lot.' But murder? He took Gilbert to the door. 'I'll see you soon,' said Edward. But he would see Eleanor Fishwick sooner. Much sooner.

Alice had gone out with the Templeton woman to choose floor-coverings for Fishwick's of Deansgate. As far as Eleanor was concerned, Fishwick's of

Deansgate was just another portion of pie in the sky. If Alice wanted to waste her bit of money, then that was her problem. A buyer for the mill had appeared on the scene; Eleanor's sole interest lay in how much money she might get and how quickly she could make her escape from Bolton.

She replaced the telephone receiver and made for the drawing room. Her solicitor had just volunteered to show the prospective purchaser round the mill. Colin Critchley had been duly advised to keep the wheels turning and to make the place look efficient. It was ten minutes past two. Eleanor reckoned that the tour would last until about four o'clock, after which time she might be on her way to ridding herself of a large encumbrance and acquiring a healthy sum of spending money.

The drawing room door opened and Edward stepped in.

'Good Lord,' exclaimed Eleanor. 'The black sheep returns. Who let you in?'

Edward, who had waited for Alice to leave the house, showed his mother-in-law the keys. 'I let myself in,' he said.

'But you are persona non grata,' said Eleanor, mockery in the words.

'Perhaps I am.' He walked right up to her, stood over the chair in which she sat. She was frail, with delicate bones, thin hands, transparent skin and eyes that might have bored holes through sheet metal. 'I want to give you some advice,' he began. On the one hand, he felt rather foolish but, at the same time, he would take no chances. 'Leave my children alone.' His voice was deceptively quiet.

Eleanor raised perfectly executed eyebrows. 'I beg your pardon?'

He swallowed his misgivings. 'Morphine,' he said simply.

Eleanor clutched at the arms of her chair. 'What? What on earth are you talking about, Edward?'

He saw the whiteness around the knuckles, the uncertain drifting of black pupils in pale blue, age-rimmed irises. 'You killed Samuel, probably with an overdose of morphine.' He waited, saw her throat constrict, relax, tighten again. 'It was easy enough, I suppose. The morphine was there and you used it, plenty of it. In fact, I remember quite clearly the day when you accidentally broke three phials. I suppose you broke them after draining off the contents.'

The old woman's back was suddenly straight. 'How dare you?' she cried feebly.

But her protest came just a fraction of a second too late. 'He was dying, was already soaked in drugs,' continued Edward. 'If we dig him up, perhaps a pathologist might discover your crime.'

Eleanor gasped for breath.

'But what did you do with Peter Turnbull?' asked her son-in-law. 'Where is he? Oh, I hated him just as much as you did. He bled us for years, as did his uncle, but I never thought of murder. It was clever of you, I suppose.'

Eleanor groped for the shattered remnants of her composure, forced herself to speak. 'I killed no-one,' she muttered quietly.

Edward nodded. He placed one hand on each arm of the chair, using his body to create a cage from which the old woman had no chance of escaping. 'Listen to me, Eleanor. There are documents with my lawyer. If anything happens to Gilbert, or Constance, or Alice, or to me, you will be investigated. Do you understand? It is all written down.'

She glared at him.

'Do you understand?' he repeated. He shook the chair until he imagined that he heard old bones rattling inside parchment-yellow skin.

'Yes,' she answered finally.

He straightened, ran a hand through his hair, then turned towards the window. 'You never forgave him, did you? It was all an act. And so well done. Really, you deserve congratulations on a wonderful performance. The show ran and ran, didn't it?'

Eleanor breathed evenly once more. 'You know nothing,' she spat. 'Nothing concrete.'

'I know enough, Eleanor. And one day, your deeds will catch up with you.' He wheeled round and faced her again. 'One day, if you live long enough, you will hang.'

Long after Edward had left, Eleanor remained motionless in the chair. She had to get away, could not remain here for much longer. Ah well, business could be conducted from London, she supposed. Tomorrow, she would get the maid to pack her bags. Then, Eleanor Fishwick could go and find a better class of company, a decent bridge partner and a few shops worth visiting. Bolton and all who lived in the wretched town could go to hell. As for Shawcross – he was bluffing.

FIFTEEN

The sea seemed to have several moods and guises. In the summertime, when Vera had arrived in Blackpool, the water had been clean, a mixture of blues and greens with white-foamed waves that licked the shore gently and rhythmically. Splashing at its edge, Vera had allowed the water to cool her feet, had been reminded of long-ago washdays when her mother had stood in the back yard with her dolly tub and washboard. The lather on Mam's laundry had been clean and white, had frothed and bubbled with the pounding of the posser and the scratching of an old, splintery-backed scrubbing brush.

Winter sea was different. It was lead-coloured, ugly and heartless. It battered the sand, worked its hungry, dark path ever nearer to the promenade, roared angrily, unforgivingly, was seldom placid. A million filthy items might have been boiled in this massive, grey cauldron, thousands of dirty clothes that had deposited their mess into the scum-crested turmoil.

She sat on a damp bench, stayed near its edge because her centre of gravity had shifted with advancing pregnancy. Soon, her baby would be born. Strangely, her closest ally was Maisie Cunningham. That fat, apparently idle female had been good to Vera. When summer had ended, Vera had been invited to stay. 'I'm not too clever on my feet,' Maisie had said. 'So I shouldn't really be alone all winter. I'll feed you and pay you a wage if you stop on here with me, Vera. I reckon we need one another.'

'I'm pregnant and single,' had been Vera's bald reply.

Maisie asked no questions. She read her books, listened to the wireless, did pretty bits of embroidery and made endless shawls and matinee coats for the 'little stranger'. The little stranger was limbering up for the big day. He or she practised somersaults while Vera tried to sleep, then chose to rest whenever Vera walked. It was a big baby. Mrs Cunningham's doctor had expressed concern about the child's size, had mumbled on about hospital and surgical intervention.

Vera rose, turned and looked at the splendid hotels that overlooked this portion of the Irish Sea. They were not empty, because older, richer people often wintered here, attracted by the bracing air and the relatively low price of out-of-season room and board. Some of them sat like prisoners at windows, their vacant eyes fixed on Vera. Few people ventured out when the weather was so ill-tempered.

Along the Golden Mile, shops and places of entertainment had been battened down for the winter. The tower pointed its girders towards a heavy sky, its highest finial threatening to pierce low-lying cloud. Blackpool was probably the most miserable place to spend winter, yet Vera loved it. The ozone was fresh, pungent, invigorating. She had developed an appetite for food and for life, was beginning to plan her future.

Where would she live? She had saved most of her wages, and the bank account was topped up regularly by Edward Shawcross, father of the child, lover of the mother. Vera could scarcely remember his face, because she had become too wrapped up in herself and her baby. Within weeks, she would give birth. Mrs Cunningham had offered to keep her on, but Vera did not want to raise her son or daughter in a boarding house. Working with a young baby to rear did not promise to be easy, yet Vera did not want to depend for ever on Edward.

Sometimes, she wondered about his daughter, was glad that the girl had survived, hoped that Edward was taking care of his family. But she did not miss him. Vera was an incubator and a companion to Maisie. Soon, she would need to find a place for herself, but for now, steady exercise and good food were all she needed.

She loitered near a shuttered rock shop, remembered the laughing summer faces of children as they had paid pennies for sweet souvenirs of Blackpool. That man had painted her sitting on a deckchair just across the road from here. Behind her, the sea had sparkled in answer to a hot and happy sun, and children had scampered to and from the sands with buckets, spades and beachballs.

He had promised to say nothing. James Templeton was one of those people who could be trusted, whose honesty shone like a visible halo around an open, hurtable face. She had told him the truth, had allowed him to know that his neighbour had been her lover. And James had reassured Vera about Constance's improving health.

James, too, had unlocked his heart. James loved Constance, the poor girl whose leg had been trapped beneath that lorry. Vera remembered blaming herself, recalled James Templeton's response to her expression of guilt. 'Everyone is somewhere, always. Circumstances made all the somewheres come together on that day. You loved Mr Shawcross, Vera. How can that be wrong? How on earth could love create an accident?'

Vera breathed in the salt air, felt an icy dewdrop on her nose. She was stronger than she had ever been, was hopeful, almost happy. Maisie Cunningham, that so-called tyrant, had a wayward thyroid as a result of over-ambitious surgery years earlier. She had been as thin as a reed, hyperactive, noisy. The gland had been removed, and now the poor woman suffered another set of symptoms. She was heavy and slow, forgetful, tired. So Vera and Maisie muddled their way through winter, helped one another, kept company together, listened to favourite programmes, played cards and dominoes.

This was a strange time, thought Vera as she walked homeward. It was a never-time, a period of inner preparation, of not quite being a mother or a servant, of not quite being a friend to Maisie. Vera was sheltered by pregnancy, was wrapped up, protected, special. She was not who she used to be, was not the person she was about to become. 'It's unreal,' she whispered.

She entered Mon Repos and cooeed at Maisie. Maisie was on the sofa with one of her soppy books. Twin tears made their way down the plump face as she read the final page. When the book was closed, she looked up at Vera. 'Eeh,' she mumbled. 'That was lovely, that was. Mind, I don't think he should have died. These writers make us cry on purpose, you know.'

'A good weep's healthy,' replied Vera.

Maisie, who worried more about the people in her penny dreadfuls than she did about real folk, shook her massive head, causing all three chins to wobble like half-set blancmanges. 'You're my first friend since he died,' she complained. 'And he was no friend of mine, messing about with floozies all over the pier. Some bloody husband he turned out to be.'

Vera had heard it all before. 'Shall I make another brew?' she asked.

'Aye,' replied Maisie. 'And bring us a few of them custard creams.' She always made a beeline for the biscuits when her reading matter ran out. 'What's the weather like?'

'Cold, but nice,' replied Vera. She took herself off to boil the kettle. Maisie needed Vera. At the moment, Vera needed Maisie, but she would not be staying, not long-term. The idea of hurting her landlady and employer was not appealing, but Vera knew that in her present state of single-mindedness, she would do whatever seemed best for herself and her child.

'You will stay on, won't you?'

Vera jumped. 'Maisie, don't creep up on me like that. I'll be giving birth here and now on the floor.'

'Sorry.' Maisie grabbed a custard cream. 'Will you stop here and bring your baby up? The air's healthy for a kiddy round Blackpool.'

'I'll think about it,' promised Vera. She stirred the tea, lifted the tray. 'Come on, Maisie. It's nearly time for *Mrs Dale's Diary*.'

They sat down, drank tea and ate biscuits while Mrs Dale worried about Jim and while Vera's sitting tenant did his or her pole-vaulting.

*   *   *

The marriage between Maude Templeton and her sweeping brush was not a happy one. Sadie Martindale eyed the near-aristocratic female warily, watched clouds of dust rising towards the ceiling. 'Yon floor wants damping,' said the expert.

Maude raised her flushed face and blew at a strand of hair that hung dead centre of her face, all the way down the elegant nose. Wound around her head like a turban, a red-and-white spotted scarf lent Maude a gypsyish air. 'Damping?'

'Aye. With water.' Sadie laughed. 'I don't know what you look like, Maude, but that's never Mrs Templeton under my owld scarf. See. Stop messing about and give me the flaming brush.' Whenever Sadie thought about life's recent turns of events, she could scarcely believe what was happening. She called Mrs Shawcross and Mrs Templeton by their given names, was invited to meetings regarding company policy and the colour of tablecloths, got consulted about recipes.

Maude snatched back her weapon. 'Your bunions, Sadie.'

'Bugger them. It's onions, not bunions what we should worry about. This is a bloody kitchen, you know, and we're opening up in three days. They'll be eating dusty custard at this rate, 'cos you're making more mess than what you're cleaning up.'

Maude blew out another puff of air, hooted with glee when the tress floated back yet again into the same position. 'You know, Sadie, it's so hard to get good staff these days. I suggest you fire me and put a small ad in the newspaper.'

'I'll think on that,' promised Sadie before tackling the dirty floor.

Maude floated off on a cloud of Chanel and washing soda. This was the most fun she had experienced in years. Even Eric had been swept along on the tide of everyone's enthusiasms. He had imported a tailor from London, a time-served chap whose previous workplace had been just a short bus ride from Savile Row. Eric had also invested money in Templeton and Fishwick of Deansgate. Alice and Maude had played around with names, and Alice Fishwick had opted to come second on the gilded sign. 'Templeton's much nicer than Fishwick,' Alice had admitted.

Maude had not expected to become so involved in the department store. At first, she had been happy enough to guide Alice, to offer suggestions, to travel to London in the company of her neighbour. 'It's infectious,' said Maude now to a dummy in a blue frock. 'I came just to have a look, and now I own half of the shop.'

'Talking to yourself again, Mater?'

Maude swivelled. 'James, where have you been?'

He clattered a box of tools. 'I've been doing things,' he said darkly.

'Which things, James?'

'Oh, just things.'

Maude caught sight of Alice. 'Alice, this son of mine is up to no good. Do talk to him, please.'

Alice smiled and carried on supervising the carpet fitter.

James Templeton's eyes were fixed on a huge side window. The glass was covered so that no passers-by would get a preview of goods that were not yet on sale. Connie was dressing the window. A professional dresser poached from a Manchester store was teaching Connie how to put on a good show.

'Her leg is doing very well,' Maude whispered to her son. 'Any other progress to report?'

He shook his head. 'Haven't proposed to her since Wednesday. Ask me tomorrow.'

Alice arrived on the scene. 'Well, James?'

'Very well, thank you.'

'He's running wild again,' said Maude. James had claimed half of the second storey. He was to be found quite often muttering under his breath about selling dreams, and he had made a huge sign for his portion of the shop. 'Art and Soul?' asked Maude for the umpteenth time. 'Are we poor, uneducated northerners ready for your play on words, James?'

He awarded his female parent a look that was meant to wither. 'Art is the expression of the soul, Mother.'

'But you intend to give lessons, James. This is a store, not a school.'

'Do not compartmentalize,' replied James. 'Learning, buying, what is the difference? Anyway, we're closed for a whole day each week, and on that day I shall ply my true trade.'

There was no shifting him. James would run his department in his own way. 'Never mind, Maude,' said Alice. 'At least he's given up on the insurance.' The truth of the matter was that the insurance had given up on James.

He tried on a pale imitation of a hurt expression. 'I felt sorry for them. Someone had to help.'

'Not by lending them their payments,' replied Maude. 'There's still overtime available at Wesleyan and General, because no-one has managed to get to the root of the damage. I hear that the area manager has gone quite grey with worry.'

'Then he should be pleased about that, at least,' said James. 'Because he was as bald as a coot the last time I saw him.'

Connie looked round when James laughed. He owned a deep, booming guffaw that was at odds with his appearance. She winced slightly as she stepped down into the shop, tried to keep the grimace from her face. Months in hospital had quietened her, had made her appreciative of things she had once taken for granted. Like legs. 'What are you up to now?' she asked the man who tormented her daily with flowers, silly poems and proposals of marriage.

He smiled angelically. '*Moi?*' he asked.

'Yes, *toi*.' The pain in Connie's leg eased as she walked. James often said that her refusal to marry him was attributable to his animal magnetism. There was a great deal of metal in Connie's lower leg. 'I'm so positively electric that you would stick to me,' he usually quipped. She shook her head at him. 'James, what are you planning for this Art and Soul thing?'

He raised his shoulders. 'I intend to make people aware,' he announced airily.

Mary entered the arena. 'Where's my wind-up potato peeler?' she asked. 'That thing with a handle like a mangle. And I haven't enough wine glasses.' She rummaged through a packing case and extracted an item that looked like an instrument of torture. 'Here's the peeler,' she said.

'Gil's gone for the glasses.' Connie tried not to laugh at Mary, who had a streak of dirt down one side of her face and a blob of paint on her nose. 'Aren't you sorry you gave up your job in the Market Hall, Mary? At least you managed to stay clean.'

Mary Martindale was in her element. She was going to run a proper restaurant with a wine list and a foreign cook. The latter spoke just a few words of English, but his pastry was manna. 'I wouldn't have missed this for the world,' she answered.

'Mam's singing her head off in the kitchen.'

Alice was pleased about Mary and Gil. Mary was a natural lady. She had been born into a slum, yet she fitted just about anywhere because she was unpretentious and generous. Sometimes, Alice wished that Mother had stayed around for the opening, but Eleanor had gone south, had bought herself a smart, ground floor flat in Kensington. Alice pulled herself together. She did not need to prove anything to Mother. Mother was never impressed anyway, so it was perhaps as well that she had left the scene.

Gil fell in at the door with a large box, flinched when the musical sound of breaking glass reached his ears. 'Sorry,' he said to Mary.

Mary made no reply, though she held his gaze while cruelly twisting the handle of her potato peeler. This was the man she was going to marry. He was about as much use as a rubber knife where practicalities were concerned, but he would charm the customers into parting with their cash. 'Don't pick it up again, Gil,' she advised, nodding towards the container of tumblers and wine glasses. 'We don't need any more breakages.'

The door opened again and Edward Shawcross stepped into the arena. 'Good afternoon, everyone,' he said. 'I've come to take your orders for opening day.' He looked hard at Alice. The patching up of their differences was the result of her efforts, not his. She had visited him, had suggested that the two of them might even help one another. Alice never failed to amaze him these days.

Connie and Gil had ceased to be surprised about their parents' relationship, though they continued glad that Mother and Father were getting on tolerably well. Some people were better apart, Connie thought now. Mother had deliberately chosen to order bread for the restaurant from Father's Bromley Cross bakery. Alice was a cool customer, a woman with a purpose. Taken all round, Mother had turned out quite nicely after all. Gil and Connie agreed that they had made quite a good job of bringing up Alice. Whenever James Templeton complained about Maude's flutterings, he was told by Connie that children were always to blame for the behaviour of their parents.

Edward went into the restaurant with Mary. He had become an old man during recent months, had spent every second of his spare time searching for Vera. The Tintern Avenue house was occupied now by another family, and Sheila Foster insisted that she had not heard from Vera since the day of her disappearance.

'You all right?' Sadie asked him.

He nodded. 'And you?'

'The same,' she replied. 'I miss the lads. Tommy got married too young, you know. They're already expecting.'

Edward knew that his smile was fading. Vera's baby was due at any time. He felt geriatric, yet he was about to become a father again.

'No word?' asked Sadie.

'None.' He placed a sheet of paper on a table. 'Just fill in this order form as soon as you can, Sadie. We'll have to work in the dark at first, because no-one can tell how much of anything you will need. Try to give me an idea as soon as possible.'

Sadie bled internally every time she saw Teddy Shawcross. He had lost so much through carelessness and because of the particular weakness that often seemed to attach itself to hard-working, successful men. 'I wish I could help you,' she said.

'You are helping, Sadie. Being here with Constance and Gilbert is helping. Keep an eye on Alice, too. If there are any difficulties, send for me.'

She surprised herself and him by planting a kiss on his cheek. Sadie entertained a suspicion that Edward was growing fond of his estranged wife. 'You're a good lad, Teddy Shawcross,' she told him as he walked away.

When Edward left the restaurant and re-entered the shop itself, he found James Templeton lingering in Perfumes and Toiletries. Edward greeted the man who wanted so badly to marry Constance.

James gazed sadly into the careworn face. James had the answer sought by Edward. He knew where Vera was, even wrote to her once every month. But he had pledged his silence, and a gentleman's word was inviolable. 'How's business, Mr Shawcross?'

'Edward, please, James. Booming in its own small way. I have an excellent baker. In fact, she has taught me so well that I can now do my own early batches. She's pleased about that, because it gives her an extra hour in bed.'

James rattled coins in his pocket. 'I know it's none of my business, but have you not thought about going back to Aston Leigh? You and Mrs Shawcross are getting on so well.' He bit his tongue. 'Sorry,' he said lamely.

'Alice and I are good friends,' Edward said. 'It would be a great pity to spoil that.' His eyes moved until they rested on Alice. She was a slimmer, smarter version of the woman who had tipped him out of the house. There was certainty in her spine, self-confidence in the tilt of her chin. 'The best thing I ever did for Alice was to leave her,' he mused quietly.

'She's definitely a survivor,' said James.

'Oh, she's more than that,' murmured Edward. 'She's clever and gifted. The sad fact is that I never noticed, never cared enough.' He pulled himself together. 'Work to do, James.'

'Will you come to the opening?'

'I wouldn't miss it for the world.'

'Where is that blessed dog?' Ada Dobson shook the kitchen tablecloth outside the rear porch. 'William?' she yelled.

Lottie Bowker joined the maid, her hands encased in a towel. She dried her fingers, thrust the piece of terry into Ada's hands and fastened her winter coat. 'I bet you he's at Top o' th' Moor or in them bloody woods. He'll get himself shot one of these days, just you mark my words. There's folk hunting rabbits and taunting badgers every bloody day now, even in the middle of winter when most sensible things is asleep till the weather warms up. Any road, you stop here, Ada, and I'll go and fetch him.'

Lottie marched round the side of the house, down the drive and into The Rise. There was no sign of the dog, so she set off for the big house. Maude Templeton remained the love of William's life, though he had become more fickle of late and was paying court to Connie and to a very ladylike standard poodle from one of the smaller houses lower down the lane.

The cook stopped from time to time, cupped her mouth with her hands and called the dog's name, but she got no response. At the back door of Top o' th' Moor, she had a quick word with Hilda Ainsworth, the Templetons' housekeeper. William had not reported for duty, and Mrs Templeton was out with her husband at a concert in Manchester.

Lottie Bowker didn't like the woods. Although the area was too small to be a forest, it was dense, dark and smelly. Lottie was not a fanciful woman, yet she recognized this as a place where ghosts and suchlike might gather if they existed. Which they didn't, of course. She shuddered, hovered nervously on the rim of the copse. 'William?' Her voice was less than steady.

A muffled woof made its way through skeletal branches that reached up like stripped fingers to point towards the darkening sky.

'Hell's bells,' cursed Lottie. 'Come here, you rum beggar,' she yelled. 'Get over here now.'

William whimpered, whined, barked again.

So, he was in the woods, and there was something wrong with him. William was a gregarious chap who thrived on human company. He usually responded within seconds to a call, as he was a dog who actively sought the companionship of mankind.

Concerned for this lovable rogue of a dog, Lottie forgot her nervousness and launched herself into the blackness. She shouted the dog's name every few seconds, was almost oblivious to a series of sharp, splintery barbs that touched her face and ripped greedily at her coat.

William emerged from his hide, a dark item clutched between his teeth. He whimpered, came to Lottie's side and dropped the burden. Lottie took a box of matches from her pocket, lit a cigarette to calm her nerves a bit, then used the flame to examine William's latest find. He had a habit of finding things, things which were not always lost. A collection of garden gnomes culled from down the hill was assembled in the rear porch of Aston Leigh.

Soon, there would have to be an open day with notices pinned to trees and fences, IDENTITY PARADE AT ASTON LEIGH, or HUNT THE GNOME.

'Give it here, then.' Lottie bent and picked up William's discovery. It was a shoe, a man's shoe. There was something inside, something off-white and embedded in darker, softer . . . oh, no! She screamed, dropped the shoe and the match, allowed the Woodbine to fall from her lips to the ground, then felt herself tumbling downward into a sudden and very welcome silence.

The dog wagged his tail, licked Lottie's face, pawed at her hand. She was asleep. Confused and excited by his newly acquired treasure, he bounded off, returned, ran away, came back again for his shoe. Once more, he fussed round Lottie's inert body, then he pranced in the direction of home.

Lottie dragged herself back to the hem of consciousness. A bone. William had come up with a bone, and that bone was from the lower leg of a man. The shoe had been masculine, dark in colour. Protruding from rotted flesh and decaying sock, the metatarsals had lain side by side, a perfect scaffolding that had once supported a foot, an ankle, a whole, unviolated leg, a human being.

She vomited quietly, looked round for William, found that she could not get to her feet. He had taken the article with him, it seemed, as it was not visible in the immediate vicinity. With her eyes adjusting to the meagre light from a quarter moon whose poor efforts were further diminished by trees, Lottie searched all around herself, discovered nothing except hard ground and twigs.

Where there was a foot, there was a leg. And where

there was a leg, there was— She stopped thinking, raised her head and screamed, every ounce of her energy feeding the dreadful sound. For the first time ever, she would have embraced the noise of gunshots, but the place remained silent. She was alone, was the only person here except for . . . Lottie moved her head and stared in the direction from which William had fetched the shoe.

A very old tree reached for the sky, its roots bared by the erosion of soil at its base where animals had dug, played and nested. Was there a body in that hole? Had the ancient tree taken recent nourishment from the dust to which man was compelled to return? She screamed again. An owl answered, then a rush of wings disturbed the overhead canopy of branches.

The pain began, a throbbing in her left ankle. She had broken it or twisted it while falling. Whatever the condition of the joint, it refused to bear her weight. 'Mrs Shawcross!' she howled. 'Somebody, anybody! Help, help!' For several minutes, Lottie screamed and shouted.

'Mrs Bowker?' It was Ada's voice.

'Thank God,' mumbled the injured woman. Lifting her head, she cried, 'I'm over here.'

Ada arrived on the scene. 'I heard you screaming,' she said. 'Even from halfway down The Rise. I was looking for William.' She shuddered when she recalled Lottie's blood-curdling yells. 'John Duncan's coming,' she added. 'I called for him on my way up.'

Lottie breathed a heartfelt sigh. John Duncan, handyman and gardener at Top o' th' Moor, was a strong fellow. He would get her out of here.

He arrived quickly, pushing aside dead or sleeping

wood until he reached Lottie's side. Alerted moments earlier by Ada, he had put on his boots and dashed out of Top o' th' Moor as quickly as he could manage. 'What have you been up to, Missus?' he asked.

Lottie flinched when he tried to move her. 'I've done my left ankle in, John. It was William, he—'

'Aye, William. He ate my tea yesterday, just sauntered in without as much as a by your leave and pinched my pork chop. Not the first time, either,' chuckled John.

Lottie nodded impatiently. 'He found something.'

The man sighed heavily. 'If yon dog finds owt else, there'll be nowt left round these parts.'

'It's serious,' insisted Lottie. 'He found a bone.'

'Aye, the bone out of my bloody chop, I shouldn't wonder.'

Lottie was growing weary and cold. She was glad of the trees now that company had arrived, because they offered some shelter from a whipping easterly blast that promised snow. 'Human, John. William found a man's shoe with the foot still in it. The leg bones had come away at the ankle, but it was real. I'm not imagining it, honest. Fair scared me, it did. That's how I came to fall over, and I've gone down awkward, like.'

John Duncan straightened his spine and looked around. 'Where?' he asked.

Lottie waved a hand in the direction of the large tree. 'Don't leave me,' she implored. 'Don't touch anything, 'cos the police'll have to be fetched and they won't want the place disturbed.' In truth, she didn't want to see any more, to know any more, not yet. 'Just get me home, please.'

John carried Lottie Bowker out of the wood. He brushed aside anything in his path, caused switches of timber to crackle as he removed them by kicking or by pushing himself and Lottie through them. When they reached Top o' th' Moor, he turned into the driveway and hammered at the front door.

Hilda Ainsworth opened it. 'John? Eeh, Lottie, have you been hurt?'

John Duncan swept past the bemused housekeeper and deposited his human burden on a sofa. 'Brandy, Hilda,' he said. 'Look at her left foot, see what you think.' He lifted the telephone and barked at the operator. 'Police, right away,' he said. 'I think there's a dead body in the Top o' th' Moor woods. This is John Duncan. I'm the Templetons' manservant. Tell them to get theirselves here before this snow comes.' He slammed home the receiver.

Ada Dobson ran in from the kitchen. Unlike John Duncan, she had entered the Templeton house by the servants' door at the rear. 'Mrs Bowker?' Her voice was high-pitched. 'Are you all right, Mrs Bowker?'

Lottie lifted her head from the cushion. 'Get Mrs Shawcross, love. And find William, because he's got a man's shoe with a man's foot-bones still in it.' She closed her eyes briefly against the look of horror on the maid's face. 'Get gone, Ada. Hurry up. Some poor bugger has died in them woods.'

Ada fled from the scene, panic quickening her movements.

John brought a stool and sat next to Lottie. 'I wonder who the hell it is?'

Lottie closed her eyes. 'Never mind, lad. Whoever he is, he'll not be going anywhere.'

*   *   *

There were police everywhere. They swarmed along The Rise, some with dogs, others with torches and sticks. William, who had buried his treasure in the vegetable patch at the edge of Aston Leigh's rear garden, stood with his front paws on the window sill of the drawing room. His tongue lolled and he panted excitedly as he sensed the nearness of other canines.

On the sofa, Lottie Bowker was stretched out, her foot resting in the careful hands of Hilda Ainsworth, who had accompanied Lottie and John Duncan from Top o' th' Moor to Aston Leigh. 'It's not broke,' declared Hilda. 'But it's a right nasty sprain. This can hurt worse than a fracture, you know.'

Lottie did know, though she said nothing. All she could see in her mind's eye was that shoe and its terrible contents. She would not sleep tonight, would not sleep for many nights to come, she warned herself.

Connie and Gil stood at the window with William. Shadowy figures distorted by torchlight passed the end of the driveway. 'Why didn't they wait until morning?' asked Gil of no-one in particular. 'From what Mrs Bowker says, the chap must have been there for some considerable time.'

Connie shuddered. 'Shut up, Gil. We've been living right on top of the poor man. Anyway, there's a possibility of snow, so the police have to get on with things. How long have we lived next to that dead body?'

'The Templetons are nearer.' Gil looked over his shoulder as a detective sergeant re-entered the room. This was a shabby, lumbering man whose sartorial inelegance did little to promote confidence in the guardians of the law. He wore a creased suit, a nasty brown raincoat and a battered trilby hat. 'Thank you,' he said to Alice Shawcross. Alice, who was sitting silently by the fire, nodded at the latest intruder.

Sergeant Barford, having availed himself of bathroom facilities, loomed over the prostrate figure of Lottie Bowker. 'Are you sure it was a man's foot?' he asked.

Lottie fixed him with a glare. 'I've never yet met an animal what wears brogues, Sergeant,' she replied smartly.

'Quite.' He scribbled in his little notebook. 'What time was the discovery made?'

Lottie closed her weary eyes. 'I couldn't say. Ask William,' she suggested. 'He's the one as found the shoe.'

The man gazed around the room. 'William?'

Connie pointed to her canine companion.

'Oh.' The policeman wrote some more. 'Where is it now? The shoe, I mean.'

'Ask the dog,' snapped Lottie. Her ankle felt as if somebody had stuck a red-hot poker into it. 'He's likely buried it outside somewhere.'

'So he didn't bring it inside?' The sergeant waited for a reply.

'I hope it isn't in here,' said Alice. 'If it is found, I shall let you know.'

Gil placed an arm round his sister's shoulders. She'd had a rough time recently, was missing Father more than Gil had expected, was still suffering pain from that appalling accident. She wore her clothes slightly longer these days, as her right leg from just above the knee to mid-calf was scarred and misshapen. Fortunately the Paris fashion houses had created the new look to cheer up Europe now that the Second World War was fading into history, and the dresses were worn long. Those abbreviated dresses of the 1940s had been shortened by shortages. The New Look suited Connie.

She grinned ruefully at him. 'This is just what we need to cheer us up on the eve of the opening, isn't it?'

Gil shrugged. 'It's just a very unhappy coincidence,' he told her. At least Connie's legs matched each other for length. Connie's accident had forced Gil to consider very sympathetically the state of James Templeton's leg. From birth, James had been deformed. For twenty-odd years, since learning to walk, poor James had suffered discomfort, stares and comments. 'How is the leg?' Gil asked now.

'OK-ish,' Connie replied. 'Heavy. I think they stuck me together with lead piping.' She glanced over her shoulder. 'He doesn't inspire confidence, does he?' she whispered, referring to the policeman.

Gil allowed himself a brief look. 'Well, he probably cares more about his job than about how he looks.'

Connie listened to the barking dogs, noticed that their noise stopped like magic in response to a long blast on a whistle.

The detective sergeant stopped writing. 'They've found him,' he announced quietly. 'I must go, but I shall need to speak to you again.'

Alice, who had been quiet thus far, spoke to the policeman. 'We shall be at Templeton and Fishwick tomorrow,' she said. 'On Deansgate.'

'Oh. That new shop and cafe?'

'Restaurant,' answered Alice patiently. 'With a licence. Getting the licence held us up for weeks. Anyway,' she smoothed her skirt, 'that is where we shall be.'

The sergeant let himself out.

Lottie moaned while Hilda bandaged her injury. 'I won't be able to do me job,' she wailed. 'And how do I get up to bed?'

'Sleep on the sofa,' replied Alice. 'Ada will take care of the house well enough. When the pain lessens, you must go upstairs to bed for a few days, Mrs Bowker.'

'I wonder who he is?' mused Connie, her eyes still fixed on the lane outside.

Gil, who was walking away from the window, stopped in his tracks. A certain man had been missing for five or six months . . . He shook himself inwardly and carried on towards the drawing room door. Surely not? Surely Grandmother hadn't really killed Peter Turnbull here, right next to the house? It was late and Gil was tired. This newly awakened unease accompanied him up the stairs, into the bath and into his bedroom. For several hours, Gil lay awake. Then he dropped into a dream-filled sleep and tossed about until morning.

The grand opening of Templeton and Fishwick of Deansgate was quite a stunning event. Because of some remote ancestor with Scottish blood, Maude Templeton had hired a lone piper who held up traffic while he played 'Scotland the Brave'. Then Millhouse Brass Band rendered an almost recognizable 'Colonel Bogey' followed by 'For He's a Jolly Good Fellow'.

James and Gil, the two jolly good fellows attached to Templeton and Fishwick, had little to do. Each stood behind his mother while the two ladies handled an enormous pair of scissors with which a ribbon stretched across the main entrance was to be cut. Balloons festooned the windows, and bunting was stretched across the whole frontage of the store.

A small crowd was gathering in the vicinity, women with shopping bags and prams, a window cleaner, two rag-and-bone men and a yawning tramp.

Maude, resplendent in fuchsia hat and gloves, navy coat and shoes, stepped forward.

James dug Gil in the ribs. 'If she says "God bless her and all who shop in her," I'll die.' He grinned at Connie and Mary. Connie stuck out her tongue and withered her tormentor with a hard look.

'She loves me not,' moaned James.

'Shut up,' hissed Gil from the corner of his mouth.

'Such sympathy.' James put his weight on the good leg and prayed that the ceremony, such as it was, would soon be over.

Maude smiled benevolently upon the increasing congregation. 'Bolton is a large town,' she announced unnecessarily. 'Yet many of us go to Manchester for clothes, china, bags, silverware. In an effort to keep trade in the town, Mrs Fishwick and I decided to open a small department store. Feel free to browse at any time. No purchase is required, and the store is very well heated.'

The window cleaner dragged on his hand-rolled cigarette. 'Pricey, too, I'll bet.' Some bystanders chuckled.

'Not at all,' answered Maude. 'We cater for all purses.'

'Not mine,' called a woman. 'It's empty.'

'Then I pray that your fortunes will change,' said Maude. She guided Alice's hand to the ribbon, and the two women cut the length of satin. 'We are open,' declared Maude as cameras clicked and flashed.

Maude and Alice had great plans for the new business. There was a need for a wedding specialist. Templeton and Fishwick was about to offer a unique service, a cheaper and more sensible way of enjoying the great day. Wedding dresses and bridesmaids' clothes would be made on the premises, as would suits for gentlemen. The restaurant would cater for the guests, while invitations and flowers would also be handled by the shop.

Maude smiled at her partner. Soon, a hairdressing salon was to be opened on the first floor. Beauty experts could make up the bride and her attendants either in the store or in their own homes. 'We should branch out into wedding cars,' said Maude.

Alice nodded. 'And we could buy back the dresses, hire them out at a very low price.'

Maude agreed. Her descent into the world of commerce had been painless and exciting. 'Come on, partner,' she said. 'Let's have a glass of wine and toast our dream weddings.'

With a sigh of relief, Gil opened the double doors and followed the two mothers inside. The near-deserted shop looked almost eerie, as if the world had suddenly ended mid-sentence. Behind tills, newly employed girls were dressed in uniform, a plain blue blouse, navy skirt, Templeton and Fishwick badge on a lapel. An archway beckoned shoppers through to fashions, while the immediate area contained perfumes and toiletries, handbags, luggage, scarves and gloves, umbrellas.

A lift announced access to further floors, on the first of which men's clothing, china and silverware could be purchased. The upper storey housed patterns, dress and furnishing materials and arts and crafts. James commandeered the lift and went up into his eyrie.

A few potential customers drifted inside. Young women clustered round the fashion jewellery counter, and the first clatter of an opening and closing till was heard. 'There,' said Maude to Alice. 'We are in business.'

Gil, whose unease about the body in the woods had not diminished, went through to the restaurant where Sadie, Mary and an incomprehensible man called Mario were embroiled in cooking and table-setting. 'What's that smell?' asked Gil.

'Meat and potato pie Italian style,' replied Mary. 'God knows what he puts into things, but they taste great.' She kissed her lover's cheek.

'We'll have none of that.' Sadie bustled past on improved feet. She had scraped together enough to afford a weekly visit to the chiropodist, and her various problems had abated somewhat. 'Get yourself into that kitchen,' she told her daughter. 'He's messing about with summat called paprika.'

'It's just pepper,' replied Mary patiently.

Sadie was unsure about all this fancy-sounding stuff. 'We'd be best sticking to what we know,' she muttered. 'There's nowt wrong with fish and chips, pie and peas. Any road, I've made apple crumble. You can't go far wrong with English baking apples.'

Gil left them to it. When he re-entered the store itself, he found it busy. Yet he noticed the sergeant immediately, picked him out right away. He walked across to the man. 'Any news?'

'Yes.' The policeman took Gil to one side. 'It's probably a chap called Peter Turnbull, missing since July or August. They've got the details at the station. Did you know him?'

Gil's heart pounded like a bass drum. 'No,' he replied truthfully. 'No, I don't know anyone of that name.'

'Lived on Halliwell Road, had some sort of private income, never worked. Mind, his private income could have been a bit dubious, because we did know him.'

Gil cleared his throat. 'How did he die?'

'Shot.'

The single word cut right through Gil, made him almost breathless. 'Really?' he managed.

'It was murder, not suicide.'

Gil leaned against the wall, tried to ensure that his stance was casual. 'There's a lot of shooting in those woods, Sergeant Barford. People kill rabbits for food.'

The man nodded thoughtfully. 'Poachers don't often use handguns, Mr Shawcross. This was not a shotgun job.'

'Oh. I see.' Gil waved at his mother, hoped that the weakness in his body was not obvious. 'Well,' he said eventually. 'There will be a big investigation, I suppose.'

'Yes.' The detective paused for a split second. 'The murderer could be anyone, but we have to start somewhere, so I'm checking on those who live nearby.'

'Naturally.'

'You see, the sound of a pistol would differ from that of a shotgun. Probably louder.'

Gil shrugged. 'We hear all kinds of sounds from the woods. Some loud, some not so loud. It would be difficult to differentiate, as none of us are experts.' Grandmother probably knew her stuff. She had accompanied her husband on many expeditions, had seen animals shot down for fun, for their skins, for their ivory.

'I must let you get back to your work,' said Barford. 'This is a big day for you.'

Gil straightened. 'Yes,' he replied. 'It's a very big day.'

SIXTEEN

In the first week in February 1951, all hell was let loose at Aston Leigh. The day started ordinarily enough. It was a Wednesday, and the department store was closed. Maude Templeton had volunteered to travel down to Stoke to replenish stocks of china and earthenware, while Connie Shawcross, who had learnt to drive her brother's car, had set off to choose fabrics and patterns for the dressmaking counters.

Gil, remaining troubled, borrowed Alice's Morris and drove in the direction of Bromley Cross. Things needed saying, things he had said before. The enquiry regarding Peter Turnbull's murder continued, but little had been reported in the newspapers thus far. Edward had tried to shrug off his son's theories, had advised him to get on with life and stop hypothesizing about an old woman who was scarcely fit to lift a champagne glass to her mean lips. Edward did not want to hurt the wife who had thrown him out, the wife for whom he had been such a bitter disappointment. For the first time within living memory, Alice and Edward were almost at peace with one another, were communicating as business associates.

Gil drove through the town, heard the faint sarcasm in Father's voice. 'Eleanor's a champagne and caviare lady to the core, Gilbert. She could never fire a gun – it would be far too messy, unladylike and unseemly for a person of her calibre. Leave it alone, please. With any luck, Alice may be spared the knowledge that Peter Turnbull was her father's son.'

Peter Turnbull had been Alice's half-brother. Gil knew enough about life to realize that his mother would inevitably find out the truth, especially if Peter Turnbull had been registered as the son of Samuel Fishwick. Gil was nursing the whole problem, was unwilling to place any burden on his sister, who had suffered enough. Today was the watershed; today Gil would use any means available to him to force his father into talking to Alice.

He parked outside Edward's shop, watched for a few minutes while customers were served. Edward Shawcross had made a success of his second career, because people travelled miles in cars and on buses to take home one of his cream Victorias or half a dozen individual trifles as a treat for Sunday tea. Even travelling salesmen and truck drivers were wont to go out of their way for a meat pie, a cream crisp or a Bavarian slice.

When the queue had dispersed, Gil entered the shop. He would never get used to seeing Father in white apron and hat, the full set of whiskers incongruous now, out of keeping with the shop.

Edward looked up from the task of wiping down an empty display case. 'Hello, Gilbert,' he said. 'Will I ever get it right? I've been cleared out of meringues, and I had a dozen left last Wednesday.'

'Are you closing now?'

'Yes,' replied the expert baker. 'Wednesday afternoon is my own, thank goodness.' He got rid of the cloth and told Gil to lock the door and turn the sign to CLOSED. 'I'll put the kettle on,' he said.

Gil went upstairs to wait for his father. The flat was more comfortable these days, with a green brocade suite, matching curtains, a new dining table and chairs. But the only ornaments apart from a couple of Toby jugs were photographs of Edward's children. Gil saw himself on horseback, on Blackpool sands, playing on the swing in the back garden of Aston Leigh. Connie, too, was frozen in various instants of time, was three, then four, then a gap-toothed seven-year-old.

'Gilbert?'

The younger man sat down. 'Father, I am going to talk to the police. There's no point in trying to stop me, because I need to tell someone in authority about my theory.'

Edward sighed and shook his head slowly. 'Hasn't your mother been through enough?'

'I suppose she has,' replied Gil. 'But my grandfather and Peter Turnbull paid a far greater price. I don't want to hurt my mother any more than you do, but I can't sleep. This is on my mind all the time, interfering with my work. Mother and Mrs Templeton are just getting this Dream Wedding business off the ground, and they need help. I can't even help myself, because I'm worn out, can't think properly, can scarcely walk in a straight line.'

Edward was glad that his son was such a stalwart, decent citizen. Above all, he found a degree of joy in the certainty that Gilbert was not weak or shallow. But poor Alice. Why should she suffer the effects of her parents' sins? 'And if you are wrong, Gilbert? What then?'

More than anything in the world, Gil wanted to be wrong. 'A murderer is on the loose,' he said. 'If I'm wrong about Grandmother, then there is another dangerous person in the vicinity.'

'I see. And I cannot dissuade you?'

'No.' Gil shifted uneasily in the chair. 'And I want you to be there when I talk to Mother. I'm too young to know the details about my grandparents. Mother should be told that she had a brother.'

Edward paced about the floor. 'She may know already,' he said. 'When I told her about Vera, it came as no surprise to her.'

'Nevertheless, this still has to be done,' insisted Gilbert calmly. 'Will you come up to the house this afternoon? Mother and I will be there, but Connie has other plans.'

Edward wheeled round and faced his conscience. 'Three o'clock,' he said. 'I'll be there.'

Connie let herself in at the side door. The shop was strange when closed, as if it still housed the ghosts of yesterday's customers. A cleaning lady dragged a mop across the floor. 'Hello!' she shouted. 'No rest for the wicked, eh?'

Connie laughed. 'I've had a great morning, Ida. There are a couple of decent cotton fents thrown in for nothing, so I'll give you first grabs when the order arrives.'

'Eeh, you're a good girl. What are you?'

'An angel,' trilled Connie, who had heard it all before from Ida.

The stairs were not easy, yet Connie refused to be defeated. Taking the soft option was not always right, she reminded herself. When the store was densely populated, she used the lifts, because the fear of falling was always strong. She had been ordered to take good care of herself and, particularly, of the miracle that had been achieved by surgeons. Just a couple of years ago, Connie's leg would have been written off within minutes of her arrival at the infirmary. She must not jeopardize that limb again.

Resting on a landing, she strained her ears and listened to a muffled laugh. James. He was up there doing what came naturally, performing to a select audience of would-be artisans. James was such a show-off that he really ought to have been an actor or a teacher, because he invariably played to the gallery.

Connie pulled a scrap of paper from her pocket and read in a whisper. 'I love thee Connie, love thee muchly, glad you walk no longer crutch-ly, if you would only walk with me, strong as Samson's hair I'd be. Don't forget to order ink, may I take you for a drink? Yours sincerely with much love. By the way, I found your glove.' He was as mad as a March hare on gin.

After her short rest, Connie continued all the way to the top of the building. When she reached James Templeton's little world, she stopped and peeped through a crack in the door. He was talking to a short, elderly woman in a flowered smock-styled overall. His and her hands were dripping in watered-down clay; sou'westers and raincoats might have fitted the bill, thought Connie when she saw the state of James's brown coveralls. 'Get the speed up gradually, Monica,' he said patiently. 'There's more on the wall, on you and on me than there is on the wheel. No, don't get upset, no need to clean the wall, clay gives the place atmosphere.'

There were others there, people drawing and

sketching, several threading beads onto wire, a man painting at an easel, a young girl working with charcoal. This was James's work room. This was his heaven, his private place.

'I'm going to owe you a fortune one way and another,' wailed the would-be potter.

'On the house,' replied James. 'Who knows? One day, department stores such as this may be selling cheap copies of your creations.'

Connie felt a smile threatening to break out. He was adorable. He was a thorough nuisance, he was infantile, eccentric, gifted, completely out of his tiny mind. She watched him struggling with silver wire as he showed a woman how to create earrings to match her string of beads. He had paid for that wire out of his own pocket, had bought oils, canvas, frames, paints, inks, paper, clay, wheel and all manner of media in order to give people a chance to create something of their own. Connie wiped away a tear and swallowed a little sob.

For as long as she cared to remember, James had been a part of her life. He had been another Gil, another brother and playmate. Gil and Connie had been James's legs, had performed his naughtinesses for him. The proxy vote, James had called it.

The poem rustled in her pocket. At home, there was a drawerful of nonsense rhymes, a boxful of other verses in which nonsense had played no part. One day, he would ask her when exactly she had realized the depth of her love for him, and he would savour the answer. 'I fell for you one Wednesday when your hair and face were covered in filthy, wet clay.'

She opened the door and stepped into chaos. 'Your inks will be here tomorrow,' she announced.

Her missing glove had been stuck like a cock's comb on a plaster bust of Mozart.

Everyone stopped working and looked at the new arrival.

'This is Miss Shawcross,' he advised the congregation. 'The love of my life, but she's sensible enough to spurn me.'

Some devil of Connie's own reared its head. 'If you would care to take a bath some time, Mr Templeton, I shall be pleased to accompany you in an orderly fashion to the altar. At which venue, you will be read your rights. Anything you say will be used in evidence against you until the day one of us pops our clogs.'

James blinked. 'Eh?' he managed.

Connie tutted. 'So common, too. Close your mouth, Mr Templeton.'

The lady in the flowered smock grinned broadly, advertising the fact that a front tooth had gone AWOL. 'You two engaged, then?'

'Yes,' replied Connie sweetly. 'At least I shall be able to keep an eye on him. You see, his mother is quite worn out. She has promised to pay me five hundred a year if I take him off her hands. Oh, and I am to have all her Co-op dividend stamps, too.'

James blinked again, this time dislodging a small amount of wetness from a disobedient duct. Yes, he told himself. Yes, this was exactly how it should happen between him and Connie. Neither of them wanted or needed wine, roses and privacy. Here was a scene he might have written for himself and for her, a pledge made in public, the accompanying music consisting of honest-to-goodness human laughter, the atmosphere laden with paint fumes and that unmistakable, earthy aroma of soggy clay.

Connie grinned. 'We might as well keep all the cripples in one box, don't you think?'

James picked up a paintbrush and forced his arm to stop trembling. Deliberately, he turned his back on Constance and carried on with the near-completed portrait of Sadie Martindale. His heart fluttered like a confused bird in a cage, but he maintained as much dignity as a muck-spattered man could muster. She loved him. She was beautiful. He would deal with her later.

Edward pushed the key back into his pocket. He would not enter as master and owner; like any other visitor, he rang the bell and waited for Ada.

'Come in, sir.' Ada had been a bit nervous since the night when the body had been found. If the master would come home, there would be two men in the house, two males who could protect the household from all the marauding criminals who currently lurked in black corners of the maid's imagination. She took his hat. 'Mrs Shawcross is in the drawing room with Master Gilbert.'

Edward nodded absently, then walked slowly towards the meeting he dreaded. Gil was beside his mother on the sofa. 'You expected me?' The guest directed this question at his estranged wife. 'Gilbert asked me to come,' he added.

Alice smiled faintly and gestured towards an armchair.

Edward sat, felt like a victim of the Spanish Inquisition as he faced the two of them. How much had Gilbert said? And did it matter? Whatever had been said would need repeating, Edward supposed. He cleared his throat. 'It's about the disappearance of the man known as Peter Turnbull.' He paused, wondered where he was going to find the language to encompass the horror of Gilbert's theory. Perhaps Gilbert would speak up shortly?

'The body in the woods,' said Alice. The police had discovered the missing foot and the shoe, had incurred the twice-weekly gardener's wrath by wreaking havoc all over the vegetable patch. 'Do go on,' she said.

Edward noticed that Gilbert was holding Alice's hand. Gilbert was leaving the explanations to his father, and rightly so. 'Peter Turnbull was your father's illegitimate son,' said Edward, nervousness elevating the pitch of his voice.

Alice flinched, hung onto Gilbert's hand. What was this nonsense? Her parents had been utterly devoted, had even ignored their only child because they had been so wrapped up within that mutual adoration. There were no other children. Father would never have betrayed Mother.

Edward continued. 'When I met your father, when I took him into my rooms in Goldsmith Street, he had been the victim of an assault. The men who had beaten him were the brothers of a woman named Molly Turnbull. Molly died after giving birth to a child, your father's child.'

'Peter Turnbull,' whispered Alice. New seeds of unease rooted themselves in her mind. The Fishwicks' sudden departure had been hasty, unexpected. Was this the reason for their escape to foreign parts?

Edward stared at his shoes. Eleanor had been so supportive, so loving. She had made a new life at the other side of the world, had uprooted herself in order to put space between Samuel and his mistakes. Could she have committed murder? Was Gilbert right in assuming that the old woman had actually killed?

'Father helped Grandfather,' said Gil. 'Hid him so that those men couldn't get to him again.'

'Samuel arranged the . . . for you and myself to meet,' Edward told Alice. 'I didn't know that he intended to leave the country so soon after our wedding. He seemed to like me, was very grateful because I had taken him in after the beating.'

Alice inclined her head. So much information to process. She felt a dribble of cold sweat making its way down her spine, and she shivered convulsively. A brother? A dead half-brother?

Gil patted a trembling hand. 'Mother? Mother?'

She left Gil's words hanging in the room. Things began to tumble into place. Questions suddenly answered themselves, though Alice derived no comfort from her deductions.

'Mother?'

'I will be all right in a moment,' she replied through lips that had stiffened with shock. Her parents had run away from Peter Turnbull's family. Father had betrayed Mother. That perfect marriage had been flawed, had been a sham, a play on which the curtain had descended only with the death of Samuel.

'I'm so sorry,' whispered Edward.

She gazed blankly at him. Ah, yes, here was Edward. Her eyes focused on him at last. He had been caretaker, had acted in loco parentis, in loco husband, in loco millowner. 'But Peter Turnbull's dead,' Alice managed. 'They are both dead.' Her father and her half-brother were no more. She stared hard into the eyes of the man who had fathered her two children. 'What was your excuse,

Edward?' she asked. 'What part did you play in the drama?'

He hung his head for a few seconds. 'I have no excuse and no answer,' he replied.

She smiled wryly. 'At least you try to be an honest man, Edward. You are, perhaps, a weak fool, but you seem to know yourself quite well.' She pulled away from Gil, rose and walked to the fireplace. 'So, the body in the woods, this Peter Turnbull, used to be my half-brother.' Her stomach felt queasy, so she inhaled deeply and gripped the mantelpiece.

'Who was only slightly older than our son,' said Edward.

Gilbert glanced at his father. 'That is your part done,' he said before rising and joining his mother near the fireplace. He took hold of both her hands. 'Mother, I think . . . I'm almost sure that Grandmother helped Grandfather on his way. With an overdose of morphine. She spilled some, broke phials. Ada had to mop up the mess. But Grandmother might have saved the drug, might have pretended to . . .' His voice died. This was so terrible, so nightmarish.

Alice, who was still battling to come to terms with the concept of a dead half-brother, blinked slowly as she digested Gil's words. Inside her head, two factions did battle. Had Father really betrayed Mother? No, no. They had been in love, had always been in love. 'Perhaps he suffered too much,' she said, almost to herself. Then she addressed Gil. 'They were so much in love, Gilbert. She could not have borne his pain. If she killed him, then it was an act of kindness.' She smiled hesitantly. 'Even I, their daughter, was surplus to requirements at the deathbed. They had eyes only for each other.' She nodded thoughtfully. 'My mother would have wanted to kill his pain.'

'No.' Gilbert's voice was low, barely louder than a whisper. 'Grandfather was asking for Peter Turnbull. Of course, I had never heard of the man. Grandfather directed me to a new will he had compiled abroad, asked me to have it verified. For a while, he seemed to mistake me for his . . . his son.'

'Go on,' said Alice.

'Well, she was listening. She grabbed the will and gave me a story about Grandfather's confusion. He was confused, I suppose, because he was already quite heavily sedated. But she was so anxious.' He swallowed. 'After that, no-one was allowed into the bedroom. He died the next day.'

Alice gazed into Gilbert's eyes. 'What are you saying? That my mother is a murderess?'

Edward coughed, stood up and took a step towards his wife and his son. 'Alice, if Eleanor did put an end to Samuel's life, then such an action could possibly be interpreted as a kindness. But there is more.' He took a deep breath as if refuelling himself for what came next. 'As we all know, someone else disappeared very soon after Samuel's death, and that person was found a few days ago. According to the police, the body in the woods had been there for at least six months.'

Alice shook her head as if trying to deny the implications behind her husband's words.

Edward carried on. 'I drove Eleanor to the house where Turnbull lived. She was angry.' He pondered for a second or two, recalled Eleanor's interest in shopping for cheese. Eleanor was a cool customer, indeed. 'Very cold, very furious,' he said. 'I wondered at the time whether she had carried that anger in her heart since hearing about your father's infidelity. She certainly mentioned drugs, said that Samuel would shortly be sedated so strongly that he would not be able to express himself. Perhaps she waited calmly during all those years . . .'

'Waited to kill him?' Alice's voice was touched with panic.

'To get a revenge of some kind,' said Edward. 'Who knows? We never saw Eleanor and Samuel, seldom heard from them. Perhaps she began to dislike him—'

'Rubbish.' Alice snatched her hands out of Gilbert's grip, clenched them to her breast. 'They loved one another. No, no, my mother could never hurt him.' Although she spoke the words, Alice doubted their veracity. For the first time in her life, Alice Shawcross suspected that all had not been well inside her parents' fairytale marriage.

Edward shuffled about uneasily. For this one time, he had to be brave, had to be firm. His son could not be allowed to say the rest of it. 'Gilbert believes that your mother shot Turnbull.' There, it was out. He had saved Gilbert a little trouble, then.

Alice's eyes were round with shock and disbelief. 'Isn't this taking assumption into the realms of fantasy?' she asked her son.

Gil swallowed. 'She's clever. There was something in her eyes, something odd. It was as if she cared for no-one at all. I looked at her, watched her—'

'Stared at her,' snapped Alice. 'Connie was always telling you to stop staring at your grandmother.'

The young man glanced from Edward to Alice, tried to find more words to underline his feelings. 'She's icy, Mother,' he said finally. 'Cold enough and tough enough to wait for a chance or to create a chance. She killed Grandfather because I was getting too close to the truth, not because he was in agony. And she shot Peter Turnbull because he was the human embodiment of that same truth.'

'And what, pray, did she use as a gun?' Alice folded her arms, as if protecting her body from the answer.

'I don't know,' answered Gil truthfully. 'But I can guess.'

'There are no firearms in this house,' continued Alice. 'Ever since you were young, your father has refused to keep a shotgun. How on earth did Mother get hold of the weapon?'

'She brought it with her from Africa,' said Gil. 'They had dozens of trunks and cases. It could have been hidden at the bottom of any one of them.'

Alice sat down abruptly. 'This is all too much for me to think about,' she muttered. 'You tell me after all these years that my father had another child, one I never met?'

'We supported that family for years,' said Edward quietly. 'The young mother died just after the birth, so Peter Turnbull was raised by his grandparents. Mr Turnbull was in a wheelchair even then. He and his wife did not reach old age, then Peter stayed with his three uncles. Two died in the war, while the third opened a business of some kind in the south – Bedfordshire, I believe. The mill supported all of them and your parents' lavish lifestyle. It has been quite a struggle.' As he said these last words, Edward realized how much his working life had improved. The tension had lessened. He was his own master at last and his labour was honest.

Alice Shawcross jumped up, walked to the window and stared through it, though she saw little. Her mind was a jumble of questions, while her emotions were a bubbling cauldron of fear, disbelief, anger and bewilderment. 'It is still a long stride from Africa to murder.'

Edward cleared his throat. 'Someone killed Peter Turnbull, Alice. He was not a particularly pleasant young man, yet he did not live the sort of existence that invites murder.' He paused for a moment. 'Also, consider the location, think about where his body was found. Who goes into the woods? Poachers, children who ignore their parents' warnings, the occasional tramp. With the exception of those of us who live on The Rise, few people travel to this area. The murder was committed by someone in the vicinity. The police will be back, I'm afraid.'

Alice swivelled and faced him. 'I cannot allow my mother to be dragged into this, Edward.'

'Then we shall all have mud on our faces,' said Gil. 'And in the end, Turnbull's uncle will come and he will tell the police about the circumstances surrounding his nephew's birth. We should inform the police now, immediately.'

Edward was beginning to see the intelligence in his son's idea. 'Last week, a body was found,' he said. 'The coroner and the courts will want some answers.'

'Then we shall wait for the questions,' replied Alice.

'You may wait if you wish,' Gil said. 'But I want to keep you, my sister and my neighbours as safe as possible. Why should we all be suspects? Grandmother must be sent for and questioned – after all, she did live here at the time of Peter Turnbull's disappearance. Can you imagine the commotion if Maude Templeton is implicated, dragged into this because she lives nearby? Or her husband?' He inhaled a stiff draught of oxygen.

'Grandmother did this. I am almost certain that she did away with Grandfather in order to get rid of his will, a will newly created to include Peter Turnbull. And after that, she removed Turnbull himself from the scene.'

'No,' said Alice.

Edward surprised everyone, himself included, by speaking up again. 'If your mother is innocent, Alice, then there is nothing to fear. However, we are withholding evidence in a murder enquiry. The fact that we have withheld will be noted and held against us.'

'No,' she repeated.

Edward persisted. 'Gilbert is not going to walk into a police station announcing to all and sundry that Eleanor is a killer. He simply wants to fill in the gaps about Peter Turnbull's past. Let the force make what they will of the truth, but give them the information first – don't wait until Micky Turnbull arrives from the south to make his noise.'

Alice remained unconvinced. 'But—'

'The uncle is capable of blackmail,' announced Edward firmly. 'Do not allow him any power over you. For years, I was in the Turnbulls' grip and—'

'And you told me nothing,' Alice said.

'I made a promise,' Edward told her.

Slowly, she approached him. 'You made promises to me and to God in a church, Edward. Did you keep them?'

'No.'

'Yet you went along with my father's wishes.'

Edward raised his hands in a gesture of helplessness. 'There would have been too much hurt, Alice.'

'And what is this?' she asked quietly. 'I am hurting, you and Gil are hurting. This is bloody painful.' Her voice rose towards hysteria.

Gil's jaw was drooping slightly. Mother had never sworn before.

'For years, you kept quiet about this, Edward. I should have known, should have been told. This has come as a . . .' The word 'shock' was not adequate. 'This is devastating,' she informed her husband. 'I have suddenly acquired a murdered half-brother and a mother who may have committed that very murder.' She turned her attention to Gil. 'I hope you are wrong,' she whispered.

'So do I,' mumbled Gil.

Alice pushed a lock of hair from her face. 'Go home,' she told Edward wearily. 'Go and bake your cakes.'

Gil stood as still as a rock. Never in his life had he known Mother to be so thoroughly shaken.

Alice sank onto the couch, folded herself almost in two as if all the air had left her body. The tears began, and she sobbed like a child on the first day at school.

She had never cried like this, thought Edward. It was sheer terror, hopelessness, a reaction against all she had just heard. She was suddenly so small, so vulnerable, and he could not comfort her. The loss of weight was noticeable, and her hands shook as she tried to wipe the wetness from her face. 'I'm very, very sorry, Alice,' he mumbled.

She raised her head. 'So am I, Edward.' If only he knew how sorry she was. 'Oh, God,' she moaned. 'So am I.' Mopping her face with a handkerchief, she fought for composure. 'Please go, just for a couple of hours,' she managed finally. 'Both of you.' She needed to be alone, wanted time, a space in which she might think. Seeds of doubt were taking root. Perhaps the relationship between Eleanor and

Samuel had been less than perfect. But murder?

After an hour or more of solitude, Alice fell asleep, unanswered questions tainting her dreams.

Sadie Martindale was trying to put a few finishing touches to her Sunday hat. Sadie's Sunday hat had suffered finishing touches for just about a decade – a bit of ribbon, an imitation flower, new netting, a feather or two. But now, the close-woven navy straw was starting to wear through. 'This'll never see me past another Easter.' She draped a length of emerald green ribbon across the battered item. 'There's only so much as can be done with a yard of petersham,' she informed the fireplace. 'And I can't darn it. Who the heck can mend bloody straw when it breaks? A thatcher?' She giggled to herself. 'Hey, mister, when you've finished patching yon roof, can you thatch me hat for me?'

The door opened and Ethel Hyatt pounded her flat-footed way into the house. Since her abandonment by the little, henpecked Denis, Ethel had started to depend on Sadie. 'I told you,' she said, a triumphant edge to the words. 'He's gone and got her in the family way.'

'Eh?' Sadie cursed her own forgetfulness. She really would have to start remembering to bolt the door. 'Who?'

'Denis's piece of fluff. She's pregnant. I wouldn't care, she's forty if she's a day, all dyed hair and peek-a-boo bloody sandals, even in the middle of winter, piece of trash, she is.' Ethel dropped heavily into a chair. 'I've took more hours on at the pub, Sadie. I can't manage.'

For a woman who couldn't manage, Ethel Hyatt

was looking remarkably robust. 'That's terrible,' said Sadie.

'Yon hat's had it,' pronounced the visitor.

'I know.'

Ethel breathed in deeply, causing an audible creaking of whalebone and elastic. 'Can you not get me a job in that cafe down Deansgate, Sadie?'

If Mary had been in the house, she would have corrected Ethel, might well have informed her that the eating place attached to Templeton and Fishwick was a licensed restaurant, all à la carte except for lunchtime specials and with a wine list as decent as any in Manchester. But Sadie merely sighed. Ethel had put on a lot of weight, and the aisles between tables were hardly avenue-width. With Ethel's girth, she would be serving on one side and clearing at the other with her rear end. Sadie forbade herself to laugh at the vision of Ethel stuck between two tables with her serving trolley. 'There's nowt going, love.'

'Just part-time would do, a few hours a week.'

Sadie was soft-hearted and she knew it. 'Look, I've been thinking, like. With you cleaning at the pub mornings and being at home the rest of the day, you could happen do a bit of our cooking, pies and that. We have fancy stuff like nice fish, and that there Italian boils enough spaghetti to knit a million string vests, but we still have our old faithfuls.'

'Meat rationing's in a mess again,' said Ethel gloomily.

'I know. And us housewives know how to make stuff stretch, 'cos we've been stretched to transparent since the war started. See, you can do potato pie and Lancashire hotpot, make a bit of meat go further, use a nice suet crust. You cook them and one of the lads could pick them up.' The lads. They were Gilbert Shawcross and James Templeton. One was the son of an ex-mill boss and the other was landed gentry. Mind, he was eccentric, was James, living in a prefab and giving drawing lessons every Wednesday. He was a nice fellow, but on the daft side.

'That would be smashing,' said Ethel. 'Eeh, I don't know how I would have coped without you.'

Ethel would have coped, all right. She was one of that strange breed of woman who liked to moan. She was at her happiest when she was miserable. Miserable as sin was as good as it got for Ethel Hyatt.

'I need a new hat,' said Sadie.

'You can afford one.' There was emphasis on the 'you' and the 'afford'. 'Can't remember when I last got owt new.' The uninvited guest rose, used a huge fore-arm to push a wedge of bust free from a length of whalebone. 'Still, mustn't grumble.' She waddled to the doorway, stopped, turned round. 'How's your lass?'

'Getting engaged, I think,' replied Sadie. 'Gil's chased her for long enough, ever since last summer, and I suppose she's got fed up with running.' She knew that Ethel was annoyed about Mary 'going up'. Ethel was always saying things like, 'Your Mary won't want to know you once she gets a nice new house.' 'They've asked me to go and live near them when they get wed. I'm thinking on it,' said Sadie.

'Oh. Well, I'd best be off.' Ethel looked deflated, as if somebody had let the air out of her shoulders. 'Ta for the chance of a bit of work.' She waddled out, slamming the front door in her wake.

Sadie threw the hat on the fire. It curled and crinkled into a mass of black within ten seconds. She'd

436

had some good times in that hat. She'd been to church fetes and concerts, she'd gone to Bolton Fair every June holiday with a bit of something new added to the perennial bonnet.

She closed her eyes and remembered their Bernard, their Mary and young Tommy staring at a bad-tempered article called 'The Smallest Woman In The World'. She'd been a nowty, nasty-humoured little bugger, about two and a half feet in height and with resentment mapped deep as unmined coal into the shrivelled face. The Fat Lady had been a bit more cheerful, all pink and powdered in a satin frock that might have housed a small circus. Black peas in cracked cups, children bending backwards to avoid being burnt on the furnace in the tent flap that served as a doorway. The man had ladled out the peas, had been liberal with the vinegar, sparing with the change. Many a kiddy had got cheated on the fair.

Roll-a-penny, darts, hoop-la, swing boats, the caterpillar and the dodgems. A tear rolled down Sadie's cheek. Bernard was in the army, Tommy was wed, Mary was all but engaged. The burning of the hat had been a symbol, a ritual, because that life was over now, was finished for ever. Sadie's turn to be young, to be a mother and a wife was ending. It was someone else's turn now.

She thought about Teddy Shawcross and Vera. Vera had been missing for ages and she had a child in her belly, Teddy's kiddy. He'd started looking his age, had Mr Shawcross. Mind, he was doing very well as a baker. Everybody was doing all right. Mary had her restaurant, Sadie had a good job in the kitchen. Mrs Shawcross and Mrs Templeton were making a great success of the store.

'So why am I crying?' she asked herself aloud.

Mary fell in, cheeks pink from the cold, arms full of packages. 'Mam, I've got you another present.' She placed the box on the table. 'Go on, open it.'

Sadie sniffed back the self-pity, got up and opened the box. Mary always knew what was needed. Out with the old and in with the new, she thought as she gazed into the circular container. It was a grand hat, still a sensible navy, but properly shaped and in a velvety cloth. 'Eeh, Mary. I could turn right rumbunctious in a hat like that.' She pulled it on and looked in the mirror. 'That's a real hat. That's a very dear hat, Mary.'

Mary looked over Sadie's shoulder and spoke to Mam in the mirror. 'It's for a real and very dear mam, Mam. And guess what?'

'What?' Sadie swung round.

'I went down to the restaurant to clean a couple of cupboards, and Connie came in.' She stopped deliberately.

'So what?' Sadie punched her daughter playfully. 'Town Hall clock struck nine this morning, but nobody got excited about it. What's new about Connie going into work on a Wednesday? She gets through her paperwork quicker when the shop's empty.'

'Sit down, Mam.'

Sadie sat.

'They're getting married. Connie and James. She proposed to him in the middle of his pot-throwing.'

'Eh?'

'While he was showing somebody how to use the potter's wheel. There was a roomful, Mam. In front of everybody, she said she'd marry him. I suppose she didn't really propose, but she accepted. Ida was that excited she knocked her bucket over in men's underwear. The water was everywhere, right up to ladies' unmentionables.'

Mary had a turn of phrase that could make the coalman's horse laugh. Sadie howled till she thought her sides would split. When she sobered up, she asked, 'And what did James say?'

'Nothing,' answered Mary. 'He just picked up his palette and finished you off. I hear you were wearing a nice smile by the time he got you done.'

Sadie removed her new hat and placed it reverently in its tissue-lined box. 'I knew she'd have him,' she said. 'Sometimes, she'd get that mad with him – you know – when he sent her all them daft poems and dandelions out of Queens Park. And when she were mad, the love showed.' She nodded in a satisfied manner. 'They'll be all right, them two,' she muttered. 'It's one of them things as just had to happen, Connie and James. I reckon they've both always known, only she's had to take her time thinking it over, like. They're made for each other.'

'What about me and Gil?'

'Depends.'

'Depends on what?'

'On how furious he gets when you tell him he's to call round to Ethel's twice a week. I've set her on doing pies and hotpots at home.'

'Well, you can tell him,' laughed Mary.

'Oh no,' replied Sadie. 'I've got a new hat, love. I'd like to stay alive to enjoy it.'

Detective Sergeant Ian Barford looked as if his face, like his clothes, was in desperate need of ironing. He was altogether rumpled and ruffled, was clearly discommoded by Gilbert Shawcross's poor timing.

He had been in the middle of a nice piece of cod, and he didn't take kindly to being disturbed during his very irregular meal breaks.

'My grandmother's living in London now,' volunteered Gil in answer to the man's question. 'With the exception of Grandmother, everyone who lived in this house at the time of the murder is here.' Connie was sitting near the window. She knew about Gil's theories regarding Eleanor Fishwick, but she had not expected her brother to go out looking for trouble. She had said nothing about her engagement to James, because she had walked into Aston Leigh only to find a policeman, her parents and Gil discussing the death of Mother's half-brother. So Gil had been right; there had been a connection between the Fishwicks and the Turnbulls.

Barford looked round the room, saw money in every corner, on every wall. Why did people like these need to go messing about with murder? 'As a matter of fact,' he said slowly, 'the boys in the laboratory came up with some funny stuff yesterday.' There again, he reminded himself, most one-offs were committed within a close group. Family life caused a fair bit of bloodshed, what with jealousies and folk getting on other folk's nerves.

Edward, who had remained at Aston Leigh in spite of Alice's harsh words, shook his head at the infuriating man. 'Funny stuff?' he asked.

'Bits of crocodile,' replied the policeman. 'Not the sort of thing you find every day in these parts. They were bits on the ground. Dirty, but they were definitely crocodile skin. In fact, there was even a little bit on the bullet. It got picked up under a microscope. Whoever shot him had the gun hidden, possibly in a crocodile bag.'

Alice closed her mouth tightly. Mother had a crocodile bag.

'So the killer might even be a woman,' drawled the sergeant. 'Or a very unusual man.'

Edward glanced at his wife, saw the whiteness round her lips. 'My son came to you because of the . . . involvement of our family with the victim,' he said.

'We must search your house,' answered Barford. 'Shall we wait for a warrant, or are you prepared to allow the search?' This question was directed at Edward.

'My wife owns the house,' he said.

Alice nodded, then turned away from the unsavoury scene. But she could not turn away from her own thoughts. She was trying to remember when she had last seen Mother's crocodile handbag. It was a huge thing, easily large enough to conceal a hand gun. But she could not pinpoint the occasion on which she had noticed Mother carrying the bag. Eleanor was always attached to some kind of luggage containing her reading spectacles, handkerchief, boiled sweets, comb, perfume and powder compact.

A car pulled up in the driveway. 'My men are here now, Mrs Shawcross,' said the policeman.

'Go ahead,' whispered Alice. 'Do whatever needs to be done.'

Gil joined Ian Barford. 'One of the empty bedrooms might be a good place to start.' He left the rest of his family in order to direct the law towards the room in which his grandfather had died. 'Up the stairs, follow the rail, second on the left.'

Gil stood in the hallway and watched four uniformed men climbing the stairs. They bore hammers, screwdrivers and small brushes with dustpans.

'We shall endeavour to leave the place as we find it,' promised Barford. He knew what this young man was trying to tell him, had received the unspoken message. Toughened by years of exposure to the seamy side of life, the detective was not easily impressed. Yet this stalwart young man was a person of good character, as he plainly knew right from wrong, was concerned with justice rather than with protecting himself and his relatives. 'Thank you, Mr Shawcross,' he said. 'We shall be as quick as possible.'

When Gil returned to the drawing room, the loudest sound came from the ticking of a clock. Mother had angled her body towards the fireplace, while Father sat rigidly in an armchair, each hand clasping a knee. Connie had remained near the window. She looked at Gil, then turned her head away and carried on staring through the glass.

'I had to,' said Gil. 'They would have discovered the facts about the dead man's connections, and they would have asked us why vital evidence had been concealed.'

Edward cleared his throat. 'There is that uncle. I happen to know that Peter Turnbull's neighbour gave the uncle's address to the police. I visited the neighbour in question as soon as the body was identified. She told me that Micky Turnbull had visited, then gone off to look at properties in the London area. He is expanding his empire, it seems. The police will have left messages for him, I'm sure.'

'He's doing well on our money,' whispered Alice.

'Yes,' agreed Edward. 'He should be back in Luton, I suppose, because he has a thriving business to supervise before he breaks into new territory.' He paused. 'Peter Turnbull's neighbour was the only person who knew of our . . . arrangement. The Turnbulls' silence was a condition I imposed in order to protect us. But the lady next door knew all about Molly's death and the baby's birth.'

'How well you have succeeded in protecting us,' said Alice.

Gil stepped into the arena. 'Please don't blame Father,' he said. 'It was Grandfather who strayed . . .' His voice faded away.

'Like father-in-law like son-in-law,' muttered Alice very softly.

Edward lowered his head. How true those words were. Somewhere, Vera was reaching the end of her pregnancy. The same pattern, the same mistakes, the same God Almighty mess.

Although Aston Leigh was not a small house, sounds from above began to reach the family's ears. Furniture was dragged about, carpets were being rolled, drawers and cupboards were opened, closed. A different sound took over as the police used hammer-hooks to prise up floorboards.

Edward looked at the clock. This endless search had lasted just five minutes. Then the silence arrived. It sat on the shoulders of the four people in the drawing room like a heavy, dark cloud. Carpet-softened footfalls padded down the stairs, then Ian Barford entered the room and closed the door.

'Well?' asked Edward.

Barford nodded. 'A loose board next to the bed,' he said. 'We found a gun and what was left of the crocodile bag.'

Alice swayed slightly before pushing herself into an upright position. 'Connie?'

Connie's face would have made a bleached sheet seem dirty. 'Yes, Mother?'

443

'If you feel up to it, find Grandmother's address. It should be in the davenport.' She looked at Edward. 'The show's over,' she told him. 'Go back to your new life.' Then she swivelled away and stared again at the wall.

'I'm sorry,' said the detective.

'So are we all,' mumbled Connie. Then she left the room to seek out information that could put her grandmother in prison. Or worse.

SEVENTEEN

Vera Hardman had been allocated a room on the first floor. In the final weeks of her pregnancy, she was too cumbersome to be hauling herself and her bump right up to the top floor of Mon Repos, so she now had just one set of stairs to tackle.

Maisie Cunningham lived on the ground floor. Shortness of breath and diminishing energy dictated that Maisie should remain on the lower level for the rest of her life. But things were different this winter, as Vera was in residence. Maisie liked having Vera around, was glad of the company, especially during the long evenings that seemed to stretch on for ever. In Maisie's opinion, Vera was a solid and sensible girl, too sensible to get herself into trouble. Where was this baby's father and why was Vera so reluctant to discuss her predicament? She seemed an open enough sort, not the type to hug secrets to her chest.

A kind of routine had developed between the two women, a tacit agreement that suited both of them. As she rose first, Vera did early morning tea, then breakfast. She picked up the mail and the newspaper from the mat, telephoned orders to the grocer, pleaded with the butcher for an extra cut of black market meat, did a bit of dusting and polishing, tidied the kitchen. Maisie was a very late riser. She took her breakfast in bed, read the newspaper from cover to cover, then got up and prepared lunch. Evening meals were made by whoever felt like cooking, and both women were in their beds early. Any real cleaning was done by the daily, who was, during the off-season, a mere once-a-weekly.

The newspaper was invariably second-hand by the time Vera got hold of it. On 16 February 1951, she smoothed out Maisie's clumsy creases and scanned the headlines. Whisky had risen in price by one shilling and eightpence, while a further twopence-worth of meat was being shaved off the meat ration. Rump steak, at two and eightpence a pound, would provide just four ounces for each person. Another choice was five ounces of imported lamb for each head of population. The war had been over for several years, but rationing remained. According to one angry butcher who had written to the *Herald*, it would soon take three ration books to buy a pound of meat, and up to thirteen books for a leg of lamb. It was all connected with Argentina and the dead-lock of some talks.

Further down the page, Vera was informed that this had been the wettest February since 1870. She didn't need the press to tell her that; each time she raised her head, she saw nothing more than a grey curtain of rain beating a relentless path from heaven to earth. She never went out much any more. Her feet swelled up when she walked too far, and her back ached from time to time. Any day now, her baby would make its debut.

She flicked idly through the pages, read about another stupid boxer defending some silly title, saw a photograph of a man with a flattened nose, cauliflower ears and a blank expression. Still, he couldn't have had much of a brain to start with, because he had opted for a so-called profession that would finish off the few living cells with which he had been blessed at birth.

Then she saw the smaller heading just below the paper's waistline. A body had been found in the woods near Belmont Road in Bolton, had been identified as a man named Peter Turnbull. Turnbull was the illegitimate son of Samuel Fishwick. Vera read on avidly, her breath quickening with every word. Several people had been questioned about the death, which was being treated as suspicious. The man had been shot in the chest and hidden beneath a tree in the Top o' th' Moor woods.

So this dead man was . . . was who? She pondered. Her thought processes had slowed, were in tune with the lassitude under which her whole being had fallen. This Turnbull was the son of Samuel Fishwick, who had been Alice's father. The dead man was a half-brother to Edward's wife. And Turnbull seemed to have been killed deliberately. Murder.

Vera placed the paper on a table. Occasionally, she received a letter from that delightful but eccentric young gentleman who had visited Blackpool during the summer. He lived in a prefab in Eldon Street, a little metal hut of his own. For the privilege of solitude and freedom, James had left a very stately house and an exceptional standard of living.

It was ten o'clock. James would be at work now. He had told Vera in his letters all about Templeton and Fishwick on Deansgate, about how his mother and Alice Shawcross had gone into business together. He had also informed Vera of Edward Shawcross's movements, and had told her that Connie was almost fully recovered from her terrible injury.

Edward had a new business in Bromley Cross, had been taught how to bake, was living in a flat above the shop. Vera could have gone to him. After all, he had left his family of his own accord, had not abandoned them just to care for his mistress. Yet she had not wanted to go, had experienced no need for him. Was he in trouble, though? She read the article again, learnt nothing from it. Who was being questioned?

James Templeton's prefab was probably the only house of its kind to be fitted with a telephone. She would talk to him later, as he had written the number on a couple of his letters.

Vera leaned back in her chair and dozed. Of late, she had taken to falling asleep at the strangest times, as if her body knew about the task to come. In her dream, she saw Edward in a prison cell. She clawed at the metal door and screamed at the warders, tried to convince them of Edward's innocence. But the guards laughed, smoked cigarettes and played cards at a table. She reached for the keys, was just about to pick them off their hook when someone grabbed her hand.

'Vera?'

She woke with a start. 'Maisie.'

'You all right? You were shouting in your sleep.'

'Just a dream,' said Vera.

Maisie eased her girth into the other armchair. 'Soon be your time, love. You must be uncomfortable. That nightmare came from your stomach, because the baby's taking up such a lot of space. I reckon it's a ten-pounder. You're getting very tired. Your feet have gone all swelled up again.'

'I know.'

There was something wrong. During the past six or seven months, Maisie had learnt to read her companion like a book. The older woman did very little during winter time, so many idle moments had been spent studying the mother-to-be. 'Have you got pains?' Maisie asked.

'No, no. Like you said, I'm just tired.'

'There's more to it than that, Vera. You look down in the mouth, as if you've had some bad news.'

Vera sighed. Keeping her privacy was not easy. 'I shall need to make a phone call tonight, Maisie. There's somebody I must talk to as soon as possible.'

'Oh, I see. Is it the baby's dad?'

Vera shook her head.

'Is it that daft bloke who painted your picture? An unusual man, he was. He did a few drawings of me and all, made me stockings look all wrinkled. Is it him you'll be talking to?'

'Yes. Yes, I'll be talking to James.'

Maisie snorted. 'What sort of a name is that for a young man? Why can't he be Jim or Jimmy like anybody else?'

'Because he isn't like anybody else.' Vera sighed to herself. This was promising to become one of Maisie's silly, circular conversations. 'He's landed gentry.'

'And he landed in Blackpool and all. I've never known the upper classes to enjoy Blackpool. Blackpool's for working folk, them as have toiled hard all year, them as likes a bit of fun—'

'He came to paint the holidaymakers.'

Maisie chewed on the rubbery lower lip. 'Vera?'

'What?'

The older woman took as deep a breath as her

corset would allow. 'Is he really not the father?'

Vera found herself grinning. 'Maisie, he isn't, I can promise you that.'

The landlady continued her probing. 'But he knows the father, doesn't he?'

Vera shook her head impatiently. Sometimes, she regretted telling James about Edward. But James Templeton was one of those rare people who always got what they deserved, and James merited the truth. He was trustworthy. He was a gentleman in every sense of the word.

'Is he married?'

'No, James is chasing the girl next door.'

Exasperated, Maisie snorted. 'Not him, you daft bat. The father of your baby.'

'Separated,' answered Vera. 'Living on his own.'

Under different circumstances, Maisie might have suggested that the 'wronged' woman should chase the man of her nightmares for money, but Maisie had an agenda that she had not quite managed to hide. She wanted Vera to stay. Even a mewling baby would be tolerable if Vera would remain in Blackpool and at Mon Repos. 'I see,' she said at last.

Vera knew what Maisie wanted, understood the woman's need for company, for a bit of help, for someone with whom she could chat and drink tea. Occasionally, Vera thought about staying with Maisie, as the decision to stay would involve no real decision at all. If she stayed, she would need to do nothing but sit tight and carry on as before. But until the onset of this terrible lethargy, Vera had wanted to move on.

'So what's the problem?' asked Maisie. 'What's different all of a sudden?'

'With a bit of luck, I'll find out tonight,' replied

Vera. 'Until then, your guess is as good as mine.' With an air of finality, she picked up the newspaper and hid behind it, pretended to be riveted by the meat crisis.

Maisie struggled to her feet. 'I'll just go and make the morning coffee,' she said before leaving the room. Her heart was heavy as she warmed milk and thickened it with a pinch of salt. Vera was changing, was perhaps thinking of leaving. Life without Vera promised to be bleak.

Vera folded the *Herald*. In a few hours, she would try to find out the truth. The small corner of Vera that still loved Edward Shawcross was fighting its way through layers of exhaustion, and Vera hoped that he was not in too much difficulty.

It was well after seven o'clock when the disembodied voice made a connection between Vera and James. The operator had maintained her dignity and her patience while Vera had tried, every ten minutes or so, to make contact with James Templeton. 'It's me,' Vera shouted into the receiver.

'Hang on,' replied James. 'You nearly blew my head off. Speak normally. Is that you, Vera?'

She nodded before remembering to identify herself with words.

'Is there a problem?'

'What's happening?' she asked. 'I read in the paper about that body. Is Edward all right?'

James hesitated fractionally. 'Yes,' he replied.

'No, he isn't. I know he isn't. They're saying he did it, aren't they?'

'How on earth did you reach that conclusion?' Everyone was being questioned. Even the residents of Top o' th' Moor had been interviewed by the police. 'Vera, you must look after yourself. Stop worrying about this business. Just settle back and take care. Isn't the baby due?'

'Yes. It's due tomorrow. The doctor said it could be a fortnight, though.'

'Then think about the baby, concentrate on him. There is nothing you can do, anyway.'

Vera closed her eyes for a split second, saw Edward's face. She had not thought about Edward in ages. 'James?'

'Yes?'

'Is he still on his own?'

'Yes.'

She pondered for a short time. 'Come and get me,' she pleaded finally. 'Bring me back to Bolton.'

'To Edward?'

Vera's brain was spinning. 'To Sheila. She's my next-door neighbour on Tintern Avenue. Will you come for me? I want Edward to see the baby, James. I've changed my mind about everything.' That last sentence was untrue, because her mind seemed to have changed itself, almost secretly, without consulting her about its decision.

He coughed. 'But that was the last thing you wanted. You ran away, Vera. Are you really sure about this?'

'I'm sure,' she said quietly. 'If the bloody police start blaming him, I'll tell them. Edward Shawcross wouldn't hurt a fly. He might need me, you see. He might need somebody. Will you come for me? Please?'

After a short silence, James answered in the affirmative. 'When?' he asked.

'Tonight.'

'Really?'

'James, I could be in labour by tomorrow. Please,

please come and pick me up.'

'All right,' he answered. 'I'll leave in about half an hour, so I should be with you by about nine-thirty.'

Vera replaced the receiver and turned to find Maisie Cunningham hovering in the doorway. 'I have to go,' Vera explained sadly. She saw the dread in the woman's eyes, wondered how Maisie could possibly manage alone. But Vera's first loyalty was to her baby, and her second, it now seemed, was to the child's father.

Maisie sniffed. 'Will you be coming back? After the baby's born and you've sorted things out?'

'I don't know. Probably not.'

The landlady reached out and touched her guest's arm. 'If he didn't want you in the first place, why should he want you now, after all this time?'

'He did want me,' answered Vera. 'But things happened. I needed time to myself, time to think.'

'So what's altered?'

Vera shrugged. 'I have, he has and life has.' She smiled grimly. 'Apart from all that, other bits and pieces are still the same.' She felt sad for Maisie, was almost guilty about leaving her. 'He's in trouble, Maisie. You've been so good to me, and I feel terrible about going off like this. Thanks for keeping me on,' she said. 'I'll be in touch, I promise.'

Maisie Cunningham watched Vera climbing the stairs to pack her bags. She felt panic in her breast, wondered who would help her now, who would shop and cook for her. The months between February and May were going to be very long, and Maisie didn't know whether she would have the energy to keep going through another summer of guests. With Vera, she might have managed. Without her, Maisie doubted her own ability to cope.

*   *   *

James steered the car through ice and fog, his eyes glued to the fraction of road that he was able to see, his mind fixed on his passenger. Vera, still basically thin, looked as if she might explode at any moment. The baby made her huge. Her belly stuck out in front of her like a balloon that was ready to burst. 'Are you all right?' he mumbled from the corner of his mouth.

'I would be if you'd stop asking me,' she replied smartly. 'I'm sorry about this, James. I should have stayed in Blackpool until tomorrow.'

'I shall be at work again tomorrow.' He slowed even further, was travelling at walking speed. 'We may be forced to hole up somewhere,' he told her. 'The journey could take hours, and this weather invites accidents.'

Vera cursed herself. She had been in too big a hurry, should have found some patience. But Edward was in difficulty, so she needed to get to him as quickly as possible. 'Has he been charged?' she asked now.

James shook his head. 'Don't start getting upset. He was questioned for quite a long time, because the police were interested in his sudden departure from Aston Leigh. Evidence was found beneath the floor-boards in a bedroom. It seems that the gun was fired from inside a handbag of some sort. Of course, that fact should suggest that a woman had committed the crime, but the law is not so easily fooled. Perhaps a man had deliberately taken a handbag in order to implicate a woman.'

'But he wouldn't, not Edward.'

'I know that,' answered James. 'You know it and the police do, too, I think. They are looking for Mrs Fishwick.'

Vera's head shot sideways and she peered quizzically at her companion. 'His mother-in-law? She's old.'

'Quite. Aged, but not decrepit. Wily, cool as a cucumber, and she's done a disappearing act. She was living in London and most of her belongings are still in her flat. But she isn't, not any more. It's my belief that she read the press coverage and left the scene pretty damned quickly.'

'But . . .' Still, at least the law wasn't interested in Edward. 'So he's out of danger now?'

James shrugged. 'Unless the police decide that this was a plot of some kind. The fact is that even apart from this new business, Mr Shawcross has seemed unhappy and harassed for quite a while. In fact, he has not been himself since you left. So when you asked me to fetch you, I was more than willing.'

Vera stared through the windscreen into a blanket of sepia fog. It had been raining in Blackpool, but conditions were deteriorating as they journeyed towards inner Lancashire. 'It's like having your eyes closed,' she commented. 'You'd see as much with them shut as you do with them open.' Had Alice Shawcross's mother committed murder? And would they ever get past this horrible fog? 'This is awful,' added Vera.

James agreed. Everything was awful, though he said nothing.

'We'll have to stop,' she said.

'Where, though? We don't know whether there's anywhere to stay for the night. And if we do stop, another car might hit us, because visibility's down to about six feet.'

'Then we have to get off the road.'

'I'd get off the road if I could see where "off" is.

455

We may not be on a road. We could be just about anywhere.'

'Stop!' yelled Vera.

He slammed on the brakes.

'A light,' she cried. 'Over there.'

James saw nothing. 'Right. I think there's a verge or a pavement just to our left. I'm going to pull over, but we must both leave the car. It's important that we stay together, and if one of us remains in the car, the other might not return. Also, there's a chance that some other vehicle might crash into the back of us.' He turned the steering wheel, manoeuvred the vehicle up a slight rise and onto what might have been a verge. 'Get out,' he said. 'And hold onto the door.'

Vera stood by the passenger side and waited for him. She clutched at his hand and felt the fear rising in her chest. Where was the light? Had she imagined it, had it been born out of hope and terror? 'This way,' she said with manufactured confidence. 'It's very near.'

They groped their way along, each clinging to the other, each searching the ground by means of sliding feet. 'A wall,' said Vera at last. She placed a hand on the masonry, felt twigs overhanging the structure. 'It's a boundary wall,' she said. 'There must be a house nearby.'

After several minutes of painfully slow progress, they reached an open gate. 'There,' sighed Vera. 'A glow.' More optimistic now, they walked towards the light. It was a massive searchlight, a huge structure similar to those used during the war. Behind it, a house loomed, its front door illuminated by a pair of carriage lamps. 'Civilization,' breathed Vera.

The door was opened before the bell's noise died

away. 'Come in,' boomed a male voice. 'I knew I'd find a use for that light. Monica?' he roared. 'Customers.'

Monica appeared. She was small, daintily dressed in a frilly white blouse and a blue skirt. 'Dreadful night – do go through,' she trilled. 'There's a roaring fire in the drawing room. Dreadful night,' she repeated as she followed them along the hallway.

They made their way into the house, were shepherded by the fluttering Monica into a comfortable room with a log fire and burgundy-coloured chairs. Vera lowered her bulk into the nearest seat, was surprised when the man of the house hastened to stuff cushions behind her spine. 'Thank you,' she said.

'Thought there'd be someone who needed shelter,' said the man. He beamed down on Vera. 'Charles Bainbridge,' he said. 'Major. Retired now, of course.'

Vera accepted a spoonful of brandy in a crystal globe.

'You shouldn't have too much,' smiled Monica. 'In your condition, a little must suffice.'

As Vera sipped on the warming fluid, her back began to ache again. She wriggled deeper into the cushions, but the gnawing discomfort continued. Her spine had been the victim of some distress for several months. But this was a different pain, a positive pain. Hot fingers curled outwards from the lower vertebrae, coiled their vicious talons round the hips and into her belly. The mound hardened, slackened, hardened again.

James sat opposite Vera, his eyes fixed on her. 'Vera?'

'I know,' she replied to the unspoken question.

'And this time, James, I'm not all right.' She should have stayed with Maisie. There had been no fog in Blackpool, and the doctor was just minutes away, as was the hospital. 'I may need a Caesarean section.'

The major stepped forward. 'There's a doctor just a small distance from here. I shall go and fetch him.' He nodded at James. 'Stay with your wife.'

This was no time for explanations. Promoted to the position of father-to-be, James knelt by his 'wife' and held her hand.

'We shall try to get you upstairs,' said the major's Monica.

Between the two of them, Monica and James steadied Vera and helped her ascend the wide stairway, stopping occasionally when a pain impeded progress. She was placed on a double bed with a canopy and drapes, then Monica fluttered round chattering about hot water and towels.

'What am I supposed to do?' Vera asked.

The major's childless wife did not know. 'Wait for the doctor,' she suggested brightly.

Vera was quite happy to wait, though her passenger seemed ready to disembark at any second. The interval between spasms was shortening. 'This baby won't stay where it is much longer,' she said. 'And what if I need an operation?'

James was at a complete loss. He closed the bed-curtains and left Monica sitting next to Vera within the tent-like structure. 'Get her ready,' he told a length of dusty red velvet. 'Remove her under-clothing.'

'But she's your wife,' replied the reed-like voice. 'Shouldn't you be holding her hand?'

'She is not my wife,' replied James, exasperation raising his tone.

The curtains parted and a small, blonde head appeared in the gap. 'You aren't married?' Eyebrows arched themselves above childlike blue eyes.

'The baby is not mine,' retorted James. Behind every great man, there was a good woman, he told himself inwardly. The walls on the landing were crowded with photographs of the major posing in all his glory, poking his stick at a tank, sitting round a camp fire in the company of lesser beings. Behind this particular man, there was a totally brainless, silly, immature, yellow-haired idiot.

China blue eyes blinked. 'Where is her husband, then? Why is she out on a night like this?'

James slapped a hand to his forehead. 'Can we save the questions for later? Vera needs help.'

Monica's fluffy head disappeared, and some fumblings took place behind the drapery.

'James?' It was Vera's voice.

'Yes?'

'She's fainted.'

Fury and frustration bubbled to the surface as James threw back the drapes. The major's Monica was in a decorous heap at the bottom of the bed. Vera's situation was rather less presentable. Her legs were bent at the knee, and the unmistakable crown of an infant's head was just visible. James dragged the inert Monica away and dumped her none too gently on the green Wilton.

'I've got to push,' screamed Vera.

'You just do what you think is right,' replied James. The human reproductive process had been carrying on for years, he reminded himself. Babies were born on trains, in paddy fields, under trees, during advertising intervals at the cinema. This was merely another birth. Yet he felt uneasy, unsure. No amount of inner platitudes could erase his fear. Her whiter-than-white face was covered in a slick of sweat. She heaved and pushed, but the tiny area of infant head grew no larger, showed no sign of emerging.

Vera was racked with pain. It was horrible, unbearable. Where was that bloody doctor? Had Major Wotsisname got lost in the fog? She was ripping, was being torn apart. When this baby finally got out, Vera would be lying here in two distinct halves. 'I can't,' she moaned. 'I can't do it.'

Vera had no choice. There was no turning back, thought James as he concentrated on the top of the baby's head. It still wasn't getting any bigger. Vera was continuing to push and strain, but the exit from the birth canal was not widening. What should he do?

The door burst open. Their host and another man strode over Monica's inert body. 'Damn fool,' cursed the major, referring to his unconscious spouse. 'This is Dr Charnley,' he explained to James. 'Everything will be fine, you'll see.'

Relieved beyond measure, James withdrew from the stressful scene. The major was used to going into battle, as was the doctor, so James sat on the stairs and waited. He heard the doctor explaining to Vera that she would need a tiny cut to allow the head to free itself. 'You'll feel nothing,' he added.

James was surprised to find that his hands were closed so tightly that the fingernails were piercing his palms. Deliberately, he forced himself to relax. History would not repeat itself. The poor little mite who currently fought for his place in the world was not going to be another Peter Turnbull. This child would be accepted, recognized and loved. This child would not be shot to death in the Top o' th' Moor woods.

Connie. Connie would be waiting to hear from him. Oh, heck. They had promised each other a trip to Preston's tomorrow lunchtime so that they could browse among engagement rings. Connie needed distractions. Her whole family had been grilled endlessly about a murder, and Connie needed a break from routine. He would have to use the telephone.

Having obtained the major's permission, James stood for several moments with his hand resting on the receiver. What could he say? How might he account for his absence? 'I am with your father's mistress, dear. You remember, the lady who was in his car that day when you ran beneath a lorry. She is just about to give birth to your half-brother or half-sister. Yes, yes, history does seem to repeat. So sorry. I'll get back to you when I find the time.'

He walked away from the telephone. The truth needed telling, but it was a job that ought to be done face to face. Perhaps the fog would lift. Perhaps he could drive back during the night, after Vera's troubles had ended. He sat on the fourth step and waited.

A thin scream floated down the stairs, grew louder, became the unmistakable fury of the newborn. James smiled. It probably was the most tremendous shock after nine months of darkness and luxury. Once the pain of birth was over, the poor little mite would be exposed to sound and light, would have his senses swirling in a cauldron of new and not altogether desirable sensations.

The major walked out onto the landing and

glanced down at James. 'It's a girl,' he said. 'A healthy, strapping child.'

James smiled again. 'How is . . . ?'

'Your wife?'

'She is not my wife.'

The older man descended the stairs slowly. According to Dr Charnley, the woman's chances of survival were not good. Had she been admitted to hospital, she might have had a slight chance, though the doctor had expressed his doubts. 'Is she a friend of yours?' the major asked. He sat down next to his visitor.

'An acquaintance,' replied James. He searched the old soldier's face. 'I was taking her home. She is on her way home.'

Bainbridge nodded.

'Well?'

'It doesn't look good, sir.'

James felt his lower jaw hanging loose. 'But she can't die. We were on our way back to Bolton to see Mr Shawcross – Edward, I mean. Vera has everything straight in her head now. Edward has a bakery. She is taking the baby to see him.'

The major lowered his head. This man was in shock, and Charles Bainbridge had witnessed the effects of trauma too frequently.

'No,' muttered James. 'No. History repeated? That would be too cruel.' Peter Turnbull's mother had died soon after giving birth. God was sticking to some predetermined pattern, it seemed. Or was this the work of Lucifer, that darkened angel?

'Would you like a drink?'

James shook his head. Vera? Vera dying?

'Is there anyone – someone who should be told?'

'No. Vera had no-one. Except a landlady in Blackpool and a friend on Tintern Avenue. I must go to her.'

Major Charles Bainbridge shook his head. 'Not yet. Let the doctor do his best. What a bugger,' he said. 'She went out like a light, you see. One minute, she was all smiles, looking at the baby and giving her a name.'

'What was the name?' For some reason, this was terribly important.

'Susan. She wants her to be Susan Jane.' The older man paused, dragged a hand across his face. 'She suddenly fell back onto the pillows. She was still smiling. Of course, I've seen injuries and so forth many times in the army, but this is . . . different. She isn't meant to get hurt. She hasn't volunteered, hasn't been conscripted. The gal is simply procreating.'

Monica stumbled onto the landing. 'Charles?' she wailed.

'Good God,' muttered Charles. 'The lady of the house has risen.' He turned. 'Come down, Monica. It's all over. The baby is born, dear.' It was plain that he was both husband and father to Monica Bainbridge.

Monica reached the two men and sat behind them. 'Who will take care of the baby?' she asked. 'That poor woman's not at all well.'

James felt as if his head would explode at any minute. 'There is a father, of course. He will have to be told that Vera is ill, but I'm sending out no messages tonight, because that fog is terrible. I shall have to leave everything until the weather clears.'

The doctor appeared. In his arms, a tiny bundle

mewled. 'This little soul needs food,' he said. 'Fortunately, we have a young one at home, so my wife will send round the powder and the bottles. Some clothes, too.' He reached for his bag and began to descend the stairs, his eyes fixed on Vera's 'husband'. James and the Bainbridges stood up and went down into the hall so that the doctor could walk down the final few treads.

'There you are.' The doctor passed the little scrap of new life to James.

James looked down into the blanket. 'My God. I had no idea. Are they all as small as this one?'

Dr Charnley smiled sadly. 'That's a huge baby,' he said. 'She must be nine or ten pounds. Some are less than half that size.'

James stroked the child's downy cheek. 'Vera?' he asked softly.

The medic placed a hand on James's arm. 'Pulmonary embolism, I'd say. She felt nothing, believe me.' When he saw the colour of James Templeton's face, the doctor grabbed the child. 'Steady on, old man.'

'Would she have lived had I got her to a hospital?' James asked.

Charnley considered the question for a brief second. 'I doubt it. The baby would have been delivered surgically, but the embolism might well have happened anyway. Don't blame yourself, please.'

When the medic had left, James looked once more at the child. She lay peacefully in Monica Bainbridge's arms, a tiny fist pushed against a rose-tinted cheek. James smiled gratefully at Monica and went upstairs.

Vera's sheet-covered body lay on the bed. James

crept in and lifted the cover from her face. She seemed to be asleep. He touched her skin and found that it was still warm. 'Vera?' he whispered, half expecting a response.

He saw her on the beach with the wind in her impossibly red hair, watched while she chased a ball, while she helped a child with a sandcastle. The deckchair had given her a great deal of trouble, and she had collapsed in a heap of wood, canvas and hysteria. She had fed crusts to the donkeys, had chased the waves at the sea's edge, had dribbled the contents of an ice-cream cone down her blouse, had shrieked when the cold confection hit her skin. Underneath the nervousness, a vibrant, life-loving woman had resided. Edward had courted her, had given her the child.

The tears flowed down his face as he remembered Vera's vitality. 'I'm not going back, James. They need Edward and I don't. See, I was terrified at first, because my sister died in childbirth. She had a terrible time, always produced these beautiful, dead babies. But something happened inside me, something that stopped me being afraid. It'll be all right.'

James sobbed and clung to a cooling hand.

'That lovely girl walked under a lorry because of me and Edward. I can't go back, can't take him away from his family. If he wants to leave them, then he can, but I won't be part of it. This is my baby. We'll manage.'

James mopped at his face. He would make sure that Susan was cared for. No harm would befall this tiny, newborn spirit while he and Connie breathed. 'Rest, Vera,' he whispered.

He covered her face and turned from the bed. As he did, the curtain near her head moved against its post. There was no draught in the room and everything else remained still. James reached out and stroked the velvet. 'Goodbye, friend,' he said. Had her soul lingered, had Vera waited for him? Was the movement of the curtain a final farewell?

On the landing, he stared almost without seeing, fixed his eyes on walls covered in aged prints, fading photographs and a mixture of militaria. He was in what his father might have dubbed 'one hell of a pickle', because he would have to return to Bolton in the company of a baby. Could Edward care for Susan? Would he? Connie would, but how would Connie's mother react?

He went into a bathroom and closed the door, splashed cold water into tired eyes. Below him, the child screamed lustily, hungrily. She had probably been born with her mother's thirst for life.

The major came up and guided James to a room. Monica had volunteered to stay up with the baby. 'She seems silly,' Charles Bainbridge explained, 'but she'll manage. Just get a good rest and, with any luck, the fog will have cleared by morning.'

Morning found James in his car with a drawer on the rear seat. Susan, muffled to the gills in second-hand clothes and blankets donated by the doctor's wife, was cushioned by an old pillow. 'What about your drawer?' asked James.

Monica smiled sadly. She had begged, had pleaded for the baby, but James and the major would not allow her to keep Susan, even for a few days. 'Any time,' she said now. 'When you are passing, drop it in.'

James did not know how to thank them. The ill-matched pair had been a godsend. 'If you hadn't used the searchlight, we'd never have found you,' he told them. 'And the baby, too, would have died.'

'Let us know how she's coming along,' begged the major, a suspicion of moisture in his eyes.

'I shall.' James started the car and pulled away. The fog had disappeared, but the day was grey and gloomy. With a sigh, James Templeton nosed his way towards Bolton, his mind still numbed by shock, his thoughts concentrated on his precious cargo. An undertaker had removed Vera's body. She was all alone in a coffin in a strange town, and James knew that he would have to make sure that she returned to Bolton. Susan whimpered, and James was suddenly very, very cold.

Edith Robinson, who lived in the prefab next to James's, took the baby. Her stammering husband was at work, and Edith promised to mind Susan through this first full day of life. 'What a bloody shame,' she said several times. 'New baby and no mother. What are you going to do?'

James raised his shoulders. His first encounter with feeding bottle and nappies had exhausted him. Susan was a wriggler. She had navy blue eyes, a few blonde hairs and very active limbs. Changing her had been like trying to dress a puppy, because the legs were never still. 'I must go and see the father. Thanks, Edith.'

Edith, whose husband's friends had taken James down mines and into mills, was not one for asking too many questions. She vowed to watch over this precious charge, just as Bob's mates had watched over James while he had sketched and painted for his *Working Pictures* collection. Yes, the Robinsons were good people. Edith smiled, closed her door and left James standing on the step like a man who had been wakened mid-dream. Connie.

He limped into his own house and telephoned the shop. Maude answered. 'Mother, would you get Connie, please?'

Maude was not happy. 'The poor girl is running your department, James. There has been a delivery of lamps, and they are selling well, so we are frightfully busy. Where on earth were you?'

James reined in a quick retort. 'Mother, will you get Connie? This is urgent.'

Eventually, Connie arrived and spoke breathlessly. 'How could you disappear like that, James? We were all—'

'Connie? Listen. Be a dear girl and shut up. I shan't be coming in today. I want you to come to Eldon Street when the shop closes.'

'What are you up to?' Connie sounded distressed. 'I was so worried, so terrified.'

He should have been grateful for her terror, but he wasn't. The anguish of the previous evening was still with him, had been underlined and magnified while he had tried to feed Vera's baby. The little one needed her mother; whatever he managed to do, James could never be a mother to Susan. 'It's difficult,' he advised his fiancée. 'I can't speak over the phone. Please promise to come after work.'

'Right.'

'And Connie?'

'Yes?'

'I do love you.'

There was a smile in her voice. 'I love you, too,' she replied. 'But what kind of trouble have you found now?'

'I'm not sure,' said James.

When the receiver was down, James bathed himself and found a change of clothes. Like a reluctant school-bound child, he took his time, fastened his tie three times, even went so far as to clean shoes whose surface had not seen polish since leaving Top o' th' Moor. He checked his watch, wound it until the spring's tension was almost audible. He found a clean handkerchief, plastered down his hair with water, bolted the back door.

Driving up Tonge Moor Road, he glanced down Tintern Avenue, reminded himself to find Vera's friend later. What would happen in the next half hour? he wondered. It was important that the thing was done properly, Edward first, Connie second, the friend third. As for Alice – well – Connie, Gil or Edward would have to decide whether, when and where.

He pulled into the pavement outside Edward's shop, saw him serving a customer. The shop was full. In spite of that, James entered and walked round the counter. 'Is Mrs Gore in the kitchen?' he asked.

Edward nodded, counted change into a woman's hand. 'Why?'

'I must talk to you.'

The shopkeeper grunted. 'You have my permission to marry Connie, James.'

'Not that,' muttered the intruder. 'This is urgent.'

Edward apologized to the queue and went to fetch Mrs Gore.

James left the shop and ascended the stairs. He waited on the landing until Edward joined him. 'Is it this murder?' Edward asked. 'Have they found Eleanor?'

James shook his head, then followed Edward into the flat. 'It's Vera,' he said.

Edward's eyebrows lifted themselves. 'Vera? Where is she?' He steadied himself against a table, then eased his suddenly disobedient body into a chair.

James sat facing Edward. 'Last year, when I went to Blackpool as part of my *Working Pictures* project, I met Vera. She was staying in a guesthouse. We chatted and I did a painting of her, took some photographs.'

'And you knew who she was?'

'Not immediately. She told me.'

Edward inclined his head. 'And you kept this to yourself.'

'I gave my word.'

Edward understood that. Many years ago, he had given his word to Samuel Fishwick. That promise had cost him dearly. 'Is Vera coming back to me?'

James flinched when he saw the flicker of hope in Edward's eyes. 'No,' he said quietly. 'Vera sent for me last night. She had decided to return to you, asked me to fetch her from Blackpool. The fog was dreadful, but we found somewhere to stay.' He hesitated.

'Go on, please!'

James bit down hard on his lower lip. 'Be strong, Edward. Vera died last night. She gave birth to a little girl and lived long enough to name her. But some sort of clot developed. The doctor said it was one of those terrible freak accidents that happen sometimes after a confinement.'

The till in the shop below clanged merrily as it gobbled up money. A clock on the mantelpiece struck eleven times, sounded like a churchyard knell. 'I am so sorry,' said James.

Edward was motionless for a while. Then his face

lit up as he began to speak, almost to himself. 'She sold me Aspros and ginger beer. The Andrews Liver Salts worried her, so she told me about her mother's remedies.' He paused, swallowed. 'We both knew. This world had contained us, had placed us within geographic reach of one another, yet it took Andrews Liver Salts and All Fours Cough Cure to bring us together.'

'Don't punish yourself . . .' James realized that his words had fallen outside Edward's current range.

'We both knew,' Edward said again. 'It was like an invisible chain that linked us. I could not cope with her fear of pregnancy, of childbirth. She seemed to think that a curse had been placed on her family. Perhaps she was right.'

'Edward, I really think—'

'Because I could not manage her, I avoided the house for a while and paid people to mind her. She had a holiday in Devon, but she showed few signs of improvement. Then, suddenly, she changed. Sadie Martindale said it was the hormones moving in.'

James decided not to interrupt again. Perhaps this was the right therapy for the man.

'Then there was the accident. Vera could not contain her grief and her feelings of guilt. And now . . . and now . . .'

'You have another daughter.'

Edward blinked slowly. 'I am such a weakling, James.'

'She's blonde, blue-eyed and over-active. I impaled myself on a safety pin trying to fasten her down.'

'A daughter.'

'Susan Jane. A big baby, or so I was told, though

she looks extremely tiny to me. She's yours, Edward.'

The older man gulped again. 'Samuel Fishwick had a son. Peter. Peter remained a secret from almost everyone, because he was a bastard, a cause of shame. I can't allow that to happen again.'

James leaned forward. 'We'll have her, Edward. Connie has the sweetest nature. Let us raise Susan.'

Edward tilted his head to one side. 'No. You must have your own children. This one is mine and I shall care for her. I'll get some help, but the ultimate responsibility is mine. Where is she now?'

'With my neighbour.'

'And Vera?'

James pulled a card from his pocket and placed it on the table. 'That's the name and address of the undertaker – it's on the outskirts of Preston.'

Edward nodded. 'Sheila Foster has the deeds to Vera's family grave in Heaton. She saved Vera's papers just before the new lot moved into the house.'

James prepared to stand.

'Hang on,' said Edward. 'Vera was about to come back to me?'

'Yes.'

'Why?'

James shrugged lightly. 'I think she loved you, Edward.'

'Oh, I see.'

James walked to the door. 'If you need someone to talk to, phone me or visit me. I'm so sorry.'

Edward sat for a long time after James had left. He had a second family, a second chance. There would be just the two of them, himself and Vera's Susan, but he intended to make a success of this opportunity. Later, when his pulse had slowed, when the shop was closed for the day, he would collect the child. 'Oh, Vera,' he said to the empty room, 'I wish you could have stayed to love your child.'

EIGHTEEN

Connie stared ahead, eyes fixed on nothing in particular, the injured leg throbbing as if in sympathy, her hands clasped tightly in her lap. She had left work three hours early in order to satisfy her curiosity. James was a character, but he would not have neglected his department unless the distraction had been important. And his reason was monumentally significant, because it involved a child who was not yet one full day old. She swallowed, composed herself deliberately.

'So,' she began reluctantly. 'It's Peter Turnbull all over again.' She paused, nodded to herself. 'The sins of predecessors and all that kind of stuff. Some poor dead mother leaving a little baby, the baby's father possibly wanting no contact. Will Father pay his own debts like he paid Grandfather's? Is that what men do, James? Do they pay to have their messes cleared up?' Her voice had increased in volume and tempo towards the end of her speech.

James shook his head. 'No. Your father does have a soul. He was heartbroken about Vera.'

She turned her fury on him, though she knew full well that James did not deserve it. She loved him, yet she screamed at him. 'What about Mother? She has struggled since last year to make a life for herself. She's stones lighter, very active and creative. All she needed was to stop depending, then her own existence could begin. Why can't he feel sorry about all the years when Mother was on a low light? Why should bloody Vera come into it? He was married to my mother! Yet you seem to think that Vera was so terribly important. Why?'

'I can't answer that, not fully.'

'Well, I can,' growled Connie. 'Men. It's all about men being the heroes, the successes, the star turns. My mother has a head for business, an ability that's usually recognized only in males. Even now, in 1951, we remain in the Dark Ages. Mother had to get rid of Father in order to shine.'

James sighed and glanced up at the ceiling. 'Do be quiet,' he said. 'This isn't the time for preaching. Connie, there is a little child next door. She has no mother, but she does have a father. Your father told me today that he intends to rear Susan.'

Connie's jaw slackened. 'A man?' she hooted eventually. 'What does a man know about the rearing of children?'

James sighed. 'Now, there you go, head first into a trap of your own making. You want to push women into the limelight, so why not allow a man to take a rear seat if he so chooses? You cannot pull two ways, Connie. Edward will bring up his daughter.'

'I shall believe that when I see it.'

James stood up and walked to the window, kept his back turned on his fiancée while he spoke. 'It does not take genius to work out what happened between your parents, Connie. Your mother, in her early twenties, felt unloved and uncertain of herself. When your grandparents bought Edward, they finally resigned, walked away from any remaining responsibilities towards their daughter. She became surplus to requirements, because Eleanor and Samuel Fishwick had eyes only for each other, cared simply and solely about their own pleasures.'

'And my father's excuse for entering the marriage was what? That he loved Mother?'

'That he feared being alone. He was a poor lad, an orphan who had suffered neglect and the sort of poverty that is almost unimaginable to people like you and me. He kept a promise to Mr Fishwick. Edward is a gentleman. There must have been many, many occasions on which he might have blurted out the truth. He paid the Turnbulls, sent money abroad so that his wife's parents could live the grand life. He also kept you, your brother and your mother fed, clothed and housed. The man must have been at his wits' end trying to please everyone. I doubt that he ever pleased himself.' He swivelled round on his good leg. 'For over twenty years, Edward Shawcross was a victim of blackmail.'

'Too weak to face the music,' replied Connie smartly.

James nodded thoughtfully. 'Perhaps. Though it's my belief that Edward put you and Gil first. And I'm pretty damned sure that he would not have hurt your mother, either. Then, after a long and stressful time, he met Vera. There were no clouds around Vera, no Turnbulls, no regretted promises. Vera came with no agenda attached. He must have gone through hell after falling in love. It was unplanned – an accident, almost. But Edward Shawcross would take none of it lightly. My guess is that the man has been riddled with guilt and remorse for ages.'

Connie sighed and shrugged her shoulders. She

was trying so hard to dislike her father, was aligning herself with her mother, who was brave and strong. Yet Connie still loved Edward, and that fact annoyed her greatly. 'He should have gone off with her, then.' She sounded petulant and childish, and she knew it.

'Vera ran away,' said James. He returned to the sofa, sat next to Connie, told her about Blackpool and about her father's mistress. 'I, too, made a promise, Connie. It was very similar to the vow taken by Edward after Peter's birth. I knew about the pregnancy. I knew where Vera was, could have told your father where to find her. But I had given my word to Vera.'

Connie swallowed. 'Did you like her?'

'Yes. Yes, I liked her. I was with her when she went into labour. After she died, I was the only person who said goodbye to her. Vera Hardman was not a bad woman. She simply fell in love with a married man. After your accident, she went away without telling him where she could be found. That woman was completely alone. She died in a strange house and among strangers. Even I didn't see her last moments.'

Tears ran down Connie's face. 'And now, I have a sister.'

'Yes.'

'And someone must tell Mother.'

'Yes,' repeated James. 'I'll do that if you like.'

Connie rubbed furiously at her wet cheeks. 'No. I'll tell her. Or perhaps Father will.'

James pulled the girl he loved into his arms. 'Don't cry. A new baby should not make us miserable. We have to be strong now for both your parents. Don't concentrate on sin, Connie. Think about that little piece of new life.'

He kissed her, stood up, walked to the door. 'There is something very wonderful about meeting a person who is only minutes or hours old. Like a clean canvas, Susan waits for the colours to arrive. She will be shaped by us, Connie. Her future is in our hands. If that sounds romantic and dramatic, then I make no apologies. The baby needs friends, and I intend to be among that number.' He left the house, closing the doors softly in his wake.

Connie dried her tears and practised feeling joyful. She would help with the baby, would be a good half-sister. Soon, she and James would be married. Now, that idea definitely brought joy. Life would probably be full of oil-paints and the smell of linseed. James was going to continue slightly crazy and terrifyingly gifted. Some of his recent work was truly amazing. They were to live in a farmhouse up Darwen Road, about a mile from Father's shop. It was a pretty place with several bedrooms, no electricity as yet, a paddock and stables and . . . And plenty of room for Father and his new daughter should they need to move.

She straightened the cushions on the sofa and worried about Mother, poor Mother. Connie could not turn her back on Alice in order to make Edward's life easier. And there was the shop, the responsibility towards customers and colleagues. 'Oh, what a bloody mess,' she muttered.

The door opened. James entered with a bundle in his arms. He bent over the tiny face. 'This is Connie,' he said to the child. 'She has been well brought up, so don't spit or vomit. She's your sister, though she's very, very old.' He held out his precious burden. 'Take her,' he said.

Susan was warm and sweet-smelling. 'Johnson's

Baby Powder,' mused Connie aloud. 'Mother still uses that sometimes after her bath. It smells beautiful and homely.'

'Your father will be here soon,' said James. 'He wanted to see Vera first, wanted to get her body brought home. She'll be moved to the McManus Chapel of Rest on St George's Road until the funeral.'

Two near-black eyes tried to focus on Connie's features, while a tiny hand strayed beyond the confines of swaddling and hooked itself around Connie's index finger. 'Less than a day old,' whispered Connie. 'All bright and new like morning.'

'Good God,' cried James. 'Not another poet. I will not tolerate competition, Connie Shawcross.'

'She is so lovely.'

'And she needs you,' said James. 'As does her father. Edward needs you, too.'

'My mother, the shop, Gil and Mary, Susan and Father—'

'And myself. Don't forget me, Connie.'

She lifted her face and smiled at him. 'You are easily remembered, James. But so many people need me.'

'Ah yes, but you, in turn, need them. Look, your family has been battered by so much tragedy, especially lately. If this little child can foster some love, then things will improve. Forget the practicalities – who will feed, baby-sit, dress, nurse. Those things will happen simply because they must. But Susan is a part of your father's life. How can such a pretty person be a bastard or a sin?'

'She can't,' answered Connie.

James had known all along that his fiancée's reaction to the baby would be positive, yet a sigh of relief

479

forced its way out of his mouth. Now, they had to sit and wait for Edward.

He parked the car on Tonge Moor Road, just outside the Co-op. A woman bustled out, one arm weighted down by a basket on top of which sat a blue sugar bag and a half-pound pat of butter in greaseproof. Up the side street, children played rounders, their bases consisting of the back corner of the Co-op, the back corner of Lever's Groceries, and two sets of wooden rails that marked the boundaries of a couple of council house gardens. A girl belted the ball and ran like the wind while fielders scattered. Young voices rose into the air, a discordant anthem that praised the day.

Edward shivered, tried to remember a time in his own childhood when he had been happy, carefree, adequately fed. The neighbours had saved him and his brother from starvation and cold. Vera was cold. Again, he shivered. The children ran, shouted, berated each other for cheating, quarrelled over a splintery rounders bat. So still and so white, she had been. But Vera's hair continued lively, its vibrance underlining to the point of exaggeration all that death had already taken. White skin, so pale, so dead.

He turned his head and gazed down Tintern Avenue. Sheila was still there, remained in the house next door to Vera's. Vera's house had lace curtains and a new doorknocker. It wasn't Vera's any more. Could he walk down that street, could he talk to Sheila? He must. A baby waited, but first, Edward had to tidy away the mother.

Vera had hated pink. Given a choice of coffin linings at the McManus Funeral Parlour, he had chosen pale blue. White was too stark and cold, but he had been careful not to choose the pink. Had he not been aware of her antipathy towards the shade, he might have opted for the rose silk.

How much had he known about Vera? That she had liked good music, theatre, books, fish and chips. That she had hated pink, had feared childbirth, had loved dark chocolate. No, he did not have much information about Vera. Yet he had known her in the biblical sense, and the fruit of that knowledge was just a couple of hundred yards away, in a prefab on Eldon Street.

The ball game was breaking up due to the onset of evening. Lights in Tonge Moor Library glared brightly, while the ironmonger began to take in his buckets and shovels. Edward climbed out of the car and locked the door. He did not need to pass Vera's house, as Sheila's was nearer to the road. But he would see the house in which he had been happy.

Sheila's lights were on. Edward stood with his hand on the gate-latch, watched the woman piling coal onto her fire. Alone in her little box, Sheila encroached on no-one, kept herself to herself, endured the loneliness. How many people lived like this, their soul's silence echoing in the emptiness that surrounded them? How many rattled round in these brick-built cartons waiting, waiting for the final packaging, the colour of whose lining was decided by some other person?

He shook himself, ordered his mind to settle on life, on the future and on the child. Soon, he would see his baby, yet he had to finish Vera's business first. Deliberately averting his eyes from the house that had been Vera's, he knocked on Sheila's door, saw the curtain move, heard her footsteps on linoleum.

She was pale, even paler than Vera had been. 'Edward?' She held the door wide.

He entered the house, stood by a roaring fire, cleared the emotion from his throat. 'Sheila,' he began. The words seemed to stick, so he coughed again. 'Vera . . . she died last night.'

The woman dropped into a fireside chair. 'Oh, God,' she whispered. 'Poor Vera. Poor, poor Vera.' Her voice threatened to crack.

'She had a little girl,' continued Edward.

Sheila rocked to and fro. 'I couldn't help her,' she muttered. 'To have an abortion. I just couldn't do it.'

Edward squatted until his face was level with hers. 'It wasn't your fault,' he said.

'It was.' The eyes reddened, making the white face even starker. 'Her sister died having a baby. Vera knew she would die like that. And we didn't listen.'

Edward took hold of the chair's arms. 'No, no. This wasn't the same thing, Sheila. She got through the birth, but a clot developed in a lung and—'

'What's the difference?'

He didn't know. The fact remained that Vera had died shortly after giving birth.

'The how doesn't matter,' sobbed Sheila. 'She died. She died because of having the baby.' Through a river of tears, she stared at him. 'We killed her. You got her pregnant and I made her stay pregnant.'

He held her for a few minutes, allowed her tears to wet his clothing. When she had grown calmer, he asked for the biscuit tin. Vera's biscuit tin had a crinolined lady on its lid. Vera's biscuit tin had always contained Vera's life – Co-op points, birth certificate, some old cigarette cards. 'You do have it, Sheila?'

Sheila got up with Edward's help, rubbed at her nose with the cuff of her cardigan, took the tin from a drawer. 'Grave deeds are in there. With her identity card and a bit of insurance.'

He sat down and opened the container. There were photographs of him, of her, of the two of them together, of William in various states of disarray. Vera's mother sat in a small silver frame, a frozen smile mocking the situation. 'I want the baby to know who her mother was,' he said, almost to himself. 'So I shall keep these for her.'

Sheila nodded, blew her nose on a handkerchief that had belonged to her dead husband. 'There's the insurance,' she said, pointing out an envelope. 'Enough to bury her. There'll only be me and you there, Edward.'

'She's on St George's Road,' he told her.

'McManus's?'

'Yes. Will you go to see her?'

Sheila nodded mutely.

'Thanks,' he said. He picked up the tin and made for the door. 'Sheila?'

'What?'

'Would you like to meet Vera's daughter? In a week or so, after the funeral and so forth?'

She gave him a watery smile. 'Yes,' she replied. 'I wouldn't miss that chance for the world.'

Alice Shawcross was suddenly the owner of a rather fascinating life. Templeton and Fishwick was a round-the-clock responsibility, because the selling of merchandise was less than half the story. There was the buying, there were books to check, wages to pay, department counters to arrange.

There was also Detective Sergeant Ian Barford.

Ian Barford was insinuating himself into Alice's existence. He no longer arrived in the guise of an inquisitor; he now presented himself with monotonous frequency in clothes which had enjoyed a passing relationship with a tepid iron. He poked about in the men's department, bought the odd shirt and some very odd ties, was often on hand when Alice put in an appearance between telephone calls and staff training.

Alice did not understand how this man could possibly be drawn to her. She was thinner, straighter, wore her clothes better, but dieting had done nothing for her nose. No matter how much praise she got, Alice continued to feel unlovely.

Also, the policeman was supposed to be looking for a murderer, should have been helping the London police to track down Eleanor Fishwick. When she thought about Mother as a murderer, Alice shivered, though she felt very little grief or guilt. Mother was a monumentally self-centred woman. If Mother had killed Peter Turnbull, then she must pay the price.

Being the daughter of a hunted woman was not as problematic as Alice might have expected. Maude and Eric were supportive, as were Gil and Connie. No-one at the store had raised the subject, so Alice simply carried on with the business of living. And she could have carried on a great deal faster without a certain detective hovering within the field of peripheral vision.

He was here again. Standing between Max Factor and Revlon, Alice counted lipsticks and made a note of the more popular shades for re-ordering. Ian Barford was holding a Wedgwood vegetable dish up to the light, though his eyes had strayed disobediently into cosmetics and perfumes. In the doorway that led to the restaurant, Mary Martindale, manager of the restaurant and Alice's future daughter-in-law, was wearing a knowing smile.

Alice glared at Mary, smiled woodenly at the cosmetics girls and strode off purposefully towards the lift. He joined her. She did not need to look over her shoulder, because she could smell the aromatic tobacco with which he filled his pipe.

'Mrs Shawcross?'

'Yes?' Alice pressed the lift button again.

'Might I have a word?'

Alice looked at him. The topcoat was of pension-able vintage, though it seemed to have been sponged or brushed. His face was clean-shaven, but a frayed collar and strangulation-tight tie made him less than presentable. 'Have you managed to find my mother yet?' asked Alice.

'No. Have you?'

She shook her head, drew back the lift door and stepped into the cage. 'Going up,' she said.

He joined her and held onto the rail that ran at waist height around the lift's interior. Ian Barford was not a lover of lifts, but his near-obsession with Alice Shawcross might have forced him to tackle a suspended ski elevator in the Alps. She was a grand woman, strong-featured, industrious and charming. Pretty women were all right, but they cared only about how they looked and about who was looking at them. Mrs Shawcross's charm came from within, so time would never wither her. 'I . . . er . . . just wanted to make sure you were all right. It's upset-ting, being involved in murder. People get upset, because it's very . . .'

'Upsetting?'

Scarlet about the cheeks, he nodded.

'I'm not particularly troubled,' she told him truthfully. 'Although the idea of a delinquent mother isn't attractive. She has been a poor friend to me. Of course, I continue to hope that she is innocent, but—'

'She did it,' said Barford. 'That's why she went missing. I wondered whether you might have thought of some friends, someone she might have visited?'

Alice shrugged. 'My parents' lives have been a mystery to me for well over twenty years. They had not seen my children until last summer.'

'All the same . . .' he began.

'All the same, you have a job to do, Sergeant Barford,' said Alice. 'As, indeed, do I.'

The lift stopped and Alice opened the gates and stepped into Interior Decor. Two women were holding a swatch of curtain material against a window. James Templeton's department was being run in his absence by a young man who had been courted away from Cavendish Fine Furnishings. He was demonstrating one of a consignment of table lamps to a young couple and to an unsavoury vagrant who had wandered in by mistake, only to remain in the nice, warm shop.

Ian Barford saw the tramp. 'Shall I shift him?' he asked.

'No,' replied Alice. 'He may inherit a fortune over the weekend. Anyway, everyone is welcome here.' She clutched a clipboard to her bosom, wished that the detective would go away. This was becoming embarrassing. It was bad enough having a fugitive mother; a middle-aged, sincere and shabby suitor was just about the last straw. 'I have work to do,' she advised him.

He squirmed, inserted a finger into the collar that threatened to cut off the supply of oxygen to his brain. 'I wondered if you might be free some evening. There are some concerts in Manchester, a couple of plays, too. Or the police brass band competition in the Victoria Hall.' Sweat ran freely down his cheeks. 'To take your mind off things,' he ended lamely.

Alice wished that Maude would appear, but Maude Templeton was in her element on the first floor, was dressing a bride, a bride's mother, three bridesmaids and a Matron of Honour. 'Thank you, but I am very busy these days.' She dashed off towards her small office, closing the door firmly.

Life was indeed interesting. Ian Barford kept popping up at strange times and in a variety of locations. He had searched the Top o' th' Moor woods so many times that he could probably have given a detailed description of every leaf, every branch, every patch of moss. Alice didn't want him. She didn't want anybody, didn't need a man in her life. They only got in the way, she kept reminding herself. On the whole, they were rather cumbersome and uncollectable. She pressed a palm to her mouth, squashed a giggle. She really would have to stop listening to her daughter and to Mary Martindale. Alice's future daughter-in-law was screamingly funny when she talked about a man's place in the world.

The office door opened. 'Mrs Shawcross?' It was the young man who was deputizing for James Templeton. James had gone missing, as had Connie. They were probably chasing rainbows or engagement rings.

'Yes?'

'The . . . er . . . the elderly gentleman is the worse

for wear. He's collapsed between lighting and fabrics.'

'Then revive him.'

The recruit from Cavendish Fine Furnishings wrinkled a perfect Grecian nose. 'He's drunk and covered in . . . stuff.'

'In what?'

'In vomit, Mrs Shawcross.'

Impatiently, Alice pushed past the offended assistant and homed in on the tramp. He was less than sweet-smelling, but she dragged him by the feet to the elevator, heaved him inside, then accompanied him to the ground floor.

When the cage reached its destination, she espied the back of a too-familiar head. 'Sergeant Barford? Would you escort this gentleman outside, please? He is unwell.' She managed to keep the smile from her face until Ian Barford had removed the man from the lift. Then Alice Shawcross pressed the button and glided upward, her sides almost splitting with hysteria.

In her office, she totted up the wages, ordered cosmetics on the telephone, consulted her diary. There were two weddings on Saturday, another a week later. Templeton and Fishwick of Deansgate was fast becoming the bee's knees where nuptials were concerned.

The door opened and Connie stepped into the office. 'Ah,' said Alice. 'I thought you might have emigrated.'

Connie sat opposite her mother. She had just left her fiancé and her father with a brand new baby. 'I'm sorry,' she began.

Alice frowned when she picked up the sadness in her daughter's tone. 'What on earth is the matter?'

'Vera died,' answered Connie quietly.

Alice processed the information, waited for the emotional responses to surface. 'I'm sorry.' She was sorry, too. The poor woman had run away for the sake of Connie. 'Where's James?' asked Alice.

'With Father.'

'Ah.' Alice turned another page in her diary.

'Vera had a baby, Mother. A little girl called Susan. She's almost one day old.'

Alice's finger hesitated for a second before flicking through another week.

'Father's going to look after her.'

Edward had never changed a nappy, made a feed, mopped up regurgitated milk. Alice picked up a pen. 'Three more weddings, Connie,' she remarked. 'We seem to be cornering the market, don't we? Oh, by the way, would you pop down to cosmetics? I forgot to check the Coty range.'

Connie stood up, nodded, left the room.

Alice Shawcross threw down her pen, swivelled round in her chair and stared through a high window. The sky was grey and pendulous. Suddenly, her heart lurched and tears collected in grey eyes whose tremendous beauty had never been noticed by their owner. How on earth was he going to manage and why did she care? Babies were very hard work. Oh, Edward.

She walked to a filing cabinet, pulled out some sheets bearing details of job applicants. Alice and Maude were due to interview half a dozen young people in a few days' time. Would he love that baby? Had Peter Turnbull ever been loved? She had pieced together the too-brief history of her unacknowledged half-brother, had wondered how he might have turned out had he been recognized and supported by more than just money.

Edward had done the same thing, then. He had found a lover, had lost her, had gained a child. She placed the applications on her desk, looked at the top page with its childish, over-looped handwriting. How hopeful they were, these young people who were just about to leave school. They saw the world as their oyster, no doubt. Alice sniffed, hoped that the owner of this scrawled letter would carry on looking for pearls. Even though there were none, Alice mused. A couple of tears spilled, and she mopped her face feverishly. 'He's not a bad man,' she whispered to herself. 'Edward's not wicked.'

'Alice?' Maude, perfect in navy and white, rushed to her friend. 'My dear, what is it?'

Too choked to speak, Alice leaned her head against Maude's crisp white blouse and allowed her grief to pour.

Micky Turnbull had been advised by the Bedfordshire constabulary to stay away from Bolton. But Micky Turnbull was angry. Fury had swollen and reddened veins in the thick neck, and he had been unable to sit still for days. So, against advice to the contrary, he had driven north in a temper and in order to get to the bottom of things. No-one had been arrested. Peter had been shot to death on the doorstep of the Shawcross house, yet the police were clarting about stopping traffic and telling people what time it was.

He sat at a crossroads in his battered van, fingers drumming against the steering wheel. Nobody cared. Nobody gave a toss for the fact that a young man's life had been snuffed out. Well, they'd worry soon enough, Micky told himself. As for bloody

Shawcross, he could have his hush money back, because Micky was doing very nicely, thank you, branching out, gaining respect and winning contracts. In fact, he might just shove the original couple of hundred down Shawcross's throat and bloody well choke him.

At the bottom of The Rise, he stopped and jumped out of the van. It was posh up here. His nephew should have been given a place in Belmont, a proper place at his father's table, but Peter had been dumped by Samuel Fishwick, who had then swanned off to the other side of the world. Life was bloody unfair. There were the haves and the have-nots, and the haves were getting away with murder, quite literally.

Peter's neighbour had kept Micky up to date. Maude Templeton, the po-faced daft bat from the big house, had opened up a shop with Alice Shawcross. For some reason, Mrs Shawcross had kicked her husband out, and had reverted to her maiden name as far as business was concerned. Micky nodded knowingly. Alice Shawcross wouldn't want to share her name with a murderer, would she? No decent person would want to be called Shawcross these days, because Edward Shawcross was a cold-blooded killer.

According to what Micky had gathered, Samuel Fishwick's widow had buggered off, too. She was probably aware that her son-in-law had murdered Peter, so she had packed up and made for pastures new. Why hadn't Edward Shawcross been arrested? Why was he allowed to remain free enough to open and run a baker's shop in Bromley Cross?

Micky walked up The Rise, past Aston Leigh and Top o' th' Moor, pausing when he reached the perimeter of the copse. The killer had managed to get Peter up here on some pretext, had then shot him and hidden the body under the bare roots of an old tree. Edward Shawcross, Micky said inwardly. The spoils were about to be divided, so Shawcross had made sure that Peter's name was off the list before wills got read, or before divorce proceedings could begin. After all, the Shawcrosses might have been planning their separation for a while. It was all a mystery, especially to a chap who lived nearly two hundred miles away.

Everything had gone quiet of late. Micky had spoken to his local police, had telephoned the Bolton police, had failed to get any information out of them. So, money was strangling the truth. Shawcross was probably one of the aproned brigade, a funny handshaker, member of an elite shower whose number pranced about with daft trowels and rolled-up trouser legs. The police forces were saturated with Freemasons, corrupt buggers, the lot of them. Micky wanted his pound of flesh and he wanted it immediately.

He stepped into the wood and listened to its wintry silence. Even after a mere two strides and without the benefit of summer foliage, the place was eerie and dark. Micky was not a romantic soul, but he suddenly felt lonely. His early life had been noisy and busy, the house filled by Mam, Dad, Molly and the three boys. Now, there was just Micky. Peter's house, once the Turnbull family's home, had seemed so bare last time; now, it was positively cobwebby and freezing.

From a trouser pocket, Micky took the lighter, flicked it to life, set fire to a Woodbine. This lighter was his only souvenir of Peter. Then, with the quickness of lightning, his brain jumped into gear. SF.

The initials were etched into thick gold plate. SF. Samuel Fishwick? Why hadn't Micky made the connection before? This was probably Fishwick's lighter. Had the old man seen Peter?

With his head bowed against a cold breeze, Micky Turnbull came out of the woods. He tossed the lighter into the air, caught it, repeated the movements. He had never really studied the thing before, though he used it twenty or thirty times each day. Were these initials a mere coincidence?

Micky lifted his head and braved the icy air. He would make some enquiries. And he intended to leave the police out of the whole business. This time, he was going to beard the lion in his den. This time, he knew where Edward Shawcross lived.

She was so tiny and vulnerable. Edward remembered Gilbert, born with black hair curling at the nape, wide blue eyes and a scream that could have wakened the dead. Little Constance had entered the world as bald as a coot, though the yellow curls had burgeoned within months. She, too, had been noisy, a gurgler and a giggler, had often been found with her foot in her mouth. He smiled. Constance had retained the ability to put both feet into just about anything and everything.

Susan had a few downy wisps on her head, but the irises were the most riveting feature. They were of an impossibly dark shade of blue, verging on navy. 'They'll change,' he told her solemnly.

The infant fixed the eyes in question on him and kept her gums clamped firmly to a supply of National Dried. The arms that held her were firm and strong. Already, she recognized the scent of her minder. This was the right one, this was where she belonged.

'A few days old,' mused Edward. 'And with the wisdom of Job etched into that furrowed brow.'

Connie had offered to stay with Edward above the bakery for a couple of nights, but Edward had decided to start as he meant to continue. Susan was his. He would pay for help, would make sure that this little one thrived. Tomorrow and for the foreseeable future, Mrs Gore could do the baking and the selling, because the next few months would probably be eaten up by Susan.

She slackened her grip on the rubber teat, smiled, delivered the wind as soon as Edward raised her onto his shoulder. He placed a towel on the table, laid the baby on the towel. This promised to be the awkward bit again. Seventeen and a half inches of human life had drawn herself up to a mere foot or so, legs folded neatly on the abdomen. Working out the mechanics took about ten minutes and two squares of terry, as Susan left a deposit on the first.

'You should be sleepy after that three ounces,' Edward advised his daughter. 'Three ounces is a lot for a person of your stature.' He shook the tin of Johnson's powder, sneezed when the lid fell off and produced a very white child. There was powder everywhere. The nappy was huge and the bundle was small, but he managed to combine the two without impaling himself or Susan with two wicked so-called safety pins.

Exhausted, he placed Susan in her drawer and sank into an armchair. Fine particles of baby powder had settled in a radius of three feet around the accident. The room was a mass of paraphernalia – nappy bucket with the price still stuck to the handle, bottles, teats, dummies, gripe water, packets of new terry nappies, a pile of muslin liners, three teddy bears, a kangaroo and the components of a cot stacked in readiness for construction.

How did women manage? he wondered. The little one was the least of his problems at the moment – it was all the equipment, the nightdresses, vests, mattress, blankets. And, of course, she would be hungry again in a couple of hours. On top of all the immediate business, there was a shop to organize and a funeral to arrange.

He wiped away a tear. Vera. Her laugh, her jokes, her thin, childlike limbs, the way she had always listened, the fact that she had never demanded much. 'I killed her,' he whispered. 'As surely as if I had taken a knife to her.' He remembered how she had ranted and raved early on in the pregnancy, how she had pleaded to be released from a contract whose clauses she had never read, from an agreement that had never been signed or witnessed.

Susan whimpered. Edward looked at the clock, wondered how he was going to muster the energy to clean up the mess.

The doorbell sounded. Perhaps Connie had returned after all. He suddenly realized that he did need company, that he wanted help. But when he reached the foot of the stairs and opened the side door, he found Alice standing there. She looked smart in a dark blue suit with a warm scarf draped across her shoulders. 'Hello,' he said uncertainly.

Alice nodded, pushed him none too gently out of the way and ascended the stairs. She had never been here before, but Connie had described the layout of Edward's new home. 'Good heavens,' she exclaimed when she entered the living room. Would he ask her to leave? And what on earth had possessed her to come?

Edward sighed and climbed the stairs slowly.

'She is lovely.' Alice was gazing down on the newborn. 'Lift the drawer onto the sofa,' she advised. 'Draughts tend to whip round at floor level.' She removed her jacket and flung it on a dining chair. 'What happened?' she asked.

'Baby powder.'

'Ah yes. And those silly holes in the lid get clogged, you know. Keep it in a dry spot.' She picked up soiled nappies as she spoke. 'Bathroom?' she asked.

Edward pointed towards a door.

She returned some minutes later with a towel wrapped around her waist. 'Would you care to make a pot of tea?' she asked. 'And I shall try to instil some order into this chaos.'

He went into the kitchen, closed the door and leaned on it. Alice was the last person he might have expected. He felt stupid, clumsy and very guilty. While his mistress lay in a coffin at the funeral home, his wife was keeping house. He brewed tea, messed about with cups, jug and sugar bowl, found some spoons and a few battered biscuits.

Alice looked up when he re-entered the living room. She was on her hands and knees sweeping powder into a pile. 'No sugar,' she said.

He poured the tea, sat down in a chair and waited for Alice to arise from the floor. She was so much thinner, happier, calmer. In fact, she was a different person, a new woman altogether. 'Biscuit?' he enquired.

She shook her head and stood up. 'No. I'm still fighting a losing battle.'

'You look . . . very well, very nice.'

'Thank you.' Compliments did not sit happily, but she was learning to keep her composure, was no longer subjected to deep blushes. 'I shall stay for a few nights,' she said between sips. 'The sofa will do very well for me. We'll organize the cot shortly and the baby can sleep in it. But you need help, Edward, since you must have a great deal to do. You cannot care for the child while . . . there will be the funeral and so on.' After the burial, Alice would sort out the details, would find hired help.

'Yes.' Edward did not want Alice here, because it felt wrong. The baby was terrifying, but Alice's intrusion was making him uncomfortable. 'I can manage.' These words emerged stiffly and without grace. 'Eventually, I shall have to cope. You have a business to run—'

'As do you,' she replied. 'After the funeral, I shall go home.' She looked him up and down. 'You look dreadful,' she announced baldly. 'Go to bed, or you'll be of no use whatsoever to the child if you become ill.'

Alice had never been bossy. She had scolded the children when necessary, but she had not confronted her husband for years. Edward studied her, watched the new ease with which she held herself. Even with an old towel wrapped around her middle, she managed to retain a degree of some quality that was no stranger to elegance. 'I did you a favour, didn't I?' he muttered.

They had not talked about themselves for years, if ever. Alice searched her memory, rooted round for an occasion on which they had discussed who they were and what they wanted, but she came up with nothing. 'I'm stronger since you left,' she answered. 'Though I started to work on myself some time before that. But you didn't notice.'

Edward piled the dishes onto the tray. The

doorbell rang anew. This place was turning into a replica of Trinity Street Station. He descended the stairs again, opened the door, saw a face that rang a distant bell. 'Yes?'

Micky Turnbull lunged at Edward Shawcross. 'You killed him, didn't you?' yelled the intruder.

Unprepared for the attack, Edward fell against the bottom step.

'You killed our Peter, you bloody rat. That's why your missus threw you out. She couldn't stand the thought of living with a murderer.' He kicked out, was surprised when his ankle was grasped by the prostrate man.

Edward dragged the uninvited guest down beside him. 'I killed nobody,' he said. 'Nobody.'

'Don't come the innocent,' snapped Turnbull. He raised a balled fist.

'Stop that immediately!' Alice came down the stairs with a poker in her hand. She raised it above her head and glowered at Micky. 'My husband did not kill your nephew,' she said with deliberate slowness.

'Then who did? And why aren't the police trying to catch the swine? Is it because you've money? Is it because our Peter was just an ordinary bloke?'

Edward pulled himself free and climbed a couple of stairs. 'He was an idle, work-shy fool,' he said. 'And I wouldn't have wasted my time on him. The gallows is not the means by which I plan to die, Mr Turnbull.'

Micky rooted in his pocket and produced the lighter. 'Look,' he shouted. 'SF. Samuel Fishwick's initials. I found this in my nephew's house.'

Alice bit down on her lower lip. She recalled seeing that lighter beside the bed in her parents' room during the previous summer. She had even used it when setting up a coal tar burner to relieve her father's chest. 'There are many SFs in the world.'

Turnbull scrambled to his feet. 'Somebody did it!' he yelled. 'The coppers are telling me to keep my mouth shut, to stay away from Bolton, to toe the line. My nephew's dead. He was stuck in a bloody ice-box for ages before getting buried. And who's to gain from his death, eh? Not me, that's for sure.'

'You'll get the house,' said Edward.

'It's a pigsty.' Turnbull shook his head as if to clear it. 'Never mind the house. You're the ones who stopped paying conscience money now. Your family must have wanted him dead.'

'He's no loss,' said Alice softly. 'But we are not criminals. Now, I suggest you leave before I get the police.'

When the man had slammed the door in his wake, Alice and Edward remained seated on the stairs. 'She did it,' said Alice. 'She must have got into his house, too.'

Edward nodded wearily. 'Where the hell is she, Alice?'

Alice rose, the poker still in her hand. 'Don't let this baby go, please. Perhaps my half-brother could have been a decent man had he not been a Turnbull.' She turned, began to climb the stairs. 'By the way,' she added. 'Buy some more nightdresses and some bibs. They spit a lot and spill a lot.'

He lingered for a while, his fingers pressed against drumming temples. But when his baby cried, he jumped up and ran to her side.

NINETEEN

May had always been Alice's favourite month. The heat of summer was still a promise unfulfilled, but the earth became green and happy during this, the prettiest of seasons. Almond blossom fell, mingled with apple and cherry flowers to pattern the lawn in various delicate shades. But the May of 1951 was different, because Alice's mother was in prison. The trial was expected to take place in the autumn, and Alice had been forced to make a terrible choice.

Bail had been offered. Alice had consulted with her estranged husband and with her children, and had decided to leave Eleanor exactly where she was. The killer of Peter Turnbull had been arrested in Brighton at the beginning of April. After several days of questioning, and in the face of so much evidence, Eleanor Fishwick had reluctantly admitted her guilt. However, the old lady continued to express no remorse for her actions.

'It was just another nine-day wonder,' said Maude Templeton. She was walking with Alice through the rear garden of Aston Leigh. 'Most of the excitement and speculation has died down, so you must return to the shop, dear. Wonderful things are happening. James has come up with an idea about arranging honeymoons – travel tickets, hotels and so on. Oh, and Connie is making bridal bouquets and button-holes from flowers bought at Bolton market. Buying them in ready-made was proving so expensive. Did I tell you about the wedding cars?'

Alice nodded mutely.

'So now, with our new hair and beauty department, we handle every aspect of a wedding from the dresses to the meal. Of course, we are booked up right through to the end of August. We need you, Alice.'

'I know and I'm sorry.'

Maude understood Alice's disinclination to show her face in public. The last few weeks had been nightmarish, because some dreadful creature named Micky Turnbull had sold a story to the press, had produced a lighter and some garbled nonsense about the item having been found in his nephew's house. The newspaper in question, together with Mr Turnbull, had been warned about broadcasting such information while a murder trial was pending, but the damage had already been done. Then, days after the publication, Eleanor had been arrested, and Alice had refused to stand bail.

'Please try not to become depressed,' said Maude. She hated to see her friend so low in spirits. Their relationship was close, because Alice had done a great deal for Maude, so the traffic had not been just one way. Maude was an excellent businesswoman who would never have achieved her full potential had Alice not been around.

'Being cheerful isn't always easy,' Alice said. Chocolate had beckoned again of late. Alice had stood outside a sweetshop with her mouth watering at the sight of a bar of Fry's. 'But I have to visit

Mother. There is no point in putting off the evil day, Maude. Whatever she has done, she is my mother.'

'You won't bail her?'

'No.' Gilbert had been right all along. The old woman had even confessed to murdering her husband 'to put the suffering soul out of his misery'. 'She killed my father in order to stop him making a bequest to his illegitimate son. But I must go to see her, Maude.' Alice could not get back into the swing of things until her duty had been done. 'I want to tell her why I refused the bail guarantee.' She was also discovering that she needed to find out who Eleanor really was and what made her tick.

'Yes. Well, just try not to upset yourself. Would you like me to come with you?'

Alice stopped walking and placed a hand on the arm of this good friend. Maude Templeton had seemed so distant and aristocratic, yet underneath the veneer, Maude had a heart of gold, a centre that had been sorely damaged by the birth of her handicapped son. 'There are some things that can't be shared, my dear. This is my burden and I must carry it alone.'

Maude nodded. Poor Alice had been through the mill several times over. Connie's accident, Edward's infidelity, the discovery of a dead half-brother, the birth of her husband's now motherless baby daughter. And now, Alice's mother was behind bars. 'If there is anything we can do, Alice, anything at all – just ask. Eric and I are here for you, as is James.'

Alice smiled. 'That's one of the two good things that have happened. Connie and James, Gilbert and Mary.'

'Double wedding, too,' said Maude. 'We shall pull out all the stops. And you'll be wearing that wonderful silk. Do you remember it?'

Alice remembered. All the chocolates had gone into the waste bin, and the silk had been wrapped in tissue and placed in a drawer. 'Such a delightful colour,' Alice mused. 'Yes, I shall wear it.'

'You will be happy again, you know. This run of bad luck cannot last for ever.'

They turned and walked back towards the house. 'How is the baby?' asked Maude.

'She's well,' replied Alice. 'Three months old now. I called in yesterday afternoon. A young woman cares for Susan in the daytime, so Edward is able to run his business.'

Maude wondered whether she would ever understand Alice Shawcross. She had seemed such a bitter, dried-up person, dull, unimaginative and slow. Yet here she was, born all over again with a slimmer, elegant figure and a nature sufficiently forgiving to adorn the curriculum vitae of the average saint. She actually supported her errant husband, visited him, bought clothes and toys for the child, talked of him as if he were an old friend.

'Maude?'

'Yes, dear?'

'Is James going to set up home with my daughter in that dreadful little prefab?'

Maude hooted with extremely unladylike glee. 'I shouldn't be at all surprised. I can well imagine your daughter standing in the open doorway wearing a turban scarf, ragged slippers, steel curlers and a flowered apron—'

'With a cigarette dangling from the lower lip, of course.'

'Of course. And James will come home and scream for his dinner.' Maude pondered for a second. 'Where did we go wrong, I wonder? How on earth did we manage to give birth to such eccentrics? They aren't like any of us. James is the absolute antithesis of his father. And he isn't like me.' She shook with laughter again. 'Please, please say he isn't like me. Oh dear. Where did James and Connie come from?'

Alice shrugged. 'Blame it on Lancashire's soft water, Maude. I always have.'

Farnsworth Women's Prison was situated in a place called Eccles. Eccles sat on the fringe of Salford, which, in its turn, lived cheek by jowl with the city of Manchester. The jail was housed in a grim Victorian monstrosity with a high wall at its perimeter and huge, solid metal gates designed to keep the prisoners inside and the public outside.

On visiting days, the large, steel doors were opened to display an inner set of gates through which a small reception yard could be viewed. This narrow, yellow-paved area was out of bounds to prisoners, whose exercise sector was situated within the boundaries of an inner court. In a building between the two sets of barriers, warders waited to take visitors' passes from those who arrived to share a small part of the time being served by friends and relatives.

Alice was sandwiched between a young man who stank of beer and a woman with a withered face into whose furrows cream and powder had settled unhappily. Others among the motley throng wore anxious expressions and cheap clothing. To Alice, they embodied all that was hopeless and desperate in society. She wondered how Mother was coping.

This was the most awful place, yet it was strangely reminiscent of those crass mansion houses in some of the better parts of London. But Farnsworth was no block of apartments built to house the Kensington set. Inside the walls of the women's jail, there were killers of husbands, murderers of children, die-hard thieves and felons. Alice's heart missed a few beats.

'What's in your bag, missus?' asked a uniformed man.

Alice stared hard at him before thrusting forward her handbag. 'See for yourself,' she suggested sharply. Did he think she was smuggling the Crown Jewels into Farnsworth?

The man pulled himself up when he heard the modulated tones. 'That won't be necessary,' he informed her. 'You may proceed, madam.'

She retrieved her property and bequeathed him a dark and withering look.

The inner gates opened and she found herself being pushed forward by the other visitors. They seemed so eager to enter this awful place, while she wanted to turn tail and run for the hills. Mother had been held in the south for the first few weeks after the arrest, but her transfer to Farnsworth meant that Alice had no excuse. Although she nurtured no love for her mother, Alice was determined to do the decent thing. She inhaled deeply and went forth through an archway and into the prison proper.

By following the more experienced members of her group, Alice found herself in the visiting room. Cheap, scratched tables were surrounded by sad-looking chairs. At each table, a woman sat. Some smiled when the door opened to admit their nearest and dearest, while others wiped moisture from their eyes. Mother, in a corner, kept her face expressionless. She was of the old school, was the female equivalent of those stiff upper lip-styled men who strutted about in the corrupt corridors of power.

Alice sat down and gazed at Eleanor Fishwick. The older woman wore a dress of plain navy cotton and a heavy blue cardigan that looked scratchy and uncomfortable. Grey, untreated hair stuck out around her features in an unmanageable frizz, and her face was devoid of make-up. 'Hello,' said Alice eventually. 'I trust that you are as well as can be expected.'

Eleanor sniffed. 'How good of you to call,' she replied. 'After all, you have such a busy schedule these days.'

Mother's hands were red, while dirt-rimmed nails wore no polish. She looked exactly like the other prisoners, except that she was older than most. 'I have had the house decorated,' Alice said, feeling rather stupid. What was one supposed to discuss with a probable murderess? 'And the shop is busy.'

'Bail me,' snapped Eleanor. 'If I am found innocent due to extenuating circumstances, you could find yourself without a house to live in. Oh, yes, I shall sell Aston Leigh if you don't help me. So get me out of here at once.'

'No.' Alice was suddenly calm. If Mother took Aston Leigh, what did it matter? There were other houses in which Alice could live.

'Why not?'

'Because you murdered my father and Peter Turnbull. The children and I have discussed this, and none of us wants to take responsibility for you.'

Eleanor nodded slowly. 'I could bail myself if you would simply transfer the money from my account to yours. My lawyer could handle the business, I am sure.'

'Your account is frozen, I expect. And really,

money is not the issue,' replied Alice. People at the next table were listening.

Eleanor's eyes narrowed. 'Why do you hate me, Alice?'

'I don't.' This response tripped readily from Alice's tongue. 'But I don't love you, either. You have never loved me, so I feel no guilt.' Alice could almost sense the ears straining to hear the discussion.

Eleanor rose from the table and gestured in the direction of a female warder. 'If you are not here to get me released, then I have no use for you,' the prisoner told her daughter. She hesitated, sat down again. 'We had to give you to Edward Shawcross,' she spat. 'No-one else would have you. You were so fat and slow and miserable—'

'As were you, Mother,' answered Alice. 'Until you dieted. You were never naturally slender, and—'

'Except for me and your father, you would have been an old maid,' spat Eleanor.

Alice put her head on one side and studied the creature who had birthed her. 'Were you always nasty, Mother, or is this a skill you developed over the years?'

Eleanor Fishwick's eyes narrowed. 'He went to bed with that trollop. How do you think I felt after that? Oh, he was a man, so he was forgivable. Because of your father, I spent most of my life abroad. Because of his wish to die at home, I was forced to return to this mess. And was I going to sit back while he left money to the whore's bastard?'

Alice stood up.

'Wait, lady,' commanded Eleanor.

'Why? What's to be gained?'

'The knowledge that I paid him back, Alice. I had many lovers, too many to number.'

Temporarily winded by this latest shock, Alice did not find her reply immediately. 'And you killed him.' The silence in the rest of the room was deafening. It pounded in Alice's ears like a hammer on steel.

Eleanor dropped her chin for a second, then lifted her face again. 'Yes, because he killed me in 1927. I loved him. I loved him and he mated with a cheap tramp, and I did my mourning then. Since his affair with the Turnbull woman, I have been a widow.'

'Lively enough for lovers, though.'

Eleanor smirked. 'Men are enormous fun. You must try one some time.'

Alice took a step away from the table. 'Mother, I came to see you because I felt I must. However, it is plain that you neither need nor want visitors.' She walked towards the door.

'That's right, you run away,' called Eleanor. 'Whatever I did, I did for you and your children.'

Having reached the door, Alice wheeled round. Ignoring wide eyes and gaping mouths, she addressed prisoner 258617. 'Mother, you never did anything for anyone. Only for yourself. It has all been for your own sake.'

Outside, Alice gulped down mouthfuls of oxygen. Eccles was not a place that enjoyed particularly fresh air, but it tasted as sweet as honey because it was unconfined. For a second or two, Alice Shawcross stood outside the gates of Farnsworth and tried to feel sympathy for her mother. But she could not manage to pity the creature in the navy blue dress.

As she opened the car door, she allowed the ultimate horror to enter her mind. Mother might hang. Not for an instant did she worry about the old woman. Foremost in her mind were her children and their intended partners. It would be nasty for them, because there was a killer in the family.

Had it not been for Connie's anxiety, James Templeton might have managed to be almost content. But all was not well with the world, because all was not well with Connie. She was deeply concerned about her mother, as Alice had scarcely stirred out of Aston Leigh since Eleanor Fishwick's arrest. Connie kept muttering darkly about chocolate and other love-substitutes, was clearly in a state of worry. 'Mother needs to keep going,' she said repeatedly. But Alice had not yet returned to the store.

Maude was maintaining a very close watch on her son, was trying to ensure that he dressed properly. He had a definite leaning towards cravats and shirts that hung open because of missing buttons. However, he was decently attired for once, in grey suit, blue tie and a sparkling white shirt from the men's department.

This evening, there was to be an exhibition of work in the home decor department of Templeton and Fishwick. Maude hovered to make sure that James did no damage to merchandise while arranging his exhibits. The trouble with a genius was that he had no respect for velvet at two or three pounds a yard, so Maude had taken the trouble of covering all the stock counters and displays.

James ran his home decor section adequately, though Maude had to keep a weather eye on him as he was wont to order copious quantities of odd things like humorous toby jugs and colourful plant pots. He was happiest on Wednesdays when the shop was closed. On Wednesdays, he and a dozen or so would-be artisans did adventurous things with clay, beads, water paints and oils. He was proud of his Wednesday Brigade, as the group of amateurs had produced some quite astounding pieces.

A small London gallery had expressed an interest in displaying James's work for sale. But like many northern inverted snobs, James would have no truck with the south. 'They're all pin-stripes, daft hats and investment,' he told his mother now. 'Paintings aren't paintings to those soulless morons. They're things that get bought, stored in attics and dusted occasionally while the owners pray that the artist will die young and suitably notorious. They can bugger off, Mother.'

Maude sighed and shook her head. 'But who on earth will come to this exhibition of yours?' she asked.

'The discerning,' he replied. 'And anyone else who needs to shelter from the rain. If London wants me, it can come and get me. But I'm not budging.'

Maude wandered round the large room, much of which had been cleared for this evening's function. Downstairs, the restaurant kitchen was awash with chilled wine and Italian curses, as the cook had been roped in to produce dainty finger foods and small sandwiches. The home decor department had been pushed to one side to make way for bits and pieces produced by James and the Wednesday Brigade. Maude loved order, hated chaos, so she was pacing about a lot and staying out of the highly charged kitchen.

She lingered next to a portrait of Sadie Martindale, noticed how beautifully the woman's expression had been captured.

Gil arrived. 'James? Connie and Mary and Sadie

want to know if you really want vols au vent.' He grinned ruefully. 'And the cook's given notice again.'

'That's all right,' replied James. 'He resigned six times last month. For goodness sake, let him make an Italian pudding of some sort.'

'You can't have dishes and spoons up here,' said Maude. 'Think of the fabrics.'

James leaned on the net curtain counter, his elbow dislodging the protective cover to display a roll of cream lace. 'Gil, tell the cook that we love him immensely, then ask him can he make a finger-held Italian pudding. I don't give a damn about vols au vent, but how is my poor Connie getting along?' Connie had been quiet since her grandmother's arrest.

'She's fine,' answered Gil. 'And we need some paper napkins.'

James began to wish that he hadn't bothered. Then he cast an eye over all the work, found the reasons behind his lunacy. There was jewellery, wood-carving, sculpture, coil pottery, wheel pottery and photography. James and a very keen window-cleaner had stolen a cupboard as a dark room, and some of the window-cleaner's photographs were remarkable. The walls were lined with paintings, most of them James's. 'I'm going down to sit on the chef for ten minutes,' he told his mother before following his soon-to-be brother-in-law to the lift.

Alone, Maude wandered about and examined the exhibits. Of late, she had begun to entertain the suspicion that her son's work was rather fine. She stopped and looked at a group of James's paintings. Each canvas was small, not much more than eighteen inches square, but the subjects were riveting and boldly depicted. She scrutinized every one, found an early morning street scene, a spinning room, a mine, a huge number of bent figures marching with banners. The last two paintings were of an old man in a public house, then a funeral cortége.

At the centre of this group and in perfectly executed italic script, she discovered a poem. It was entitled 'THEY'. She read it aloud.

Cap pulled over watery eye
Cigarette smoke as grey as sky
Clattering clog, good morning cry
They walk.

Endless cop on endless spool
Cotton bondage hard and cruel
Memory of breezes cool
They spin.

Crawling, blinded, human mole
Enslaved in Satan's blackest hole
Everlasting quest for coal
They sweat.

Broken boot, a hundred mile
Starvation greeting, death's head smile
Government obscene denial
They march.

Creaking bone, a pint of ale
Weary telling of the tale
The hammering of one last nail
They die.

For a reason she could not have explained in a year, Maude felt dangerously close to tears. She was not a weeper by nature, had never used or abused the more obvious wiles of her sex. But the verses seemed to cut right into her, giving extra insight into the complex character of her son. He was special. The limp had refined him, had served to make him aware of the burdens of mankind. Perhaps Maude might begin to forgive herself for her son's birth injuries.

She turned away and straightened a cover on the chintz counter. It was strange being in the shop after closing time. She was tired, was worried about Alice, about Connie and about this evening. It had to be a success, especially now, after all that dreadful business with Eleanor Fishwick.

With her head shaking slowly, Maude Templeton wondered how on earth she might have reacted a year or so ago to the troubles at Aston Leigh. James was marrying into the family of a murderer. Strangely, that didn't matter now. She hoped with all her heart that people from other towns and cities would come out for James. Because he certainly would not take his work south. 'Let the mountain come,' he had told her earlier.

It would not matter. Maude dried her eyes and forced a smile. If no-one came, James would not mind. Really, he was a man of simple tastes. All he wanted and needed was Connie, his paints and his camera. 'He's brilliant,' she told a length of velvet. 'But I do hope he can be happy, too.'

The evening was a roaring success. Local press photographers fought for space, light and angles, jostled each other until food and wine arrived. The Top o' th' Moor servants were out in force, the oldest retainer, John Duncan, leading in a handful of maids and dailies. Hilda Ainsworth, the Templetons' housekeeper, discussed suet puddings with her counterpart from Aston Leigh. Sadie Martindale, splendid in a mauve suit with matching veiled hat, served refreshments with her daughter, Mary.

Maude and her husband presided next to the lift, shaking hands with everyone who alighted. Jessica Barton and Irene Cawley, bridge friends to Maude Templeton, were clearly impressed by the quantity and quality of the Wednesday Brigade's work. Members of James's class hovered near their exhibits, their minds suddenly turned into war zones where desire to hang on to their exhibits fought bloody battles with the need for money and recognition.

Sadie, who was having a fight of her own with a very crumbly chicken vol au vent, suddenly found herself staring at her next door neighbour. Ethel Hyatt, clothed in a supposedly slenderizing black, beamed triumphantly upon Sadie. 'Well, you should have served them one of my hotpots, love. That crumbly pastry'll be everywhere.'

Sadie snapped her mouth into the closed position. Next to Ethel, thin and puny in an oversized pin-striped suit, Denis Hyatt smiled timidly.

'He's come back,' announced Ethel. 'This afternoon. Haven't you?' These last words were bellowed into Denis's ear.

'I have,' he said.

'Needs me,' boomed the large woman. 'Don't you?'

'Aye,' agreed Denis.

Mary ran away. She stood in a corner and suppressed her laughter while the cabaret continued.

Poor old Mr Hyatt had returned to his loud wife because she would draw a map for him each morning, would steer him with certainty through the day's various confusions.

'She weren't pregnant.' Ethel's dulcet tones found Mary quite easily. 'Anyroad, she were a trollop, weren't she, love?' Imagining Denis's quiet 'yes', Mary bit down on a smile and stayed where she was.

Connie made a beeline for James. 'How's it going?'

'Don't ask.' He was flustered.

'I am asking and you are telling.'

He shrugged. 'I've sold most of my work. And the Wednesday Brigade's up to its neck in orders. At least two of them have been offered jobs.' He looked at his paintings. 'All gone,' he moaned. 'Except for the 'THEY' group, and I had to fight to keep that. I shall be going to London after all. At least, my work will go south.'

Connie understood. She knew how much of himself went into his painting. 'Never mind, sweetie,' she whispered. 'You're a success.'

James raised an eyebrow. 'Yes, I suppose I am.'

Connie awarded him a kiss before walking back into the fray.

Edward Shawcross sought out Maude Templeton and took her aside. 'Alice didn't come.'

Maude shook her head. 'I didn't like to say too much, Edward. We don't want Alice to feel pushed or forced back into life. Some things one has to do for oneself.'

Edward sighed deeply. It had been an unhappy day. Little Susan had grizzled for hours against the agony of swollen gums, and Edward had learnt that his brother, Paul, had died out in Australia. While baking his cakes, Edward had spent the day back in Delta Street, had watched Paul begging for food, putting his drunken parents to bed, trying to make a meal out of rotten carrots and potatoes.

'Edward?'

Edward Shawcross smiled sadly at Maude. Edward Shawcross had become an almost-millionaire this afternoon. Paul had never married and had bequeathed his fortune, made in Australia's abundant minerals, to his little brother. 'She'll start to eat chocolate in her room again,' Edward told his wife's dearest friend. 'That was how she gained the weight. They made her like that, the Fishwicks, made her depend on food. Her parents grew tired of her, then I made things so much worse. I'm worried about her, Maude. I'd hate to think of her slipping back again.'

'Yes,' she replied. 'I understand your concern.' A wise smile hovered for a split second on Maude Templeton's lips. Edward was worrying about Alice; Alice had been worrying about Edward for quite some time.

He looked at his watch. The baby-sitter, a seventeen-year-old girl, was clearly a responsible type, yet Edward did not like to leave his little daughter while she was teething. 'I'll mingle for a few minutes,' he called as Maude was dragged away.

In the doorway, James and Connie almost collided with the Murphys and the Robinsons, James's immediate neighbours from Eldon Street. Danny Murphy, uncomfortable in collar and tie, grinned broadly at the couple. 'We're here for the free wine,' he said.

Mona Murphy dug her husband in the ribs. 'We are here because we are proud of you, James.' She dragged Danny and her two children into the room.

Bob Robinson stammered a greeting, had the words finished off by his wife, as ever. Their twin girls dashed off to look at jewellery, then James and Connie sat alone on the stairs.

He kissed her and stroked her hair. 'Connie? We'd better give up the prefab.'

'As you wish. Or do you think we should keep it as a holiday home? After all, anyone can go to Southport or Morecambe. We could have a fortnight in Eldon Street. You'd be able to sit in the doorway with your trousers rolled up. We could paddle in puddles.'

James sighed dramatically. 'We shall live on the moors,' he said. 'In that farmhouse. Our children will need to run about.'

'OK.' She stood up and smoothed her dress. Whatever James decided, she would go along with him. 'We are in danger of being very happy, James.'

He agreed. 'Grim prospect, what? To paint, I must suffer.'

'I said nothing about your sufferings,' she informed him smartly. 'If you need to suffer, I shall be happy to oblige. It will be my wifely duty to heap difficulties on your head.'

James thought about that. 'Does it have to be my head, Con? Only I've been reading something about the Marquis de Sade, all flagellation and masochism. Ouch.' He rubbed a boxed ear. 'You're a terrible woman. I could go deaf if you keep doing that.'

She stood up. 'Come on, we'd better put in another appearance before the show finishes.'

James clambered into a standing position. He was always painfully aware of his clumsiness when Connie was near. In spite of her own accident, she managed to be so graceful, so sure—

'I don't mind about your leg, James,' she whispered. 'You'd be too, too perfect, my love.'

And so capable of reading his mind.

'Connie?' A voice floated up towards the couple on the stairs.

Both turned and looked downward. Alice Shawcross smiled up at them. 'I decided to let myself out,' she explained.

Connie knew that her grin was Cheshire-cat-sized. Mother looked wonderful in a green suit with black accessories. She had made an effort, had found enough energy to make up her face and arrange her hair. 'We're so glad to see you.'

Alice climbed the last few steps. 'I needed the time and the space to myself,' she said. 'So much has happened and I wanted to think.'

James inclined his head in agreement. 'If more people took time to think, Mrs Shawcross, there would be fewer wars. And may I be the first to congratulate you on that wonderful colour. Green is definitely you.'

Connie hooted. 'There speaks the fashion expert.'

They entered the department together, Alice flanked by her daughter and James. Inside the large room, people continued to chatter, eat and drink.

Maude rushed across, relief showing in every line of her face. The nine days' wonder had run its course, and Alice was back in the land of the living.

William was a fine dog until he got bored. Due to his positively superior intelligence, William usually found something to do but, occasionally, he ran out of ideas. Having dug over the herb garden and rearranged a few young lettuce heads behind a strawberry patch, he sat and scratched an ear. Maude, who remained one of his favourite people, was not in the next house. She went absent without leave almost every day with Alice, Connie and Gil. There was nothing to get excited about, nothing to wag a tail for. William had given up dragging washing from the lines, because Ada Dobson packed a fair wallop when she was not best pleased.

He spread himself flat and pretended to be dead, but nobody came to mourn his supposed passing. A punctured ball lay just beyond his reach, yet he couldn't be bothered. Once the air came out of a ball, it stopped being lively, just landed where he tossed it, didn't bounce off all over the place.

Rabbits were a sort of fun, except that they ran very fast and, on the single occasion when he had caught one, William hadn't known quite what to do with it. In fact, he had probably been more scared than his prey. He yawned, thought about that other time in that other place. The place was still there. Sometimes in the mornings, when the dew was fresh and the breeze skittish, he caught the faint smell of the other place.

A visit would do no harm, he supposed. If he cut through the fields and made no room for distractions, he could be there and back in time for his evening feed. With a last accusatory glance at the window of Lottie Bowker's domain, William set forth in pursuit of his destiny. Lottie would not fret about him, as the Aston Leigh cook had lost sausages, chops and even best rump to William.

He flew through meadows, ignored cows and a couple of stray mongrels, galloped over sprouting crops, cleared fences, walls and stiles like a steeple-chaser training for the National. From time to time, he paused to leave his mark, as he had not travelled long-distance before.

Eventually, he reached Tonge Moor Road. There was little traffic, so he crossed the road easily and trotted down Tintern Avenue to Vera's house. She would be in the kitchen, he supposed. She would make a fuss, would find him a biscuit and a bowl of water, might produce a ball with a bit of bounce left in it. Whatever she did would be more fun than meeting Lottie Bowker after just a little bit of digging.

But no, something was wrong. She wasn't here any more. The house remained the same, yet it was different. William sniffed the air, found the scent of Sheila's cats, caught a whiff of tripe and onions. Why did things have to change? Where was the woman, the one who had fed him and taken him out?

He slouched near the gate that had been Vera's, stood up after a while and urinated for no particular reason. Home was far away. He could find it, because he had left a trail, but there was . . . there was unfinished business.

At the top of Tintern Avenue, he spread his nostrils and inhaled deeply. The large ears were pricked to capture any sound, any clue that might lead him to whatever and wherever. Eventually, he turned right and headed towards Crompton Way. Ignoring a boisterous queue outside the cinema, William continued onward, onward until he reached the Royal Oak.

There was a fork in the road. The right-hand prong was not attractive. Something pulled William to the left, and he carried on along Darwen Road until he reached the place. It was special; it was connected with the house where Vera no longer lived.

A woman opened the door of the bakery and emerged with a basket of bread. William lunged forward and squeezed past her into the shop. Edward, who was just about to close for the evening, saw the large animal. Intending to remove the unwelcome guest from his premises, he stepped forward, stopping in his tracks when he recognized the intruder. 'William?'

The thick tail wagged hesitantly. William had found his new place. He loved Edward, because Edward was his hero, was the one who had rescued him from a contained existence, a tight collar and a chain that had restricted his movements. But there was another life here, a fresh life that was linked with Vera.

William wagged his tail again. At last, he knew where he truly belonged.

Edward spoke into the phone. 'I've tried,' he told Alice. 'William's an amenable chap, as I'm sure you know, but he won't budge. Short of using phenobarbitone and a straitjacket, I can't think how I'm going to remove him.'

Alice laughed. 'So he's standing guard?'

'Yes. He won't leave Susan for a moment longer than absolutely necessary.'

'They know things, Edward. I'm not sure what I mean, but they have some sort of sense, an instinct. Perhaps he realizes that the baby is Vera's.'

How easily Alice spoke about Vera, about the woman who should have been a rival. Perhaps Alice accepted the situation so easily because she had not loved her husband. Edward found himself in awe of her tranquillity. 'Alice, this is a bakery. William can't live here. I'm not sure that he should be near Susan, either.'

After a brief pause, Alice came up with her answer. 'Edward, dogs and children have lived in harmony since we were cave people. Just keep him away from the food. He's a thief, a very clever thief, and he has a particular affection for meat. So watch your pies, the steak and kidney in particular.'

Edward Shawcross didn't know what he wanted. He was a mixed-up man, a man with just a single aim in life. There were no money problems; he had just inherited three quarters of a million pounds from a brother he hadn't seen in decades. Beyond Susan's safety and Susan's education, he had no sights toward which he intended to aim.

'Edward? Are you still there?'

'Yes.' Perhaps he wanted a family, a support network for himself and his tiny daughter. Perhaps he wanted . . . 'I'll call again later,' he said, replacing the receiver quickly. Perhaps he wanted Alice, the new Alice, that vibrant, hard-working and humorous woman who had risen, phoenix-like, from the ashes of a previously lifeless existence.

He turned and looked at the dog. William, suddenly as good as gold, was lying beside the cot in which Susan snoozed. Joan Shacklady, the young girl who looked after Susan, had gone home for the day. Joan, a seventeen-year-old, had helped to raise her eight siblings, was a trustworthy and capable nanny. 'William, you are surplus to requirements.'

William raised a doggy eyebrow. William intended to stay exactly where he was; William could howl and scream with the best of them. He stared hard at Edward, maintained eye contact for a determinedly long time.

Edward sighed and sank into a chair. It had been one hell of a day. The meringue mix had gone wrong, and Mrs Gore had dropped a tray of meat-and-potato pies. Now, this alsatian was lying here as if he owned the place and, in particular, the baby. Dogs did not stare like this; dogs could be quite embarrassed when humans fixed their gaze on them. 'You know, don't you?'

William whimpered.

'She's Vera's. She's all that's left of Vera.'

William grinned, his daft tongue lolling sideways.

'But this is a bakery. We have to be very clean, old son.'

The large dog lifted his head and listened. There was no anger, no threat in the voice. A bud of hope burst open in the canine heart, blossomed when the man smiled. Would William be able to stay here with the little creature?

A dog's task was to be companion to man. The tiny being in the cot belonged to the man as well as to the woman, and the woman was dead. William walked to Edward and placed a paw on his knee. He watched the little drops of water as they ran down Edward's face. The smile had gone.

Edward patted William's head. 'I haven't told her about Paul's money, you know. Alice, I mean. Do you think she'd let me buy my way back into her house?'

Recognizing that his friend was sad, the dog raised himself onto his hind legs, placed his front paws on Edward's shoulders and licked away the salty water.

'Your breath stinks,' said Edward. 'I must get you some garlic tablets from the vet.'

The dog dropped down, scratched, stopped after a few scrapes of the paw. Two-leggeds didn't like scratching. Scratching meant baths in disinfectant and soap that stung the eyes.

Edward managed a smile. 'You are a dreadful dog,' he said.

Knowing that he had won, William settled back to do his real job. Guarding the human puppy was to be his life's work. As long as William lived, no harm would come to Vera Hardman's daughter.

TWENTY

Gilbert Shawcross and Mary Martindale were a pair. They had eased themselves so effortlessly into their relationship that neither was able to imagine life without the other. When Mary cast her mind back to the Hen and Chickens and the tennis balls, she suspected the existence of God. And now, with the success of Templeton and Fishwick, Mary had everything. She had a good job, a mother who was comfortable and a wonderful man. 'I don't deserve all this,' she told him as they walked up the path of Aston Leigh. She still remembered, just about, that she had wanted to succeed in her job more than she had wanted him. But she had been different then, had not begun to love him.

'Yes, you do. You deserve the best of everything.' Gil had escaped from university. He felt like a condemned man who had been reprieved at the eleventh hour. The social side had been fun, and he had enjoyed all the union activities, but Gil was a born persuader. He liked buying, selling, talking to people and catering for their needs. And above all else, he loved being with Mary.

Mary saw Connie and James inside the house, waved at them as she neared the window. Mary and

Gil both knew that they would never be as exciting a couple as Connie and James. Gil's sister was a character, as was Maude and Eric Templeton's son. Their relationship would be volatile, active, unusual. James would paint his way to stardom – or not, if his mood changed, while Connie might just drift into writing or mountaineering, might decide on a whim to become a piano tuner or a poet, but James and Connie were definitely right for each other.

Gil squeezed Mary's hand. 'At least he's giving up the prefab. We must be thankful for small mercies.'

Mary frowned. 'No, I liked the prefab. It was James to a T. You see, Gil, James is a humanitarian.'

'You mean he eats people? I've heard of vegetarianism—'

Mary dug her beloved in the ribs. 'I think the word I'm looking for is really egalitarian.'

Gil whistled. Mary was a great reader. She appeared to have given up on *Good Housekeeping*, was absorbing dictionaries and encyclopaedias for pleasure. The fact was that Mary Martindale would have benefited greatly from a college education, but such luxuries had not been on offer to her.

Mary nodded pensively. 'James turned his back on wealth and decided that everybody is the same. Which is fine if you're rich. The well-heeled can choose to exist among equals, but the poor have to be invited to join. The poor can only be equal to the poor. So James, bless him, lives in cloud cuckoo land.'

'Exactly where he belongs,' laughed Gil. 'And my sister, too.' Mary should stand for parliament, he decided. Like her mother, she would probably run the country with one hand and the rest of the world with the other.

'I do hope they're not thinking of giving up all their funny ways,' she said. 'They're something to talk about, aren't they?'

'We'll have plenty to discuss, and a lifetime to chatter,' Gil said contentedly.

Ada Dobson opened the door. The afternoon had been what Mrs Bowker called flusterful, as William had disappeared and there had been five to cook for. Alice made sure that her offspring and their partners ate once a week at Aston Leigh. 'The dog's gone off,' Ada told Master Gilbert.

'You should have kept him in the fridge,' quipped Gil.

'Run off,' said Ada patiently.

Mary shook her head. 'Oh, I hope he's all right.'

'He will be, miss,' said Ada. 'He's gone living in a blooming bakery. There'll not be one cake or pie left in Bromley Cross come morning. He ate his way through three pairs of kippers last week, bones, skin, even the paper they were wrapped in. And they weren't even cooked. And he's dug up all our mint. Mrs Bowker was furious when she saw what he'd done to the herb garden again.'

Gil and Mary entered the drawing room. Connie was seated in a chair by the window, while James had his nose in the newspaper. He folded the *Evening News* and hailed the latecomers. Connie continued to stare at the driveway. 'Mother?' she said.

'Yes?'

'Your boyfriend seems to be on his way again.'

Alice bit down on her lower lip. This was beyond a joke. Ian Barford was always telephoning, arriving at the shop, wandering up and down Deansgate as if crime didn't exist any more. 'I wonder when he finds time to do his job?' Alice asked of no-one in particular. 'It's becoming easier these days to understand how criminals thrive. Guardians of the law should not be roaming about with nothing to do.' He was finding things to do, though. He was finding theatre tickets, concert tickets, cinema tickets. Alice straightened her spine and marched out of the room before giving the man a chance to ring the bell.

He stood on the top step, a battered trilby turning between nervous hands. 'Mrs Shawcross,' he began.

'Yes, that is my name.' She folded her arms and looked sternly upon her unwanted suitor.

He heard the impatience in her tone, reddened slightly. 'It's about your mother, I'm afraid.'

Alice felt a chill running the length of her back. Mother was in prison. Surely she hadn't managed to summon up the energy to escape? 'Go on,' urged Alice. 'We were just about to sit down for our meal.'

'I'm sorry.' He was sorry, very sorry. The news he carried would not improve with keeping, and no cushion of words would make it easier for this wonderful lady. 'Mrs Fishwick has tried to kill herself. She's in hospital, in the Manchester Infirmary. She isn't very well, I'm afraid.'

Alice steadied herself against the jamb. It was strange, she thought, because she had no love for Eleanor Fishwick, yet this news had hit a weak spot inside her. Parents were a part of the life pattern, she explained to herself. The loss of a mother was a reminder of one's own transience. 'Is she going to die?' The words emerged evenly, no tremors, no wavering of the voice.

Ian Barford lowered his head slightly. He did not like to think of Alice Shawcross in pain, could scarcely bear the idea of her being hurt. 'I don't know. She's having transfusions. Would you like me to take you to the hospital?'

Alice considered the proposition. She had been about to sit down for a meal with her children. She had been about to begin her life over twenty years ago, then Samuel and Eleanor had passed her on into someone else's hands. Should she stop again for the sake of that self-centred, nasty old murderess?

'I'll get my coat.' Conscience prevailed, as ever. Conscience, and the need to act in a manner that could be interpreted as civilized and humane. She left the man standing outside. Back in the drawing room, she spoke to the four young people, told them that they must remain here and enjoy their meal. 'Life should carry on as normal,' she advised. 'My parents have been responsible for too many interruptions.' She pondered. 'I do hope that you never have to say that about me or about your father.' They were so happy, these four, so hopeful and alive.

She climbed into Barford's car. There was some evidence of the policeman's attempt to tidy up, as most of the mess had been thrown into the rear seat. The vehicle stank of vinegar and hair oil.

He walked round the Ford and got in beside her. She was a woman and a half, and Barford suspected that he was not fit to lick her boots. 'It happened a couple of hours ago,' he volunteered. 'She found something sharp and opened her wrists.'

Alice nodded, made no reply.

'She might just survive it.'

That was a definite possibility, Alice thought. Mother was a tough old bird with just one item on her agenda. Mother was the single bright star in her own small sky.

'So don't worry. Let's just see what we find when we get there.'

Alice had one near-regret – perhaps she should have broken up the family gathering, should have asked Gil to do the driving. But no, she replied inwardly. She didn't want her son to be affected yet again by the old witch. He had seen, had judged, had been correct. It was better to tolerate this would-be Romeo than to heap more worries onto Gilbert's head.

'So how are you?' asked Barford. He wished that he could cut out his tongue. He was taking this lovely woman to her mother's sickbed, yet he continued to ask stupid questions.

'I am well, thank you.'

'Oh.' She didn't seem in the least upset. Perhaps that was a part of the strength he admired so much. Well, he would be with her, would be there if she became upset. He pictured a quiet little pub somewhere between Bolton and Manchester, imagined himself buying a brandy, drying her tears, holding on to her trembling fingers, offering words of wisdom and consolation.

Alice stared ahead into the evening sky. She felt as if her life had spun out of control again. Control. That was the key word. Of late, she had taken charge of her own direction, had organized her diet, had invented an exercise plan, had taken the reins as far as her own body was concerned. She controlled half of a department store, fifty per cent of a restaurant, had been a prime factor in the development of the Wedding of your Dreams department.

This sad figure of a man was driving the car, but Mother, in slitting her wrists, was doing the steering again. 'No, no,' Alice shouted without thinking.

'I beg your pardon?'

Alice sensed the heat in her face. 'I felt a run in my stocking,' she muttered by way of explanation.

Women, thought Ian Barford, were a breed apart. When you arrested one, she often combed her hair and applied lipstick before coming along quietly. He had seen women laughing, not always hysterically, when their husbands had died, had observed several females celebrating once their other halves had been arrested. And now, while driving towards her mother's bed of pain, Alice Shawcross was worrying about a ladder in her nylons.

'Nearly there,' he said.

Alice clutched at her handbag. She didn't want to see her mother again, didn't need to. If Eleanor Fishwick had made a suicide attempt, then death was what she wanted. Selfish to the end, the old woman was pleasing herself.

'You don't like your mother, do you, Mrs Shawcross?'

To this understatement, Alice answered simply, 'No.'

'Is it . . . because of what she's supposed to have done?'

She considered the question. 'It's because of what she did and what she didn't do. She's horrible. To be perfectly frank, I have yet to meet anyone who does like her.'

'Oh.' Well, it wouldn't matter if the old girl died, then. He cheered himself with the knowledge that Alice Shawcross would not be mortally wounded if Eleanor Fishwick popped her clogs.

When the car was parked in the shadow of yet another Victorian monstrosity, Alice allowed herself to be guided into the hospital by the detective. He held her arm so gently, almost tenderly. At the reception desk, he explained himself, then they waited in two green-painted chairs for a nurse.

'Mrs . . . er?'

Alice looked up, saw a woman in blue. 'Shawcross. Eleanor Fishwick is my mother.' She turned to Barford. 'Stay here, please. I need to do this alone.' There would be no chance of being alone. Mother was probably under guard even now.

After walking through a maze of corridors, Alice found herself standing at the closed door of a ward.

'It's just the one bed,' said the nurse, clearly embarrassed by the situation. 'We wanted to put her away from . . . from—'

'She has to be separated from the rest of your patients. I understand.'

Alice turned the knob and entered the room. It was small, containing just a narrow bed and a couple of chairs. In one of these sat a prison warder, while the second was occupied by a young policeman. He jumped up and offered Alice the chair.

The woman in the bed was white and wrinkled. A tube through which blood ran was attached to her arm. Eleanor Fishwick's matted hair was spread across a bleached white pillow case. Gnarled, liver-spotted hands lay on the coverlet, the wrists heavily bandaged.

Alice sat. 'Is she unconscious?'

The guard nodded. 'She lost a lot of blood.'

While the evening wore on, Alice maintained her vigil in the company of two complete strangers. Occasionally, one or other of the men stepped out for a smoke, but Alice was never alone with the patient. She tidied up the contents of her bag, wrote a small shopping list, folded and unfolded her handkerchief several times. She even found herself making plans for the double wedding of Connie to James and Gil to Mary. It was simply a matter of passing the time. The parchment-skinned woman in the bed was a stranger, a person from another time, another life.

It had been all right at first. She remembered being tossed in the air by Father, being dressed up for outings, having her photograph taken at Mother's knee. There had been birthday parties, Christmas parties, days by the sea. Then, one night when she had been about twelve or thirteen, Alice had overheard her mother. She had stood on the stairs and listened to words whose harshness had cut through her like a butcher's cleaver.

'She's lumpy,' said Eleanor.

Samuel laughed. 'So were you, dear, until you lost the weight. Give her time.'

'It's her nose, Samuel. The fat may disappear, but the nose won't. And she's so . . . so unimaginative, so dull. I sometimes wonder whether they gave me the right baby.'

'That's my nose,' announced Samuel. 'She's definitely a Fishwick.'

'She's a bore,' snapped Eleanor.

To this accusation, the subject's father had attempted no response.

'So you came.'

Alice jumped, dragged herself through thirty-odd years and into the present. Mother looked terrible. The whites of her eyes were threaded with so many veins that they were turning pink. Her mouth looked dry, the lips cracking and peeling, while her cheeks were the colour of plain beeswax candles. 'Yes, I came.'

'Why?'

'I don't know. Because you are my mother, I suppose. It is what those in my circle might describe as the right thing to do in the circumstances.'

'And you are waiting with bated breath to get your hands on my money.'

Alice could not be bothered. She did not rise to the bait, because she refused to disturb herself any further.

'It's for your children. Handsome creatures. I have willed every penny to them.'

'I know,' replied Alice. 'And I'm sure that Gilbert and Constance are grateful for your concern.'

'They got their good looks from their father, of course,' breathed Eleanor.

The door opened. Alice felt the draught on her legs as someone entered the room.

'Hello, Eleanor.'

Surprised beyond measure, Alice realized that Edward had arrived. He stood behind her, placed a hand on the back of her chair. A feeling of relief swept right through her body, almost overwhelming her. He had come, and she was grateful.

'I'm dying,' said Eleanor quietly. The eyes burned like twin coals, and the mouth stretched itself into a terrible smile. 'I paid him back, Edward,' she muttered. 'I gave him as good a life as he wanted, then I killed him. He would have left money to . . . to the creature. And I killed the creature, too.'

Edward nodded. 'Yes, we know.'

A doctor bumbled in and placed a stethoscope on Eleanor's chest.

'Bugger off,' she told him. 'Let me die in peace.'

'You have an excellent chance of surviving,' scolded the doctor.

'No.' Eleanor's voice was weakening. 'No, thank

you. I am going to die. I have made the . . . decision.' She looked at Edward. 'You got a raw deal.' The eyes wandered across the face of her daughter. 'No oil painting, is she?' A dry, cackling sound emerged from the parched throat.

Edward stepped forward to stand beside Eleanor Fishwick's daughter. 'Alice is a fine woman, Eleanor,' he said quietly. 'No man could wish for a finer wife. I was not good enough for her, and that was the seat of our difficulty.'

Amazingly, the old woman giggled. But the laughter grew fainter, changed to a choking sound that lasted for a mere second or two.

The doctor pressed the stethoscope against the hollow chest, listened, then stepped back. 'She's dead,' he announced, eyes straying towards a clock on the wall. It was two minutes after ten, and a death certificate was required.

Alice stared at Mother's face for a few moments, then she rose steadily from her chair. 'Right,' she said. 'That's that, I suppose. We may as well go.'

Edward took her arm. 'Are you—?'

'I'm fine,' she replied almost snappily. 'Please take me home.' She could not bear the idea of being confined in a small space with Barford all the way from Manchester to Bolton. 'That policeman brought me,' she said.

Edward coughed behind a hand. 'Connie told me about him. He seems to be very taken with you.'

Alice pulled her arm out of her husband's grasp. 'I am tired,' she said. 'Just get rid of that dreadful man and take me home.' A thought struck her. 'Who's looking after the baby?'

'Connie is,' he answered. 'She telephoned and I decided to come to the hospital.'

She stopped, waited until his footsteps slowed. 'I'm glad you came, but I don't need looking after,' she explained. 'I have not needed that for years, because I learned a long time ago to take care of myself.'

'I'm sorry.'

She shook her head. 'Don't be. It was the best preparation I could have had. Neglect is a good teacher, Edward. It develops the character.' He looked so crestfallen that she reached out and touched his arm. 'Please forgive me,' she said. 'Self-pity is always so ugly. And although Eleanor was no mother to me, I have just closed a chapter of my life.'

She remained in the corridor while Edward went off to dismiss her unwanted beau. It was very strange, she thought, how she had managed to travel into her forties without ever seeing a glimmer of interest in a man's eye. And now, with a suitor who was plainly head-over-heels, she was not in the slightest bit interested.

Edward returned. 'He was not thrilled,' he told her. 'But I managed to send him away.'

Alice smiled. 'He is a pleasant enough soul, but I do wish he would clean himself up a bit. It's embarrassing having a shabby man dogging my heels. The girls in the shop have begun to notice.'

'Aren't you flattered?'

'Of course I am. But he's no Valentino, is he?'

They walked through the dismal hospital and got into Edward's car. For several miles, they travelled in silence, then he spoke. 'There'll be another funeral,' he said. 'Will you go?'

'Of course.' Doing the right thing again, she told herself. Always, always, doing the right thing. 'Will you go?' she asked.

'If you wish.'

'I wish,' she replied.

When the car was parked outside Aston Leigh, Alice showed no immediate desire to alight from it. She sat motionless for a few moments. 'Shall I come in with you?' Edward asked.

'No.' She fiddled with her handbag. 'I was thinking as we drove home – what a pity that we didn't always get along as well as we do now.'

He nodded mutely.

'Still, we had two lovely children.'

'Yes. Are you sure about me not coming in?'

She looked at him. 'I'm sure. Thank you for everything.' Alice got out of the car and ran into the house. In the hallway, she stared at her reflection in the coatstand mirror. Ridiculous, she said silently. Absolutely ridiculous.

Edward Shawcross locked up his shop and climbed the stairs. This had been a terrible year, he mused. Samuel, then Peter Turnbull, Vera and Eleanor, all dead. He wondered sometimes what might have happened had he not kept Samuel Fishwick's great secret. Peter Turnbull would probably have survived. All that to-ing and fro-ing with money for Peter and for his uncle, all that secrecy would have been eliminated.

He sat in an easy chair and closed his eyes. Susan and William had been taken out for their daily constitutional. He was weary to the bones, was tempted to get rid of the shop and move right away. After all, he had his brother's legacy. But Edward knew that he would never understand a world without work in it.

He reached, picked up the afternoon mail from a side table and opened it. There was a gas bill, a phone bill, a reminder from one of his suppliers about a special reduction in the price of bulk-bought flour. The last envelope was manila with name and address executed in a beautiful copperplate script. He tore it open and drew out a single sheet of paper. A solicitor in Blackpool wanted to see him, because a woman called Cunningham had left a boarding house to Vera's child. James Templeton had informed the landlady of Vera's death.

Edward smiled sadly and shook his head. He had all the money he would ever need. His little daughter, now four months old, was a Blackpool landlady-in-waiting. Yet there was something missing from Edward's life, something of vital importance. He closed his eyes again and dozed off.

'Edward!' Someone was shaking him none too gently. 'Connie, send for the doctor immediately. His head's hot enough to run a central heating system.' It was Alice's voice. He tried to open his eyes, but they seemed glued and weighted down.

Alice felt his head again. She could hear the wheezing in his chest, yet the man was too weak to cough. 'Edward,' she said again. 'Edward, please try to wake up.' He was on the sofa with his upper body propped against cushions.

Really, Edward was miles away, was walking through a field with Constance and Gilbert. The former wore a blue dress and little red sandals. Alice was calling his name, but he could not see her. The children rolled about like puppies, pushed and stumbled over each other, played tig, threw a ball.

'Edward?'

Vera came. Behind her, a large alsatian dog panted, the stupid tongue lolling sideways. Vera threw a stick for the dog, turned round and smiled at her lover. Constance was under a lorry. Gilbert lifted the wheel, and Edward saw the shattered leg. He called to Vera, but she had run away, was disappearing over the horizon. 'The world is flat,' he muttered. 'And she's dropped off the edge.'

Connie hovered anxiously. 'What did he say?'

Alice put a hand to her mouth. 'Oh, Connie.'

'What did he say, Mother?'

'Something about the edge of the world. He's ranting. We should get him into bed.'

'No.' Connie knew very little about medicine, but she felt that her father should not lie down when his chest was so congested.

Alice looked at the clock. Twenty minutes, and still no sign of a doctor. James, Mary and Gilbert had taken Susan to Aston Leigh. It was important to keep the child away from germs.

The doctor banged at the door, was admitted by Connie. He fiddled about with a thermometer and a stethoscope, diagnosed single pneumonia. 'We shall keep him here,' he said. 'Bed, drinks when he wakes. Plenty of pillows, and burn some coal tar in the room. Wash him down every hour. When he asks for food, give it to him.' He glanced at his watch. 'Twelve hours,' he said. 'He should be out of danger by tomorrow, or . . .'

'Or dead,' said Alice. Well, she wasn't going to allow him to die. He could not die, not when both his children were getting married in a few weeks. There was to be a grand double wedding, and Edward would be giving away his only daughter. She thanked the doctor, waited for him to leave.

With cool water, Alice sponged the body of her husband. He was raving again.

'No, no,' he yelled. 'She killed him! She killed him, she killed him. Morphine. Gilbert knew.'

Alice bit down hard on her lower lip. She would not cry.

'Wicked old witch,' shouted the patient.

She wet his lips with an ice cube.

'Waited quietly for many years to kill him. Only a woman could do that. Alice?'

'Yes?' But he was talking to the other Alice from the other time.

'Speak to me,' he continued.

She shook her head and carried on with her task.

'You never talk to me.'

Connie came in and sat at the table. 'The doctor left this.' She handed over a bottle of brown medicine. Mother was being so careful with Father, was washing him slowly and gently and with . . . with something that was not a stranger to love in her eyes.

Feeling like an intruder, Connie announced her intention to rest, then she went to lie down on her father's bed. Parents were indeed strange creatures.

Alice prayed all night. She changed his clothes, forced the glutinous medicine between his lips, rubbed ice against his mouth, spooned minute amounts of water into him. 'Don't die, Edward,' she said repeatedly. 'Don't leave me again.' The fact that she loved this man so fiercely was hard to explain, especially to herself.

'You're a crook, Turnbull,' he yelled. 'Bleeding us dry.'

Alice's tears flowed at last. Edward had fought for more than two decades to save the good name of Samuel Fishwick. 'I mustn't cry,' she whispered, but her eyes were not listening. He had paid and paid and paid. His nerves must have been stretched to breaking point. 'Live,' she pleaded.

Connie touched her mother's shoulder. 'It's only one lung, Mother. If it doesn't get to the other one, perhaps he'll be all right.'

At about four in the morning, the doctor returned and announced that the worst was over. 'You've done an excellent job of work,' he told Alice.

Dawn came eventually, was heralded by a mutinous blackbird outside the window. Edward opened his eyes and saw his wife and daughter. 'Connie?' he said.

Connie clapped her hands in relief. 'Yes?' She rubbed fiercely at her nose, refused to weep.

'Make some tea,' he said.

Alice sat and gazed down at him. 'This is all very silly,' she whispered. 'I think it's time you came home.'

He blinked slowly. 'And Susan?'

'It's time she came home, too.'

'Are you sure?'

She was sure. At last, she knew who she was and what she wanted from life. He was the husband she had just begun to love, the man whose affection for her was plain in his eyes. 'We'll take things very slowly,' she said.

Edward looked at this very real woman and managed a weak smile. 'Thank you, Alice,' he muttered. Then he fell into that special, dreamless sleep, the sleep that heals.

THE END

THE BELLS OF SCOTLAND ROAD
by Ruth Hamilton

To the Liverpool of the 1930s came Bridget O'Brien, a young widow with two children, about to be forced into marriage with a man she had never met. Her destination was the infamous Scotland Road, with its noise, its colour, its poverty and humour, where the people lived lives of deprivation and courage backed by rich tradition and a folklore they had themselves evolved.

For Bridget, straight from Ireland, fleeing from a brutal and bigoted father, Scotland Road was, at first, noisome and terrifying. Her sense of isolation was made worse when she met her bridegroom, Sam Bell, a middle-aged pawnbroker whose twin sons were older than she was. Grimly, thankful that at last she and her daughters had a roof over their heads, she settled to make the best of it she could.

It was the rough and vibrant Costigan family who first made her welcome. Diddy, a huge warm-hearted Liverpudlian and Billy, her docker husband, did their best to ease the young widow into her new life. Anthony, one of her so-called stepsons, also held out the strong hand of friendship, but Liam, the favourite of his father, had the power to terrify her. Liam was cold, compelling, mysterious and antagonistic. He was also a priest.

Against the backdrop of a unique culture, through the depression of the 30s and the savagery of the Second World War, the story of Bridie, her daughters, and the two men who were to shape her destiny was played out.

0 552 14385 5

PARADISE LANE
by Ruth Hamilton

There were only four houses in Paradise Lane, and young Sally Crumpsall lived at No.1. If it hadn't been for the kindly inhabitants of the Lane she would have been even more neglected than she was, for with a father too ill to care for her, and a mother who was to abandon her, she led a ragged and lonely existence. When – finally – both mother and father had gone, then the Lane moved in and, with the help of Ivy, Sally's old and stubbornly aggressive grandmother, they decided to raise Sally as best they could.

But Paradise Lane was built in the shadow of Paradise Mill – and Andrew Worthington, owner of the mill, loomed menacingly over the lives of everyone about him. A corrupt, evil and greedy man, he had totally destroyed his own family, and soon his venom was directed towards Ivy, her friends in Paradise Lane, and finally threatened the very existence of young Sally.

As events moved towards a violent and terrible climax, only the combined efforts of all who loved the young girl were able to save her.

0 552 14141 0

A SELECTED LIST OF FINE NOVELS
AVAILABLE FROM CORGI BOOKS

THE PRICES SHOWN BELOW WERE CORRECT AT THE TIME OF GOING TO PRESS.
HOWEVER TRANSWORLD PUBLISHERS RESERVE THE RIGHT TO SHOW NEW RETAIL
PRICES ON COVERS WHICH MAY DIFFER FROM THOSE PREVIOUSLY ADVERTISED IN
THE TEXT OR ELSEWHERE.

14060 0	MERSEY BLUES	*Lyn Andrews*	£4.99
14453 3	THE DARK ARCHES	*Aileen Armitage*	£5.99
13313 2	CATCH THE WIND	*Frances Donnelly*	£5.99
14442 8	JUST LIKE A WOMAN	*Jill Gascoine*	£5.99
14096 1	THE WILD SEED	*Iris Gower*	£5.99
14537 8	APPLE BLOSSOM TIME	*Kathryn Haig*	£5.99
13897 5	BILLY LONDON'S GIRLS	*Ruth Hamilton*	£5.99
13755 3	NEST OF SORROWS	*Ruth Hamilton*	£5.99
13384 1	A WHISPER TO THE LIVING	*Ruth Hamilton*	£4.99
13616 6	WITH LOVE FROM MA MAGUIRE		
		Ruth Hamilton	£5.99
13977 7	SPINNING JENNY	*Ruth Hamilton*	£4.99
14139 9	THE SEPTEMBER STARLINGS	*Ruth Hamilton*	£4.99
14140 0	PARADISE LANE	*Ruth Hamilton*	£5.99
14385 5	THE BELLS OF SCOTLAND ROAD	*Ruth Hamilton*	£5.99
14529 7	LEAVES FROM THE VALLEY	*Caroline Harvey*	£5.99
14486 X	MARSH LIGHT	*Kate Hatfield*	£6.99
14220 4	CAPEL BELLS	*Joan Hessayon*	£4.99
14397 9	THE BLACK BOOK	*Sara Keays*	£5.99
14333 2	SOME OLD LOVER'S GHOST	*Judith Lennox*	£5.99
14320 0	MARGUERITE	*Elisabeth Luard*	£5.99
13910 6	BLUEBIRDS	*Margaret Mayhew*	£5.99
14498 3	MORE INNOCENT TIMES	*Imogen Parker*	£5.99
10375 6	CSARDAS	*Diane Pearson*	£5.99
14125 9	CORONATION SUMMER	*Margaret Pemberton*	£5.99
14400 2	THE MOUNTAIN	*Elvi Rhodes*	£5.99
14549 1	CHOICES	*Susan Sallis*	£5.99
14548 3	THE GHOST OF WHITECHAPEL	*Mary Jane Staples*	£5.99
14476 2	CHILDREN OF THE TIDE	*Valerie Wood*	£5.99

Transworld titles are available by post from:

Book Service By Post, PO Box 29, Douglas, Isle of Man, IM99 1BQ

Credit cards accepted. Please telephone 01624 675137
fax 01624 670923, Internet http://www.bookpost.co.uk
or e-mail: bookshop@enterprise.net for details

Free postage and packing in the UK. Overseas customers: allow £1 per
book (paperbacks) and £3 per book (hardbacks).